COLLEGE OF EDUCATION

THIS edition, issued in 1955, is for members of The Companion Book Club, 8 Long Acre, London, W.C.2, from which address particulars of membership may be obtained. The book is published by arrangement with the original publishers, William Heinemann Ltd.

Also by
KATE O'BRIEN
★

FAREWELL SPAIN
LAND OF SPICES
THE ANTE-ROOM
MARY LAVELLE
WITHOUT MY CLOAK
PRAY FOR THE WANDERER
THE LAST OF SUMMER
THAT LADY

THE FLOWER OF MAY

"A blessed companion is a book"—JERROLD

THE FLOWER
OF MAY

★

KATE O'BRIEN

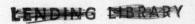

THE COMPANION BOOK CLUB
LONDON

*Made and printed in Great Britain
for The Companion Book Club (Odhams Press Ltd.)
by Odhams (Watford) Limited
Watford, Herts
S.755.ZT*

CONTENTS

CHAPTER		PAGE
1	LILIAN'S WEDDING	9
2	GLASALLA	40
3	VILLA DES GLYCINES	58
4	AT DANIELI'S	77
5	WEST FROM VENICE	87
6	AT DANIELI'S AGAIN	125
7	MÈRE GÉNÉRALE	159
8	HOMEWARD TOMORROW	172
9	MESPIL ROAD	183
10	THE LIGHTHOUSE	210
11	VIGIL	256
12	CRAHORE AND EVENING	281
13	'WHITE COLD VIRGIN SNOW'	299

There's one that is pure as an an - gel and

fair   as the flower of   May, . .

CHAPTER ONE

LILIAN'S WEDDING

LILIAN's wedding went without a hitch. This is an unusual fact to set down of any wedding. But, as Lilian's father was fussy and a shade exuberant; as Lilian's mother often looked abstracted; as Lilian was their eldest child and the first to go to the altar; as the younger children knew nothing about weddings; and as the wedding guests were mixed and lively of temperament, the smooth procedure of the day was more than customarily remarkable.

The Morrows' parish church, St. Mary's, Haddington Road, Dublin, lacks beauty, and therefore adds no fortuitous gift to such a ceremony as a wedding. But neither Lilian nor her father, as they walked up the aisle together, considered this.

For Joseph Morrow, whatever by the accident of habit was added to the progress of his life became thereby decorated. He had been baptised, confirmed and married in St. Mary's Church; he had brought each of his six children to be christened there; he had attended its eleven o'clock Mass on almost every Sunday of fifty years; he confessed his sins there once a month, made his Easter duty there, and paid his dues to its priests. He had given it some altar vessels in memory of his brother. So for him it was an endowed place; and he led Lilian to its Communion rails to give her to Michael O'Connor, the eldest son of his old friend Sam O'Connor, with his sense of proprietorship in her and his sense of occasion happily enlarged by the rifted story of himself that the church contained. And Lilian, in bridal white, clouded in lace and silk and orange-blossoms, carried her beauty tranquilly to the sanctuary gate, and was aware that it was enough for the hour and the event.

The occupants of the front left-hand pews—the Morrows let them be called, whatever the names acquired by marriage

—agreed for that day and in principle with Lilian's confidence.

There were murmurs along the files: I entreated Julia *not* to let her do her hair that way . . . The bouquet is too large . . . She's plumper than I thought, poor child . . . Grandmother's Carrickmacross will be ruined—but then I said it would be.

Natural and fair these observations; but unity commanded them. Lilian was *their* lamb, led, in a manner of thought, by them to this fine sacrifice; and all feelings added up they looked with a gentle emotion on their offerings. Some of their eyes were wet as they beheld her fairness, and as they remembered what they believed to have been their own. And, though reflecting that the O'Connors were just a little rough, they noted the furs and white gloves of the right aisle meditatively, and remembered that Lilian was making an excellent match, and that no one can get everything, after all. And some of them bent their heads and said a prayer for her. Others watched Canon Phelan come down the sanctuary steps, and hoped in God's name that the poor old man would not fall.

Bill Morrow tiptoed into the church and reached the last of the family pews in better time than he had reckoned on. Indeed, recognizing four rows ahead of him his wife's crisp hat and flushed ear, he knew by them that he was believed to be still disgracefully absent from this family duty, and he smiled as he made the sign of the Cross and spread his silk handkerchief under his knees. Then he peered, half-closing his short-sighted eyes, towards where the bride and groom were waiting to speak their vows. Canon Phelan and the assisting curate were in position, the best man was where he should be; Lilian's father was at her side. And Lilian herself, a radiant cloud of beauty, appeared exactly what young women desire to be on this, their one, day—a white symbol, among black frock-coats, of that which, having been wooed, can never again be realized after the folding-away of the Carrickmacross.

"No man goes to bed with his bride," said Bill.

The ceremony went through, as has been said, without a hitch.

Afterwards at the reception in Mespil Road there were moments of embarrassment which, recurrent though their kind are in Irish bourgeois society, nevertheless persistently take that society by surprise.

Toasts, for instance—as, 'I wish you health, I wish you joy, And every year a bouncing boy.'

It was noticed that this unfortunate enunciation, by Michael O'Connor's Uncle James, rich, friendly and head of the powerful O'Connors, did not disturb Lilian. She smiled at Uncle James, lifted her glass to his suggestion and then left the room to go and change for her wedding journey. Everybody admired her tact.

"*Viri, diligite uxores vestras sicut et Christus dilexit Ecclesiam . . .*" said Bill.

"I beg your pardon, Cousin Bill?" said Lilian's brother, Joey.

"Paul to the Ephesians," said Bill. "You should have followed the service, Joey. I don't know why anyone who reads it gets married."

Joey, who was twenty, smiled. This Cousin Bill of his was thirty-five years old; a barrister, growing bald, always half-drunk, and married to a woman whom he sometimes insulted in public.

"I think," said Bill, "that it's conceivable that Christ loves his Church in some better terms than your sister Lilian, for instance, has up her sleeve for Michael O'Connor."

Joey was wearing morning dress for the first time. He was a mathematician and studying to be a chartered accountant. He imagined that this speech came from a drunken man. As he backed away he brushed against his sister Fanny.

"Bill is drunk," he said softly. "Don't talk to him."

Fanny smiled at Bill. She and her misty blue dress looked pale and far-away to him; but he knew who she was. She was his young cousin.

"Why are you dressed up so grand, Fanny?"

"I'm Lilian's bridesmaid, Bill."

"Ah, I see. That's all right. Don't ever set up to be a bride, dear Fanny."

"Come on, pet," said Joey. "Lady Rawlinson wants to meet you."

The two went towards Lady Rawlinson.

Bill observed his young cousins as they talked to an old bundle that he took to be Lady whoever-it-was that Joey had mentioned. 'Fanny is hardly visible,' he thought. 'Yet she was the bridesmaid, or so she said.' He half-closed his eyes, and for a moment did see her. She was slim and childish. The blue chiffon of her bridesmaid's dress made a wraith of her; she had a mermaid quality. 'My poor little cousin,' said Bill, 'I think if a man could see her, if she'd get in focus, she could be decided about. But I can't see her. She's like what you take in your arms in bed when she isn't there.'

He refilled his glass with whisky and turned to the window. Beyond the garden the wide road and the canal were very quiet; the sunlight of the April afternoon was hesitant, and nothing stirred under its touch.

Bill sang to himself, and tapped his tune out on the pane of glass. *'Ah, si je pouvais Deux fois naître. . . .* It would be a fearful thing to marry Lilian,' he thought complacently while he sang.

At three o'clock the bride and groom departed for the south of Ireland in a motor-car. Their going there was a cause of great hilarity, and indeed, as one or other of the more sensitive aunts remarked, the comedy it provided was a help to the affectionate Morrow family at a moment which might, without it, have been painful and blurred by tears. But Michael O'Connor was an up-to-date young man, and he was determined to spend his honeymoon in mastering his father's munificent present to him, a brand-new 1906 Mercedes automobile. So, after teasing and fun about dustcoats, goggles and motor-caps—infelicitous wrappings for a bride, Bill Morrow thought—the two just wed were hoisted into their proud and dangerous vehicle, splendid in its dark green leather and brass fittings. The engine started, to the general surprise, and the motor-car moved forward and turned into Mespil Road and was seen to be still in motion a few minutes later on the hump of Leeson Street Bridge. Indeed, young Stephen and 'Muscle' Morrow and some young O'Connor boys who ran after it for a while reported that it vanished down Leeson Street at what must have been fifteen miles an hour.

Julia Morrow, Lilian's mother, as she kissed her first-born for the last time that day and saw the girl's beautiful blue eyes flash oddly, shadowed and disturbed, behind the motor-goggles, knew that for this bridal journey Paris and the established forms of transit would have been a happier choice than Glengarriff and a new Mercedes. But she knew, and knew that already Lilian knew, that the world was, in its appearances, designed for men and their pleasures. Also, Julia understood that although Lilian was frightened of this new carriage she nevertheless enjoyed being its mistress, for that placed her high in the esteem of her generation. And Paris would come too. Lilian would know how to graft her pleasures on to those of the man she had married.

Joseph Morrow waved his handkerchief one last time after the receding Mercedes. Then he wiped his eyes, and patted his wife's arm.

"Come in, Mother. You'll get your rheumatics again if you stand about here in that lovely dress."

The whole party moved indoors from the garden and the steps.

"I'd love to be driving away off in that contraption," said Fanny. "By myself," she added.

Michael O'Connor's Uncle James was in fits of laughing as they all moved back to the drawing-room.

"That young fellow's mad," he said. "A grand wedding night he's arranged for himself, by God! Marooned he'll be in the Bog of Allen at the psychological moment, so help me! And the little girl crying for her mother!"

"What harm?" said Bill Morrow.

"Don't mind Mr. O'Connor, Julia dear," said Aunt Edith Morrow softly.

"Have a piece of the cake, sir?" said young Joey Morrow to Mr. Samuel O'Connor, his sister's new and wealthy father-in-law.

"I'll be delighted," said Sam O'Connor. "There can't be a wedding-cake recipe in the world to touch Mitchell's, I believe."

"Mitchell's *are* excellent," said Julia Morrow absent-mindedly. "Canon, you must be very tired?" She led her

13

old parish priest to a chair. "Do sit down and let me bring you a glass of wine."

"I hate weddings," said the Canon wearily.

Fanny listened with interest to this remark. The Canon was old and did not always know whether he reflected or spoke aloud.

"But seriously, Sammy," boomed proud James O'Connor to his brother, "why didn't you advise the boy? Yourself and your present of a motor-car! Good God! I've always assumed that you *enjoyed* your wedding night, Sam? You know a thing or two, don't you?"

Sam laughed.

"So'll Michael enjoy his—he picked well, didn't he? You leave my boy to manage his own business, James! He's my son. And he knows a beauty when he sees one—my compliments, Mrs. Morrow!"

Samuel lifted his glass of whisky in vague salute towards Julia.

Father Fogarty, the curate, was worried. Young Miss Fanny Morrow, today's bridesmaid, was not yet nineteen, and he understood that she intended to be a nun. Moreover, the young Morrow boys, Stephen and Muscle, were innocent, good children, in every way a credit to Belvedere College. (Not that Father Fogarty cared very much for the Jesuits.) And the youngest girl, whom the family called Cockle— Father Fogarty understood that there was some family joke about 'Cockle' and 'Muscle'—was listening also to the observations of these loud, elderly men of the O'Connors. Father Fogarty adored the Morrow family, and wished to preserve it as in his prayers and affection he beheld it.

"We witnessed the conferring of a great sacrament today," he said nervously. "I think we can confidently leave the two who received it to God's grace."

Fanny was near the curate and heard him. 'Priests tend to say interesting, enigmatic things,' she thought. 'I suppose it's living alone that gives them that peculiarity.'

"Did Father Fogarty say something about the grace of the sacrament, Fanny?" said Bill Morrow.

"Yes, Cousin Bill."

14

"Ah! He's a priest for ever, according to the order of Melchisedech."

Fanny smiled.

"You're always quoting, Cousin Bill."

"It's a way of irony," said Bill, feeling snubbed. "But, you know, Fanny, everything relevant to human comedy has been said. So you can only quote."

"I don't know anything to quote," said Fanny, "and if I did, I wouldn't know if it was true."

Bill looked at the innocent mermaid.

"Is it possible you have a mind, Fanny?"

Joseph Morrow refilled Kitty Morrow's glass with champagne. Kitty was Bill Morrow's wife. Joseph liked her very much. She was not, perhaps, in the exacting terms of his dear wife, Julia, what was called a lady; but she was, as he rightly saw, a true and good young woman, who was served a rough deal from her brilliant, egotistical husband—and she was lady enough, thought Joseph Morrow, who was sufficiently fastidious about manners.

"Drink up, Kitty. It's good wine."

'She's ageing,' he thought. 'No wonder, married to that rattling intellectual drunkard, my brilliant nephew.' Joseph could not stand Bill, who was the eldest son of his defunct eldest brother. He had disapproved of Bill's marrying into what he called the 'small-shopkeeping element'; but he had grown to like Bill's wife, and he had never liked Bill. Now, as he poured out wine for Kitty, he saw her sad, hard eyes look past him, indifferent to his kindness. And turning to follow her glance his own fell on her husband and on his daughter Fanny.

The hour was a sentimental one for him—for he loved his children very much and the marriage of the first of them strained hard on his emotions. But out of his excellently-favoured six it happened that his favourite was Fanny. He adored his second daughter with a passion which he concealed from himself; for he was a tender-hearted man, and he could not imagine that any child could or should be preferred above others by its parents. He did not see—(he was only an ordinary sentimentalist)—that Fanny was to his ageing, watchful eye what her mother had been once to his illusion.

He did not see, in fact, the flowering in Fanny of what love had once suggested to him; that she was Julia re-made in terms of a dream he had forgotten, if indeed he had ever consciously dreamt it. He would have sworn that his first and last love was his wife, and after her in equality the fruits of her womb; but this was not so. And at his very heart—where he did not care to visit—he knew this. He knew, when he kissed Lilian good-bye, when he gave her away, that all of his emotion then was othodox and clear, sentimental without hurt. But this very fact of good-bye to the lovely Lilian, forcing him, who did not study such things, to suffer his feelings with a new attention, was making him understand now, not formally but in nervous exhilaration, how glad he was that Fanny was today the bridesmaid, not the bride.

Kitty Morrow sipped her wine.

"Bill and I ought to be going home," she said.

"Oh no! Don't go yet. Stay—we want you all to stay and have tea now. We'd feel very flat if you left us as soon as this. It'll be a sad evening for my dear wife, you know. She and Lilian—ah well, sure you know the sort of companions they've always been to each other?"

Kitty surmised that Lilian Morrow was by nature her own life-companion and no one else's. But she herself had two small daughters and an infant son, and, without hoping for much, she did sometimes dream of a possible future companionship with one or other of them, and of the tenuous compensations that might hide therein. Yet she did not think, as Joseph desired her to, that today in losing Lilian Julia was deprived of an especial filial tenderness. Her eyes still rested on Bill, her husband, as he talked with young Fanny, the bridesmaid, in the window. 'All the Morrows hunt alone,' she thought. 'This affection they trade about is only a mannerism, perhaps?'

"Very well, Joseph. We'll stay a little. Only I hope Bill doesn't get too drunk in the bosom of the family."

"'Tch, 'tch," said Joseph, and then realized sharply that it was incorrect and disedifying that Fanny, his child just out of school, should be seeming almost to enjoy the society of the family drunkard. "I'll keep my eye on him for you, Kitty," he said, and moved in the direction of the window.

16

Kitty smiled at her mistake. If Joseph was going to be solicitous, that meant that Bill would not merely become drunk but unpleasant. She turned politely to the group of ladies on her left.

The moderate-sized living-rooms of the house in Mespil Road overflowed today, as for a wedding they must, with people, voices and emotional and social situations of many kinds. Julia Morrow, who was not expansive, had invited only the close inner rings of the two families; yet that added up to an assembly of forty-six people. And she reflected now that when everyone was in his or her best clothes, that seemed, though inexplicably, to increase the bulk of a party; men certainly tended to take up more space, she thought, in frock-coats than in everyday clothes. And the men of the O'Connors were big, however attired. But Mitchell's waiters were so far getting on harmoniously with Lizzie and Nora, her two elderly maidservants; the children were behaving nicely; wine and other refreshments circulated as seemed desirable, and throughout the gathering the tide of talk and laughter swelled and did not ebb.

'However, it never does ebb at a Dublin party,' thought Julia Morrow. She was a native of the far-away coast of West Clare, and in twenty-three years of married life had not grown used to the rattling conviviality of her husband's town.

"Now, Julia, you're looking sad! We can't have that at a wedding feast, you know! Come on, try a drop of this beautiful liqueur whisky, won't you?"

"No, thank you, Mr. O'Connor. Lizzie is bringing me some China tea, I think——"

"China tea! God help us! China tea at your daughter's wedding! And you married to the most famous wine-shipper in the whole of Ireland! Ah, sure you're mad, woman dear!"

"You've often told me that before, Mr. O'Connor."

"True for you. And I suppose I will again. As Joseph's oldest friend I have privileges. But the day has come, Julia—after twenty-four years' acquaintance, mind you!—when you must make up your mind at last to call me Sam! After all, we're related now someway, aren't we? Father and mother of the bride and groom!"

Julia, taking a cup of tea from the salver Lizzie brought,

17

smiled at the big red man whom she had known since the days of her engagement, and had always found tiring and unattractive. 'Will his son Michael be as predictable and obvious?' she wondered with a pang of anxiety.

"Why, yes—I think we will seal our new association as you suggest, Sam," she said.

He roared with laughter.

"Well done! I must tell old Joseph that I've whipped you over that fence at last! Joe, old boy, do you hear that? Your lady wife has called me Sam at last, in the evening of our day!"

He went roaring off across the drawing-room towards Joseph Morrow.

Joseph Morrow was not the most famous wine-shipper in the whole of Ireland. He was the present head of a wine-shipping firm which his grandfather had founded in 1830, and which in the lifetime of its founder and of Joseph's father had held its place creditably among the best of such firms in Dublin. That its business had declined in its last twenty years was due to the simple fact that Joseph was lazier and less shrewd than his immediate forebears had been. Had his elder and more astute brother William lived, the Morrow business might still have kept its old level of prosperity; but he had died of pneumonia in his early thirties. Of his five children, whom he left well provided, three daughters had married well, a fourth was a nun in the order of the Sacred Heart, and his only son, Bill, had chosen the Bar for his profession. The family wine-shipping had descended therefore to Joseph, and sentimentally it meant much to him; he talked often and lovingly of its tradition, and he believed that he served it well. He looked forward to handing it on; but Joey, his eldest son, had hurt him very much by refusing to enter it, protesting that he intended to make real money. So Joey studied for actuarial examinations, and smiled at Morrow & Co. However, there were Stephen and Muscle. They might yet be famous wine-shippers, Joseph thought.

The O'Connors all knew—and none better than Samuel, Joseph's life-long friend—that in the world of business the well-respected Morrows had been slipping gently down while they were vociferously coming up. The O'Connors were auctioneers of lands and live-stock, and in the Dublin cattle-markets and across the fat acres of Kildare and Meath they made fine fortunes. But though the Morrow name was no longer as sound in business as a business name should be, the O'Connors respected more than they would ever admit its seventy-year-old registration, and its place among safely accepted Dublin names. Moreover, there was no insolvency or anything like discreditable penury associated with it, so far as they knew; Joseph and his relations were able to live in a condition that might still pass for well-to-do, and there seemed to be no skeletons in the cupboard. Julia indeed, Joseph's wife, was a Delahunt and landed gentry class, though without a penny to her name, naturally. But it was unquestionably a good name, Delahunt. So, except for that conceited drunkard, the barrister-nephew Bill Morrow, and whatever disgrace his bad character might bring with it—and he had already done ill by marrying the daughter of a small shopkeeper on the North Side—the O'Connors saw no danger in this Morrow connection, but mainly social advantage. True, Lilian Morrow brought Michael nothing but her beauty, her European education and some exquisite household linen and old lace. But these things were novelties to the O'Connors and they were shrewd enough to appraise them as assets. And they really liked the girl for being so beautiful, and Samuel had always had a true affection for her father. So now it pleased them, led by Samuel, to be gracious, and to make exaggerated and over-exuberant statements on this day about the high status and merits of the Morrow family.

Julia understood all this. So—less precisely and more affectionately—did Joseph. He was very glad of this wedding, because he liked his friend's son Michael, and he liked prosperity and liveliness. Julia accepted it; it was presented to her as Lilian's choice and wish. It had surprised her; but even had she seen any reason for gainsaying it, it was uncertain that she would have spoken that reason aloud.

So there this wedding party was, going forward smoothly, as has been said, and with its bride and groom already departed into the lonely, experimental pleasure of a honeymoon.

Joseph, his hand on Fanny's arm as he led her away from

her drunken cousin in the window, smiled affectionately at his big friend Samuel O'Connor.

"Well, so she's called you Sam at last, has she? And I suppose you expect me to be jealous, do you?"

"Maybe I do then! She's a beauty to this day, faith! And didn't I always say, from the first hour I saw her, that you had too much luck, you divil, you?"

"I don't think you know Fanny, Sam——"

"Not know Fanny? Sure, man alive, wasn't I at her christening?"

"I mean, since she's left school. She's home for good now, you know."

Fanny's eyes darkened, and it seemed to Samuel, who was still sharply observant of women, that she grew in a second taller than she had been. 'Spirited,' he thought in sudden heedless intuition. 'What's stung her so suddenly? By Jingo, she's grown very like that curious mother of hers, with the China tea.'

"Sure I gathered that, man, when I watched her at her bridesmaiding below in the church. I'm getting old indeed, said I to myself, for here's young Fanny in the market now, I thank you!"

Fanny slipped from her father's light hold. "I want to talk to Kitty," she said.

"She's lovely, Joe; you won't have her long," said Samuel.

Joseph frowned. 'Fanny won't be easy to woo,' he thought in jealous love. But he did not say this, lest it might seem to reflect contemptuously on Lilian, so quickly won, or on his friend's son, who had won her. He was intricately sensitive, at once to himself and to the feelings of others. This dual nervousness caused him often to desire to wound while yet unable to drive a blow. But he was not very intelligent, so he found comfort from intuition in his well-fixed sentiments.

In so artificially-poised an assembly as a wedding party, where behaviour simplifies itself into mass formations, momentarily—as a hint may dictate of unaccustomed tribe loyalty, or momentarily, again, of rash and random embracement of the new, which cannot be helped—in such a

20

social moment it is difficult to pick out and follow one theme; more difficult to espy and follow one constant, one truth. Yet the story here to be told is of a constant, a truth; or rather of a vessel, a carrier of truth—seeking its groove, as it were, its rail, its inevitable direction; and certain moreover that the quest is normal and will be justified. But the laughing hubbub of the Dublin drawing-room drowns, for this hour at least, the theme; flowers, feathers and laughing faces hide the quarry; yet whoever seeks anything, or even looks curiously or intuitively about, must be patient and delicate with such as these. For they are visible life and its mirrors; and they and their multiple reflections—which are which?—contain us and our questions, in the natural order of things; and for better or worse they are what we have to study from in our first open-eyed morning.

Fanny did not stand back at all from the humming zestful party. Being at home, she felt at home. She ate the smallest *éclair* she had ever seen in her life; delighted with it, she ate its twin. Far off in the hall, supposing themselves sheltered by the door of the back drawing-room, Muscle and one of Mitchell's waiters were downing two full glasses of champagne. The sight surprised her, for Muscle was only twelve, and expressly bound by their parents not to drink wine, even today. She looked quickly from her youngest brother to her mother. But Julia, in all her lines expressive of a politeness which Fanny recognized as automatic and therefore perhaps without virtue, had her back to the hall and her head bent resolutely into the hot, florid stream of talk arising from Mrs. Jeremiah O'Connor. Fleetingly Fanny wondered what Mother would say—or would she even then say anything?— if sweet Muscle grew up to be a drunkard.

> "... *Mon beau printemps et mon été*
> *Ont fait le saut par la fenêtre*...."

Cousin Bill was leaning against the mantelpiece.

"You again, Fanny? You know, someway you're out of place here today."

"At Lilian's wedding, Cousin Bill?"

"Yes. You're an annoyance at a wedding, I'd say."

Fanny smiled.

"If you drink much more you'll be an annoyance at this wedding——"

"I daresay. They tell me, Fanny, that you want to be a nun? Is that what's wrong with you?"

Fanny took a glass of champagne from the waiter whom a moment ago she had observed drinking with Muscle. She had never drunk champagne before. She studied it now, its pallor and sparkle, and tried to guess how it might taste.

"You don't get the tune of that song quite right, Cousin Bill," she said.

"Excuse me, but I do. I'm incapable of singing out of tune."

"That's not the same thing as *knowing* a tune."

"How do you know that song?"

"We learnt it at school."

Bill laughed delightedly.

"Schools are funny, by God."

Fanny tasted her champagne with care.

"The classic thing for the *ingénue* to do is to take an almighty gulp, and then choke amusingly. My God, Fanny, how you're going to fail to amuse!"

Fanny eyed the wine in her glass with appreciation.

"But whom shall I have to amuse, Cousin Bill?"

"The mistress of novices, I suppose."

The important day was dying. With suddenness the room proclaimed this. At one moment it was full of flowered and gloved sustainers of its significance; at the next, it was surrendered to evening and dispersal. This one and that one was gone, and seen to go with a pleasure which enhanced the painful hour; quiet, torn by far-off news-cries and clatter of cabhorses, slipped over the cheerful scene.

"It's time to be gone and at home," said old Canon Phelan. "It's time, Mrs. Morrow. Good luck to Lilian, and may the Holy Spirit help her tonight and always. But I'm tired, so I am, and I don't greatly care for weddings—so let us all be gone and at home now, in the name of God!"

'The evening, trailing sad light along the waters of the canal, answered the Canon's feeling,' Julia thought, as she stood and waved to receding wheels. 'It's time to be gone and at home. To be gone—ah, maybe,' thought Julia, as she went back to the drawing-room. 'To be gone should be easy; to be at home is something other.'

Julia crossed the threshold of the room which in twenty-three years had been the centre of home to her. It contained her adult life. Chronicling more literally, it held at this moment her husband, her three sons, two of her daughters, as well as the gear and appurtenances that such relations and relationships imply. Yet, now she entered the shabby, pleasant and most familiar room, the words 'at home,' the Canon's weary, hungry words, which she was pondering, did not take her to this place.

They took her further.

Julia was fifty. She was fond of her husband, and grateful to him—often passionately grateful in a measure which at once surprised and moved him—for his unquestioning and loyal love of her. She loved her children strongly, yet with detachment—a detachment born perhaps of timidity but which, estimated, might have yielded the measure of her great wonder before them. She had never felt, as she gathered many mothers did, that she possessed them; and as they developed she could only stand aside and guess about them; and those of them who, growing, pleased her best, increased in her her sense of far surmise.

Once, in the days when old Canon Phelan had still been sufficiently sociable to like a game of whist, he had spoken an aphorism about Julia, at the Morrow card-table, which had hurt and offended Joseph.

"They say of mad people," had said the Canon, "that they aren't all there; but you could say of Julia, I think, that she's never been all here. Anyhow, never all in Dublin, Joe."

Joseph was incapable of expressing pain or indignation to the old parish priest, but it had taken Julia many hours and nights of gentle reassurance to smooth this wrinkle so carelessly made in her sensitive husband's bed of roses.

It was true that, try as she might, her habit of living, her nature, kept her outside what might be reasonably called the immediacies, the actualities of her life. That she attended to all these and, as has been said, loved their causes, her husband and her children, was plainly true; yet a film she could not

23

brush away, a film which, unwilled by her, her own soul spun —in dreams, in the night, in her walks, unseeing walks, along the streets—floated always between her and all the people, the dreamt figures with the least apprehended, of her adult years.

She was not vague. Her perspective, though her own, was clear and constant. She saw her duties and relationships, and she fulfilled and enjoyed them; but she saw them at a distance which differentiated her, all against her will, from other people; and life brought to her such response and explanations as it had to offer along airs and channels unsuspected by her nearest, but vital, secret and known to her from the long past, from her earliest looks and breaths. Life spoke to her out of its atmosphere rather than through faces and voices; and mostly she understood and loved it at the remove her especial long-sightedness exacted, the remove of memory or guess; seldom, if indeed ever, could she fix its shape or the character or movement of its creatures while it was what is called happening, while they were living it before her eyes.

Sometimes she reflected with a smile that, paradoxically, it was because of this defect in her that she was normally and safely married, and that her husband and children—and she as well—were happy. But she did not often ponder on this accidental felicity. She knew it for an accident, was grateful to God for it, and was willing to let it be, and keep her characteristic distance from it.

But what is most characteristic in us becomes exaggerated under stress. So this evening, tired by social effort, moved by the day's decisive action, the marriage of her forthright, beautiful first-born child, and saddened by she knew not what of mingling languor, emotion and uncertainty in the hour and in the thinned-out family group, her spirit turned away almost cruelly from the moment in its sad half-light, and sped for homelier contact far away.

She seated herself in a corner of the old green velvet sofa. They were bringing in lamps, but the curtains were still open and there was only one star as yet in the rose-bright sky.

"They should be past Monastrevan now, the pair of them," said Daisy O'Connor.

24

"Monastrevan how are you!" said Sam. "What'll you bet they're sitting in Inchicore this minute, and Lilian crying her eyes out?"

Everyone laughed.

"How tired you look, dear Julia," said her husband.

She smiled at him lovingly, and gave him without effort the negation he desired. He would not cease until he died to be a most sensitively demanding husband.

The tide was out at home. She knew that because, from where she stood above the artichoke bed, she could not hear the last small suck of it below the Golden Rocks. That was always the sign it was full out. When the wind was down and there was no sound of water to hear, then the boys would be after the crabs and shouting below in the hurry of harvest before the turn. Yet if it wasn't home to you, you might hardly know from that high end of the garden that it was the sea, the Atlantic, that made the slight sighing below. There was no sight of it through the broken mulberry tree in the angle of the wall. No one in West Clare but the Dela-hunts had a mulberry tree against the sea. The lighthouse—'the last glimpse of Erin' they called it—was four miles away; but sometimes on autumn evenings from this place in the garden it seemed to be no more than beyond the coach house. Often, waiting for it to light up, Julia considered how it might be to look back at it for the last time as she went west-ward on the tide in emigration—never to hope to see that cold white tower again. It marked for Julia the boundary, the only one she noticed, of childhood, and so of life. For all of Glasalla, her father's house, seemed to look only westward, toward 'the last glimpse of Erin'; garden and fields and windows seemed to her to strain that way past the green and black water—over bent hazel trees and tossing fuchsia hedges. The white tower with its finger of light controlled Glasalla, and exacted silence of it, Julia thought. For her home, swept indeed by sounds of sea and wind and bird, was yet a silent place, silent as she so awkwardly was herself, and as her father was and her dear sister Eleanor. And silently now, salvaging her from loneliness, the place, the faithful place, encom-passed her. The tide was out; the deep and weed-wrapped garden lay asleep, and the blank, bright windows of the house, though expressive to her of all they guarded, let none of the beloved gentle voices out to reach her where she stood.

'How quiet we are in Glasalla,' Julia thought contentedly. 'Even when a swan squawks in the night on the little lake at the back it still surprises me; I think it surprises Father too.'

She forgot that she sat on the green sofa in Mespil Road. If she leant forward she could touch the nearest of the artichoke heads; they pleased her in their hieratic September pride.

"Ah! Belladonna! Dear girl!" Julia's unsocial, lovely old tabby cat had braved the crowds and was on the sofa, purring.

"I don't mind admitting, Joe, that I breathe easier in your house, now that old—pervert is out of it."

It was James O'Connor who spoke, head of the O'Connors and uncle of the bridegroom. He had drunk at his pleasure, and now held a glass of whisky in his hand. He spoke loudly, as was his custom, and his remark caused some anxious surprise in the room.

"Old pervert? Who, what have I been missing?" asked Bill Morrow.

"Careful, James," said Sam O'Connor.

"Careful my eye!" said James. "Joe Morrow is friend enough to know what his friends are thinking. Sam."

Aunt Edith Morrow cleared her throat.

"If you are referring to Lady Rawlinson . . ."

"I am, Miss Morrow."

Aunt Edith looked anxiously towards Julia on the sofa. Bill Morrow swayed away from the mantelpiece.

"What is all this loose and interesting talk?" he asked. "Who is Lady Rawlinson, and in what sense is she a pervert?"

James O'Connor measured this question.

"She *was* a Catholic lady of the name of Miss Norah O'Dwyer, and properly educated by the Sisters of the Holy Child in England. *But* she married the late Sir Stanley Rawlinson in St. Patrick's Cathedral of this city, sir—a Protestant place of worship, as you may know? That is who she is, and why she is a pervert."

26

"She is a near cousin of my wife's," said Joseph Morrow, half anxious and half cold. "She cares for the family connection, and insisted on being present today."

"No, Joseph," said Julia. "She simply said she'd like to come. She is fond of Lilian. And *I* am fond of Cousin Norah. She loved my father very much. Indeed, I think she would have liked to marry him. I was glad she was able to be here today. She's old and ill. She won't be at many more weddings —and she likes them."

Silence fell for half a minute. Even Dublin's social ease was not entirely sure of itself before that simple speech.

"It must have been some time ago," said Bill Morrow. "This marriage in Saint Patrick's?"

"Thirty or more years ago," said Joseph, soothingly.

"But it was a scandalous action just the same, Joe," said James O'Connor. "You must remember quite as well as I do the widespread scandal of the thing?"

"Widespread scandal?" said Julia. "Oh, hardly that, Mr. O'Connor! Of course the family didn't like it. But Cousin Norah was an obscure person—and almost elderly——"

"Sir Stanley Rawlinson was elderly beyond a doubt, Mrs. Morrow—but he was by no means obscure, let me tell you. Indeed, it's no lie and no harm for me to state that the unfortunate man was a—well, God help him, he was a very prominent freemason."

Aunt Edith Morrow gave a little screech.

"Oh no. Mr. O'Connor," she gasped. "Oh no—*not* that!"

Others of the ladies screeched also.

"A freemason?" they cried together, from sharp to very flat.

"That's bad, Aunt Julia," said Bill Morrow. "A freemason, God save us all! But sure, it might have been that the poor knight was a Ribbonman on the quiet, or even a member of the Confraternity of the Holy Innocents!"

This piece of irony was in bad taste, but could not now be paused for by the startled group of Morrows and O'Connors.

"A freemason is what I said, Miss Morrow," said James O'Connor. "And one who had the devilry to force a respectable Catholic maiden lady into an act of public apostasy, here in this city!"

27

The Morrow children drew around. 'Apostasy' was a word with the ring of history in it. There had been great apostates. So much was not only admitted at school, but had been sometimes discussed there at length and with gravity. But, Lady Rawlinson . . .

Julia was truly devout, and therefore much displeased by the incontrovertibility of Mr. James O'Connor's plain statement.

"I beg you . . ." she began.

Joseph, her husband, was no less devout, and he was the master of this house, where he expected to hear no dictation from anyone else on any law whatever.

"When I invite you, here, James," he said, "I'll trouble you to reserve your pronouncements on such friends of mine as you may meet until, at least, you are outside my gate again."

'Well spoken, Joseph,' Julia thought—amused at him, not surprised. Her husband was no quarreller, but she knew that sometimes bad manners could prick him to a testiness that could even sound foolhardy; and today he was not calm, no one should expect him to be calm. Moreover, she reflected, he is doubly exasperated now; he hates quite simply such gross ineptitude as this in which poor, tipsy Mr. O'Connor is indulging himself, but also he hates it that his respected old friend, whom I dislike, should behave before me in a manner for which he can see no defence.

"You'll trouble me, will you, Joe?" said James O'Connor, and his rich, broad voice was expressive of inebriate enjoyment of his own crude mischievousness. "So you'll trouble me to reserve my pronouncements on faith and morals, even when I see these flaunted in the house of a Catholic, and on the occasion, the sacred occasion, of my own nephew's wedding?"

"Easy now, James," said his brother Sam. "Easy there like a good fellow."

" 'Easy' is easily said, Sam! 'Tis you're the easy one, by God!"

Father Fogarty stood up.

"Be so good as to be quiet, Mr. O'Connor. There are young people present; and in any case all that you've been saying is quite uncalled for——"

28

"That's so," said Bill Morrow, "since you're not in the running for the Chair of Peter——"

Fanny gave a little laugh.

Julia placed her teacup on a table and stood up.

"Mr. O'Connor," she said, "discuss the sins, the apostasy, the perversion of my friend and cousin, Norah Rawlinson, wherever else you please on the free fields of Ireland—but *not* in this house. And, Joe," she went to her husband smiling—"Joe, won't you sing for us? It's been a difficult day. It would give me great pleasure to hear you sing."

"If you like, Julia," said Joseph. "Yes, of course I'll sing for you, dear."

Julia opened the piano, sat down and ran her fingers over its yellow keys. They were in tune—had been tuned for the party.

"Sing 'The Gentle Maiden', Joe," she said.

"Fanny's song?" said Joe, "but this is Lilian's day!"

"Lilian's gone," said Julia. "We'll have Fanny's song."

She began the accompaniment, thinking of the lightness of men. Joe had courted her with his sweet singing of 'The Gentle Maiden'. Now it was Fanny's song.

"There's one that is pure as an angel. . . ."

Joe sang any song he knew with a purity that was absolute. His voice was light and of no account, but he had the accidental gift of true pitch. He could add to that his sweet feeling for the simple songs he sang. So, in the simple situations where he sang, his singing was lovely. Nothing indeed could be sweeter than Joe's singing of 'The Gentle Maiden' just then when Julia asked him to sing, after Lilian had gone.

Julia, accompanying him, listened through a confusion of reactions which was not fair to the very beautiful, modest singing. Joe, as he sang, looked for Fanny, enjoying himself and wanting to smile at his pet. But Fanny was not looking at him; indeed, it even crossed his mind that she was not listening to his song.

He was right. Fanny did not notice that anyone was singing. She sat in folded consideration of the passage of conversation just gone over, about Lady Rawlinson. She was in some ways a kind of inversion of her mother. For instance, had she now even known that someone was singing, it would not have

29

occurred to her that the singer should desire to smile at her or at anyone, but simply to sing. She was only beginning to look out at life, and she found it fascinating, and asked no more at present than to watch it, and not be distracted. She did not know at all about the smiles, sighs and side-references of what is called 'feeling.' So far she took her natural affections for granted, but she did not pause for them; she leant on them, perhaps, without knowing that she did so, but her eyes scanned beyond them, impatiently flicking about the general sky. She found the adult scene bewildering, irrational and a feast for her surmise. Julia, her mother, had always held it to be bewildering indeed and irrational, but far beyond her surmise, and eventually an affair which she dismissed from a curiosity which preferred to examine the beautiful, clear questions raised by garden, field and seashore. Julia, except for the accident that she loved Joe and her children, was positively incurious about her fellow men, and therefore, when occasionally she had to face them and their emphatic activities, protected herself from all she could not miss by invoking a vein of delicate sentimentality.

Fanny, not yet eighteen, was perhaps more intelligent than her mother; assuredly she was never crude, and could not be blamed for her naïveté. Nor was it blameworthy in her that she was not sentimental. But it might perhaps be disconcerting that in her nineteenth year she looked, very likely, to any sensitive young man, the embodiment—hardly that, but the vision—of his dream. More dangerously than her more beautiful sister Lilian, she looked like a boy's dream.

So had her mother looked once, and without brooding on the question and searching into its value had accepted that for which she, if not all of her, had been made.

Fanny was different. She was a true innocent, in that she saw no reason to turn away from life at any moment, and had no idea at all that that which interested might engulf the soul so deeply that answer, comment—which Fanny was unconsciously bent upon already—would become impossible.

Now—while her father sang to her—she was engrossed in the Lady Rawlinson question. She saw, even without the direction of her mother's snub to them, that the O'Connors had been idiotically ill-mannered. But that, to Fanny, was irrelevant. What attracted her attention—never mind the bad taste of Mr. O'Connor—was this: the point having been raised, wherein lay the rights and wrongs of that long-ago decision of Lady Rawlinson, which was indeed a defiance of fixed doctrine, and which still, after thirty years, disturbed social relations? What was the general reference from the private action? Why did it annoy the O'Connors?

"You see," said Stephen to his younger brother, Muscle, "you see, your friend is an apostate."

Muscle's face was anxious.

"She's always nice," he said. "She gave me half-a-crown when she was getting into her carriage."

"Mr. James O'Connor would give you five shillings any time," said fifteen-year-old Stephen, who was a tease.

"That's true," said Cockle.

"She's very nice," said Muscle. "She's our cousin too. I like her."

Bill Morrow and Fanny were listening to the young ones.

"That's the awkward part, Muscle," said Bill. "Having a nice apostate cousin can be very awkward."

"Don't mind him, Muscle," said Fanny.

But Mitchell's waiter, passing near-by with a tray of champagne-filled glasses, winked at Muscle, who moved after him smiling.

". . . The sound of her voice is about me. . . ."

They became aware of displeasure in the liquid tenor notes, and Fanny looked towards her father at last and smiled. Placated, he smiled back, and Julia was relieved that the children had at least stopped muttering for his last few bars.

There was great applause for Joseph's song, and loud requests for an encore.

". . . Will follow me till I die . . ." hummed Bill. "But I've been singing a *real* song all the afternoon, Fanny," said he. *"Mon beau printemps et mon été,"* he chanted, *"Ont fait le saut par la fenêtre. . . ."*

Fanny was looking at him anxiously. So far as she could judge, Cousin Bill was now very drunk.

"I think a song should always say something true, Fanny," he said.

"So do I," said Fanny. "And that song is true, for Father. Why shouldn't it be?"

Bill dropped unsteadily on to a window-seat.

"Come here, sit down! I didn't notice you much before today, Fanny!"

But Julia from her piano-stool beckoned to Fanny. Lizzie had brought in a visiting-card on a salver and was awaiting her mistress's instruction.

Fanny read the card over her mother's shoulder.

Le Comte de Mellin.

"Some relation of Lucille's, darling?" said Julia.

"Oh, yes! Her brother, André-Marie," said Fanny.

Julia nodded to Lizzie.

"What a confusing day for him to call," she said to Fanny. "Do you know him, pet?"

"No. Only through Lucille's talk—I'm sorry, Mother."

"But he comes opportunely," said Julia.

"Delighted, darling," said Joseph. "Any relation of your dear Lucille——"

Old Lizzie, stiff and correct, returned to the drawing-room now, followed by le Comte de Mellin. She announced his name courageously but vaguely. The young gentleman advanced to his advancing hostess.

"Madame Morrow, I am very happy," he said, and kissed Julia's hand. "Monsieur," and he and Joseph bowed. Then the newcomer, turning swiftly, saw Fanny, and spoke in French.

"That—ah, you must be Miss Fanny? The dear friend of my sister Lucille?"

He bent over Fanny's hand.

Thereafter he was presented to the assembled guests and the day's occasion was explained to him. His English was good and he was able to express with grace at once his embarrassment at intruding upon a family union and his regret at not having been in time to see the bride.

The company pressed about him. He was not only opportune, in that his arrival obliterated from all minds any lingering thought of Lady Rawlinson's thirty-years-old misdemeanour; he was also a novelty, being a foreigner and a nobleman. Everyone was pleased to meet a count, and the O'Connors were thinking that truly one never could tell from minute to minute what these Morrows would pull out of their sleeves.

The young Belgian explained himself rapidly to Julia. His maternal uncle, M. Paul de Lainsade, had large interests in the manufacture of motor-cars and, in general of the combustion engine, and he, André-Marie, had recently been made a junior partner in one of his uncle's factories at Charleroi. He was now, with Uncle Paul, about to combine some business with pleasure—touring in Ireland. They had arrived in Dublin, with a touring car that morning, and he, commanded by his sister, Lucille, had regarded it as his first very agreeable duty to pay his respects to the parents of Miss Fanny.

So there he was, blond and gay, a pleasant exotic, admirably at his ease. The wedding party accepted him, and he accepted champagne, and expressed himself as fortunate in meeting the entire Morrow family at once, by happy chance.

"All save our eldest daughter," said Joseph. "Today's bride. She drove off on her honeymoon an hour or two ago in a dangerous-looking affair called a Mercedes!"

André-Marie waved his hand towards the road.

"Not dangerous, Monsieur! I drive one too."

Muscle and Stephen moved to the window.

"Is yours out there?" asked Muscle wistfully.

"Yes. I'll take you for a drive in it whenever your parents will allow me."

"Oh!"

"Lilian—that's the bride, Monsieur le Comte—is the family beauty, some of us think," said Mr. Sam O'Connor heartily.

"Indeed?" said André-Marie. "I wonder if that *could* be true?" He bowed slightly towards Fanny. "But indeed she must be very beautiful, Monsieur."

"You can take it from her father-in-law that she is, Monsieur. My son Michael had ever an eye for a girl, God bless him!"

André-Marie lifted his glass and smiled.

33

"Naturally, Monsieur," he said.

Fanny was amused by the delicate irony of the foreigner's inflection, and also by her mother's gallant refusal to wince away from Mr. O'Connor's heartiness.

"What a pity Lilian's married," said Cousin Bill softly to Fanny. "This noble sprig would have been exactly her idea of a brilliant *parti*."

"That's a silly thing to say," said Fanny. "What harm has Lilian ever done you?"

André-Marie moved near to the window-seat.

"Miss Fanny," he said, "I have many messages for you from Lucille—much to tell and ask."

"Oh yes—I'm dying to hear her news. She said you'd be in Dublin about this time."

"We must have a long talk—many long talks, Miss Fanny."

"We will indeed. Oh, Monsieur, this is my cousin, Mr. William Morrow."

The two men bowed.

"Enchanted," they both said.

"Sit down, won't you?" said Fanny, and the Belgian immediately drew up a low chair beside her, and obeyed.

The group of three, pressed into the window, drew close together quickly in attention.

Far away by the fireplace Julia sipped her China tea. Mr. Sam O'Connor had returned to his assault on her friendship. She understood his friendly need and nodded to it. But her eyes rested on Fanny in the window, and on Bill Morrow and on André-Marie de Mellin.

Fanny contemplated the handsome young Belgian visitor with a pleasure far more complicated than his aspect, were it or not attractive, might explain. He was Lucille's brother, he was visibly that; he was from Brussels; he spoke the French she had learnt in *Place des Ormes*; he would have messages for her, he would know the references of much that she was missing now. He was Lucille's brother—and heavens, how clearly that fact shone in his eyes!

Fanny had had a painful quarrel with her father in January. She had come home from her school in Brussels for the usual Christmas holiday—very gladly. During the holidays Lilian had announced her intention of being married shortly after Easter. This had taken Joseph Morrow by surprise; Lilian was very young, and Joseph liked his family about him, was in no hurry about marriages. But Lilian was fixed in her intention, and firmly backed by Michael and all the O'Connors. So, yielding that battle, Joseph decided that Fanny must henceforward stay at home. She would be needed in the pre-marital fuss, she should have these last months of home-life with her elder sister, she should be there and ready to be his dear daughter when he had to suffer the loss of his Lilian; she had had four-and-a-half expensive years at *Place des Ormes,* she would be leaving in July in any case, and Lilian's wedding was going to cost a pretty penny. So Fanny would not return to Brussels on 15th January.

The news, announced on New Year's Day, assaulted Fanny, shocked her, as nothing hitherto had done. Indeed, she did not believe that so ruthless a *fiat* could become a fact. She listened to her father, and instantly defied him, said that she would and must go back to school, that Lilian's plans had nothing to do with her, and that she could not tolerate to be so fatuously subjected to them. Her father and she were alone when he told her his decision, and clearly he was frightened by the scene she made. He was, however, obdurate. But Fanny reminded herself of her trump card. She had Mother up her sleeve. Mother would understand, and speak for her. Father would do as Mother directed.

Julia was always more wife than mother—in so far as she was aware of being either. She listened to the tempestuous stories of her husband and of Fanny, and—after much inner argument—she decided to support her husband's wish. Not without anxiety. Often, dreaming along with her shopping bag in January rain and dusk, she sought to understand Fanny's wild anger. She too had been schooled at *Place des Ormes*—that was why Lilian and Fanny had been sent to Brussels. She remembered her five happy years there, and she appreciated Fanny's attachment to the lovely place. But, the child would be having to leave in July anyhow; it was only a question of two terms, two terms the fees of which would be extremely useful if deflected to Lilian's trousseau; and if, as she and Joseph suspected, Fanny was thinking of embracing the religious life in the *Compagnie de La Sainte Famille*—a decision which would break Joseph's heart, as Julia wonderingly realised—then perhaps this arbitrary cutting-off from *Place des Ormes* might be a very good thing. Furthermore, the departure of Lilian into marriage would sadden Joseph; and Fanny was his pet, to whom he was always extravagantly kind—and Julia saw no reason why she should not therefore be at hand for her father's comfort at a difficult juncture. There were also other secret reasons why Julia thought it desirable that Fanny should now slip into the habits and exactions of home life. She conceded in her silent debates that to have to say good-bye to a whole life without being allowed to say good-bye was hard; but in adolescence, she told herself, these things must happen, and are good for us. In short, she decided wearily, hating to distress Fanny but determined to protect Joseph, that schooldays were over now for her second daughter, and that she must do as her father willed.

Fanny had therefore no choice. She did not return to *Place des Ormes*.

Her grief, great and surprised and for many days hopefully incredulous, did at first so strongly rule her that she was almost unaware of her anger against her father, or of the surprise she had suffered in her mother's decision against her. But they had in fact wounded her, and wounds are not forgotten, even by the most loving, even indeed by the most generous.

Nevertheless, self-control was not only hoped for from Fanny's class and generation; it was taught, and it was mastered, and understood by the moderately intelligent. Fanny was intelligent, therefore in clear opposition to her dreams and needs she saw and accepted her losses. She had indeed, as her parents suspected, given long thought, as still she would, to the religious life—and saw the point of the vows of chastity, poverty and obedience. Particularly, because she was intelligent, she saw the point of the often absurd-seeming vow of obedience. Not that she made an emotional confusion here. She was under no vow of obedience to her father—but she was materially helpless against his mandates. If he did not buy her travelling tickets or pay her fees, clearly she would not finish her year at *Place des Ormes*. So, angry, resentful though she might be, training would and did prevail—and if she lived in her father's house and ate his bread, and loved him and her mother, she would naturally behave as a daughter and as a disciplined person, who has learnt, and who understands, that her transitory desires are not paramount.

She had in fact, as Joseph and Julia acknowledged, been a good girl, and carried her disappointment with a cheerful reserve which may have made them remorseful at times, but which they respected. Fanny had continued some of her studies, at a private coaching establishment in Lower Baggot Street, and for the rest had made herself useful at home, and in shopping for Lilian.

But she was only marking time. She had no intention of going Lilian's way, and her mind would not long be contained between the two bridges that spanned the canal at either end of Mespil Road.

So now, in this saddish hour at the end of Lilian's wedding day, and tired with its fuss and strain, she turned with unconcealed delight to greet this sweet surprise, this bright-haired messenger from all she had forgone.

The party was mercifully thinning out. The polite Morrow aunts had taken their leave; Father Fogarty and some cousins also were gone. But indefatigable O'Connors, refreshed by the arrival of a foreign count, were refilling glasses and inventing new toasts. Julia wondered mistily how much more of Mr. Sam O'Connor's sociability she could parry without losing consciousness; Cockle and Muscle had gone down to the breakfast room and kitchen, in order to celebrate freely with the waiters and with Nora and Lizzie; Joseph, anxious for the acute weariness he sensed in Julia, and irritable because he felt an engulfing paternal melancholy about to sweep him with the fall of the light, screwed himself to a sticking point of desperate affability, ordered the gasoliers lighted and hurried about with wine and jokes. Kitty Morrow longed to go home, but could not catch Bill's eye, and did not dare cross to the window and ask him to leave with her. She was used to scenes with him, even public scenes, but did not wish to create one in this house, or on this day. And she knew from where she sat that he was drunk, and at the tricky phase of feeling obstinately, fatuously gay.

When the gas was lighted young Joey came to draw the curtains. But Fanny turned in the window-seat, to look towards the misted canal and the few stars shaken out above the shadowy houses over the water.

"Oh no!" she cried, impatiently for her. "Let's keep this lovely day a little while!"

Bill Morrow looked at her smilingly, and raised his glass in assent.

"Let us indeed, Miss Fanny," said André-Marie.

Young Stephen Morrow came to his father with a telegram. Joseph looked fussed, although there had naturally been many telegrams throughout the day.

"It's probably Eleanor's good wishes, dear," said Julia. They were always late about everything at Glasalla.

Joseph put on his spectacles.

"Well!" he exclaimed. "Well, did you ever?"

"What is it, Joe?" cried the O'Connor men.

Joseph read the telegram aloud.

"Mercedes mysteriously broken down. Staying tonight Fitzgerald Arms Hotel Monastrevan. Please send expert Mercedes mechanic early tomorrow. Very well and happy. Love to all.
LILIAN and MICHAEL."

Everyone burst into exclamatory laughter. This was a truly amusing how-do-you-do.

"But how very much to be expected," said Julia.

"Well, I'm damned!" said Sam O'Connor. "And if you knew what was paid for that affair!" (No one replied that everyone present did know, that the O'Connors had frequently told them its great price.)

There was a very great deal of joking, and surmise as to how far the happy pair had to walk from their superb motor-car to reach Monastrevan.

"All very fine," said Joseph, "but where in the name of mercy am I to find a Mercedes expert mechanic in the city of Dublin? I ask you, where?"

"There isn't such a person, dear Joseph," said Julia.

"If that boyo weren't so much in love he wouldn't need one," said James O'Connor. "Great heavens, if he can drive the thing can't he see how to repair it? Ah well, it's his honeymoon, not mine. But I told you, Sam, he was mismanaging it! Poor old Mike! Lilian in new shoes, and with blisters on her heels now—and floods of tears, and I-told-you-sos—Ho, ho!"

"The telegram sounds very happy indeed," said Julia.

"In any case," said Bill Morrow, "how far did they *want* to travel tonight, the babes?"

But Joseph was worried, though amused.

"I must make an effort," he said. "We must find someone to assist them."

"If I may say so, Mr. Morrow," said André-Marie de Mellin, "you have found him. I am a Mercedes expert—fully trained. And I have all necessary tools in my own Mercedes."

A gasp of amusement went up from the company.

"Of course," said Julia. "How very odd!"

"But Monsieur de Mellin," said Joseph, "we couldn't dream of troubling you to such an extent——"

"It is my work, Monsieur. It is what I love to do—and I am here to advertise Mercedes, and travel about and show her. If you will tell me where this Monastrevan is——"

"Oh, it's not far," said Fanny.

"Then, I will, with your permission, sir, leave for their rescue very early in the morning."

"This is extraordinarily kind of you," Julia began.

"It is indeed, Mooseer," said Sam O'Connor.

"Only I wouldn't be too damn early, if I were you," said James. "After all——"

"Naturally, Monsieur," said André-Marie, and bowed.

So the next day's rescue of the honeymooners was as by a miracle arranged. The telegram drew the party into a whole again; there had to be much joking about the episode, of which Lucille's brother was the hero. So he had to talk with everyone, and Fanny left the window-seat and went downstairs to help about supper.

The drawing-room curtains were drawn then, and Lilian's wedding day crept into the April night.

39

CHAPTER TWO

GLASALLA

In the days after the wedding Julia was tired. She could not conceal her weariness, and Joseph knew that 'home', as she always called it to his hurt, 'home', Glasalla, was the only medicine. So, a fortnight after Lilian's great day, Julia travelled to Glasalla, taking Fanny with her.

To her own surprise Fanny was reluctant to go to 'Grandfather's', whither she had gone enchantedly heretofore. But even since the unlooked-for wrench in January, her spirit had been turned exasperatedly towards Brussels, Lucille and *La Place des Ormes*. And now here had come Lucille's brother, with messages, invitations, suggestions flowing over; but somehow they were all politely shelved by Julia and Joseph. 'Later on, perhaps; we'll see. It is very kind of your mother, Monsieur de Mellin—but—well, a little later, maybe. . . .' Fanny could only bite her lower lip, and keep silent. She was in the hands of her parents. And she understood that so long as she was in that situation it behoved her to observe its conditions. But in the weeks which had accumulated between New Year's Day and the end of April the child, about to be nineteen, had had to reflect with wonder upon being in any 'situation' at all. Hitherto life had moved in a fixed, natural and mainly happy pattern. Mainly happy, because Fanny loved her roots, her home, her parents and her brothers and sisters, without having to take thought of such natural and easy-going love; happy, happier perhaps, because she loved the school she had been sent to, and could savour how sharply its excellences conflicted with the goodness of life at home, holiday life, the life of affection and tact and *laissez-faire*. But violently these two harmonious lives had been divorced. In a sentence Fanny had been instructed to understand that home was enough; and she had instantly apprehended, even as her father spoke, and without trial, that it was not. Her private argument against unforeseen cutting-off from all she had zealously pursued in four-and-a-half happy years she could not, would not, formulate for her father and mother. No child, dependent, at bay, and loving its destroyers, could ever, unless absurdly, unless unfairly, speak of private desires to worried-looking parents. 'Parents are not for speaking to truthfully,' Fanny thought. 'One loves them; since obviously they are kind, how not to love them? One does not understand them, if they are Julia. If they are Joseph, almost one does—but with impatience. And impatience is useless against a father, when one is not yet nineteen.'

But she could and did fling one argument against them. "Only let me try for my *bachot* in July!" she pleaded. "I'll get it—I swear. Write and ask *Mère* Alphonsine. Let me just get my *bachot,* Mother!"

"Child—what would you do with it, in this country?"

"This isn't the only country——"

"It's where you live, Fanny," said Joseph.

"Listen, Fanny," said her mother gently. "Your father and I have observed your progress at school with great pride and satisfaction. It is clear to us that you have benefited enormously by the excellent education they give at *Place des Ormes.* But the *bachot,* as far as Ireland is concerned, is an unnecessary *panache,* dear child—and you are not in any necessity of going abroad to teach, or anything of that sort. My pet, don't you see that we are doing you no harm in wishing to have you here with us?"

"We are losing our dear eldest girl——" said Joseph. "Your mother and I must have you with us now, Fanny——"

"Mother and you have each other," said Fanny.

The parents exchanged an astonished glance.

"We desire our children about us," said Joseph primly.

"You have them," said Fanny. "We swarm around! Oh, Father—let me just finish the year, and get the *bachot!* Let's argue then!"

"Argue? About what, dear Fanny?"

"I don't know. But we'd be on fairer ground."

"How do you mean, Fanny?" Julia asked.

"Oh, Mother, you know! You were educated in Brussels. You know that the *bachot* gives me a kind of minimum independence. I mean—if you and Father and I couldn't possibly agree about my future——"

"Your future?" said Joseph. "How could we disagree about your future, my pet?"

41

Fanny covered her face with her hands. Julia saw by her shoulders that she was crying. She touched her head, took Joseph by the hand and led him out of the room. Joseph looked back, aghast, at his weeping Fanny, but Julia took him away. She was a dreamer, and would not have fuss about such dull facts as *bachots*. She disapproved, with immeasurable gentleness, of the scenes that Fanny was making about two lost terms at school.

So, in Glasalla, Fanny sat by the drawing-room fire, listened to the sucking of the tide through the rocks below the garden, and waited for the flash of the lighthouse beam across the wide, empty room.

The smell of Glasalla held childhood. 'Only in a very accurate poem could I recollect the references,' Fanny thought, 'and I shall most likely never learn how to write an accurate poem. That will not matter, naturally. But what will matter is to find out——'

"Don't scratch him under the left ear, Fan. He can't bear that," said Aunt Eleanor, who sat in a hooded chair near the window. She was reading, by the last of daylight. A tabby cat lay on her knees. This cat's son, another tabby, lay on Fanny's lap. She conceded that Aunt Eleanor's admonition was correct, and began to stroke the lovely young cat under his chin. He purred and gradually, purring, fell asleep.

"Where are they?" said Eleanor.

"They said they'd go up round the Top Grass."

"Too far," said Eleanor.

"But Grandpa is very well," said Fanny.

"Yes, I agree. Julia isn't, however."

"She's tired, I know."

"Exactly. She's tired."

"She adores being here, Aunt Eleanor. It has a wonderful effect on her."

"We miss her very much always," said Eleanor.

"But——" said Fanny—"she's been—well, she's been living away from here for—twenty-three years."

"Yes," said Eleanor. "That's it. We miss her. It's a long time. Quiet now, Teresa—what's the matter with you, pet?" she said to the tabby on her lap.

44

"Why did you call her Teresa, Aunt Eleanor? It's not a good name for a cat."

"I agree. But when she was a baby she really did look like a flower—and you know, Fanny, there was a little nun in Normandy whose claims to sanctity are being examined."

"I don't think your Teresa bears any relation either to a flower or to a little saint in Normandy, Aunt Eleanor."

"That's because you don't know her yet, Fanny. She is the most delicate of all cats. You wait. In any case, should she prove troublesome, there is the great Teresa of Spain, you know. You could fit any character into her. Do you know anything of her, Fanny? But I expect in Brussels you only hear of vulgar, popular saints?"

"Didn't you like *Place des Ormes,* Aunt Eleanor?"

Eleanor turned in her chair and searched the shadows of the room for her niece's face

"I'm not there because I'm here," she said. "One can't be in two place at the same time."

The lighthouse beam struck again across the room. 'How do they endure it,' thought Fanny—'every minute, night after night?' The curtains could be drawn—but no one thought to do that in Glasalla. Fanny sat, considering this life of such peace that the hard beam from a lighthouse could not trouble. And when in the next minute the light flung itself in again on the quiet room, and took Aunt Eleanor straight on the face —'She's more beautiful than Mother,' Fanny thought, with shock.

Julia and Grandfather came in then.

"Cold! Oh, my feet are cold!" said Julia. When she came to the fireside Eleanor rose and, kneeling, took off Julia's wet shoes and began to rub her feet. Fanny looked on, amazed. Mother was a stranger to her here. At home everyone worshipped her, but no one took off her shoes when they were wet, and knelt and rubbed her feet.

Grandfather had pulled the bell-rope by the fireplace and was lighting candles.

"The lamps, Honoria," he said to the big maidservant when she came in. "The lamps—and we'll have supper whenever you think fit."

43

"Ya, sir, as between the supper and the lamps, let ye have the supper now—God knows it isn't much!—and let me wrestle with the illuminations while ye're masticating—and pity bind us all!"

"Whatever way you want it, Honoria," said Grandfather. "But what's contrary with the lamps tonight?"

"Divil a know do I know, sir, only that they're smelling like a hospital to the sky this instant—but sure, give me time and let ye be eating your ham and I'll have them tamed and downed for ye. Only, give me the bit of time, let you—and won't a candle or so do ye at the supper?"

Honoria seized two branch candlesticks. "Come on out of that now, the lot of ye," she said. "The tea is wet, and I've an oven-load of potato cakes nearly destroyed with your traipsing. 'Tis a shame for you, Miss Julia, so it is, to be wandering and stravaiguing this hour of the night—come on now, let you—'Tis like a death's head you are at this minute, me beauty——" She flung her arm round Julia as they all crossed the cold, wide room. "Come on now, me little wanderer, and have your tea for yourself."

The love in Honoria's voice as she bullied Julia made music of the things she said.

With spilling of candle-grease they crossed the flagged hall, and sat down to ham and potato cakes and tea.

Teresa and her son Iago placed themselves, tails folded round them, on the dining-room hearthstone with their backs to the turf fire. They fastened their eyes then on Grandfather, and roared at him. This was routine. They always ate with the family whatever was served, and Grandfather prepared their platter and placed it between them on the flag in front of the fire.

"Shut up, let ye," he muttered lovingly, and began at once to carve ham for them and mash potato cakes and milk. "Ye'll eat when it suits me, me pair of rowdies," he said, or half-said. Grandfather never raised his voice to normal volume, save when addressing Honoria, whom he erroneously believed to be stone-deaf.

Aunt Eleanor poured tea from an enormous silver teapot. Fanny began to eat very fresh home-made bread and butter. She was dizzy with hunger. Julia filled an old shallow Rock-

44

ingham bowl with milk, added a tablespoonful of boiling water from the urn, then mixed into the bowl two spoons of sugar and a half-cupful of cream from the big ewer. She stirred this mixture gently, and when her father had crossed to the hearth with his platter she followed and placed the well-known bowl to the east of it, by the fire. Always, since she was seven years old, old enough to be in the dining-room for supper, Julia had mixed the cats' milk in this Rocking-ham bowl. Always there had been two, sometimes three cats waiting for it by the fire. Always the proportion of milk, cream, sugar and really boiling water had to be the same. In her absence, in twenty-three years of married absence, her sister Eleanor saw to the cats' bowl, protesting and aware that she was only 'obliging' the cats, in Julia's temporary absence.

So fixed was childhood here, so present always the past. Fanny knew the idiom, and had nothing against it. Yet she watched it, as she grew up, from outside. She watched it lovingly—yet as a novelist might. Tonight, to her surprise, she watched the ritual with impatience.

'Fine for them,' she caught herself thinking. 'Fine for them, set on their old fads.' She did not go on, in any recordable shape, with her derivative, impatient thoughts. Yet, the gist of her swallowed exasperation was that she desired to be in Brussels and pursuing her education rather than drowsing about on the Irish Atlantic coast, with tabby cats, a muttering grandfather and an admonitory lighthouse for landmarks.

Grandfather, the cats fed, at last gave Fanny a plate of beautifully carved ham. There was a salad too, and the potato cakes, blazing hot in a silver dish on wheels with a spirit-lamp under it.

Fanny, soothed, began to forgive the cats and the ritualism of her mother's family.

"You eat well, Fanny—thank God!" said Aunt Eleanor. "When do you take your *bachot*?"

"I'm not taking it, Aunt Eleanor."

"Not? How do you mean—*not*?"

"Well, I can't, Aunt Eleanor."

"Can't? Child, you're not going to tell me you are an idiot? Any reasonable being can take a *bachot*! Don't imagine that

45

because I'm a farmer I've forgotten about the elements of education; You must take the *bachot*, Fanny. Julia, aren't you shocked at her saying she can't?"

"Oh no," said Julia. "We all know she can. Fanny would get the *bachot*, I think. But Joseph and I want her at home now Lilian's gone. And what does she want—with these—certificates? She's well educated, don't you think?"

Eleanor looked carefully at Fanny, and helped herself to another potato cake.

"I can't measure education," she said. "And if you talk about certificates—oh, most Holy Redeemer! Still, I think this child should be back at school—and I'd say, Julia—that there's something wrong with her!"

"Wrong with who?" said Grandfather softly.

The lighthouse finger flashed its minute-round again across the table, and in its flying glare Fanny caught a weak look on her mother's face, which was turned towards her. In the cold flash she grew up somewhat—because this was the first time she had seen doubt—perhaps guilt?—in Julia's disciplined countenance.

Honoria turned from the hearth, where she was tidying the fire and arguing with the cats.

"What you have to say, asthore," said she to Julia, "about Miss Lilian being away is of no account, for never did any of us know a Christian whose being here or in Killarney was of less matter to anyone except herself!"

Honoria had privileges, especially in Julia's view, so Julia laughed now.

"You impertinent old thing," she said, and beamed at Honoria. "I wish her husband heard you!"

"Faith, and I'll swear to you that I'm glad the poor man can't! Because I don't like Miss Lilian! Divil a like did I like her from the cradle, Julia darling—and I mad about you and whatever you'd breed all the length of my days! Isn't that a queer thing now?"

"It's a very rude thing for you to be making up, Honoria," said Fanny.

"Make up how are you!" said Honoria. "But how's the honeymoon going on, do any of ye know?"

46

Julia smiled.

"It's not a matter on which we have exact information, Honoria," said Eleanor. "And will you be so good as to take the cats out to the terrace now?"

Honoria had a tabby under each arm.

"In the nature of things I'll do that, what I do every night of my life. Do you remember, sir, the first time we ever heard that phrase here—'Will you be so good'?"

The family knew this reminiscence by heart, but it always pleased Grandfather.

"I remember, Honoria," he said loudly.

"'Will you be so good,' said Eleanor, and her nose not as high as that table-edge, 'will you be so good, Honoria, as to listen to what Mother is saying?' Ah, the sweet mistress, I thought herself and myself 'ud never be the better of the laughing! 'Will you be so good, Honoria . . .' she'd say to me for ever and a day afterwards, and off into stitches with the two of us! The gall of that one, God bless us and save us, and she not the height of the table! Ah, the mistress, God love her—she was the one for a laugh!"

"She was, Honoria," said Grandfather loudly.

"Mind Iago's back, Honoria," said Eleanor. "You're hurting him."

"And if I am, why not, the young eejit," said Honoria.

A slow bell began to peel in the stone depths of the house.

"Bad cess to whoever is at the back door this sacred hour of darkness," said Honoria. She tramped off with the cats, leaving the dining-room open to the draught that swept across the hall.

"Fanny, would you pass me the salad?" said Julia.

"I'm sorry I didn't take those ewes to Kilrush Fair today, Father," said Eleanor. "By what Michael Pat was saying I think I'd have got my price."

"Skewer to Michael Pat," whispered Grandfather. "I hope to God she put the cats on the terrace—*not* into the yard!"

"Do they still hate the yard?" asked Julia.

The white beam from the lighthouse flashed over and over the table, but no one, except Fanny, paid any heed to it.

47

Another bell began to jangle slowly, a minor third higher than the back door one, still twanging.

"God Almighty," said Eleanor.

Honoria and the cats reappeared on the dining-room threshold.

"Is it a swaree ye're holding tonight, or what?" said she.

"Open the hall door if you please, Honoria," Grandfather shouted. "And when you do so, will you kindly release those unfortunate cats on to the terrace."

"If I live, sir, I'll loosen the creatures," said Honoria. "But the way them two bells is tolling simultaneous reminds me unduly of the troubled times."

She marched across the candle-lit hall, and rattled at the great chain-bound door. There was a gale of laughter and cold air.

"Goodness, Honoria! Such unlocking! Didn't you get our telegram?"

The honeymooners were on the threshold—Lilian radiant, Michael O'Connor handsome and looking happy. Laughing, bright-eyed both; pleased to have descended thus on Mother and Grandfather, they swept into the dining-room, Honoria with them, flustered and amused.

Julia, Grandfather, everyone leapt to welcome them. Surprise and pleasure surged to their incoming beauty; the old, dark room was suddenly filled with fun.

"By God—sure we might have known it," said Grandfather.

"Lilian! Oh, darling child!" said Julia.

"Welcome, sit down! Are you frozen?" said Eleanor.

"Honoria," said Grandfather, "they'll have the bell-wires broken down, whoever's in it at the back door!"

"Yerrah, let them!" said Honoria. "I like to cast my eyes over a honeymoon pair. They say there's good fortune in the sight!"

"There should be, Honoria," said Michael O'Connor.

The newcomers drew to the fire, Julia with them, holding Lilian's hand. Eleanor and Fanny bustled to lay new covers at the table.

"Fresh tea, more salad, Honoria," said Eleanor, "and in God's name answer the back door!"

48

"Did you release the cats to the terrace?" Grandfather yelled.

More supper was brought—another teapot, more potato cakes—and it turned out that the ringer at the back door was only young Festus Joe with Lilian's telegram, despatched from Limerick at ten o'clock that morning. It was delayed, Festus said.

Lilian turned from the fireplace. She was dressed in close-fitting, dark attire but seemed to shine expensively, as with bridal jewels. Her air was aristocratic—always indeed she had that look, but now some new assurance stressed the easy pride of her beauty.

'Certainly she takes the shine out of Fanny,' Aunt Eleanor thought. 'Ach, the grandeur of her,' thought Honoria, coming in with the delayed telegram.

"When we got to Limerick last night I suddenly thought I'd love to show Glasalla to Michael—and then, as you were here, Mother——"

"It was a lovely idea my pet."

"I understand, from our maps," said Michael, "that we can rejoin the Dublin road by way of a place called Bally-vaughan, and then Oranmore——"

"Well, with a good sound ass and cart you could, in the fullness of time," said Grandfather.

"Did you actually drive here in this motor-car thing you have?" asked Eleanor.

"Didn't you hear us coming?" said Lilian.

"Oddly enough we didn't," said Julia.

"Oh, I'm hungry," said Michael, and everyone sat down to supper again. "Dear Fanny—nice to see *you!*"

"Yes indeed," said Lilian. "We rather understood from—from Lucille's brother that you were in Brussels now, Fan?"

"I'm due there ages ago," said Fanny.

"I've been greedy," said Julia. "I truly can't have two dear children torn away from me at once."

"Certainly not!" said Eleanor. "What did you have them for, pet?"

"Well, what *did* you have them for, Mother?" said Fanny, on a gust of impatience.

All truthful answers—and Julia was truthful—seemed

indelicate. Moreover, this mood of Fanny's was unexpected and impolite. So Julia only smiled. But her eyes rested a little while on her second daughter.

"That Belgian count fellow—he's been a great help to us, by the way——" Michael began.

"So we gather," said Eleanor.

"Well, he said, when we saw him the other day in Cork, that you must be in Brussels by now, Fan, because his sister was expecting to start for Italy with you in May."

"I know that," said Fanny. "And this is the end of April."

"But Fanny—we're going home in a day or two—we'll see then, darling! We'll see what Father thinks," said Julia.

Fanny got up.

"I hear the cats crying! Shall I let them in, Grandfather?" she said, and ran out into the hall.

"That child isn't well," said Grandfather.

"Oh, she thinks she wants to be a nun, in *Place des Ormes*," said Lilian. "You'll get her over that nonsense, Mother."

"If she meant that, it'd be no nonsense, let me tell you, Lilian," said Eleanor. "But I think myself she's rather a vain young lady."

Julia was hurt.

"Don't, Eleanor," said she. "Fanny is a very good child."

"Fanny's a dote," said Grandfather loudly, "Ah, here ye come, my pack of loves," he went on, as Fanny came back with Teresa and Iago in her arms. "Bring them over to me here let you, Fanny, and get the towel out of the drawer there —till I rub the dew off of them."

Fanny piled the two cats into the old man's arms, and went to get their dirty brown towel for them.

"You're not the only motor owner in this country tonight," she said to Michael. "There's another machine making a violent fuss below in the road."

"Nonsense, Fan—not here, at the last glimpse of Erin!"

"But—how do you mean? Are you sure?" said Lilian.

Fanny mused, vaguely. 'Lilian never used to trouble to play a part,' she thought. 'Why is she tonight being the heroine so livelily? She's charming Mother, she is being gracious all round; she is even showing some interest in me. Does marriage change people so much?' Fanny was young

50

and not yet ironic, but the mystical words 'the grace of the Sacrament' did float across her mind; however, shocked, and smiling to herself, she shook their implications off. 'I shall probably get to like Lilian more than I used to,' she thought. 'Even if for no better reason than that now I have a bedroom to myself.'

She helped Grandfather to rub the cats down.

"I'll wash this towel tomorrow, Grandfather," she said.

"Oh, do! That'll be grand, Fanny!"

The hall door-bell pealed; it had been very strongly pulled and would ring for a long time.

"Sweet Jesus tonight!" said Honoria, who was changing teapots by the hearth. "Sweet loving Lord! What affliction is about this place?"

When she opened the hall door and let in the cold April night she also let in André-Marie de Mellin.

He was charming, he was gay and blond and ruddy. He bowed over Eleanor's hand and Grandfather's. Picking up the cats, stroking them with exquisite care as he warmed himself at the fire he explained that after his last meeting with Mr. and Mrs. O'Connor in Cork it had occurred to him that, having business in Limerick, it would be simple and interesting for him to find the last glimpse of Erin and, incidentally, offer to Mrs. Morrow the hazards of his Mercedes, if she would perhaps consider them, for her imminent return to town?

Everyone was delighted with him. He sat down to supper, and ate ravenously. No—no tea—he could not possibly, he regretted; but Grandfather was happy to ramble off with his bunch of keys and come back with a dusty bottle of claret; enchanted to uncork and savour and carefully decant and warm it. Fanny's eyes shone over the prospect of the adventurous drive back to Dublin. Julia, uncertain, was not proof against Fanny's eagerness, worried as she already was by her own thwarting of too many of the child's desires.

"When did you get back to Limerick?" asked Michael.

"At lunch-time today. I had thought you were on your way to Dublin?"

"Well, we are, really."

"The car behaves well now?"

"So far so good."

"Still, it was lucky you were able to come to the rescue at Bantry again," said Lilian.

André-Marie bowed.

"A very great pleasure," he said.

"Yes, but what really brought you here tonight, Monsieur?" said Grandfather.

André-Marie laughed delightedly.

"Sight-seeing, sir, and the idea that I might conceivably be of use to Mrs. Morrow. And business. In fact, the hope that I may sell to you, sir, a very fine Mercedes motor-car!"

"When you've done that, young man, you'll go and sell a similar object to the Lama of Tibet," said Grandfather. "Nevertheless, don't misunderstand me. You're very welcome to my house."

"Still, it's odd," said Eleanor. "You going the roads selling things, I mean. You are, I suppose, some kind of an aristocrat or other?"

André-Marie laughed.

"I suppose I am. But we make money in my family. And I like money. Do not you like money, Miss Delahunt?"

"I've never thought about liking it—any more than liking this old knife and fork," said Eleanor.

"But money most of all," said André-Marie. "Without it you couldn't have even your old knife and fork."

"Oh, but she could," said Fanny. "She could make a knife and fork——"

"Any day," said Eleanor.

Everyone laughed.

"Funny old knife and fork it'd be, Aunt Eleanor," said Lilian gaily.

"That reminds me," said André-Marie. "I lunched in Limerick today with Mr. Bill Morrow——"

"Oh! that fellow!" said Grandfather.

"The Assizes must be on," said Julia. "That's Bill's circuit."

"Yes—Michael and I were rather glad we dodged him in the hotel last night," said Lilian.

"But why dodge Bill?" said Fanny.

"Oh, Fanny—don't be silly!" said Lilian.

"Well, I understand he is drinking a bit at present, Mrs. Morrow," said Michael—"and I, well, I didn't want Lilian to be embarrassed——"

"Well, Miss Fanny, this Mr. Bill Morrow——" André-Marie was amused and imperturbable—"whom, you remember, I talked to with you on that happy afternoon of your sister's wedding——' he bowed gaily to Lilian—"well, he said of you today, Miss Fanny—I cannot think how we were reminded to speak of you, and it cannot have been by the sad mutton that we ate, or by the pudding of milk——?"

"Heavens, it's frightful what people eat in those hotels in Limerick!" said Eleanor.

"Is it not, Miss Delahunt!" said André-Marie. "However as I was saying, Miss Fanny, your distinguished cousin said of you——"

"Is Bill distinguished, Julia?" said Eleanor.

"Well, I believe he could be," said Julia.

"—He said of you, Miss Fanny, that his present impression was that for your age you were alarming—and that he viewed your future in bourgeois society somewhat uneasily!"

The young Belgian meant all of this as froth; but Fanny's laugh was shy to a point which hinted almost at distress, and the elders did not know whether to resent Bill's vapouring impertinence, which was in an idiom they knew, or to reprove the insouciance of this young gentleman who, God help him, meant no harm.

"I'd advise Bill Morrow to be uneasy about his own future in bourgeois society," said Eleanor.

"Hear, hear!" said Michael O'Connor, and everyone laughed, including Fanny.

"I'm assuming," said Honoria from the doorway, "that some class of bedding will be required this night of God for all your new arrivals?"

"Naturally, Honoria," said Eleanor.

"Oh, that's grand," said Honoria. "That's grand entirely! Praise be to the living Lord!"

"Is it sarcastic you're attempting to be?" said Grandfather. "Look at here, Honoria Maguire—is this house rampant with bedrooms, bedsteads and blankets, or is it that I'm out of my mind in the heel of the hunt? Will you clear off out of my sight now, like a good girl, and make suitable preparations, if you please, for the comfort of my guests?"

"'Suitable preparations!' May our Merciful Redeemer look down on us all! But when did your honour last place a hand on anny single wan of the spare feather tickings above? Of course, if it's to send the young bridal pair to their death you want—not to mention this poor foreign gentleman here——!"

"Is the range out?" asked Eleanor coldly, "And have yourself and Mrs. Hession been struck with paralysis?"

"The range is not out, but at the boil, Miss Eleanor. And as to Mrs. Hession, as you should know full well, she is only now half-way through the Sorrowful Mysteries, after which she has to be left to grapple with the Five Glorious—and then, God help us, the poor woman has the Thirty Days' Prayer to face, and nine separate repetitions of the *Memorare*. So, *she's* dead out of it all for a while's time, sir —you might as well face that!"

Eleanor stood up.

"We don't face it," said she. "Come on, Fanny. You and I will light some fires upstairs. Mrs. Hession and you will take mattresses down to the kitchen to air, Honoria. Let there be a pause to the Sorrowful Mysteries!"

Eleanor, very aristocratic of movement, swept Fanny and Honoria across the draughty hall.

"No pause! No pause at all, Miss Eleanor! Sure don't you know?" said Honoria. "But we'll get the tickings as far as the range, whatever!"

André-Marie leapt to his feet, with Michael, as the ladies crossed the dining-room. Fanny noticed that the eyes of the young Belgian were full of laughter and that he watched Honoria's retreat with appreciation. 'He must know English very well,' she thought, 'if he can so much enjoy Honoria.'

He stayed Fanny's passage as he held the dining-room door for her.

"It is a great delight to find you here unexpectedly, Miss Fanny," he said. "But Lucille must be angry, I fear? When do you go to her to Brussels? She expects you every day, you know—and for the whole summer, Mrs. Morrow!"

'How like Lucille he is,' Fanny mused; and the thought

54

made her eyes absent and affectionate. 'More beautiful perhaps, than his sister; less true, perhaps.'

"I'm longing to go to Brussels," she said, and hurried across the shadowy hall after Aunt Eleanor.

'We are being unfair to Fanny,' Julia thought, moved by the girl's quick words and flight. 'Getting a beautiful daughter married is perhaps a dangerous sport. It seems to harden the nerve-terminals——'

"Why, Mother, what are you smiling at?" said Lilian.

"At you, pet. Come back, and eat, Michael. Come, Monsieur de Mellin."

"What does it cost, I wonder, Fanny, to drive these motor-car contraptions about the roads?"

Aunt Eleanor had sorted out linen for the guests' beds, and sent it down for a bit of a baking over the range; she was now polishing and refurbishing the marble-topped washstand in the enormous, icily-damp bedroom where Michael and Lilian were to sleep. Fanny knelt before the hearth, hopefully holding an *Irish Times* across it, and listening for a possible crackle from wet sticks behind it.

"I don't know, Aunt Eleanor. A lot of money, I suppose. Anyway, only very rich people seem to do it."

"So we may assume that Lilian has married a very rich man? Well, why should she not? She's that kind. Could you leave that old fire a minute, child, and bring me a piece of the good lavender soap from the press on the landing?"

Fanny fixed the *Irish Times* with a poker and tongs to support it at each side.

"Mind it now," she said, and went out to the landing. She met Michael O'Connor there; he was carrying a Gladstone bag, a morocco-leather dressing-case and a small, humpbacked, pretty little trunk. His shoulders were draped by a fur rug and a fur cape.

"In here, Fan?"

"Yes. And you'll need every bit of fur you own," said Fanny with a shiver.

When she came back with the lavender soap, the *Irish Times* had gone up in flames—"a good sign of the chimney," said Eleanor, and Michael was kneeling before the hesitant

55

fire, delicately using a squeaky old pair of bellows. He looked very handsome, Fanny thought.

"Tell me, Michael—I was just asking Fanny—does it cost a lot to drive these motor-cars around?"

"Well, Aunt Eleanor—I *may* call you 'Aunt Eleanor'?"

"You may," said Eleanor, formally. She was unaware that as she made this polite concession she was vigorously polishing a chamber-pot, part of the beautiful double washstand set of stone mason which was the glory of this guest room.

"Well—Aunt Eleanor—these motor-cars *are* rather expensive to run——"

"Then why in the name of God did that Belgian young fellow come all this way tonight, would you tell me?"

"Sight-seeing——" said Fanny.

"Yah, nonsense!" said Eleanor, slapping the chamber-pot into its cupboard, and beginning with passion on the polishing of its twin. "There's no sights to be seen round Glasalla, thanks be to God! And sure the old lighthouse is nothing but a curse——"

"But he's on a sort of advertising tour for his firm," said Michael. "Expenses are *ad lib.*, you know. He has to show off this great German engine——"

"To my father?" Eleanor laughed ringingly.

"Well, not necessarily," said Michael, "but to anyone he might pass on these roads. you know—poor devil, he's a travelling salesman!"

Fanny, who saw Lucille in André-Marie's merry face, resented this condescension to him of a cattle auctioneer.

"Then that must be an enjoyable thing to be," she said coolly.

Aunt Eleanor stared at Fanny.

"Are you conceivably taking a fancy to this—this foreigner, child?" she asked.

Michael amusedly looked the same question, and Fanny laughed back at them both.

"Maybe," she said mischievously. "Anyway, I find it nice —a person being *foreign*."

Honoria and Mrs. Hession staggered into the room, under the load of a feather mattress, which they flung on to the vast wooden bedstead.

"Well, the first of the damp is steamed out of it anyway," said Mrs. Hession; then she drew a small bottle of holy water from her bosom, and began to sprinkle round and over the bed, in rudimentary signs of the Cross.

"When we have the jars in it ye'll notice the last of the wetness clouding off," said Honoria. "Is the bolster below, Miss Fanny?"

"I placed it with my own hands in the bakehouse oven," said Mrs. Hession. "And let us return to our devotions now, Honoria, in salvation's name! Time enough for the jars and the bolsters!"

The two withdrew.

"Let us have an eye to the fire next door," said Eleanor to Michael. "That foreigner looks pampered. We'd better do our best for him."

The beautiful elderly woman took the young man by the elbow and marched him along the landing. Fanny stood alone in the flickering light of fire and candles. She considered the vast unmade bed, and the luxurious-seeming luggage. Less than a month ago she and Lilian shared a bed, a chest-of-drawers, a dressing-table. Now these locked and elegant travelling bags, these flung-down furs represented the never-no-more of sisterhood. There would be no regrets. Lilian had desired the grandeur that these assembled objects represented, and Fanny had longed for privacy, for an unshared bed. Both had their wish now, and no bones broken. Yet, as she looked with diffidence about the bedroom she had been helping to prepare, it still seemed sad to Fanny that she and Lilian had never even been able to play at loving each other, as many sisters managed to do.

'I'll go down to Grandfather,' she thought.

On the curving staircase she encountered through the great west window of the landing the long white stroke from the lighthouse. She crouched away from it against the wall, yet smiled at herself. Why shrink from an ordeal which swung back ruthlessly in every minute from sunset until sunrise? Almost as foolish as to deny the beats of one's own heart.

She entered the vast, dimly-lighted drawing-room. Grandfather was playing with the cats, who sat on his knees; Julia peered, under a smoking lamp, at the *Irish Times*; her silver-rimmed spectacles made her look old, Fanny thought with sudden, piercing love. The lighthouse beam struck the room as she stood on its threshold. It poured enhancement over Lilian, making briefly a myth of her as she sat in dreaming idleness near Grandfather; and it struck without mercy across André-Marie's face. His eyes were upon Lilian at that moment, and Fanny, thinking of Lucille, observed now in this white flash that her brother's face did not so very much resemble hers; it seemed hard and anxious, as she had not hitherto noticed it to be.

"How are the preparations going for the night's repose?" said Grandfather.

"I don't know," said Fanny. "Anyhow, the pillows are in the bakehouse."

Julia removed her spectacles.

"Are you tired, Fanny?" she asked.

CHAPTER THREE

VILLA DES GLYCINES

"You will spend summer with me, Fanny? You'll come to Italy? It is imperative that you do this—oh, I assure you!"

Fanny sat by the window in the bedroom she always occupied in Lucille's home. It was a warm and beautiful night at the end of May. She had reached Brussels on the evening before, and had been driven along the familiar road towards Ghent in just such a motor-car as André-Marie was so busily advertising in Dublin. She knew the wealthy and splendid *Villa des Glycines* from many Easter and half-term visits there, and because of Lucille she was not afraid of it. Because of Lucille, tall and shining on its lordly terrace, she had last night run gladly up the millionaire steps. She had been tired then, however, and with little more than the necessary politenesses to Lucille's parents had been happy to eat supper in her room, and go at once to sleep. She had slept late, and when her coffee was brought Lucille came in after it, laughing, to warn her that her father had important magnates to lunch at midday. There was barely time for Fanny to bathe, dress and be in her place in the salon to say good-morning to the Comtesse de Mellin before the German guests were announced.

The *Freiherr,* his wife and his brother-in-law ate well and slowly of the superb luncheon prepared for them—they were important business guests. And the de Mellin family had their own good Flemish appreciation of food. So the warm afternoon was drowsy, and contained no more for Fanny than an indolent stroll about the park, with Lucille and young Patrice and some of André-Marie's beautiful gun-dogs. But this languorous, slow readjustment to a life she knew only to wonder at, but which was dear to her because it contained Lucille, and dearer because naturally it was slipping back into the experiences of childhood, was a better way of approach now than could have been the old headlong, two-days-out-from-school return. Sleepy still from the forty-eight hours' journey from Dublin, made sleepier by the rich, long lunch and the surprising warmth of the day, all she could do that afternoon was moon about amusedly, adjust herself to talking French again, enjoy the lovely dogs and let the curious, thin Flemish light wash all the scene back into reality from memory.

They made their way through the great, walled kitchen-garden—so immaculately tidy and where the busy gardeners remembered Fanny and came to shake her hand—and up behind it over some mossy steps to a little mound, planted with ilex, and lavender, which the de Mellin children called 'The Hill'. Fanny accepted with amusement that for them it was—almost—a little hill. But she had always shared Lucille's delight in the small circular temple-grotto on its crest. For one thing, it reminded her of a colder, cruder hill-top belvedere at Glasalla. And it was in itself charming—slim-pillared. shabby, older than the wealth of its present owners, and tactfully allowed by them to be as it had been.

This afternoon as she sat on its upper, mossy step with Lucille, the dogs all lounging about, and young Patrice stretched flat, eyes closed and heavy gold hair falling over

them, on the lower step—as she sat there with Lucille where
so often they sat, and settled her shoulders against the little
fluted pillar of the portico, she said to herself that naturally
for Flamands the tiny eminence must be admitted to be a
hill. For looking out from it she saw what for her was
Belgium. Over the grey mass of the stables and garden sheds,
southwards lay—spread flat as in some thirteenth-century
monk's design—a still, harmonious plain, striped buff and
green and yellow in neat promise, banded by sandy tracks and
the white ribbon of a road; darkened and patterned by
poplars and their shadows, by swaying willows; warmed by
old roofs and curls of smoke. Across the long view slipped a
cool winding water. And here and there, tenderly interrupting the austere neatness, soft outbreaks of flowers—uni-
dentifiable, red, pink, and white—seemed, Fanny thought,
to ask mercy. So seemed the frequent, scattered spires to ask
—she always felt—in this gentle scene. And the sky, the
extraordinarily delicate, thin far sky of Flanders seemed to
her to give assent, as again on this hot afternoon, to the
especial, quiet appeal of this especial landscape.

Young as she was, and tired and over-happy though she felt
today, Fanny understood to some extent the traps of the
pathetic fallacy; also she had frequented the houses of rich
Belgians sufficiently already to know how vigorously wealth
contradicted at once the austerity of the Flemish rural scene
and the pure gentleness of the Flemish sky. Yet as she sat
with Lucille on the step of the grotto she looked all round
about over what *La Place des Ormes* had taught and given
her, and oddly enough, as she drank in the irrelevant beauty
she perceived, she felt strong, and suddenly anxious.

"Your hill," she said. "Your silly little old hill."

"I know," said Lucille. "But why don't you invite me to
go to Ireland and see a mountain?"

Patrice pushed his hair back from his eyes.

"You have been moved by seeing all this again, Miss Fanny.
Don't tell any lies. I've been watching you while I was fast
asleep."

"I wasn't going to tell any lies, Patrice. I—I love all this—
I love Belgium."

Patrice closed his eyes.

"My God!" he said. "You poor girl!"

Lucille, who was eighteen months older than Fanny, had taken her *baccalauréat* with distinction a year ago, and then, with regret and in anxiety, had had to come home under her imperious father's command, to the idle, pampered life he intended this eldest daughter—indeed all his daughters—to live. But she had a forthright, questing kind of intelligence; she was also as wilful perhaps as her father, and Fanny suspected that battle was engaged already between the two.

The friendship of these girls was a lucky chance for both, since by reason of age Lucille was always in a grade above Fanny; but it was now nearly three years old. It had arisen when on one October holiday afternoon some of the young ladies of *Place des Ormes* were lounging in the cloister and discussing a sermon delivered to them that morning by a distinguished French bishop—on love of God. The bishop was handsome and eloquent, and had been much moved himself by his resounding analysis of why, when and in what manner it was man's duty to love God. Most of his auditors had been as much moved as he—and on that delicate autumn evening some of them were possibly feeling a melancholy, hopeless love for the holy man.

Fanny was not subject to falling in love with the clergy, and she had really listened to the sermon.

"I didn't like it," she said. "It was sentimental. In fact, it was all casuistry too."

Everyone laughed. Ah, this Irish Fanny! We know her and her anti-sentiment bias! And what is that word 'casuistry', Fanny? Is it a Gaelic word?

A tall fair girl who was leaning against a pillar near Fanny's group looked up from her book; and looked with attention at Fanny.

"I agree with you," she said. "I wanted to interrupt several times. Have you been reading Pascal?"

"Well, yes—a bit."

"Where did you get him?"

"He's in the library here."

"Pascal! He couldn't be!" shrieked Isabelle de Chasseberg. "He's a heretic!"

61

Lucille laughed.

"Dear Isabelle! Ask *Mère Générale* for a few words on Pascal!" And then she returned to her book.

But so she and Fanny became friends—and their friendship grew to inviolability as each discovered, both being secretly arrogant, that the other was her only intellectual peer in the whole school.

Fanny smiled down now at the great, long boy, Patrice. He was her age, and would be facing the ordeal of the *bachot* in the coming weeks, as she also should have been. She had known him since her first visit here with Lucille, more than two years ago. He had seemed small, evasive and wild-animalish then, but had grown of late, mentally as well as physically, at an abnormal-seeming rate. Even last autumn he had already seemed to her formidably mature of mind, but Lucille in recent letters had reported, half-ironically, his unresting leaps and plunges into intellectual manhood. And there he lay now, a lazy giant, no more disposed to open his eyes wide than he had ever been. And certainly the *bachot* would not take a feather out of him.

"You sound very worldly, Patrice," she said.

"Yes," said Lucille. "Indeed, he's world-weary. As well as going to and from Brussels every day to school, he's been to Antwerp twice! Haven't you, Patrice?"

Patrice opened one blue eye at them.

"I've walked through the Ardennes too—very fatiguing. And—don't you remember, Lucille?—don't you remember Le Coq-sur-Mer?"

"Ah, yes! Poor Diogenes!"

"You still call him that?"

"Naturally."

Patrice stretched up to the grotto for an ivy leaf which he began to chew.

"What did you think of the son and heir, Miss Fanny? He appears to be enjoying Ireland!"

"André-Marie? He's charming—we all found him very gay and—well, a novelty, I suppose."

"He'd like that," said Lucille. "He loves being a novelty." She smiled benevolently.

"He's much handsomer than you, Patrice," said Fanny.

"Oddly enough, I don't agree, Miss Fanny," said Patrice.

"He's clearly infatuated with Ireland—and all the Morrow family," said Lucille. "Indeed, I think Mother is terrified that since you gave him the slip by coming back to me, he'll marry Cockle!"

"Cockle is under the age of consent," said Fanny.

"Cockle! What a word! What sort of a child is called Cockle, Miss Fanny?"

"A nice little child called Marie Rose."

"Ah! Marie Rose—perfectly all right. Cockle." Patrice repeated the word reflectively. "It is a pity for our alluring André-Marie that he reached Dublin too late to capture your beautiful sister, no? You *have* a beautiful sister, Miss Fanny? The newly-married one—I forget her name?"

"Lilian," said Fanny. "Yes, she's beautiful."

"Don't you think Fanny beautiful, Patrice?" asked Lucille.

He opened an eye again.

"Not yet, I think. She lacks definition, this Miss Fanny. But I have no doubt that that will come. Then—we'll see." He smiled and closed his eye. The two girls laughed. "But André-Marie has written to me—he seeks to educate me, you know!—that the beautiful sister, the Lilian, is—oh, well!" He kissed his own hand, and then stretched it up for another ivy leaf.

Fanny who had known this household well for over two years had never, as it happened, met André-Marie until he walked into the Mespil Road drawing-room at the end of Lilian's wedding day—for he was a busy young man, and lived mostly at Charleroi, where his uncle's factory was. In Ireland when she was lonely and fretting for Brussels, he had seemed to her poignantly like Lucille; now she tried to recall his charming face, but it was lost behind these two that she knew so much better. Yet how alike the three were—tall, fair, strong, and blue-eyed; and so merry, so easy to be with, gracious and quick.

She closed her eyes. The sunshine, the sweet smells and her lingering weariness sent her almost asleep against the little fluted pillar. Glasalla. Mother. It was fun, the long drive to Dublin in André-Marie's car. Yes, Father, yes, do sing. Sweet little cat, Iago—you're a sweet——

"Come indoors, Fan," said Lucille, taking her elbow gently. "You're still a very tired traveller."

"I am," said Fanny, smiling. "Goodness, Lucille, I'm like Grandfather, nodding off in the afternoon."

"We all come to it, if we have any sense," said Patrice, climbing to his feet as Fanny and his sister rose. He bowed to them and entered the shade of the little temple, taking a book from his pocket.

"How amusing he has become!" said Fanny, as she and Lucille descended through the garden.

"Yes, he's nice, with all his flourishes," said Lucille. "Ah, Fanny, it's good you're here! I'll have them darken your room completely, and then we'll send you tea—Irish tea!—and then you must sleep! Because I regret to tell you that Aunt Justine and M. le Curé are coming to dinner——"

"Oh, Lucille! Couldn't I *not* come down to dinner, just this one time?"

"If you're as tired as that I'll insist that you don't! But you do know my parents. Kindness itself, but if anyone declares herself unable to eat a large meal at the usual time, there's nothing else for it but instant medical attention, the best in Brussels! And everyone has to be frantically upset, because of the alarming phenomenon of a fellow-creature who doesn't want any dinner!"

"I know! I remember! And sometimes I've thought your parents are right, Lucille! Because look at the race of splendid Gothic giants they are raising up!"

"To the glory of God?" asked Lucille.

"Well, anyway, not to His shame."

Lucille smiled, and then grew grave.

"We live absurdly," she said. "I for one will *not* spend my one human life this way."

So Fanny had a sleep and, bathed and wearing the first dinner-gown she had ever possessed, had descended to face Aunt Justine, M. le Curé and the extravagant, excessive delights of the de Mellin dining-room.

The evening had indeed been amusing, refreshing. Lucille's relations, when one was feeling strong enough for them, were a complete entertainment, and having slept

64

in the afternoon she had felt nearly strong enough.

Moonlight flooded the terraced garden now; sweet smells crossed each other, and the tall, lacy iron gates threw black patterns over white gravel and pale grass. Hoofs, carriage-wheels sounded discreetly now and then on the road; the plain beyond was steeped in silver and silence. Far off to the left some lights of Brussels winked against the moon.

"You'll stay for all the summer, Fan? You'll come to Italy? Oh, promise, promise!"

Fanny could not answer, though she knew that her answer was "yes." She knew, with delight, that she would stay with Lucille all the summer, and go with her to Italy. Yet there were superficial as well as under-surface reasons why she could not answer quickly. Superficially the embarrassment was that it was impossible to mention money, ways and means to Lucille. Fanny could not afford to travel to Italy, let alone in the de Mellin style of travel; she knew that in these invitations and appeals she was assumed as Lucille's guest, and that Lucille would lose patience if she dared to say anything about the cost of travelling about Europe. Lucille loathed money, and all talk of it; but more attractively than most rich people, who demonstrate their dislike of their burden often to the discomfort of the lightlier laden, she was truly gracious in her desire to use that which she could command for her own pleasure, this being largely her need to give pleasure to whomsoever pleased her. Fanny, knowing Lucille, knew that she could really spoil the latter's delight in setting out for Italy if she refused to share in that delight, or set up an argument about paying her way—which certainly she could not do. So, for the moment, she brushed aside the awkward "I can't afford and can't accept" protests, which would always be embarrassing, and would always infuriate Lucille. But there were deeper-lying anxieties which held her back from immediate response to a prospect all brilliant with enchantment. And these, though they were many and strong, she could not bring to definition—at least not on this lovely, happy night. Most of them lay cloudily with Father, with Mother. Was she justified at all, was she not being unfair and selfish in merely thinking of a whole summer with Lucille and in Italy? And, since she was not to have her *bachot* she should be thinking now at home about how to approach responsibility and how to shape her life and livelihood—since she had no intention either of staying at home idly, or of marrying the first suitable intendent for her hand.

But in the foreground lay a vague desire to refuse this curiously urgent and attractive appeal from Lucille, for Lucille's sake and her own. Lucille was not over-dramatic, and in the small, various crises of their friendship Fanny had indeed learnt from her; because she was so naturally just and balanced, because she never asked too much either of fellow-creature or of situation, because her brain dominated Lucille without even quenching her live heart, Fanny had learnt from her, and knew that in everything she could trust her. So now she knew there was no falseness in this appeal. It sprang from trouble; it was a claim on Fanny, and its ring of urgency honoured her love, her free and unhesitating friendship. Lucille, in short, was in trouble, in battle—and she—the strong, the clear-headed, the fearless—she, Lucille, actually needed to have so hesitant a one as this Irish Fanny at hand.

Fanny had felt this afar off. In the invitations, in letters, even in André-Marie's gay reference to his sister's waiting, she had felt some of Lucille's urgency. She had known then that, granted her father's consent and purchase of her travelling tickets, she would go to Brussels. Yet she had been, and still was, uneasy. She did not feel equipped for what Lucille might expect of her: she felt uneasily in sympathy with whatever the cloudy battle was into which she was entreated, but sympathetically she feared that it might only too easily merge and spread and become her own battle; and, an argument which Lucille would find insufferable, she did not like the idea of being the expensive guest of Lucille's parents whilst she promoted—as her heart told her she would—every rebellious treachery of Lucille against their hopes.

"You'll stay? I have to talk to you this summer. Fanny, you are the only intelligent person I know!"

Fanny laughed.

"Oh, Lucille—what nonsense!"

"Well, the only intelligent person I trust—will that do?"

66

"It's better."

"But you see, Fan—that's what I mean! You modify, you make me think twice——"

"That can't be true, Lucille, because I always think *you're* right! It was you who taught me to think at all, you know. Honestly, it was!"

"No. Ah, no!" said Lucille.

A great dark moth wheeled in and settled on Fanny's hand.

Across the fields a clock began to ring midnight. Fanny half-closed her eyes and tried to count the Pleiades. She never could find exactly seven of them.

"What is it, Lucille? What are we to talk about this summer?"

"Me!" said Lucille. "Isn't that dreadful? But let's leave the hideous topic until we're on our way to Italy."

"Italy! But—Oh, Lucille—I've no money."

"'Sh, I beg you! We're simply swollen and sick with it here."

"May be. But——"

"Fanny, I entreat you! Do you want to put me into a fury?"

Fanny stretched out her hand and the moth flew away. She took Lucille's hand.

"You and your furies!" she said. "Ah, you dear one."

"*Mère Générale* wants to see you."

"And I to see her, indeed! How is she?"

"Uglier than ever, fatter than ever."

They laughed.

"When it comes to dying," said Fanny, "I'd like to have been *Mère Générale*."

"Perhaps when it comes to dying you will have been——"

"No. There could only be one of her. Anyway, I don't think I'm going to be a nun——"

"Thank God. Though I think a religious vocation may prove to be my only escape from Father! And if I'm driven to that, Fanny, you *have* to come too! Remember!"

"I'll remember. We'd have fun in the novitiate—but then —oh then, they'd send me to Poland and you to Canada!"

"We're not taking that risk, Fan! And we're taking no vows of any kind, I imagine!"

67

"There are marriage vows," said Fanny mischievously.

"I know, I include them. No vows, I tell you, Fanny."

"That'd be best, I agree," said Fanny. "But people seem to find them necessary——"

"I can't imagine why."

"Anyway, hers didn't seem to take a feather out of Lilian. You never saw so cool a bride!"

"She was always icy-cool. Do you remember one day when she had been awfully insolent about something or other at tennis, and old *Mère* Célestine said: 'Beware, child, beware lest your heart grow cold!' And Lilian laughed as rudely as you like and said: 'I'd rather beware of its ever growing hot, *Mère* Célestine!'"

"I didn't hear her say it, but I remember your telling me about it. Still, you know, there's more meaning in it than you allow. It's even enigmatic, if you like!"

"Nonsense, dear Fan! There's nothing enigmatic about Lilian!"

"I expect not!" Fanny laughed. "Anyhow now she's very happy and grand and rich."

"Which is exactly right for her."

Silence fell around them tenderly.

"I must let you go to bed," said Lucille. "You're still very sleepy, you bad traveller."

She stood up and moved to turn on lamps. The miracle of electric switches, in one's room, beside one's bed, still had power to ravish Fanny's wonder. She turned to smile at the illumined room and at her radiant, tall friend.

"How did you really like André-Marie?" Lucille asked suddenly.

"Well—but I told you—he has enchanted us all. He's delightful. And—he reminded me of you. Isn't that enough?"

"Rather too much, Fan. He's not a bit like me."

"Well, in temperament perhaps not. But—I didn't get to know him. Indeed I was hardly ever in his company, except when he drove Mother and me from Glasalla to Dublin. That was great fun—and he was a wonderful kind of—captain of the ship. Mother adored the expedition—and I don't think she had expected to!"

"Oh, he's marvellous with his great German cars!

68

Apparently he's making vast deals for them in Ireland, what's more. He'll be richer than Uncle Paul, I believe, before he's very old. Isn't it awful to belong to a family of Midases, Fanny?"

"I don't know. To me it's a novel idea. I'd have to try it."

"Well, do if you like. Why don't you marry André-Marie?"

Fanny laughed.

"One has to be asked! But what on earth put such a thing into your head, silly? Would you *like* me to marry your brother?"

Lucille came and took Fanny's head into her hands.

"No. I'd loathe it. And anyway, he won't ask you. André-Marie will marry a beautiful, fat German girl—some motor-car millionairess."

"Very well then! Shall I marry Patrice?"

"I don't think anyone will ever marry Patrice. I think the notion would drive him mad. And he is *very* like me, as it happens!"

Laughing, she moved to close the outside shutters.

"It's a pity to shut out all those stars," said Fanny.

"Well, mosquitoes, moths, bats—do you really want to sleep? Look, pet, here is some fresh lemon juice, see—and there's iced water in this Thermos jug—and there are biscuits in this little box. Would you like me to have them send up a jug of milk?"

"My goodness, Lucille, you make fun of your mother—but you're every bit as bad!"

"No, I'm not—but she'd eat me if I couldn't swear I'd offered you every possible nourishment for the night! I'll be cross-examined when I go to say good-night to her."

"Won't she be asleep?"

"No, no; she's in the oratory. I'll have to force her out of it now, and to her room. Oh God! How I detest being the daughter at home!"

Fanny kissed Lucille's frowning face, smiled into her brilliant, sapphire eyes.

"Still, I can see their point," she said lovingly. "If I were your mother I'd keep you at home."

Lucille laughed delightedly.

"*You* for a mother! Great heavens! Good-night now,

69

and do get your sleeping done! I'm having no mercy on you tomorrow! There are heaps of things to do, and to arrange."

"Good-night. I'll sleep, I promise. I must write to Mother——"

"But we telegraphed——"

"Yes. Oh, I'll write in the morning." She yawned. "Italy. Where are we going to in Italy?"

"To Venice first. We can't do everything this time——"

"Venice? Oh, Lucille! Oh, dear Lucille, good-night!"

The oratory door, at the end of the wide, long corridor, was ajar. Lucille stood on the threshold and contemplated the quiet little chapel for a moment before she disturbed her mother's prayers. She smiled, she hardly knew why, into the incense-burdened shadows; perhaps because she was happy to have Fanny with her again, and to be about to go with her to Italy, or perhaps because it was amusing to contrast from downstairs, where her father and M. le Curé were, the click of billiard balls, the loud laughs and the cigar-smoke—all carried up through the well of the stairs—with this ugly, silent little place of prayer, the candles flickering round Our Lady, and her mother's large form bent in faithful rapture.

But no; Lucille was not sardonic. She was too young and true to feel other than shocking the exaggerations of life in this house—and her mother's brainless piety exasperated her as much as did her father's very intelligent materialism. When she was alone she did not smile at these extremes in her parents' philosophies—if such they could be called, Indeed, they angered her—and sometimes she was touched, though always bewildered, by her mother. So, if tonight she smiled on the threshold of the oratory, it was absent-mindedly; in pleasure for having Fanny under her roof again, and in thought of Italy.

She knelt a minute beside her mother.

The one beautiful thing in this rich, over-carved and over-loaded oratory was its statue of Our Lady, Queen of Heaven. Fourteenth-century, carved in oak, crowned and smiling, her eyes bent towards the three roses which lay in her joined hands, this triumphant, quiet figure was indeed a veritable Queen of Heaven. It always pleased Lucille to recall that her father had bought the statue at an enormous price—as a present for his wife when she, Lucille, was born. And it was the only object in the house that she coveted, and prayed might one day be hers.

Now she set another tall candle on the candelabra, smiled at the Queen of Heaven and took her mother by the elbow. The latter rose, gathering up her rosary beads, and blessed herself. Together they left the oratory and closed the door, the Countess first liberally sprinkling Lucille, the threshold and herself with holy water.

"You're a great bully, my darling—indeed, you're the image of your father! However, I'll say my novena in bed!"

"I hope you don't mean that I *look* like Father," said Lucille good-humoredly, as she opened the door of her mother's room.

"You know I do, love. You're the image of your dear father in every way—and what could be more fortunate? Except, of course, that, like him, you are not quite as devout, I think, as one might hope for!"

Lucille laughed.

"No, Father isn't what I'd call devout!"

The Countess frowned and, with warning grimaces, placed a finger to her lips. Her maid was standing to attention by the dressing-table, and must hear no flippancies about the master of the house.

"I am very tired, Séraphine, and you will brush my hair slowly and carefully, so that I may sleep. Stay, darling, while my hair is brushed. I want to hear all Fanny's news. I've hardly exchanged a word with the dear child yet! All these guests today!"

Séraphine, grey, thin, ageing, undressed her large, strong mistress, wrapped her in silk, placed cushions about her in her dressing-table chair, and stood and brushed her hair gravely, carefully. Lucille watched, and marvelled, as she had done on many and many a night since she was less than ten years old.

"Is Fanny comfortable, darling? I should have gone myself to see to her, but M. le Curé was so very talkative, and then you know your Aunt Justine! And I felt that surely I could

71

trust you to see to your beloved Fanny, at least! Has she everything she wants?"

"Oh, yes, Mother. I expect she's fast asleep now."

I wonder! She ate very little at dinner, darling! Oh yes, I noticed—she just played with the sole—and I must say that I do consider Pascal's sole *véronique* one of his few perfections!"

"*Few* perfections! Mother dear, Pascal cooks indecently well!"

"I don't know what you mean by 'indecently', darling. Pascal *is* a good cook—but there is no sense in exaggerating. After all, food has to be properly prepared, Lucille! Don't you agree?"

"Would it matter if I didn't?"

"I don't see what you mean, pet. Gently, please, Séraphine. You ought to know by now how sensitive my left temple is. But, do you think, Lucille—a cup of *bouillon* now for little Fanny, and a small piece of toast?"

"Yes—send it up to her, Mother—do have it sent up!"

"Are you laughing at me, darling? But why? You saw yourself that she didn't touch her duckling, or the really perfect artichokes, or the salad. And—can you remember?— did she or did she not eat the rum omelette? I believe she enjoyed the cherries, which are delightful just now. But what are a few cherries, if you haven't eaten your dinner?"

"What, indeed?"

"You know, Lucille, that child looks delicate. The Irish seem to eat very—very peculiarly. André-Marie says that their food is positively extraordinary."

"Well, he seems to be able to manage on it."

"I wonder. It's very worrying. Supposing he were to get poisoned, darling, or to undergo a stomach upset?"

"Yes—supposing!"

"When will you begin to take things seriously, Lucille?"

"Which things do you mean, Mother? André-Marie's digestive processes?"

In the mirror Lucille considered her mother's heavy yet still beautiful face, and behind it the weary old face of Séraphine.

Oh Séraphine, she longed to say, go off to bed in God's

name, and forget this old lady and her hairbrushes and her thinning hair. But she knew that to say any such thing was to put Séraphine in an awkward position, and even perhaps to endanger her job. And she knew that Séraphine, having grown old and ill by this tyrannical dressing-table, must stay by it—if her nephew was to get through the seminary, if her niece was to have a dowry, if her old father was to be allowed to continue to occupy a cottage much needed by M. de Mellin for a gamekeeper.

There was a loud knock on the door that led to the dressing-room, and immediately upon it M. de Mellin entered his wife's bedroom, clad in a white silk dressing-gown. He was a neatly made man of medium size, a greying blond with a crisply handsome face and grey moustaches brushed in the style of the reigning German Emperor. His eyes—wherein he was seen to be Lucille's father—were magnificently intelligent, attractive, sapphire-blue. His wife turned and beamed at him. He kissed his hand to her, and smiled on Lucille.

"How many prayers has she still to say?"

"Oh, I don't know. We were discussing André-Marie's digestive system."

"Well, you could hardly be on a healthier topic."

"That's what I think."

"Do you really mean that, Marcel?" asked the Countess anxiously.

"No, dear, of course not. Obviously, the boy's a martyr to ill-health. Now, Séraphine, off with you—you're dead sleepy, and we want a few hairs left on the head of Madame—for a while."

Séraphine smiled and vanished through the bathroom door.

"I don't know why you have to make fun of me to the servants——" said the Countess, with perfect good humour.

"Lucille," said her father, "do you suppose that André-Marie is having a love-affair in Ireland—or, if you prefer me to be delicate, do you imagine that he is falling in love?"

The Countess wheeled round and stared at her husband.

"I don't know, Father. I have no evidence. I gather he adores being in Ireland—which, considering his digestive

sensitiveness, etc., must mean much. But then, he's making
money there, and he loves money."

"That is true. And Fanny, after all, is now here."

"Yes," said Lucille.

"But," said the Countess, "he would not be in love—with
Fanny?"

"Why should he not be?" inquired her husband.

"Ah, but obviously, Marcel. Fanny is a lady. He cannot
be in love with a lady, unless he marry her. But he will marry
—as my brother will arrange—he will marry, a lady of course,
but a lady for the business So he cannot be in love with
Fanny. Perhaps he has found some—some pleasure, some
kind person——"

Lucille laughed.

"Really, Mother, in spite of all your prayers, you're a very
reasonable woman."

"It is possible, unfortunately, to fall in love with a lady,"
said the Count de Mellin.

"You think so, Marcel?" asked the worried Countess. "But
—but Fanny? She is a darling, she is Lucille's sweet friend,
and we all love her. But—to fall in love with Fanny?"

The Countess opened her vast, pale blue eyes very wide in
question, and the Count, his sharp, sapphire eyes snapping,
laughed vigorously into their question.

"Dear one," he said to his wife, "to fall in love with Fanny
is so easy that even I, even M. le Curé have to be sharply on
our guard. Haven't you noticed that Fanny is enchanting,
grows enchanting? When you first brought her here, Lucille,
she was the usual little awkward foreigner from *Place des
Ormes*. But heavens, how she unfolds, how she stretches up
in grace!"

The Countess ceased massaging her eyelids.

"Poor Marcel! You're talking idiotically," she said.

"No, I'm not, my dear. But I'm only saying that a man
in love with Fanny might justifiably talk so. Still, I don't
think André-Marie is in love with her. I think he is still too
worldly to be completely attracted to a girl."

"But you—you were attracted to me, Marcel—and I was
only a girl out of school."

"I wasn't at all attracted to you, love, when you were a

girl out of school. But you were the arranged and perfect marriage, according to both our families. And I was very fortunate in that I fell in love with my sweet wife, as it turned out. Don't go over all that—you know it upside down.''

The Countess beamed. Lucille was not embarrassed. She had seen and heard this before, and knew that, for all its sentimental flourishes, it was true. Her father had, she believed, fallen in love with his wife after marriage. And clearly, until she began to get fat, the Countess must have been a very great beauty. Moreover, she would have had the charm of immeasurable silliness—very restful, Lucille guessed, to such a man as her father.

If the Countess de Mellin was nothing else, she was, to her finger-tips, a man's woman. From her cradle to her grave she would have been wax in the hands of men. Her father, her brothers, her husband, her confessor, her sons—and indeed, at a reserve, her butler, her chauffeur, her dressmaker and her cook—all of these were for her mysterious creatures with whom she felt entirely safe and in the dark. Although she did not know of this peculiarity in herself, Cécile de Mellin was truly happy only in the society of those to whose thoughts and emotional processes she had no clue. Men were just such beings, so she liked them. Women, on the contrary, had always given her the fidgets. Without being aware of it she had never liked her mother, of whom she constantly spoke with great filial reverence, and for the repose of whose soul she prayed and gave alms unremittingly. She had disliked her schooldays at *Place des Ormes*; being stupid almost to illiteracy in a society where, for its time, the standard of intellectual curiosity was kept rather high, she certainly was at a disadvantage—at school. Nuns bored her then as always they would. Her contemporaries, the young ladies with whom she 'came out', with whom she was presented at Court and whom she met at balls and hunting parties, did not interest her at all. She was in no sense unkind to them, or about them; she was not feline, and she wore no claws, but, foolish, feminine and pretty herself, she somehow took no interest in the reflection of these familiar attributes in others, or in their variegated consequences. Even when her second child was born, four years after the birth of André-Marie, and at the end of a very sick pregnancy and a perilous delivery, she had been secretly disappointed at having had a daughter. She could not understand her husband's delight. "Lucille!" he had cried out, when he first kissed the infant. "We'll call her Lucille, for my dear mother!" Had Cécile known on that day that she was to bear only one more son, and three more daughters, she would indeed have felt herself a wronged and outraged woman. However, mercifully she could not read the future. Yet, pious though she was, she did not truly think that the beautiful, extravagant, far-sought statue of Mary Queen of Heaven was the consolation prize her husband should have chosen. She never did other than venerate it, and all her children and household were educated to regard it as her treasure above all treasure. Yet the Count may have guessed that something was amiss in his gesture. For it is true that he celebrated the births of Adèle, Cécile and Isabelle respectively with diamonds, pearls and emeralds. (It was always a secret satisfaction to Lucille that she alone of his six children had at her birth wrung from their imperious father a real expression of paternal joy.)

"Did I hear the telephone ring while I was in the oratory, Marcel?"

"You did, dear. My sister Justine as usual—you'll be glad to hear she reached home safely once more."

They all laughed. Aunt Justine, Madame van Aalenhuis, always found it necessary to inform her relatives of her safety, even after so small an expedition as a four-mile drive home to Brussels after dinner.

"But also, she desired to reassert what she told us at dinner —that all the family is too much involved with German money, and that we're going to be ruined one of these days. I told her, once again, that the man to speak to about that is your brother Paul. *I'm* not importing and assembling German automobiles."

"But you have a great many German investors in the bank."

The Count was president of the bank his grandfather had founded in 1840.

"That is true—and I have some valuable German investments also. But though the Curé actually supports Justine's notion that the German Empire is riding for a fall—I am not disturbed."

"Well, of course if one were to be disturbed every time Justine got in a fuss about money——" The Countess laughed and rose from her dressing-table. "Good-night now, darling," she said to Lucille, embracing her. "Have a really good sleep—no reading in bed, mind!"

"Oh, Mother—don't be silly!"

"Your mother is not silly about that, Lucille; you know that reading in bed is not allowed."

Lucille accepted her father's firm kiss non-committally, smiled at her parents and withdrew from their room. She always read in bed and would do so tonight. She had a stack of new books of Italian history, travel and topography which she longed to share with Fanny. But there was no gleam of light under the latter's door as she passed it now. Fanny was asleep.

CHAPTER FOUR

AT DANIELI'S

"The Irish truly are naïve! Don't you agree, Lucille?"

"But how could I? Fanny is my only Irish friend, and she isn't naïve."

André-Marie smiled at Fanny.

"*Premi!*" commanded their gondolier as they swung out of the shadowy canal under the Bridge of Sighs, and into the brilliant light of the Grand Canal.

"I could enlarge on my theme," said André-Marie.

"I've no doubt you could," said Lucille, "since you live among the Irish now!" Lucille and Fanny gathered up their sun-hats and guide-books as the gondola pulled in by the *Piazzetta*. André-Marie and the gondolier gave them their hands as they disembarked.

"What a very ridiculous way of travelling about," said André-Marie, as charmingly, smilingly, he paid the smiling gondolier. But he only said it to tease the girls, because he knew that they were intoxicated with the surprising beauty of Venice. He was by no means unmoved by the strange shock of the city himself, for he was openly susceptible to beauty; but he felt traitorous to his Mercedes, forsaken at Mestre, and he felt it his professional duty to protest against Venetian transport.

"How amazing," he went on. "A city where no wheels turn!"

"You may wheel a perambulator," said Lucille.

"That would be quite a relief," he said. "I might attach a very small combustion engine to it, and have a lot of fun!"

"Up and down all those little steps, and over all the little bridges?" said Fanny.

"Yes, Miss Fanny. Will you sit in my perambulator when I try it out on Venice?"

"I will," said Fanny. "Oh, I'm hungry!"

"So am I," said Lucille. "And Mother will be raving hungry!"

They strolled past the Palace, along the *Riva*.

"I wish we didn't have to stay in Danieli's," said Fanny.

"Heavens, so do I!" said Lucille. "But you can thank your lucky stars we're not in one of those monstrous places on the Lido!"

"Anyway, count your blessings, girls," said André-Marie, "and count your hours! Because any minute now Mother is going to smell a bad smell——"

"What? Hasn't she smelt one yet?" asked Fanny.

The three laughed. They had now been six days in Venice, and were happy, and dangerously delighted.

Fanny, for her part, was only barely articulate. She walked about so far uncertain that she was Fanny Morrow of Mespil Road. Paris, where the luxuriously travelling de Mellin party had paused for two days and nights, had indeed been an encounter she would reflect upon very much—when she had time for reflection. But, confused though she was in Paris, she did fumblingly apprehend that it was a city that she must postpone; certainly she had wit enough to know that in two days and from the foyer of the Meurice she could only be confounded by the place. Almost deliberately, certainly in a

78

strong mood of self-defence, she let its first impact run over her like water. Paris was for the adult, and she looked about it eagerly, and understood that in French terms she was not adult. She would become adult, and would return to Paris. But she was relieved that she need spend no more than two extremely silly tourists' days there now.

However, in Paris the carefully arranged de Mellin plan of travel had suffered alteration. The party setting out from Brussels had consisted of the Countess, Lucille, Patrice and Fanny, supplemented by the Countess's maid Séraphine and an expensively hired gentleman, Signor Maffetoni, who was to combine the duties of courier with those of linguistic tutor to Patrice. Certainly, so far as French and his native Italian extended him, Signor Maffetoni was a fluent linguist. And he seemed to be efficient with railway tickets and Customs regulations. That he was a faded and pathetic old bore, and had already bored Patrice almost into nervous collapse, mattered nothing to Lucille and Fanny, since he was polite and companionable with the Countess and so left them free to an extent they had not reckoned upon.

But in Paris André-Marie had joined the family party— naturally with his great Mercedes. His Uncle Paul required him to visit certain new automobile plants in Milan, Turin and Vienna. Reluctantly, Lucille and Fanny apprehended, he had suspended his work in Ireland, at the command of the firm he served. So, gay as a lark in Paris, he insisted that he drive Lucille and Fanny to Milan and to Venice.

Patrice was furious; but it was clear that he must travel with his expensive tutor, and André-Marie said that he would not have that dandruffy old dandy as a passenger. Fanny would have preferred to make her first long journey through France and into Italy by train; she was greatly attracted by the tickets, coupons, and the immensely novel idea of *wagons-lit* and restaurant cars. But Lucille, more sophisticated, had accompanied her parents to Monte Carlo, to Biarritz and to San Sebastian, so she was eager to experience a long motor tour. Fanny did not want to be separated from Lucille; André-Marie begged their companionship, and undeniably it could only be more attractive to travel with Lucille and with him, by no matter what means, than with the anxious Countess, poor Séraphine, smiling Maffetoni and an infuriated, sick Patrice.

So from Paris she and Lucille had set out in goggles and veils in André-Marie's splendid vehicle. The travel had been lyrically gay and misadventurous, but safely at last, on a still, starry night, the three had reached the place where André-Marie could no longer press the accelerator and command the streets. They had descended then into a gondola.

Fanny knew that although she was young and had as yet seen nothing of the world, she would never again, however old she grew or wherever she went, make a journey to match that first, short journey into Venice. She sat in silence throughout it, and so did Lucille and André-Marie. When they reached Danieli's they were exhausted, almost in bad tempers—and after a supper which they did not like they all went immediately to bed, and slept far into noon of the next day.

But that was six days ago, and had anyone asked Fanny when she had reached Venice she would have had to take a long time to arrive at a true answer.

It was perhaps well that neither of Fanny's parents could apprehend or see into her spirit now. Always this may be well for parents, if not also for the children they love. But Joseph and Julia Morrow were especially delicate of nerve, even if unaware of this shared peculiarity, or of its threat from parent to child. So, in certain times of sharp experience it is well if physical separation adds its veils, so much more certain, to those which normally cloud spirit from spirit. And today, a day of early June in Venice, it was well that Julia could not search her Fanny's face, or Joseph seek in it the simple reassurance he habitually took from his 'gentle maiden'.

Or, was it well? Was too much happening too rapidly to Fanny?

"I think if a man could see her, if she'd get in focus . . ." her cousin Bill Morrow had said. And: "She lacks definition, this Miss Fanny," said young Patrice fourteen days ago in Brussels. "But no doubt that will come. Then we shall see."

Today, in the exquisite noon light on the *Riva dei Schiavoni* as she swung her ribboned sun-hat on her fingers, and smiled about her, perhaps there was not definition yet, but it seemed that a man, or anyone, could get her in focus. Light was upon her, at least.

André-Marie smiled at her and at his radiant sister.

"You are silly girls," he said. "This is only Venice, after all."

"Yes——" said Fanny. "Only!"

They swung into the hotel, all laughing, all ready for the absurd reproaches of the loving Countess, who whirled them to their table in the dining-room as zestfully as if none of the party had had a bite or sup for forty-eight hours.

There were letters. Fanny gathered hers up—from Mother, from Cockle, from Father. She put them away—happy to see the dear writings, but unwilling also to face the sweet dragback of them, just at this moment.

André-Marie filled all their glasses with the lovely, simple red wine of Verona.

"Oh, please do eat *something* nourishing, children! The food is appalling, I agree——" said the Countess.

"You don't agree with me," said Fanny.

"How good your French grows!" said André-Marie.

"Fanny's French was always good," said Lucille.

"I'm sure of that," said André-Marie politely. "But now, in the last few days, it is elastic, idiomatic——"

"The French of Venice?" said Fanny.

"Children," said the Countess, "what did you do this morning? What did you see?"

"Nothing, Mother," said Lucille. "We told the gondolier to take us round the back streets——"

"But, my darling—you really *must* begin to be serious! What will your father say— Oh—oh dear—it's tragic how these people cook their pastas! Oh, what mess is this ugly dish?"

"We saw everything, I thought," said Fanny.

Lucille looked at Fanny and, smiling, paused in her smile. Venice had gone to Fanny's head, and, heavens, why not? How could it not? said Lucille to herself. Hasn't it gone to mine? Who could be so deadly as to be here for the first time and not be mightily disturbed? Yet she could not in the last two days quite recognize Fanny—and since she thought that

81

they were indulging together, in harmonious joy, an experience they could not have measured in advance and assuredly would never on earth encounter again, she had gladly accepted Fanny's reaction to the extraordinary place.

Signor Maffetoni shook his wild hair above his plate of spaghetti, towards which he was bent in passion.

"Meess Fanny!" he protested, as he sucked the long ropes of pasta through his teeth.

"I bet you *did* see everything," said Patrice, in a fury. "And I tell you here and now, Mother, that if I'm not allowed at least as much freedom of movement in this town as those two senseless girls, I'm clearing off! I'm *walking* to wherever in Europe I damn well please!"

"Patrice! I beg you! The waiters! The, the—well, everyone!" the Countess exclaimed in what she believed was a wily whisper.

"He's right, Mother," said Lucille, "and if he goes off like that I'll think it my duty to follow him!"

"Oh, right or wrong, let him go, Countess," said Maffetoni, who had finished his bowl of spaghetti and wiped his mouth. "I for my part am useless to the petulant boy—he *knows* his Italian irregular verbs, and will listen to nothing that I say about literature! I dislike this Patrice, Countess, and I desire very much to explain Venezia to a *lady,* a lady of such great sensibility as you, Countess! I am not for bad-tempered boys of genius! Definitely I am not!"

"Well done!" said Patrice. "Do have him explain Venezia to you, Mother, in God's name!"

"But I'm dying to have *someone* do me that kindness, children," said the Countess. "Only, your dear father did say——"

"Enjoy yourself, Mother," said André-Marie. "Our dear father is a long way off——"

"And give the man his due, he's never been a spoil-sport," said Patrice.

"Oh, what wicked boys you are!" said the Countess. And to the head-waiter, bent obsequiously beside her, she said very prettily: "Do you truly believe this that we are eating to be veal?"

After luncheon Fanny lay on her bed behind closed blinds

82

and read her letters from home. Two o'clock rang from St. Mark's as she opened her mother's letter, and although her window looked out over the *Riva* and towards *San Giorgio* she thought she could hear the great rush down of the pigeons to the *Piazzetta*, where they must receive their ordained dinner of maize from the Venetian State. She smiled about the pigeons as she shook open the thin sheets of her mother's letters.

There were other letters than her mother's. There was a kind brief note from her father to 'My Gentle Maiden', enclosing a ten-pound note, and adjuring her to enjoy herself. There was a touching, illiterate letter from 'Cockle'. But from her mother's good letter Fanny took the family news. All was well. Lilian was very busy getting herself established in her splendid mansion in Stillorgan Road. However, everyone was helping her, and she was well and gay, and looking very pretty, mother said. Mother also said that she hoped Fanny was enjoying this wonderful tour and holiday that she was having. 'Always I wanted to see Venice,' wrote Mother. 'I shall not now, but when you come home, pet, you will tell me about it, and if it is really as amazing as it sounds. Have a happy time, and God bless you!'

Fanny was crying still when Lucille came into her room at three o'clock. They were going to Padua, taking André-Marie's car from Mestre, to see the Giotto chapel. Lucille, all love, bent over her.

"But, Fan, Fan—in tears? And you never weep, I think! Fan, my dear, bad news?"

"Oh no—good news. Dear letters, from Mother and everyone."

"Then—why—what?"

Lucille sat on the bed and put an arm round Fanny.

"What is it, dearest Fanny?" she said, in her accurate, sweet way. "What is changing you these days?"

Fanny turned away into the pillow, and shook with crying. "Nothing," she said. "Nothing. Only Venice is too much. I'm—I'm over-excited."

Lucille kissed the top of Fanny's head, and then stood up. She had had a visitation of fear, and desired to examine it alone.

"We have to catch the Mestre steamboat at a quarter to four," she said. "That gives us twenty minutes. Will that be all right?"

"Splendid," said Fanny. "But won't everything be shut when we get to Padua?"

"Apparently not — according to André-Marie — who is efficient, if no more." Lucille paused on these cold words, her heart suddenly still and cold in her. But Fanny did not stir.

"Don't cry, Fan."

"I'll stop. I'm all right now. Oh, dear Lucille, I promise you I'll be ready—I'm all right."

Lucille left the room, feeling sad and puzzled.

In twenty minutes the whole party was setting out up the Grand Canal—for Mestre, for André-Marie's deserted car, and for the road to Padua

Fanny, squashed in the back of the car with the Countess de Mellin and Patrice, contemplated in front of her Lucille's lovely head, and André-Marie's, lovely too and very like it. (Signor Maffetoni had excused himself from the Padua drive. "Well, either he or I," said Patrice. "Wherever that man is is hell for me. What a misfortune to arrive in Italy with such an encumbrance!")

"I find this landscape dreary," said the Countess.

"The Euganean Hills, Mother," said Patrice.

"Shelley," said Fanny vaguely, foolishly.

"I agree with you, Mother," said André-Marie.

"But you're going to see a lot of lovely Giottos," said Lucille.

"Darling," said the Countess. "In the last five days I've seen a great number of Bellinis and Tintorettos——"

"No use repining," said Patrice. "You committed yourself to this affair—so you have to see it through, my dear Mother."

"And anyway, isn't it nice to be moving about on wheels again?" said André-Marie. "I was afraid I'd have forgotten how to drive. Those damned, ridiculous gondolas!"

"Gondolas are exquisite," said Fanny.

"No question," said Lucille. "They are exquisite. There is no better thing."

André-Marie laughed.

"Idiotically you talk, Lucille!"

"She doesn't," said Fanny. "There could be no better thing than a gondola."

André-Marie half-turned, and smiled at Fanny.

"Miss Fanny, I will teach you sense! I will teach you the combustion engine!"

Fanny shook her head.

"About Bellini, children," said the Countess sadly. "Well, Signor Maffetoni tells me that I'm quite justified in finding him a little tiring——"

"No," said Patrice. "You can find Giovanni Bellini immensely tiring—I do, in fact—but, Mother sweet, he's not 'a little' tiring—not that at all!"

"Don't be silly, Patrice. I've just told you that *I* find him a little tiring. Are we dining in Padua, children?"

"There's a place called Stella d'Oro, I believe," said André-Marie.

"Fanny," said Patrice, "didn't you say something about Donatello——"

"Oh, I wonder which is the safer—what do you think?" asked the Countess.

"Donatello, Mother," said Lucille.

"Very well, we'll dine there, and commend ourselves to Providence. Now what *are* you laughing at, children. Really, such a set of silly gigglers!"

"And you're the silliest," said Patrice lovingly, and gave her a kiss.

They sped through the perfumed afternoon, all laughing under their breaths, and each one in his measure suffering, as every day since they had come to Venice, an unmanageable delight.

"Yes, we are gigglers," said Fanny softly. "Lucille, isn't it awful to seem to do nothing but giggle when you're confronted with Venice?"

Lucille looked back to Fanny diagonally across the car.

"But we don't 'do nothing but giggle,' Fan!" she said. "A few tears have fallen—give us our due!"

Her voice was so gently communicative to Fanny that the

latter felt almost as if a few tears might fall again, and instantly.

"But that's worse than giggling!" exclaimed André-Marie. "*Whose* tears have fallen during this expedition, may I ask?"

"You may, of course, ask," said Lucille gaily.

"I won't have people shedding tears in Italy in the middle of June! Are you listening, Mother? Do you hear me, Miss Fanny?"

Fanny heard him, but only laughed within her breast, and did not answer audibly.

"Darling boy," said the Countess. "I can truly say that so far I have not shed any tears in Italy. And that is curious, you know—because there have been a great many inconveniences and discomforts——"

"Mother, dear!" said Patrice delightedly.

"You see, Patrice understands," said the Countess to Lucille. "After all, that dish last night that they called *pizza* —dear heavens— and then those ghastly little strawberries at luncheon today! Do you think they were diseased, André, those strawberries?"

"Undoubtedly, Mother. Still, you didn't cry. You're a born traveller."

"Your dear father would be surprised to hear you say that, my son. As you all know, he is the very best of men— yet somehow, when we've been abroad together he sometimes has tended to lose his temper with me."

"Then he's not the very best of men," said Patrice.

"Oh, but he is, Patrice; I do assure you!"

"The best of men wouldn't have sent that plague of a Maffetoni on my first journey into Italy!"

"Oh, forget Maffetoni," said André-Marie. "I expect he'll get drunk this afternoon and either fall into the Grand Canal or else get taken home into the mazes of the slums by some beautiful shop girl, and never again find his way to Danieli's."

"Please, André! Your sister and her friend are in the car!"

"Oh, so they are, Mother. I'm glad you reminded me. By the way, Patrice, are you still Lycée-bound, or have you noticed how singularly beautiful the girls are in Venice, and that in fact many of them *have* the hair that Titian gave them?"

The Countess beat her tongue against her teeth in a loud noise of disapproval.

"André," she said. "It is precisely because of the kind of nonsense you are talking about that your dear father sent Signor Maffetoni with us——"

"So as to take my attention off the girls on the *Piazzetta*?" said Patrice.

André flung back his head and laughed delightedly.

"Oh, Patrice! What a fearful comment on you!" he said. "Well, Padua on your left, Mother. Here we go."

The roofs and towers of the town lay at rest against the brilliant sky.

"We're late," said Lucille. "The Chapel of the Arena will certainly be shut."

"In that case we'll just go to Donatello's," said Fanny.

Everyone laughed except the Countess.

"It will be the best thing to do, dear Fanny. A nice, cold *citron pressé* now would be delightful, after all this dust." Her eyes travelled over the mellow, encroaching town. "Saint Antony appears to have been a very holy man," she said. "I was reading about him lately, children. He was an innocent man, very good——"

CHAPTER FIVE

WEST FROM VENICE

JUNE, that June in the Veneto and about the Adriatic lagoons, was not what either Lucille or Fanny had foreseen.

Between them the two had assembled almost all known writings on Venice—from Coryat to Ruskin, from Evelyn and Lady Mary Wortley Montagu, through Goethe and Byron and Shelley to Lord Houghton, Browning and George Sand. They had Baedeker, too, and Vasari, and Howell's *Venetian Life*. Fanny had found Arthur Symons's translations of D'Annunzio's plays, but neither she nor Lucille could discover even a French translation of *Il Fuoco*. And they had no Italian. However, in Brussels and in Paris Fanny had considered that she must simplify, for the first assault, what she had to confront; so she told Lucille that she had decided that until Venice was in the past she would read Coryat for the pleasure of reading him, and Ruskin for his information. And all the others she must, if she was to keep sane, ignore.

Lucille was impressed by this clear resolution. She too was all for battling along with Ruskin—though attracted uneasily to other guides. But she was a more literal and serious student of everything than Fanny was; the latter could flash and dart about *Stones of Venice* and find what she sought, leaving what bored her, but Lucille could not read in that manner, and therefore was alarmed by the exactions of the too detailed work.

But she did not worry overlong. Once they were in Venice the books they had brought lay around the two girl's bedrooms, most of them unopened, undisturbed. True, with Baedeker Fanny did resolutely carry *Stones of Venice* about, and in gondola and church and café frequently fought hard for Ruskin's right to instruct her. But André-Marie, carrying the fat volume, had made an amusing game out of her zeal. Whenever, arguing in Florian's or in their gondola as to what church or museum next to visit, she or Lucille suggested '*Nome de Gesu*' or '*Ospidelatto*' or '*Palazzo Rizzonico*', André would flip his fingers rapidly over the pages of Ruskin's Index.

"I'm sorry, girls, but Ruskin says it's of no importance." Or—"Oh dear, Ruskin says it's just grotesque Renaissance, less extravagant than usual." Or—"How surprising. 'Late Renaissance—of no merit'." Or—"Goodness, girls—'a graceful series of buildings, of no particular interest'. Funny how *dull* Venice turns out to be, isn't it?"

Lucille and Fanny, in grave earnest before they reached Italy, surprisingly found this repetitive joke attractive as they drifted and dreamt about the city's stones. They were not entirely fooled into laziness, but they laughed and were lazy —looked about them, deep in pleasure and wonder, and opened almost never a book, and at first never a question.

Lucille did not talk to Fanny about herself, as she had said she would. And Fanny could only look about and above and, in cold moments, pray her astonished sensibilities to keep still.

The days and nights flowed through each other; there never seemed an angle or a mark on time.

"Do you sleep, Lucille? You know, I'm not sure that I sleep——"

"Or wake? I'm not sure about waking, Fan."

"Oh, isn't it maddening? There's so much that it's obligatory to examine——"

"St. Mark's, for instance, Fan—when are we really going to study St. Mark's?"

"I dislike St. Mark's," said Fanny.

"Goodness, Fanny! Haven't you read Ruskin?"

Padua, Chioggia, Vicenza. After the day at Vicenza the Countess gave way, and could not face supper.

"Those ceilings, darling Lucille. Oh, I am so very ill from staring up at idiotic ceilings."

"I'm not surprised, Mother. I'm rather ill of ceilings myself. Would you like me to send for Father?"

"I don't know, pet. You know he did warn me to be good, and not bother you children. And I've done my best not to, Lucille. But truely, if anyone ever again troubles me with Tiepolo or a ceiling—no, no; don't worry your father."

Lucille kissed her, and left her to Séraphine's devotion, and downstairs she ordered carefully a large *plateau* of invalid foods to be sent to the Countess's room. Then she joined Fanny and her brothers at Quadri's in the *Piazza*.

The four were hungry, happy and tired. They sat a long time in their little open, painted parlour; they ate a vast, late supper, drank their adored Verona wine, and came to a splendid plan—André's great plan.

He had to visit Milan and Turin on his uncle's business; he was not in Italy for his health, he said. But he thought it would be fun if Lucille and Fanny could visit those cities with him. He would require to be about two or three days in each —they would be absent from Venice, say, a week, could fit in whatever sightseeing the places afforded, and he would bring

89

them safely back to Danieli's before he had to set off again for Vienna, and for Ireland.

The girls' eyes shone, though neither saw how such an arrangement could be carried through. Patrice, however, sat rigid in his place as André talked, and when the elder brother paused he spoke at once.

"If you three go off on this trip without me I shall never speak to any one of you again! Do you hear? If you do this, and leave me with Maffetoni——" Almost he was in tears.

Lucille took his hands.

"I won't go unless you come, Patrice," said Fanny.

"Oh, dear Fanny!"

"Truely, it wouldn't be fair," said Lucille.

"I agree," said André. "But what are we to do with Maffetoni?"

"Much more important," said Lucille, "what about Mother?"

"I've thought about Mother," said André. "The dear one is being marvellous, but she is absolutely exhausted. Even Venice itself is on her nerves now, let alone Bellini and Tiepolo! I'm going to suggest that while we're on our travels she takes herself off with Séraphine to the Lido, to the Hôtel des Bains. It's very comfortable there, and rather French— and not a work of art for miles around. She can have a thorough rest, and come back to Danieli's to meet us—and almost ready to look at another fresco!"

"And Maffetoni? Does he go to the Lido?" asked Patrice.

"Oh, no! He'd spoil it for her. We'll give him a week off with pay, I think—and if he never turns up again, who's going to cry?"

Patrice banged on the table.

"You're a marvel, my beloved André!" he said. "Oh, let's have some wine!"

Lucille sipped slowly from her glass.

"Is it a good plan?" André asked eagerly. "What do you think, Miss Fanny?"

Fanny, from the velvet bench she sat on against the back wall of the little painted room, looked about her, at the gleaming wine, the flowers, the happy, beautiful faces of her friends—and beyond, through the colonnades, she looked out to the moonlit *Piazza,* to its crowds and its brash music, its brilliant light and deep, dramatic shadows.

"So long as we come back here," she said.

Lucille smiled at her.

"Yes; that is the *sine qua non.*" But even as she spoke Lucille was pondering André-Marie's efficiency. How subtly were balanced in him wilfulness and tact!

Patrice was mad with joy.

"When do we start? Oh, when?"

"But, Patrice, how can you want to leave Venice?" said Fanny.

"I want to come back, Fanny! And I want to lose Maffetoni! And I want to go around enjoying myself with you and Lucille! Don't you understand?"

Today was Tuesday, André was saying to Lucille. "I thought we might all see Mother safely settled in the Lido on Friday—and set off for Milan early on Saturday morning?"

"I wonder what opera they are singing on Saturday night?" said Patrice.

"The Scala's shut," said André. "But we'll find something amusing for Saturday night"

"They're playing Glück's *Orphée* at the Fenice tomorrow night," said Patrice.

"Yes," said Lucille. "And this unmanageable Fanny has taken places for us all for it!"

André and Patrice leapt in their chairs.

"But, Miss Fanny! You can't! You *can't* do that!"

"Oh yes, I can," said Fanny. "How old-fashioned your brothers are, Lucille!"

"I love the music of *Orphée,*" said Patrice. "Thank you, dear Fanny."

The two boys smiled at her and lifted their glasses.

"Do you really think we can leave Mother at the Lido, just with Séraphine?" Lucille asked André. "Won't she be hurt, a little?"

"Not when I've talked to her. Besides, she needs the lull. She's been simply heroic now for a whole fortnight. I did think that the picnic to Torcello yesterday was so exacting for her that she shouldn't have faced Vicenza today——"

91

"She's a great girl," said Patrice.

"But truly, Lucille, she needs the interlude; she doesn't like Danieli's and is being very good about it because you æsthetes *must* be in Venice.

"And we can telephone her every evening, can't we?"

"Of course we will. And if there's the least thing wrong we'll just come tearing back to her. I'll write and give Father the whole plan tomorrow, when I've settled it with Mother."

"Yes, do that," said Lucille.

"Surely it's a very long way from here to Milan?" said Patrice. "Will the contraption do it in one day?"

André smiled.

"Two hundred and thirty kilometres? My dear fellow! But we will start early—for comfort's sake. About eight o'clock. So as to get to Verona about eleven—before the day gets hot. And if we leave Verona at six we should be in Milan certainly before nine o'clock. That's not too tiring, is it? What are you smiling at, Miss Fanny?"

"Oh—I was thinking, if we get to Verona, why need we go on?"

"Well—only that the whole pretext is that I am about my uncle's business in Milan——"

"But not on Sunday," said Patrice.

"True enough," André agreed.

"Let's stay in Verona until Sunday evening," said Lucille.

"By all means—I hadn't thought of it. But why? Is Verona attractive?"

"There were those two gentlemen," said Patrice.

Lucille and Fanny laughed.

"I'd forgotten them," said Fanny. "But there were the Capulets and the Montagues too."

André looked puzzled.

"Romeo and Juliet, André," said Lucille.

"Ah! Of course." He smiled.

"I've read in some of these books," said Fanny—"no, not Ruskin—that Verona is the most beautiful place round here, after Venice. And it belonged to Venice once."

"I think at least one day and night, André?" said Lucille.

"As you will; I'll inquire about a hotel tomorrow," he said.

He filled the glasses again. "What day of all these days has been the best?" he asked the three.

"Padua," said Patrice. "Because there was no Maffetoni."

"Today was marvellous," said Lucille. "I adored Vicenza. But I'm still under the impression, I suppose."

"What do you say, Miss Fanny?"

"I think—the days we stay in Venice are the best."

"Ungrateful creature!" said Patrice. "Here we are slaving to be good tourists with you——"

"If I'm ungrateful for all this? Oh, goodness!"

"Still, which of the organized days, Fan?" Lucille asked her.

"Torcello and Murano."

"Sad places," said André.

"But in sight of Venice," said Patrice. "That's why, perhaps, Miss Fanny?"

Fanny laughed.

"Very likely," she said.

"In fact, you are in love with Venice," said Patrice in a severe tone.

"In love?" Fanny laughed. "I don't know. Lucille, are we 'in love' with Venice?"

André swooped in.

"Would you choose to live here, let us say, Miss Fanny?"

"Live here? Oh, no!"

"Why, Fan?" asked Lucille.

Fanny laughed at the three.

"Don't glare at me!" she said.

"Still, why wouldn't you live in this Venice you're so insane about?" said Patrice.

"Heaps of reasons. Well, there's Mother and Father, and everyone at home, and Glasalla——"

"But—say you could visit them, say you were free and rich——" said Lucille.

"That's not the point. I mean, I couldn't live, in the sense of spend my life, in a place so foreign to all that I mean by them——"

"Still, you wouldn't rule out life outside of the family span, would you?"

"Ah, Lucille! How silly! I said there were heaps of reasons

—I gave you the first. As between Venice and what I loved before I came here, of course I'd choose what I loved first! But that's easy. Anyway, if I was an orphan, if I was nameless and rootless, I wouldn't *live* in Venice—unless I happened to be born here."

"You say that strongly," said Patrice. "You are growing up, Miss Fanny."

Fanny felt tired and lonely. She had a sharp visitation of anxiety about Mespil Road.

"Lucille, why must they hold this inquisition? I'm sleepy."

"So am I," said Lucille.

"We must finish the bottle," said Patrice.

"You're welcome," said André, as the young brother emptied some dregs into a glass.

As they crossed the *Piazza* André put his hand on Fanny's forearm.

"Miss Fanny, what have you against your—your feeling for Venice?"

Fanny paused. She looked back over the now quiet, empty *Piazza,* then down along the *Piazzetta* to the silky, pale lagoon, and to *San Giorgio* afloat against a hint of daybreak.

"Nothing," she said in a contented voice. "I couldn't be more delighted than I am. Only——"

"Only what?"

Fanny moved forward to where Lucille and Patrice were strolling. She stretched her hand out and took Lucille's before the latter knew she was so near her.

"I think all I mean is that being delighted is a passive condition," she said.

Lucille laughed.

"You're being epigrammatic, Fan!"

"I wouldn't call that remark an epigram," said Patrice.

Fanny realised now in the cold air that her head was aching fiercely. The day at Vicenza had been long and exciting, and at supper she had drunk more wine than she was used to.

"It was only a flat observation," she said, and walked away ahead of the three.

André stood and looked after her. 'How feather-like,' he thought; 'how beautiful, how like her sister.'

But Lucille and Patrice ran after her.

"Are you annoyed about something, Fan?"

She took their outstretched hands.

"Oh, no! Oh, no, my dears! I'm sleepy! Let's go to bed. Venice could drive you mad, you know!"

They went past the Palace and down the *Riva*, happily hand-in-hand.

"Sing Fanny. Sing Moore's melodies," said Patrice.

"Oh yes," cried André and Lucille. "Oh yes, indeed. Please, Fanny!"

But Fanny would not sing.

André's plan was accepted ("as all his plans are," said Lucille) with relieved and anxious blessings from the Countess, unashamed expressions of satisfaction from Signor Maffetoni, and telegraphed approval from the Count.

"It *is* a somewhat unconventional thing to allow these two girls to do in a foreign country," the Countess said. "But then you are so very reliable, André. Very like your dear father in that. And you all promise to be very, very good, don't you, children? And to obey André in everything, no?"

Lucille and Fanny laughed delightedly.

"I don't know what they find amusing in that injunction, Mother, dear," said André. "Because I assure you that they *are* going to obey me in everything!" He shook his fist in their faces.

The Countess was so happy to know that there was not a single work of man which she need admire on the Lido, save the excellent Hôtel des Bains, that she could hardly wait for Friday evening and her installation there. Séraphine and the baggage were dispatched over the lagoon in a *vaporetto* in the afternoon, and Signor Maffetoni, delighted with his prospect of well-paid freedom, had the grace to accompany the maid and to undertake to supervise arrangements for the Countess's comfort; and later in the evening the de Mellins and Fanny set off across the water in a noble, two-oared gondola.

They dined in splendour. The cooking of the hotel was French, as André had promised, and almost won the Countess's approval. The rooms were large, with Séraphine housed in a little dressing-room. The children had crowded all the tables and shelves with flowers, bon-bons, perfumes, restoratives, and many kinds of light but, they hoped, edifying literature. The balconies overhung the hotel's rustling, palmy garden, and the silver strands and quiet shelving waters of the Adriatic. Venice was away to the rear, out of sight.

"Children, how lovely this will be! If only you'd all stay here! Couldn't you? I'll miss you so much, my darlings!"

"You're to *rest*, my girl—and *forget* us," said André.

"But I couldn't do that, André!"

"We'll telephone you every evening," said Lucille.

"Punctually at nine, remember," said Patrice.

Fanny was thinking, 'How tenderly dutiful they are. We are not one-fifth as good to Mother, and yet she's ten times more important than this sweet, foolish Countess. But perhaps Father is very good to her—I hope he is. Certainly he loves her. I hope she knows that we also love her.'

"And remember further, Countess de Mellin," said Patrice, "that you are to be in Danieli's on the afternoon of tomorrow week, to welcome us back, and renew your struggle with fine art!"

"Oh dear—I know, Patrice!"

"It's a long way off, Mother," said Lucille, "eight whole days! Just rest now, and paddle about in that lovely water down there."

"And collect shells," said Fanny.

"*Are* there shells?" cried the Countess. "Séraphine, do you hear? We'll have to find some really lovely shells—I wonder when the tide is out."

"It's out now," said Patrice, from the balcony. "Ah, what a sad old sea this Adriatic is!"

"Sad, darling boy?"

"Don't mind him, Mother!" said Lucille. "It's reaction from the *bachot*."

At noon on Saturday the Mercedes triumphantly swept its four passengers into Verona and to the Hôtel Royal et Deux Tours, in the *Corso Santa Anastasia*.

"Astounding!" said Patrice as he dismounted. "Truly,

96

André, you have the luck of the devil." For they had in fact reached Verona with only one breakdown, and André had been able to overcome that—Patrice seeking no explanation of it—quickly and good-temperedly.

In the early evening, tired of *St. Zeno Maggiore* and *San Giorgio in Braida,* tired of the gaieties of the *Piazza delle Erbe* and very tired indeed of looking vainly for the house of the Capulets, Juliet's house, the four strolled by the Adige and over the *Ponte Navi.* The evening was exquisite; the lovely town was clamorous with summer joy. Patrice leant on the parapet of the bridge and looked backward.

"What is that, Lucille?" he asked, pointing towards a Gothic façade.

Lucille studied her map.

"It should be *San Fermo Maggiore,*" she said.

"It looks lovely. Must examine it—but I'm tired now. Are you?"

"Yes. This is a lovely town." Fanny and André, ahead of them, had disappeared from view. From her map Lucille surmised that they were seeking either the Pompei Palace or the Giusti Gardens—both probably closed. For herself she felt disposed to return to the hotel, and to drink iced lemonade in her room, in silence.

"Shall we go back, Patrice?"

"In a minute." He folded himself over the parapet. "Funny, but this irrelevant town—and it is far more irrelevant to me, let alone Fanny, than Venice is—still it's started me fussing about the future. Isn't that odd?"

"Odder than you think!" said Lucille. "Because it seems to be doing the same thing to me! I don't know—but I feel depressed. Do you?"

"Terribly!"

Lucille laughed into Patrice's shining, happy eyes.

"Let's go towards the hotel; it's getting cold, and I feel a little sick."

The two recrossed the bridge; Patrice took his sister's arm.

"You'll be at the hotel in a minute, Lucille."

"What's fussing *you* about the future, Patrice?"

He shrugged.

"God knows! I suppose I'd best read history for a year or

two, until I sort myself out! After all, history should teach one *something*."

"That's what I think."

"Would Father ever let me go to Oxford—or to Harvard?"

"I think so—especially he might like the Harvard notion. And after all, you're not only a son; you're a *younger* son."

"You envy me that?"

"Do I not, Patrice!"

"I think there's a fight coming up between you and Father."

Lucille laughed.

"It'll be hard on Father," Patrice went on. "Because you are his pet, poor man!"

"He has three other daughters, sweet little things, to make pets of," said Lucille.

"And he's given his wilful heart to you."

"Anyway, don't *you* get depressed, Patrice. After all, there's heaps of money, and Father does enjoy already the legend of your intellectual promise."

"Yes, but he is rather a clucking hen about us, isn't he? And *he* holds the money."

"He's awfully generous."

"As long as you're doing what he suggests—oh, marvellously generous. But not all Mother's wailings will drive me into the University of Brussels next term—and I'm not at present attracted to the Sorbonne."

"Have you thought of Germany?"

"Yes. I think of all the places where one might find out what to do. Like you, Lucille. The one place one won't find out in is Brussels, living at home. Why, even André knew that!"

Lucille laughed.

"He's curiously lucky," she said.

"In love, is he lucky, would you say?"

They were crossing the *Piazza dei Signori*. Lucille paused and looked about. She leant, wearily for her, against the base of the statue of Dante.

"He's not concerned with love, I think," she said. "Perhaps he won't be, ever."

"So you call him 'curiously lucky'? I agree that he's not

'concerned with love', as you'd mean love. But he has—I *think*, Lucille—a variety of complicated feelings, sentiments, sensations—many more than you or I could imagine, perhaps. And they have to be aired and exercised—in the name of hygiene."

"You're being unkind," said Lucille. Her face was clouded; her eyes were anxious.

Patrice took her hand.

"Come, we're near the hotel," he said. "We'll go to your room, and order ourselves champagne! What do you say?"

"I say you're a crazy boy."

Fanny and André, in the Giusti Gardens, looked over Verona and wondered where they had lost the other two. And strangely their thoughts and words—at first surrendered to the ancient cypress trees and Roman statuary through which they moved, and afterwards, from the terrace, directed across the twisting river to the spread of Verona's roofs, to the delicate evening sky and the silent landscape—strangely they escaped into irrelevancies, into the very irrelevancy of their own fortunes.

André had said something conventional about the beauty of these days of beginning to discover some part of Italy.

"Yes," said Fanny, and went on with more feeling than, had she been older, she would have allowed herself to betray to a chance companion. "But it's only a postponement, you see, a terrible self-indulgence. Indeed—oh, don't think I'm being ungracious about the marvellous holiday your parents are giving me—but the whole business does sometimes make me desperately anxious!"

He could not help laughing at this, but his laughter was kind.

"What on earth do you mean?" he asked. "Why should you not have a happy holiday with Lucille, your greatest friend?"

"Happy holiday? Oh, why not hundreds of them? But—this being, out of the blue, in Venice, no, not Verona, Venice—being in Venice, I tell you, and without responsibility, and free, and with Lucille——"

"Yes——?"

She turned to him and laughed. "I can't explain! It's temptation, I suppose!"

"Temptation? In temptation there must be a tempter?"

"Venice is the tempter."

"But what is she offering?"

"Oh, nothing! Certainly one couldn't or wouldn't live in Venice—but that certainly makes one feel small and common and miserable. And one must go back to all one loves so much at home, and find a way of living there. For true reasons, one must. So, all this disturbance is temptation. You Belgians are not Catholics in our Irish sense—but I know my catechism and I know the meaning of the word 'temptation'."

"You're eloquent and explicit this evening, Miss Fanny."

"I'm often very talkative. Ask Lucille. And Verona is irritating me by looking so beautiful. I wanted Venice to be the only beautiful place, for the present!"

Gently he took in his hand the little finger of her left hand.

"I never saw so small a finger-nail," he said. "Honestly, I find it difficult not to laugh at it."

Fanny looked at the finger-nail.

"It's always seemed a reasonable size," she said.

"It isn't at all reasonable. Your sister, Mrs. O'Connor—have you noticed?—she has just such small, delicate finger-nails."

"Lilian has very pretty hands—I haven't. But I don't remember the size of her finger-nails."

They both laughed, and Fanny withdrew her finger from André's entangling.

"You are going through some disturbance about Italy, about Venice, Miss Fanny," said André. "But you are young and very sensitive, and I am sure that you have to go through many disturbances."

Fanny turned to look at him; he was looking at her and his expression was grave; his eyes shone deeply blue, and reminded her of Lucille.

"Naturally. Everyone has to," she said.

"Yes, Miss Fanny. Venice is disturbing you. Ireland has disturbed me "

Fanny laughed.

"All you mean is that you've enjoyed Ireland."

"I don't. I haven't, so far, enjoyed Ireland. I mean what I say. Ireland has disturbed me."

"I should never have thought it could *disturb* you!"

"I won't examine what you've said—it might hurt me."

"Ah, no! Honestly—I was only surprised."

"How odd you are! I shall be back there in a fortnight or so. I have persuaded my uncle to allow me to establish the assemblage and promotion of the combustion engine—for all purposes—in Dublin. I'll make fortunes of money through the idea, I think; and I shall live in a country worth fifty Venices——"

"Oh, please! Don't make an impossible argument of that kind! No Irish person could be annoyed with you for liking Ireland or for wanting to seek your fortune there—still, it's very queer in you, I think——" She laughed suddenly, looking sideways at his handsome profile.

He turned and smiled at her.

"You ought to understand," he said. "You are, after all, exceptionally intelligent. Oh, Fanny, you are strange!"

He put his arms about her, and drew her up against him, smiling bravely into her darkened eyes.

'I am bemused,' thought Fanny.

From over the river the sounds of evening in Verona came, but all immediately around was still, and the air blew coldly. 'This is,' thought Fanny, 'a part of what I was saying; this is, like Venice, because of Venice, temptation.' His beautiful face bent close to her; his fingers moved delicately through her hair.

Fanny placed her two hands on his face and looked into his blazing eyes.

"No," she said. "No. Not this mistake. Please, don't."

He held her still.

"I entreat you," he said. "Kiss me—once, once only."

She laughed softly, and drew away from him.

"I know nothing about it," she said. "But I imagine that there's no such thing as once, if you kiss a person. After all, it is a most extraordinary thing to do. So don't cheat about it."

He dropped her, let her go. She was distressed to see how very white he looked, how weary.

"I'll try not to cheat," he said.

She took his hand.

"It's cold. Come, André, let's go and eat a great lot."

"Mother's panacea," he said. "How odd, from you!"

"Oh, I didn't mean it," she said wearily. "It was just something random to say. You—you had, after all, embarrassed me."

They were walking back towards the bridge, and the wind was cold.

"You are grown-up in your mind, I have noticed," André said irritably. "So why should my—my love embarrass you?"

"Love? André, don't speak falsely."

"Falsely? Of all the arrogance! What do you know of me, that you dare use such a word? For that matter, what do you know at all of love, outside of literature?"

They were crossing the *Ponte Navi*. Fanny stopped, laid her hands on the parapet and looked across Verona. The wind swept her hair away from her high white forehead. Her eyes were bright and stern.

"Of the kind of love you are talking about, André, I know nothing outside of literature. But I read mostly good literature," she laughed cruelly. "And so far I trust what I learn from it."

"Prig!" he almost sobbed. "As ruthless a prig as Lucille!"

"To be comparable to Lucille in anything makes me happy," said Fanny.

"But life isn't as Lucille would order it, you stupid child! Life is as men—I say *men*—make and feel it!"

"I've noticed already," said Fanny, "that that is men's idea. But my life is mine, and it will be more or less what I make and feel it, I hope."

"That doesn't make you sound very attractive."

"For heaven's sake, why should I sound attractive, André?"

"Because you *are* attractive! Oh, Fanny, you are ravishing!"

She covered her face with her hands, and said nothing. The cold wind whipped the river below them. André noticed that her shoulders were shaking He took her hands and pulled them down from her face, down which tears were streaming.

"Oh, what is it, what is it? Forgive me, Fanny! Explain!"

"Most certainly I won't. Be quiet, please."

"Very well," he said. "I'll be quiet."

He leant his elbows on the parapet.

"Would you mind if I smoked?"

He inhaled deeply the fumes of a Turkish cigarette, and he grew calm. He considered her young profile, enclosed between her hands. She looked tired, almost ill—but extraordinarily young and pure. 'She is not yet as beautiful as Lilian,' he reflected, 'but when she is thirty, when she is forty, she will almost certainly be the more beautiful of the two. She will age, very likely,' he thought, 'in the distinguished and somewhat alarming way of her mother. That,' he admitted to himself, 'might well be too much of a good thing. Brain and spirit can divinely mark an ageing face, but what of the sustenance of love in the flesh, what of love's adventure, what of all the questions, all the years, of *interim*?'

Yet, as he searched coldly through his own multiple desires, he was in parallel motion invaded, as constantly now, by painful tenderness for this lovely face of Fanny. (He was indeed, though alert and intelligent, a young man very dangerous to himself.)

"May I speak now? May I ask you something, Miss Fanny?"

She inclined her head.

"What are you at this moment wishing?"

Fanny turned dark, surprised eyes upon him before she answered. And when she spoke she looked away again over Verona.

"I'm wishing I was at home in Mespil Road," she said, "with Mother and Father."

"Ah!" André stubbed out his cigarette on the parapet, and dusted it off into the river. "We could arrange for you to go home at once," he said. "Talk to Lucille, and we'll make the necessary reservations."

If this answer surprised Fanny, if it chilled her as he desired it should, he could not tell. All she did was incline her head.

"Oh it's cold," she said then. "Why do we stand here shivering?"

"Why, indeed? Why not go and eat, as you suggested ages ago?"

They crossed the bridge and turned nothwards towards the *Corso Santa Anastasia.*

They joined Lucille and Patrice in the little salon that separated the girls' bedrooms.

"Champagne, indeed?" André cried amusedly.

"We were feeling so lonely for you," said Patrice.

"I was tired," said Lucille. "And now I'm very glad I yielded to the wicked boy's idea. Because, Fan, you're tired indeed! Come here!" She made room on the little silk sofa.

"Now, Miss Fanny." André was quicker than Patrice in reaching her with a brimming glass, but as she took it her shadowed, shining eyes thanked the two young men.

"I'll get tipsy," she said, "because I'm awfully hungry."

"And cold," said Lucille as she touched Fanny's hand lightly. "Shut the window, Patrice."

Silence fell for a second. Lucille noticed that the wine-glass shook in Fanny's hand. Involuntarily she looked then at André. He was savouring his champagne with cool pleasure; he looked very handsome.

"Where did you get to, indomitables?" asked Patrice.

"Only as far as the Giusti Gardens," said Fanny.

"That would have been the last straw for poor little me," said Patrice. "Lord! *What* tourists we've been today!"

"Are they good, Fan?"

"Lovely. And the view over Verona and out across the plain is—oh, well, I can't get the exact word now. None of the obvious, large ones would do, Lucille. But—it got cold suddenly. Ah, this champagne is marvellous!"

"Anything like the view we saw, Miss Fanny?" asked André.

"Not in the least," she said, and the two laughed involuntarily, as if at some small secret, Lucille thought. Small and silly, I hope, prayed some dark part of her intuition.

At dinner, however, no observer would have taken them for

weary tourists, or perceived any shade at all upon their gaiety. During it André commanded a telephone call to the Lido and when it came through all four ran to the instrument in the foyer, and spoke into it almost simultaneously. They heard with relief that except for missing them the Countess was enchanted with her rest cure, had walked along the sands, and written to their dear father, had made some pleasant, French-speaking acquaintances; and that to her amusement a very charming elderly man had introduced himself to her as none other than Raymond de Chamboisel—"You remember, children, a friend of my girlhood? You've heard your father tease me about him?" "Now, now," said Patrice. "You be careful! You don't want him teasing you again, do you?" "Oh, silly children! Your poor, old mother! He's got his wife with him, of course—a German lady, very devout." And were they all well, and happy—and eating properly? Dinner in her hotel had been—for a hotel—quite surprisingly excellent. And now she must go to her room and begin her night prayers—and God bless them all, her good children.

*   *   *

They trooped back to their table and began to eat in earnest.

"Mother's the one who knows how to live!" said Patrice. "And here are we with that Duomo on our hands for to-morrow morning!"

"And the Scaligeri Tombs," said Lucille.

"Oh, lay me in one of them!" cried André.

"And the *Museo Pompei*," said Fanny. "And every piece of San Michele architecture!"

"Indeed, every piece of architecture in the place!" said Lucille.

"That can't be true anyway," said Patrice. "Or else, what were we slaving at today?"

"It's a kind of madness, dear Patrice," said André. "It can't be helped. It's a way some girls get." He filled Fanny's glass with a beautiful golden wine.

"Prigs?" asked Fanny, laughing at him. "Lucille, André told me this evening that you and I are prigs!"

"I call that really handsome of you, André," said Lucille.

"Lovely prigs, two really lovely ones," cried Patrice. "See, I toast you!"

"What prompted the tribute, Fan?"

"I think we were talking about literature——"

"*I* wasn't," said André.

"But Fanny was. Ah well, then what more natural?"

"Ah, Miss Fanny," said Patrice, "if you're going to add literature to the burdens of this tour—I'll *have* to go back to the Lido!"

"There's a convenient train you could catch tomorrow, dear boy," said André.

"Yes. Or I might even walk, nice and slowly."

Fanny poured a little wine from her glass over her plate of strawberries, then leant across and poured some on Lucille's.

"Doesn't it sound a good idea, Lucille," she asked—"to be walking slowly back to Venice?"

"No Mercedes?" said Lucille.

"No Milan? No Turin?" said André.

"I'd chance them," said Fanny.

"But, Miss Fanny, Ruskin says they are both of supreme importance!"

They all laughed at this ever-welcome chestnut.

"One thing at a time is what I like," said Fanny.

"And do you know," said Patrice, "I think that nothing at a time is what I like."

"But, at that rate, life will never be long enough for you, Miss Fanny!" protested André.

"It won't, in any case. I know that. Still——"

In Milan they stayed at the quiet Hôtel Cavour, by the Public Gardens. André explained that he had taken rooms there because the centre of Milan was unbearably noisy.

"I know it's a bit far from the Duomo and things——"

"Thank God!" said Patrice.

The girls smiled at each other, because Lucille had told Fanny that the night before in Verona she had seen the light burning very late under her younger brother's door and, feeling restless, had knocked and gone in to talk with him. He had not heard her knock; he was bent over his table, writing in a large notebook with a pile of similar notebooks near-by—and there were several learned-looking books about the room. He had smiled guiltily when he looked up.

"A few noble thoughts I'm jotting down," he said. And Lucille had said nothing, and gone away.

"He doesn't waste anything, that queer Patrice," she said to Fanny. "And already he seems to know how to conserve his vitality, how to hide himself. I—I envied him, Fan——"

Late, and hungry from the long drive, they went downstairs to dine. All four were tired.

"No, don't look round, André," said Lucille in a very quiet tone of disgust. "Guess who are at a table at the far end of the room. The von Langenbergs, mother and son!"

"Oh, Otto the Magnificent?" said Patrice.

"But how amusing!" said André. "He's probably here on more or less the same business as I am. No use looking like that, Lucille! We'll have to be affable!"

"That's as may be," said Lucille.

Fanny raised a questioning eyebrow at Lucille, who half-winked to indicate that she would explain these German acquaintances later. But André turned in his chair, looked down the room, and then rose and advanced to where an elderly straight-backed lady and an equally straight-backed young man sat at a table by a window.

"Always the business man, our handsome André," said Patrice.

The tall young German leapt to his feet smiling, as André approached and bowed before the elderly lady, kissing her hand. The three who watched from afar could follow the pantomime of exchanged courtesies and explanations; they saw André indicate them and saw Frau von Langenberg raise an affable lorgnette, smiling in their direction. And then, while André lingered politely with the lady, they saw the tall young man advance with strides to them. It was now Patrice's turn to rise, as Otto von Langenberg bent in greeting over Lucille's hand. There was polite laughter about the unexpected encounter, Herr von Langenberg was presented to Fanny, there were promises of pleasurable meetings on the morrow, and with further bows to the young ladies and a friendly nod to Patrice the civilities were concluded for the time being, and André came back to his interrupted dinner.

"Well," he said, "that's amusing."

"You don't often repeat yourself," said Patrice.

"It's funny how individually people apply the word 'amusing'," said Lucille.

André cocked a slightly exasperated eye at her; then he drank some wine and called for more asparagus.

The von Langenbergs were a wealthy German family, rivals of the firm of M. Paul de Lainsade, André's uncle, in the promotion of the motor-car in Europe. But the rivalry was amicable, and as the interests of the two successful companies met in certain ways, their Chairmen sometimes walked cautiously round the idea of amalgamation. They respected each other, and the families of von Langenberg, de Lainsade and de Mellin had long exchanged a friendly social intercourse. And as André de Mellin, his uncle having no son, was heir-apparent to his firm, so Otto von Langenberg stood in relation to his father's wealth and responsibility. And the banking house of de Mellin in Brussels handled a large proportion of the enterprises and investments of both firms. It was obvious therefore that the two groups, meeting accidentally in the Hôtel Cavour, would be reciprocally affable.

"I have asked them to lunch with us tomorrow," said André.

"Oh Lord!" said Lucille.

"I must find out what is the really good restaurant in Milan," her brother went on. "It is our only opportunity to be polite to them, as they have to leave for Ferrara in the evening."

"Oh!" said Lucille.

"They're full of regrets, but unfortunately they are due to stay some days with friends who have a villa near there—a beautiful place on the Po, Frau von Langenberg says."

"How charming for them," said Lucille quite enthusiastically.

"Yes—praise God!" said Patrice. "By all means let's give them the best lunch in Milan, André!"

When they had drunk coffee André fixed his eyes commandingly on Lucille.

"You must come with me now, Lucille, and make your bow to Frau von Langenberg."

"Nonsense, dear André."

"But you must! After all, you're in Mother's place——"

"I'm certainly not in Mother's place, you silly! And wild horses won't get me marching the length of this dining-room to bow to that old bore."

André usually knew better than to press forward into defeat, so now he laughed.

"You're a very naughty girl!" he said. "I'll tell Father."

"He knows that already," said Patrice. "But I tell you what—here's a compromise. When we get up you and I will stand back reverently, André, and these two girls will step a little forward facing towards our German friends, and hand-in-hand they'll sweep to the ground in the famous *Place des Ormes* curtsy."

"Yes—we'll do that," said Lucille.

"I hope I haven't forgotten it," said Fanny.

"It'll be a charming surprise for all the diners," said Patrice.

"What fools you are!" said André good-humouredly. "But anyway, you do promise to be very polite at lunch tomorrow?

"Exquisitely polite, you dear André," said Lucille. Then, lifting her glass, in which there was still some golden wine, "And here's to Ferrara and the Valley of the Po!"

When they left the dining-room they inclined their heads solemnly in the direction of the Germans, and were rewarded by the sight of tall Otto leaping to his feet, and bowing from the waist.

The Countess had instructed André, in regard to the safety of Lucille and Fanny during this tour, that the two must either share a bedroom or have communicating rooms, so that either could shriek for the other or dash to her in the event of there being a man found under a bed.

"It's a very frequent occurrence in foreign hotels, André—and of course we know what Italians are——"

"We do indeed, Mother. Do you think I should get them a brace of pistols?"

"Well no, dear boy. That would worry me even more than

the bandits. Because they don't understand firearms, naturally. And they might have an accident, you see. No, no pistols, I think. But the greatest of care about their rooms, which you will of course examine every night before they retire. And *very* strong locks on the outer doors, dear boy——"

In the Cavour André could reserve only one large room for his two precious female charges. They were well content with it; it was a beautiful room and its long balconied windows opened out to the rustling freshness of the Public Gardens and to a starlit sky. As they lay in their beds and listened to the clang and the singing of the city they found that although tired they were not immediately sleepy.

As they undressed Lucille had explained the von Langenbergs to Fanny, and as the latter listened she remembered amusedly Patrice's comment: "Always the business man, our handsome André." 'Indeed that is true,' she thought, with a condescension that had an odd undertone, as of relief, in it.

"The three families have always been friendly, I think," said Lucille. "Gertrud and Augusta von Langenberg were at *Place des Ormes*—but before our time. Gertrud's married now, to a Brazilian industrialist—Heavens, you should see him!"

The nineteenth-century fortunes of the von Langenbergs, as of the de Lainsades, had derived from the building of locomotives and rolling-stock generally, in which they still had large interests, but the firms, influenced by their younger directors, were now chiefly concerned with the combustion engine.

"I think Otto von Langenberg is just like André in that— crazy about motor-cars—as money-makers, I mean. Boring, isn't it—in young men?"

"Yes," said Fanny. "Yes, it is boring."

"Old Herr von Langenberg isn't a bad old fellow, all the same. Anyway, he's quite a musician—could have been a very good one, they say, if it wasn't for the rolling-stock!"

"Of course, *we* have what I suppose you would call **no** money at all, Lucille—so sometimes all this wealth calling to wealth that I find in your walk of life does stun me a little!"

Lucille laughed as she jumped into her bed.

"It isn't *my* walk of life, Fan! Anyway, I swear it isn't going to be!"

They switched off their bedside lamps, so as to cheat moths and mosquitoes.

"I'm getting shockingly used to switches and having everything within reach and all the rest of this corruption," said Fanny as she leant back and looked out to the dark blue, jewelled sky. "I don't know what they'll make of me when I go home. Mother! Dear Mother, she's truly austere, you know, Lucille."

"I can well believe it. You'll be austere too. I'm sure you're like her. When am I going to be invited to Dublin?"

Fanny laughed.

"Any time. But—we live very simply, in a small house. You'd—you'd have to share my room."

"Well, aren't I doing that now?"

"True enough."

Silence fell.

"Gone to sleep?" said Lucille.

"No. I'm thinking—about you. You said, that first day in Brussels, that you were going to spend the entire time in Italy talking to me about yourself. And so far there hasn't been a word."

"My attention was deflected, Fan—you'll be surprised to hear! Oh, not only by Venice! But don't worry. I'm liable to begin any time now!"

"I wish you would."

There was silence again.

"You're smiling, Lucille, aren't you?"

"Yes. How did you know?"

"I felt it somehow. What are you smiling at?"

"I think I'm laughing, really. How would I look, Fan, married to Otto von Langenberg?"

Fanny turned on her pillow and searched Lucille's profile outlined against the gleaming summer midnight.

"You'd look magnificent," she said half amusedly, half in fear.

"Would I? He's a handsome animal, undoubtedly."

"Do they intend you to marry him?"

"'Intend' is an amusing word sometimes. But I'd say that

111

André 'intends' me to marry this German *vis-à-vis* of his. Father—well, Father is different. He has been reflecting on it for much longer than André, and I think he hopes that it will happen. I don't know exactly why."

"The von Langenbergs would jump at it?"

"I don't know about jump. I believe the old man would be really pleased, for softer reasons than my dowry and the business alliance. But I think that Frau von Langenberg says to herself that as girls go nowadays—well, I'm a lady, I'm a Catholic, I have good health and they know all about me and my safe, wealthy relations—so, I might almost do for her princely son."

"And the princely son——?"

"Oh, Otto! For him we can use that word 'intend'. I believe that Otto intends to marry me, Fan, when he feels inclined!"

They both laughed softly. Fanny did not like to ask any more leading questions; moreover she knew that Lucille did not 'intend', at least at present, to marry anyone.

"That seems to simplify everything, for men," she said, drowsily. "Feeling inclined, I mean."

It was Lucille's turn to search Fanny's face.

"What an experienced-sounding statement!" she said gently.

"Oh, it was only a sort of question," said Fanny. "Forgive me if I seem silly. I've told you that—that your way of life stuns me a little. And oh, all this Italy! It *is* Milan we came to tonight, isn't it? I'm like an American tripper in *Punch*, I think——"

"Very like."

"I must write to Mother tomorrow, Lucille. A long, long letter."

"Homesick?"

"No—not that exactly, not yet."

"But sometimes—I don't know, I think you feel at bay amongst us, Fan—defenceless?"

Unaccountably tears stung Fanny's sleepy eyes. At bay? Defenceless?

She stretched her hand across to Lucille's bed and ruffled her friend's gold head.

"Sometimes," she said. "But never when you're with me."

Lucille heard the withheld shake in Fanny's voice. She took the hand that had ruffled her hair, and kissed it lightly.

"I'm always with you, Fan," she said.

Fanny's hand fell away gently. She was almost asleep.

"There is a good deal of noise in Milan, but it's far away," she said. "Don't marry anyone, Lucille——"

"Wasn't it nice, what *Mère Générale* said to us the other day?"

"You mean: 'I'll be disappointed if either of you two does the obvious thing'?"

"Yes. I wonder how many of the possible things she would call 'obvious'?"

"She's a great charmer," said Fanny very sleepily. "You have to be wily——"

"You couldn't be wily enough for her. I suppose she's about the ugliest woman in Belgium?"

Fanny did not answer. Lucille lay awake only a little longer.

*   *   *

Fanny enjoyed the luncheon comedy the next day. The formidable Frau von Langenberg was an amusing monument of dignity whom she could observe in safe detachment; Herr Otto, dignified also, she watched for symptoms of his 'inclination' towards Lucille, and these, she thought, were not wanting; and it entertained her to contemplate André in what she supposed she might call his 'public' rôle, as the man of affairs, the man of worldly power and guile whom he was assiduous to become.

He had indeed taken trouble about this small luncheon party. He had secured the best placed, quietest table in Savini's, and had chosen the food and wines with perfect judgment. And the friendly waiters were perhaps, thought Fanny—who was already beginning to know something of the character of Italy—a shade more disciplined and alert under his tranquil eye than might have been their daily habit. 'He is not only being the brilliant business man,' she thought suddenly; 'he is also quite babyishly showing off to his grand friend, Herr Otto.'

A flat dish of red and white rosebuds lay in the centre of the table. The restaurant was coolly shadowed from the noonday, and it rang with the gay polyglot voices of many travellers.

The language at André's table was French, because although Lucille, Fanny and Patrice studied German none of them was fluent in it, whereas Frau von Langenberg's very remarkable North German French was equal to any possible demand.

"Yes, thank you, André-Marie. I find these shrimps exactly to my taste. Correctly chilled."

Fanny could see Patrice thinking that that was how the German lady would like many things—correctly chilled. She caught his eye but did not smile at him.

"One eats well in Savini's—for Italy, I mean. Do you not think so, Miss Lucille?" said Otto.

"I've never been here before," said Lucille. "But it looks as if people do," and she waved a slightly contemptuous hand towards the crowded room.

Looking at her, Fanny thought that André could only feel that the lamb he was leading to market was worthy of the trouble he had taken today. For Lucille was looking positively lovely. She was always beautiful in a careless, noble style, but this morning, in a spirit of pure mischief, Fanny guessed, she had taken trouble to get what she called, mockingly, 'a suitable effect'.

Lucille wore a simple dress of pale gold silk, that matched her hair and enhanced the pale gold of her skin; her shady hat was of gold straw, and her only ornaments were a necklace and bracelet of small topazes strung on thin gold chains. And Fanny, studying her and deciding that she looked perfect, had a moment of foreseeing sympathy for her parents and her elder brother, since it was clear that Lucille could, if she chose, flower into such an adornment of the de Mellin way of life as almost to be a justification of it.

"But you are now grown-up, Miss Lucille?" Otto was saying. "When I was last in your father's house, you were still a schoolgirl——"

"I left school in the summer of last year——"

"And quickly you have entered the great world, eh?"

"No— I haven't entered it yet, Herr Otto."

"I should think not!" said Frau von Langenberg. "Young ladies have much to learn, my son, before they are fitted to enter society."

"Yes," said Lucille, in a soft tone which Fanny and Patrice knew to be mischievous. "Yes, alas, Frau von Langenberg, there is much to learn."

"As I have said, Lucille, But do not be uneasy, my child. You have received an excellent moral and mental training at *Place des Ormes*, and for the rest you will trust yourself in all things to the guidance of your wise, good mother."

Patrice sat between the German lady and Lucille, and facing Fanny, who sat between André and Otto.

He permitted himself a cautious smile at her now, since no one, he surmised, was paying attention to her or to him at this party. He thought he had Fanny to himself for consolation while the German lady boomed her wonderful French, the idiom and accent of which he was happily memorizing.

'Lovely Fanny,' he thought as he did his best to get an incautious smile from her. 'She wore that dress in Brussels once, and I think she said she had got it for her sister's wedding. I don't suppose Frau von Langenberg sees her, the pale blue wraith. That hat shades her eyes too much from here; I could make her laugh easily if she didn't have it on.'

It was a wide-brimmed Leghorn hat, bought in Venice; it had a narrow pale blue ribbon round the crown; Fanny loved it and was glad that she had it to wear on this day of sudden elegance. And Patrice was wrong if he thought that nobody was observing him or her; because, however busy as host and man of affairs André might just then be, he was aware of the girl at his side, and though he could not turn often from his chief guest to look at her he too was thinking, in his fashion, lovely Fanny. And Lucille was playing comedy chiefly for Fanny to catch. And Fanny could have told Patrice that nothing and no one at the table was going unobserved by Frau von Langenberg. But he would find that out.

They were eating trout *à la Lombarde,* a speciality of the house, André said.

"And I trust I shall be forgiven, Frau von Langenberg, but I found in the cellar book here a very promising Moselle of

1898—just the right age? I hope you do not think it foolish to drink Moselle in Italy?"

"Not necessarily, André-Marie. It depends on the condition of the cellars here, and on how long it has been at rest."

"But since there is no wine on earth to match it," said Otto, "I for one would choose to drink it anywhere!" And he smiled graciously at André, and lifted his glass. "Drink, dear Mother," he said, "to this very graceful thought!"

Frau von Langenberg obeyed her son, and pronounced the wine to be worthy of its label.

"I confess it is somewhat surprising to me, Lucille, to encounter you and your Irish friend in this manner. The world is changing, of course, and a little judicious travel is possibly a useful finish to a young lady's upbringing. And indeed I am sure you could have no wiser or better escort than your brother, André-Marie. But—have you no companion, no chaperon with you?"

"We have a splendid chaperon," said Patrice, "but we left him in Venice for a rest."

"'Him'? You left 'him'?"

Lucille laughed.

"Patrice is talking about his tutor, Frau von Langenberg. No, Fanny and I are not chaperoned."

"It's only for a week, and they are strictly under my orders, Frau von Langenberg," said André.

"Well, we can only allow your good parents to judge for you, I suppose," said the German lady handsomely. "But this young man, for instance——" she rapped Patrice's hand sharply with her lorgnette, for she did not like him. "May I ask why he is travelling about so luxuriously with a tutor, when surely he should be in his classrooms in Brussels?"

"Oh no, he shouldn't," said Lucille, and Patrice put both his hands into safety under the table. "He left the Lycée last month having taken a brilliant *bachot*, and every possible prize and honour he could win, Frau von Langenberg!"

"Indeed, the poor old tutor is only a joke!" said André.

"And you're having a well-earned holiday, eh?" said Otto to Patrice.

"That's what I think," said Patrice, still keeping his hands under the table.

116

"I see," said the German lady. "Well, I repeat that your dear parents must judge in these things for themselves. Yes——" she indicated to the waiter that she would have some chicken breast in cream—"yes, this dish appears to be quite excellent. And you, Miss—er——" she turned on Fanny.

"Fanny's name is Miss Morrow," Patrice said, with a sudden Teutonic hint in his French which made André frown, and which compelled Lucille to pinch his hand reprovingly under the table.

"Miss Morrow—coming as you do from such a country as Ireland, this tour must be a very extraordinary surprise to you?"

"It is indeed," said Fanny. "More of a wonder than a surprise, however."

"It's a great wonder, as Fanny says, to us all," said Lucille. "It's our first sight of Italy, Frau von Langenberg."

"Yes, but—to a person from Ireland, my dear Lucille——"

"Do you ascribe especial sensibility to the Irish, Frau von Langenberg?" asked Patrice innocently.

"Why should I, young man?"

"Oh, but indeed one might," said Otto, bowing gallantly to Fanny.

"I don't," said André, and he laughed gaily and kindly into Fanny's eyes, leaning near her to fill her wine-glass. "I live among the Irish at present, Frau von Langenberg, and let me tell you they're a cool-brained and superior lot! Isn't that true, Miss Fanny?"

"I hope so," said Fanny.

"You are talking nonsense now," said Frau von Langenberg, "and that is a tendency I never understand—do you, Otto?"

"No, I confess, Mother. But——" smiling at Lucille, "it might be well to try to."

"I cannot imagine why, my son. Yet, do you know, Lucille, that I have sometimes heard your dear mother talking nonsense?"

"Mother talks it often," said Lucille.

"Most excellent nonsense," said Patrice.

117

The German lady waved her lorgnette dangerously, but Patrice was ready, and took cover.

"I cannot help thinking," she said, fixing him with an instructive eye, "that a little more respect for your parents would not be out of place."

"That's odd, Frau von Langenberg," said Patrice in a gently reasoning tone. "Because *we* would find it quite out of place. We're very fond of them, you see——"

'He is being really naughty now,' thought Fanny. 'She is not going to be forgiven for rapping his knuckles.'

"I should hope so, foolish boy!" And he was brushed aside as if he were a fly, while André engaged the enemy swiftly for him in respectful queries about her comfort and pleasure on Lake Como, where she had been resting for some weeks.

Patrice leant back in his chair and winked broadly at Fanny, who at last allowed herself to smile.

Herr Otto was engaged in expressing to Lucille his bitter annoyance about the Ferrara engagement and, Fanny gathered, was trying to extract some information as to the de Mellin plans for the coming weeks. But Lucille appeared to be completely uninformed about them. "It all depends on Mother," Fanny heard her say, in a docile, floating kind of voice. 'If she goes on that way,' thought Fanny, 'he'll be "inclined" to marry her before we get to drinking coffee.'

Frau von Langenberg looked amiable as she discoursed to André about the amenities of Lake Como and of the Hôtel Grande Bretagne. She really likes him, Fanny reflected. During lunch she has, whether she knows it or not, snubbed the rest of us very heavily, including Lucille—yet she has only smiles and flourishes for André. She is almost as indulgent of him as she is of her glorious Otto. I wonder why? Oh, of course—Augusta. It must be Augusta. Lucille didn't say that she had hooked an industrialist yet. She'd like André for Augusta. Well, if the young lady is even half as handsome as her brother—granted the other advantages—my goodness, all these rich, tall blondes, all blooming away in perfect health, and intermarrying, and breeding masses more of the same, and making money all the time—oh, goodness, how foreign and strong it seems as a programme! How it would astonish

Mother to contemplate! Indeed—Fanny smiled again—how it would fatigue her! Even more than all the poor simple O'Connors.

Patrice leant over the rosebuds and spoke to her softly, not interrupting Otto's flirtatious efforts with Lucille or Frau von Langenberg's hypnotising of André.

"What are you smiling at, Irishwoman?"

"I'm only thinking how vast and godlike you all are—and all your friends! Look at you!"

"It fatigues you?"

"Sometimes it's like being in Valhalla." He chuckled. "Am I being rude, Patrice?"

"Very rude."

She pulled a red rosebud from the dish, and laughed at him as she smelt it.

"Forgive me, will you?"

She leant back out of his range as a waiter poured coffee for her. But he stretched for the rosebud.

"I'll think it over," he said, as he fixed the flower in his buttonhole.

Frau von Langenberg was unable to understand why André had allowed his mother to stay in such a notoriously unhealthy place as the Lido. Now Bellagio, where she had had the wisdom to repose herself——

"Oh, but Mother is having great fun on the Lido, Frau von Langenberg," said Patrice. "She's met an old admirer there, you know——"

The German lady gasped. Were she not so perfectly trained a lady she would indeed have spluttered her coffee. But before she could speak Lucille, giving Patrice a small slap on his wrist, came laughing to the rescue.

"We must beg you to pay no attention to this extremely foolish boy, Frau von Langenberg! He's such an innocent for his age that half the time we think he doesn't know the meaning of what he's saying! Truly!"

Frau von Langenberg and Otto both stared now in some misgiving at Patrice. Could it be that—but sometimes of course one did hear that these brilliant young examinees——

Lucille enjoyed her effect, and looked forward to Patrice's assault on her later. But he delighted Fanny and her now by assuming as she spoke a softly foolish expression, gazing wide-eyed at the German lady.

The latter, authoritative but not cruel, looked back at him thoughtfully, nodded her head and said: "I see. I see."

André thought this turn of pantomime excessive, and felt angry with Lucille. But he laughed his most charming laugh.

"More of this nonsense that they talk, Frau von Langenberg! I assure you they are quite a plague sometimes!"

The German lady thought it best to accept his graceful screening of a possible family anxiety, and also to say no more about the Lido.

So luncheon ended, a little languorously. It was now the hour of siesta, and in two pretty canopied victorias the party drove to the Hôtel Cavour, Otto and Patrice escorting Lucille and Fanny, and André taking care of Frau von Langenberg.

Farewells were spoken in the foyer.

"Miss Lucille, it has been a happy meeting. I shall remember today. I shall remember Milan." Herr Otto bowed over Lucille's hand, and stood proudly smiling towards her until the lift carried her away from his sight with Fanny and Patrice.

The girls pulled off their beautiful hats and sighed with relief.

"I think she broke one of my knuckles," said Patrice, examining his left hand with tenderness.

In the cool of late afternoon they felt recovered from the luncheon party, and prepared to begin on their postponed duties of sightseeing.

Patrice came to the girls' room with a message from André, who regretted that he had business engagements, and begged all three to chaperone each other carefully until he rejoined them in the hotel at seven o'clock.

"And if you'll tiptoe cautiously on to this balcony," said Patrice, "I'll show you a pleasing sight."

Below them on the *Piazza* the two von Langenbergs sat stowed away in a large touring car, the lady's back and feet and veils and goggles being reverently adjusted and secured by a strong-looking maid, while a powerful chauffeur attended to Herr Otto's comfort and took his crisp instructions. Presently maid and man mounted to their posts, the hotel porters made low bows, the motor-car emitted some roars and, to loud horn music, moved slowly out of the *Piazza* and out of sight.

"Well, André's the better man," said Patrice. "He can drive the thing himself."

They withdrew from the balcony.

"Next stop Ferrara," said Lucille with a brilliant smile.

"Happiest of towns!" said Patrice. "And now to work, my ladies. There's a cathedral in this place for one thing!"

That was on Monday afternoon, in Milan.

They had to leave Turin on Friday while the day was still hot.

"Well, this carriage of André's always knocks up a nice breeze," said Patrice.

"But pity the poor driver," said Lucille.

André laughed. He was normally of equable temper, but never more so, Fanny noticed, than when in charge of his huge motor-car.

"It would have been fun to take you back by Cremona and Mantua," he said. "But I don't like to risk those secondary roads."

Fanny sighed inwardly over the lost chance of Mantua, but she was too polite and grateful to admit her pang.

"I'll have to drive fast and rather dustily, girls, for Milan, as we must dine there early and quickly, and then press on for Verona. I'm afraid you'll be half-dead before we get there!"

"Oh, no," said Fanny. "It'll be heavenly to be in Verona again."

"I agree indeed," said Lucille.

"Then you didn't take to the big cities, girls?" said Patrice.

"I thought we had terrific fun in both of them," said Fanny.

"Still, two nights and one day of Turin were quite enough —for now," said Lucille.

"But you saw all your necessary merchant princes, I presume, André?" asked Patrice.

André nodded.

"We were negligent about sightseeing," said Fanny.

"I like that!" exclaimed André. "Considering that I cut a most important business engagement in Milan so that you could be escorted to the top of the Cathedral tower, Miss Fanny! Was that negligent?"

Fanny laughed softly at his audacity in reminding her of that expedition. It had not been happy.

"But that is any tourist's minimum," she said. "Even you, a business man, would have had to go up that tower, with or without a companion!"

"Funny that they'll only let people up in twos," said Lucille.

"Yes. I was sorry about your business appointment, André," said Patrice. "But I simply couldn't go up that frightful tower twice. I'm not strong. Since Frau von Langenberg I'm not at all strong."

"I wouldn't have dreamt of putting such a strain on you, dear boy," said André.

"Still—we were awfully lazy," said Fanny.

Patrice turned right round in his front seat to face the two girls accusatorily.

"Listen, you Irishwoman! We had exactly forty-eight hours left to spend in Milan when those Germans let go of us, and in that time, some of which had to be given to eating and sleeping, did we or did we not examine the Duomo inside and out——"

"Examine?" laughed Lucille.

"How much suffering did you put me through in the Ambrosian Library?"

"Oh, but you could spend whole years there inadequately," said Lucille.

"Well, then? And, didn't we traipse all round the Brera——"

"I didn't," said Fanny. "I hardly saw a thing. I was dead tired. Anyway, I think I'll remember a few of the pictures we saw in Turin——"

"But one will hardly forget *Santa Maria della Grazie*, Fan?" said Lucille.

"The Last Supper. Ah no! Still, I'm afraid I'll remember Milan as having been just great fun, won't you, Lucille?"

"Yes, and I didn't expect it to be like that. All those pretty little carriages we drove about in!"

"We'd have been corpses without them," said Patrice.

"And that amusing concert in the Café Biffi," said Fanny.

"That was delicious," said André.

"And the shops—wonderful bookshops," said Patrice.

"You too!" cried Fanny. "You were disgraceful in the shops!"

Lucille and Patrice had gone mad among the beautiful shops in the *Corso* and in the Victor Emmanuel Gallery. Fanny had only a little money to spend, and was also determined that such presents as she took home from Italy would be bought nowhere but in Venice. So she had kept her head. But the other two became extremely frivolous, bought exquisite trifles for everyone, including themselves, and lavished delightful follies upon protesting Fanny. André, in the daytime bound to his business schedule with the merchant princes of Milan, all of whose handsome invitations his obstreperous three charges refused to consider for one moment, had had no time either to visit the shops himself or to exercise restraint upon his sister and brother. But when he joined his party at the evening *apéritif* hour, he had been good-humouredly entertained by the spoils they displayed before him.

Fanny was for ever marvelling at the serene temper of the de Mellins. Did they ever get ruffled? Were they ever rude to each other? She thought sometimes as she watched them of the life of her own family—so affectionate, so close-bound, so vulnerable—by contrast with this other pattern, so precariously balanced between mutual understanding and mutual exasperation. It was something which naturally she understood much better than she ever could this sunny serenity. Yet what a rest, what a bath its atmosphere was—even while she wondered at it. For she knew Lucille to be both grave and hasty in her real heart; she was sure that Lucille's father was not so much the amused and easy man he seemed as one in crisp control of himself; she knew Patrice to be at least as impatient as he was sweet; and in private quite lately she had been allowed to see how near his smooth surface lay in André a cruel kind of wilfulness. Yet to make this Italian

journey with them and not consider them too closely would
be to accord them as a group an all but seraphic equanimity.
They have, of course, extraordinarily good health, she told
herself sometimes; but had to laugh a little at that explanation, because assuredly there was nothing wrong with her own
health, or for that matter with Lilian's or Joey's or her
father's. Yet they, the Morrows, could certainly not have gone
travelling about together for a whole month without a few
squalls, some misunderstandings, a few tears. It must be a
racial difference, she thought, or perhaps it is accounted for
by their always having been so smoothly rich. Or it may be
only that they are detached persons; in spite of their obvious
pleasure in each other perhaps they are much more separated,
isolated persons than any of us Morrows could ever be?

"Where shall we dine in Milan, girls?" asked André.

"Oh, the Cavour, please!" said Lucille.

"So long as it's not Savini's," said Patrice with a shudder.
"That's haunted for me!"

"Me too," said Lucille.

"Agreed, no Savini's," said André. "You disgraced yourselves there, as well you know."

"Couldn't we go to that café, the one under the chestnut
trees in the Public Gardens?" asked Fanny. "Just above that
great fountain?"

André half-turned his head.

"You liked it there, Miss Fanny? So did I. We'll have our
apéritif under those trees—but you'll have to eat a really
good dinner in Cavour's. The drive on to Verona will be an
ordeal."

"For you, indeed," said Fanny. "But truly not for us."

"We'd better telephone Mother from the Cavour," said
Lucille. "Because heaven knows where we'll be on the road
at nine o'clock."

"We'll do that," said André.

"Won't it be fun to see her again tomorrow evening?" said
Patrice.

CHAPTER SIX

AT DANIELI'S AGAIN

So on Saturday evening they were in a gondola on the Grand Canal.

"Ah, the sweet air!" said Lucille. "It's like—it's like a sort of home-coming!"

"How radiant you look, foolish Miss Fanny!" André said softly.

Fanny smiled in vague answer, but did not try to speak to anyone, did not wish to.

This 'home-coming' was only for farewell. A few days now, they could only be a few, and they would all be for the north, and she on her way to Ireland.

She desired to go home, not only because she was dutiful, not only because she often missed her own people and her own way of life amid all the strange and lovely ways and places, but because she was sane and knew that life lay for her there where she was her familiar self; at least that it must stem from there, be planned from there, and that almost any time now it must in reason's name begin.

She was grown-up. She had been considering that fact in gravity and perplexity ever since her father had refused in January to let her return to Brussels and take the *baccalauréat*. And Lilian's wedding, that very grown-up, expensive and serious sending-off into the hitherto remote world of contracts, vows and matron-status of someone who was only three years her senior and who had always seemed, whatever else she was, a silly girl, had brushed away some mornings mists for Fanny, had sobered if it had not dismayed her.

And these weeks of dreaming, of golden dalliance and of first tasting of the world's delight, had not been irrelevant to her preoccupation. Indeed, the crowded, vivid experiences and impressions, lightly though she had perforce to take them—they being too many and too rich, as reason told her —were nevertheless an educative force within her, and for all their semblance of dream, of passing music, were in fact no such matter, but solid food for her growth, accretions that

125

were working change from day to day in the very substance of her nature. These weeks of holiday pageant in which so little happened save what was pleasant, easy and amusing, were, against appearances, carrying her forward as soberly and ruthlessly to adult life as every event had seemed to do since schooldays had closed behind her in December.

And André? He too, a part of these recent months, was hurrying her forward to the status of young woman in the world, understanding the world. André was educating her indeed, if not exactly as he thought to. But perhaps there was nothing exact about his educative plan or his intention.

But now, making this journey over the golden water, through sails and gondolas, between flower-hung walls and red and gold and silver palaces, towards the great turn at the Rialto, through peerless evening light, through calling, shouting and singing all around of the cool Venetian hour —Fanny was not consciously sorrowing to find herself grown-up, or troubled by any aspect of her education. Simply she was wrung with delight to be in Venice again, and she foresaw that every hour of this delight in the days ahead would be grief-shot, a delicate, sustained experience of pain.

Patrice lay low in the gondola, his gold hair untidy on his forehead, his eyelids down as if he slept, but that there was a narrow blue glitter through his lashes.

"The place could not possibly have been looking more beautiful," said Lucille, and to Fanny her face seemed as brilliantly surprised as if this was her first ride into Venice.

"I wonder which will turn out to be best," said Fanny. "Remembering—or being here?"

"You might easily think you were remembering it now," said Patrice.

"Yes," said Fanny. "That's true."

"We're a dusty lot to be entering the earthly paradise," said André amusedly as he contemplated his oil-stained hands.

"Yes, Mother will take us for a lot of tramps," said Lucille.

"Oh, there's water in Danieli's," said Patrice.

"Water everywhere," said Fanny contentedly. "If gon-

dolas weren't so irresistible, wouldn't it be lovely to swim
down the Grand Canal, Lucille?"

"Wonderful. Ah—we'll be at the Academy Bridge in a
second——"

"Yes—I can see *Santa Maria della Salute*! Can you?"

They all straightened up, and tried to shake away a little
of their travel-dust.

"There's Mother on the *Molo*!" cried André.

"The sweet lady!" Patrice sprang up and waved his arms.
"Maffetoni, too, alas! But what do I care! Hi, there,
Countess!" he shouted. "Look this way, you silly one!"

"She must have seen our luggage coming in from the
vaporetto," said André.

"*Stáli! Stáli!*" commanded their gondoliers to the out-
coming traffic of the *traghetto*.

The four were on their feet now, looking inward happily
to the familiar *Piazetta*.

"There's quite a group to meet us," said André. "Do you
see Otto von Langenberg?"

"Oh, no! Oh God!" cried Lucille, and the happy light
her face had worn vanished as if switched off. Fanny flashed
her a look of true compassion, and Patrice groaned aloud.
However, the business of the moment was to step ashore,
and, Germans or no Germans, they did so with delight.

*   *   *   *   *

"I wonder where we are," said Fanny.

"Does it matter?" asked André.

"*Stáli!*" warned the gondolier.

"Ah, *now* I know! I think I recognize this little narrow
Rio we're turning into. It looks like *San Giovanni Laterano*.
If it is, we must be near *Santi Giovanni e Paolo*—you know,
where the Colleoni statue is. The horse—you remember?"

"I believe I do. Heavens, what an exhausting guide you
could become!"

"Are you laughing at me?" asked Fanny gaily. "Lucille
wouldn't! I wish she had come out, the silly!"

"I thought she was coming."

"Yes, but then—well, she said she had a headache——"

"She seemed to me to develop it only when von Langen-

127

berg crossed the lounge and suggested himself for going with us!"

"Perhaps she didn't want to leave your mother the first evening?"

"But Mother was just off to bed. Is Lucille going to be shy of male admirers, do you think?"

"No; not shy. Yes, look—there, up to the right! You can just see Colleoni's helmet—ah, it's gone!"

"Do you want to go that way? I suppose these affairs have a reverse gear?"

"No—I'd rather see it again properly by daylight. Let's go on past *Santa Maria dei Miracoli*, and into the northern canals. This is really the part of Venice I'm mad on—this shabby east and north part. Lucille is mad about it too."

André laughed.

"But with all this twisting and turning how on earth do you know you're going east or north in this labyrinth?"

"I can't explain. Father says I'm a natural compass. Anyway, I think I usually know my bearings, even in the dark."

"How unattractive of you!"

"Is it?" She laughed, and leant back lazily against the cushions, holding the curtain of the canopy aside. Her hand lay white as moonlight on the dark silk. "I don't care. One doesn't compete with Venice, or the Venetians."

"You should. You must always compete. Everywhere. You're fit to."

"Nonsensical." Her voice was shy, but she flicked him a half-smile. "You're talking to an obscure ignoramus from Dublin!"

"Am I? Well, do you know, I find Dublin ignoramuses rather to my taste. When do you return home, Fanny?"

"Ah, soon! Indeed I shall have to go immediately we get back to Brussels."

"And that should be in about ten days, I'd say. Mother's getting a bit restive for her stable now."

"Naturally. You're leaving Venice tomorrow, aren't you?"

"I hadn't thought so. Do you want me to?"

"Why ever should I?"

He did not answer her question.

"I shall have to leave some time on Wednesday—for

Vienna," he said. "And after I've called at Charleroi and Brussels, I hope to be in Dublin by the end of the following week."

"A lot of travelling," said Fanny. "Isn't this a lovely little square?"

"Yes, indeed! Shall we tie up awhile, and drink something in that low-looking tavern?"

"I'd love to."

As they crossed the square Fanny recognized it.

"*Santa Caterina*," she said. "There's a picture in that church we ought to see——"

"I daresay, but we can't see it now, you crazy tourist! Are you cold, Fanny?" His hand lay lightly under her arm and he felt her shiver against the small scuffling breeze. The trees shivered too, very softly.

"No; it's delicious air."

They sat in the screened angle of the *terrasse* and drank rough red wine out of heavy glasses. Two tired-looking workmen were at another table; there was a boy with a flute under a tree, trying over a few notes; their gondolier, invited to drink by André, sat a little way off and lifted his glass to them with a smile.

"I'm glad the others didn't come," said André. "Would it worry you if I smoked?"

"No; it'd keep the mosquitoes off—and your cigarettes smell deliciously."

"Have you ever smoked a cigarette?"

"Heavens, no!"

"Would you like to try one?"

"No, thank you. And you'd be extremely embarrassed if I did—even here!"

"Would I? Do you know, Fanny—if you're going home to Dublin so soon, I think you might as well travel with me. What do you think?" His eyes were very bright with mischief.

"Well, suggest it to your mother! And wire and ask my father what he thinks of the idea!"

"I'm sure they'd all entrust you to me as to your old nurse! After all, I've been chaperoning you all these weeks—haven't I? I'm a trained duenna, that's what I am!"

"And you look the image of one."

"We'd have fun in Vienna—and in Paris, and all along the road! Isn't it silly that such an obviously convenient thing is impossible?"

"You're a mischievous character," she said with amusement. "But even if it were a perfectly correct arrangement, I shouldn't want it."

"Why? You're homesick now, aren't you?"

"Yes. But all the same, I want to be with Lucille, and I want to go back to Brussels with her."

"You'd rather travel with Lucille, in *trains,* than with me in my motor-car?"

"I'd rather travel with Lucille in anything than with almost anyone else in anything else!"

"That's a remarkable sentence!" They both laughed. "So you won't run off with me to Vienna on Wednesday?" She laughed at him again over the rim of her wine-glass. "Oh well, another time perhaps? When you're a little older, no? It would be better then——" he mused audaciously.

Fanny shut her eyes, and pretended not to hear these last fooleries. She was suddenly tired. 'Why does he have to rattle and be nonsensical always?' she asked herself. 'Why can't he be quiet sometimes about his own frivolous whims? Why can't he listen to all this—to Venice? He's spoilt; truly he's a silly man.'

Then she opened her eyes and looked at him. He was looking at her, and his expression was grave, even mature; his eyes were anxious. She recognized uneasily this unfamiliar aspect of his face; but when had she seen it before? She could not remember.

"It's late," she said. "It's a little cold."

"Yes. Come, Fanny." He took her hand and they went back to the gondola.

The gondolier sang gently, in time to the beat of the water. Within the little shadowy tent Fanny's eyes shone; her forehead gleamed dramatically white, as the breeze lifted her hair.

"You haven't talked to me since we went up the *Duomo* tower at Milan," said André.

"But—haven't we been talking now?"

"Ah, now! But I tricked you into this."

"I don't think so. I—I was glad to revisit these canals tonight. I wanted to."

"I wasn't fretting for the canals, I only wanted to be with you, Fanny."

Fanny looked down at her hands.

"Then—then we've both had what we wanted," she said. Her voice was hesitant.

"I haven't," said André.

His arm was lying along the back of the seat; now he touched her shoulder lightly with the tips of his fingers. She leant forward and cupped her chin in her hands, staring along the water-way.

"He's taking us northward still," she said. "If he turned left we should get into the Grand Canal somewhere——"

He tried to draw her hands away from her chin. Laughing he bent over her.

"Fanny, listen! You are lovely! Almost no one has the luck to be so lovely, you innocent! Why on earth can you not enjoy that wonderful stroke of fortune——?"

She could not help laughing.

"I'm not convinced about it yet—as I've told you before! But I'm not inhuman. It's—it's nice to hear it said, anyway."

"It's a responsibility," he cautioned her.

"I'm almost beginning to believe you! Ah, André, let's stop talking about *me*, please!"

"No, we won't. You were very cross and unreasonable on the roof of the *Duomo*——"

"It was you who were cross and unreasonable."

"I was cross, I admit. Oh, foolish child!" He took her in his arms and laid his mouth against her hair. Fanny twisted herself back from him, her hands on his shoulders.

"André, I beg you not to go on teasing yourself in this wilful, foolish way—about a nothing!"

"It's not a nothing." His voice tightened and his eyes grew narrow. "I'll make you understand that——"

"You couldn't."

"Oh, I know you're only eighteen!"

"That's irrelevant. If I were twenty-eight I'd say the same."

131

"No, Fanny—you wouldn't, if you were twenty-eight."
His arms hardened about her again—and she drew back
to the side of the gondola, her hand on the silk curtain,
pulling it back. "No good!" he insisted. "The gondolier's
on my side! The whole of Venice is!"

"Take away your hands, André." He obeyed and she leant
far back in her corner. "Venice is a libertine," she said.

"And you love Venice."

She laughed at that, conceding her weakness.

"But not to imitate, not to live with, not for keeps."

He paused, and lit a cigarette. The match illumined his
features closely for a second, and showed them coldly handsome.

"If we were always to wait for those three qualifications,"
he said, "I wonder how much loving there would be?"

"Enough, I'd say. Perhaps the right amount."

"Oh prim perfectionist! Would you rob life of all its
graces? Would you take away, for instance, all that this
wanton Venice has expressed?"

"No, André, I wouldn't. That's the trouble. But, thank
God, I'll never be consulted!"

He leant across and took her hand with mock caution.

"That's where you're wrong," he said. "You're being consulted at this very minute, Fanny—in a small way."

"Mischievous creature!" she said, yielding her hand to his
in her amusement. "You can always make me laugh!"

He kissed her finger-tips.

"Flirt!" he said.

She pulled her hand away.

"Flirt—I? André, how dare you? I assure you I hardly
know the meaning of the vulgar word!"

"Indeed? Then what do we do whenever we are alone
together?"

"Oh, I suppose you flirt! I don't know—But I have never
sought these private conversations in which you persist in
embarrassing me!"

"That isn't true! You like me, Fanny."

"Certainly I like you, and it's because I do that your
nonsensical wilfulness embarrasses me. Why can't you be
like Lucille and Patrice?"

"Patrice, indeed! Patrice is crazy about you, child!"

She stared at him—then turned away with a sigh of exasperation.

"You're mad," she said wearily.

"I'm not in the least mad."

"Then you're—to say the least, you're lacking in judgment."

"In what way?"

"Well——" she paused. "You apparently have a—a hedonistic habit of life, which you're free to pursue. And I'm sure it's extremely easy for you to find those who share your tastes. Yet you will go on being—discontented, because you can't convert an awkward creature like me to your notions. That's a silly way to upset yourself, surely?"

"Your observations are shallow," he said.

Fanny smiled in the shadows.

"No doubt," she said, "since we're in shallow water."

"You have only as much right to say that I am silly and lacking in judgment as I would have to say that you are."

"No, André; I have the right to comment on an attitude to life which you are forcing on my attention. But I haven't ever asked you for a single thing, or exposed a solitary one of my ideas to you."

"So you have ideas?"

"A few, to be going on with."

"And one of them is, I suppose, that it would be a sin to kiss a man, to let a man kiss you?"

Fanny laughed outright.

"Do you truly want to discuss sin, André?"

"You are convent-trained, so I was merely trying to talk on your plane," he said with pomp.

"Don't try," she said cruelly. "But since you ask me, and leaving my convent training out of it, I do think that to kiss is frequently a wrong thing to do—a sin, if you like."

"Ah! You see!"

"I see—but you don't, André. Oh, don't be silly, let's leave it!" They had swung at last into the Grand Canal, and the summer night poured radiance on their faces.

"For now let's leave it, Fanny," he said, all his customary sweet temper in his voice.

133

"Look," she said. "I think that's the house where Wagner died."

"Ah! Which one? Now, there was a man who stood no nonsense, Fanny!"

"I don't think that *can* be true," she said amusedly. "He was far too great not to have been at bay and thwarted over and over again!"

"Indeed? Poor fellow! Then perhaps I'm on the way to greatness, would you think?"

"Who knows?"

"And if I am, Fanny, it follows that you can't be—because your rectitude will prevent you from ever being thwarted or at bay."

"Very likely. So you win."

"But I don't want to."

"That's a pity. What time is it? Lucille will think the gondolier has drowned us."

"Or that we've eloped?"

"She knows my rectitude."

"But I could have gagged and chloroformed you."

"True enough."

They fell silent. Tired. Even the Grand Canal was almost quiet now. André took Fanny's hand again and counted her fingers.

"Cold heart," he said, pinching her thumb. "Cold, superior, Irish lady," he went on, flicking a word off to each finger.

"Superior Irish lady, I hope," said Fanny, "but not 'cold heart'. Still, what have the Irish ladies been up to, I wonder, that makes you always insist that they're superior?"

"Ask no questions, Fanny. You're a puzzling race."

"That's gratifying to hear. Oh, I'm sleepy! Verona seems a long way in the past, doesn't it?"

"As far as yesterday. That's one o'clock striking. I've only three days left."

"Goodness, how we'll miss you, André! We're sure to get into fearful muddles!"

As they went through the hall of the hotel they saw Patrice stretched, half-asleep, in an arm-chair, a book on his knees. He opened his eyes at them and rose.

"Is it bedtime?" he asked innocently.

The three entered the lift; as they went towards Fanny's room she saw a light shining under Lucille's door.

"I'll say good-night to her," said Fanny, and as she knocked André and Patrice bowed and went on down the corridor.

Lucille was sitting up in bed, with books flung around the coverlet. Her eyes shone welcomingly on Fanny.

"If you had a headache, you should have gone to sleep ages ago!"

"It was only a German headache, Fan."

"Are you going to have many of them—every day that's left?"

"I think not. Frau von Langenberg loathes Venice. She told Mother that it is the two things she most abhors—frivolous and insanitary!"

"She sums things up rather neatly, doesn't she?"

Fanny slid on to the bed, leaning against its foot. Lucille flung her a pillow.

"Put that behind your back," she said, and Fanny smiled as she did so, thinking that kind Lucille was in some small points quite clearly her mother's daughter.

"Yes, she does. You'd be surprised!" Lucille laughed mischievously. "When she came to say good-night to Mother in the lounge she told us that it was incorrect for you to walk in the streets of Venice at night escorted only by André."

"What did your mother say?"

"Oh, something gentle and vague, which really meant 'Mind your own business, you old bore!' But the real fun was that Patrice almost gained favour in her sight because he bowed very low and said that he agreed with her, that it was entirely incorrect. All with his usual air of innocence—very amusing!"

"And you, my girl," said Fanny. "What about this air of innocence you're assuming now? I find that amusing!"

"I thought you would. I'm sorry, Fan. But I couldn't resist telling you about your German censor."

"I'd have said she hardly knew I lived—but of course, I'd forgotten, she is aware that André does!"

"Yes—poor André! Where did you go?"

"Through the inner canals up to *Santa Caterina,* and then home along the Grand Canal. I hope you weren't worried —didn't think we were drowned?"

"Oh, no! About ordinary things, such as not having accidents and getting people home safely and so on, André is quite first class. And——" Lucille paused and smiled a little, "—as to less definable issues, dear Fan—I don't think that anyone who knows you would be so impertinent as to worry!"

Their eyes met in a grave shy look. Fanny ran her hand over the silk coverlet.

"I wish you'd been there," she said. "It was our particular, favourite journey in Venice."

"I was dying to go. But I couldn't have stood it with Otto von Langenberg."

"What on earth brought them to Venice?"

"Oh, I think he wormed it out of André in Milan that we were coming back in a few days to Mother. So after Ferrara he forced his unfortunate mother here—they came yesterday. But I'm not worrying. I'm certain that she'll insist on leaving this place of sin and pestilence any minute now."

"On the other hand he might do a bit of insisting, Lucille! And he is her god."

"Yes, he might—if he wanted to. But does he strike you as a man on fire?" They laughed. "No; I think that it has interested him to see me in my more or less grown-up state, and to look me over carefully. And I think this turning up in Venice is meant merely to indicate that, so far, he approves of me and that he is thinking about me. Our unexpected encounter in Milan had simply reminded him that I would be a suitable wife; I'll even go so far as to guess that this second look-over tonight has made him almost certain of that! But he'll have to think for a long time, and very carefully—there's no hurry at all. I'll be there waiting when he feels inclined for me. And meantime, he knows how, and how moderately, to take his solemn and hygienic pleasures."

"Ah, Lucille!"

"Silly Fan! It all has nothing whatever to do with me— that's the delicious, pathetic comedy of it! And anyway we can rejoice, because I know he's had what he requires of me for now, and will think it judicious to leave Venice exactly when his mother wishes to."

"And that's the man that André would have you marry?"

"Yes. And he will choose his own wife by exactly the same rules."

"I suppose so. Will it be that sister of Otto's?"

"Augusta? Well, secretly I think he'd rather it were not. Oh, she's handsome, she has her brother's handsome, cold face, but she's fattish. By all accounts she's had the bad luck to miss her mother's elegant figure and to inherit her domineering and prudish nature."

"Oh, poor André!" Fanny laughed.

Lucille leant back on her pillows and ran her strong, beautiful fingers through her bright hair.

"If I were to marry Otto I think that André would side-step off delightedly after some more alluring heiress than Augusta. But if I don't land a von Langenberg he certainly won't let that business alliance slip. He'll do his duty."

"You're hard on him."

"He wouldn't mind. If he heard me now he'd approve of my realistic good sense!"

"But he's so charming and quick, he's such good fun, Lucille! Somehow, in spite of all his frivolity and—and hedonism, one does feel his relationship to you and Patrice. After all, he's always very sweet-tempered and brotherly—isn't he?"

"Yes, he's those things. And if he had something of Father's passionateness as well, something more from Father's strong brain and heart, he could be ruthless to more purpose, I think. I mean, he might then go ahead and be the terrific business magnate in the family pattern, and yet be lovable, as Father is."

"He's young. Perhaps he'll learn to discipline himself?"

"Perhaps. But you and I are younger. Patrice is younger."

"Patrice might be—a troublesome person?"

"Yes, indeed. Especially to himself. But he begins by being aware of other people."

"That's true. Are you sleepy now?"

Lucille nodded.

"So are you, Fan."

"I'm dead. But heavens, it is good to be going to bed in Venice again! When do we leave it?"

"Mother thinks she'd like to start for home on Monday week——"

"Oh, but that's very good of her! By now she must be awfully tired of being away from your father."

"I think they're both getting restive. They don't like being apart, and aren't at all used to it."

"And she's looking so well after the Lido that we really mustn't take the bloom off with any more mosaics or Tintorettos——"

"No; we mustn't. Father would be delighted if he saw her as she was tonight. You'll stay awhile in Brussels, won't you, Fan?"

"Only a few days, pet—at home they must be thinking that I'm crazy!"

"Nonsense!"

"It isn't nonsense. Still, the whole purpose of this glorious visit was that we were to talk, interminably I think you said, about *you*!"

"That's true, dear Fanny. There's a lot to say, and I've a lot to ask you."

"And I'm here waiting. But now," she slid off the bed, "it's after two o'clock."

"Yes, there's no hurry—when André is gone——"

"What has he to do with it?"

Lucille took her hand.

"He's confused me sometimes, Fan. He's been a bit in your eyes——"

Fanny, who was bending to kiss good-night, paused and looked grave.

"No," she said. "That isn't true. I promise you."

"Ah!" Lucille put her arms round Fanny's neck and kissed her.

"Good-night," they both said. "God bless you."

The Countess de Mellin understood well that the great business house of von Langenberg had long been a formidable factor in the industrial schemes of her brother, Paul de

Lainsade and in the international transactions of her husband's bank, and she knew that in recent years the German firm and the directors at Charleroi were feeling around, with reciprocal friendliness, for some form of trade amalgamation that should simplify their European undertakings, cutting overheads and increasing profits on both sides of the Rhine. Moreover she knew—but only intuitively, because Marcel had never put this into words—that Otto von Langenberg would be encouraged, now that she had left school, to proffer his suit for Lucille; therefore, during this chance encounter in Venice, she observed the young man with more attention than heretofore. She might as well do that, she told herself, since, if her husband wished things so, here before her certainly stood her first son-in-law. She noted that he was handsome, as he had always promised to be, that he bore himself with distinction and had fine, formal manners. If the habitual immobility of his noble features contrasted almost comically with the sweet expressiveness of her own children's faces, she reflected that Lucille after all had enough radiance in her to light up twenty husbands; and if the cloudy word 'uncharming' sometimes crept into her notes, she blurred it away, and chose 'reserved' in its place. And summing up, because she would in all things please her husband and see what he desired her to see, she told herself that Herr Otto was a man of honour and high principle; that he was young and in perfect health; that he was the eldest son of an old and respected Catholic family of the Rhineland, and heir to a great industrial fortune.

So she approved of André's desire to show suitable courtesies and friendliness to their German friends, knowing that such would be his father's wish; and therefore dutifully refused to laugh at Patrice's grotesque descriptions of the luncheon party in Milan.

"I suppose if she had actually broken my hand, as she desired to, you'd still tell me that she's a lady of virtue and importance?"

"But, Patrice, your huge strong hand could not possibly be broken by anyone's lorgnette!"

"She slapped me, I tell you!"

The Countess laughed.

"You're a very naughty boy! You really must not make fun of our friends in this way."

But, although she was not going to admit it to Patrice, she shared his distaste for the company of Frau von Langenberg. In spite of its fatigues and what she called 'discomforts,' she had very much enjoyed the expedition into Italy with her dear, amusing children and with Fanny, but the immanence about her now of the German lady was having a dispiriting effect, and she was secretly beginning to consider that for the present enough had been done on the de Mellin side in the cause of Flemish-German amalgamation. She had listened with rising hope the day before to Frau von Langenberg's expression of cold disapproval of all things Venetian. She had indeed subtly encouraged the German lady in her multiple censures of the hotel, of the canals, of the gondolas, of the flies, of the terrifying smells, of the absurd little shops and, above all, of the uninhibited conduct of the citizens. She implied her agreement with these fault-findings, so that Frau von Langenberg was moved to ask her why, if her eyes were indeed wide open, she had considered staying so many weeks with her family in a place overcharged with dangers both physical and moral?

The Countess was inwardly flustered by this attack; but she countered it deftly enough, saying that she saw to it that every precaution was taken, but that Lucille and Patrice both required to be in Venice because of some special studies they were engaged upon, and that she had the greatest confidence in Signor Maffetoni, who was not only a learned man, but a person of strict morality; a very pious, careful gentleman, said the Countess. However, she added that she would be glad to return home within another week, and she said nothing about how thoroughly she had enjoyed the Lido.

Frau von Langenberg was not entirely satisfied by this defence of an unwise stay in a vicious and insanitary town; but she admitted to herself that there had always been perceptible in this Belgian lady a streak of frivolity. And she continued to catalogue the horrors of Venice.

Therefore on Sunday afternoon, as the Countess talked with Patrice, she was secretly confident that Frau von Langenberg was considering flight and pondering how to persuade her obstinate son to it. But—the Countess did not know this—she was the more disposed to snatch him away from the malodorous vapours and the flaunting street-girls all about, in that in these two chance meetings she had not taken a great liking to Lucille.

"Shall I pour more tea, Mother?" asked Patrice.

The two were seated at a window of her sitting-room and looking out over the Lagoon.

"Do, please, darling. Do you like these little cakes?"

"Exquisite."

"Then you'd better ring for more."

Patrice shook his head, his mouth full.

"Where are the girls?" his mother asked.

"I think they're writing letters. Fanny said she had to write home."

"Naturally. What a sweet child she is, that Fanny! One wonders what will become of her!" The Countess sighed.

Patrice smiled, and bit into another little sugar cake.

"How do you mean, 'become of her', Mother? Now I wonder sometimes what she will become."

"Are you trying to confuse me, darling boy?"

He nodded.

"Well, you shouldn't, because it's so very easy to do it to me, Patrice!" He blew her a kiss. "It would be nice to look forward to seeing dear Fanny a very happy wife—and mother; or else, of course, she might become a good, holy nun."

"Now you mention them, those are, of course, two possible careers for her!"

"Do you think that Fanny has a religious vocation?" asked the Countess.

"No—I shouldn't think so," said Patrice. "Do you think Lucille has, Mother?"

"Oh! my dear boy! Lucille? Of course not!"

"Truly? Are you sure?"

"But—I'm certain, Patrice!"

"Oh! Then, in that case, what do you suppose will 'become of her'?"

" 'Become of her'? What will become of your sister Lucille? But what on earth do you mean, dear boy?"

141

"Only what we were meaning about Fanny, Mother. You were wondering what will become of Fanny. So I go on to wonder what will become of Lucille. What will they become, either of them?"

The Countess paused, faintly embarrassed.

"They are differently circumstanced, Patrice. Lucille is very fortunately placed, and her life is settled for her. She need not give it a thought, thank God! But—I understand that the Morrows are not at all wealthy, and so I was feeling just a little sad for our sweet Fanny. Things cannot be so smooth for her, I suppose, as we would all desire them to be——"

"I wouldn't especially desire smoothness for her——"

"But, Patrice, how unkind of you! How unlike you! I thought you had grown quite fond of Lucille's charming friend?"

"I have," said Patrice, "in my fashion."

"Then, if that is true, don't say such selfish-sounding things about her, pet—or indeed, about anyone!"

He kissed his mother's hand.

"I'll be careful, darling goose," he said. "I wish those two damn Germans would clear off, don't you?"

"Patrice, did you hear yourself swearing?"

"I did, and I beg your pardon, Mother. But they're on my nerves, and they look idiotic in gondolas. They were clearly terrified they'd drown on the way to Mass at *San Giorgio* this morning!"

The Countess smiled.

"Yes, I did notice they were a little nervous."

"Of course I know why the old woman is hanging on, risking pestilence or violent death. Simply and solely for André!"

"For André? What on earth do you mean, child?"

"I mean that she's crazy about André, Mother, and that if it's the last thing she does she's going to marry him to her fat daughter Augusta!"

"She's—what? Augusta, for André?"

"But of course! And why not? It would suit both families perfectly. What a simpleton you are, dear Mother!"

If he wanted his mother to turn against the von Langenbergs, if he wanted to promote for the last week in Venice the untroubled, light peace of the first days there, he had played the ace of trumps.

The Countess de Mellin, preoccupied with Otto and Lucille, had forgotten that Augusta von Langenberg existed. But now in a flash she saw the dangerous likelihood of what Patrice suggested; now she reminded herself of what she had unconsciously noted during last evening and this morning, that whereas Frau von Langenberg had not seemed especially to remark or admire Lucille, she had been consistently adulatory of André, gracious and responsive with him, making him talk of his plans and concerns, and even flattering him to his face. She had indeed disapproved of his leaving the hotel to walk on the *Piazza* with their dear little Fanny last evening, but her censure had been directed pointedly against 'young ladies who allowed themselves such freedom', and she had contented herself with saying of André, almost indulgently, that he was 'unwise'.

Now whereas the woman was not born, nor ever could be, who would be a worthy wife for either of her two sons, the Countess was cheerfully determined that both were to marry young, happily and as suitably as could in an imperfect world be arranged for them. But she had always so naturally and freely disliked the womenfolk of the von Langenbergs that her benevolent mind had made itself almost unaware of them, until here in Venice she had been compelled to reflect that Frau von Langenberg would be a somewhat dispiriting mother-in-law for Lucille. Yet she had consolingly reminded herself of the unimportance of mothers-in-law, and also that Lucille was too bright and strong of heart to be troubled in her married life by a flaw which could only be external.

A wife, however, André's wife whom he would take for better for worse, was something other than a mother-in-law. And, if the Countess could help it, no son of hers was going to espouse the cold and fat, the charmless and sanctimonious Augusta von Langenberg.

She stared at Patrice.

"I had forgotten her existence," she said slowly. "But—— such a calamity could *never* happen to André!"

"Could it not?" Patrice laughed at her. "It's women who

143

do the marrying, Mother! All history proclaims that. And
I warn you that if they want him, that mother and daughter,
André will marry Augusta!"

"Oh, is it settled?" asked Lucille.

Her knock had gone unheard, and she and Fanny had
walked in on Patrice's last words.

"What nonsense!" said the Countess, greatly embarrassed,
and grimacing in what she believed to be a subtle fashion, to
convey to her children that in the presence of an outsider,
even dear Fanny, there must be no more flippancy about
Augusta von Langenberg or André's matrimonial intentions.

"You know this foolish Patrice, dear Fanny! He is still a
great baby and likes to weave romances!"

Fanny smiled at him.

"I thought he was such a baby that he hadn't got to that
stage yet," she said.

"What greedies you two are," said Lucille, and she took an
éclair from the tray and bit into it. She was amused, and
grateful to Patrice; she thought she saw what his game had
been about the von Langenbergs. Judging by their mother's
flushed cheeks and startled eyes he had done well.

But her young brother, while he smiled at the three, was
thinking that women, mothers, could be unpleasantly
illogical. 'This mother,' he thought, 'does indeed love us; yet,
if it is our father's wish, most certainly Lucille must marry
a conceited bore, whereas for no consideration need André
embrace a pious fatty.'

"Well, ladies," he said. "Shall we go out and be dissolute
among the bad smells, as Frau von Langenberg might say?"

"Fan and I are going to post her letters, and then on to
the *Accademia*——"

"Ah, I won't go there, my darlings," said the Countess.

"No, of course not, Mother."

"I'll take you for a drift along the *Riva*, if you like, Mother
—in a luxurious gondola?"

"That would be lovely, dear boy. You'd better ring for
Séraphine——"

"Well, we'll be going," said Lucille.

"Don't overdo things, girls," said Patrice. "You know
there's the concert at the Goldoni tonight—and we're all

invited to it, Maffetoni and all, by our German friends!"

"I thought André was taking us?" said Fanny.

"So he was. But when Herr Otto heard of it he insisted it was to be his party—*and* supper afterwards, at that German place in *Ventidue Marzo*—you know?"

"Oh, good Lord!" said Lucille. "Why have we to do everything in cavalcades? We even had to go to Mass with them!"

"Well, it's kind of—of Otto to wish to entertain us, dear."

"It's one thing to *wish* to entertain us, Mother. It's another to succeed!"

"Lucille! That doesn't sound polite! But of course *I* shall not dream of going to any concert—*or* to supper. I shall explain to our friends that I am not well enough——"

Fanny laughed.

"You'd better do it from behind a heavy veil, Countess —because you're looking simply wonderful after the Lido——"

"And I confess I feel wonderful, Fanny—but I must conserve myself now—run along, children——"

"And give her respects to Giovanni Bellini," said Patrice as he held the door open.

Said Lucille to Fanny, as they descended in the lift: "If we can only get out of the hotel and across the *Piazza* without meeting either of our attendant cavaliers!"

"It's almost too much to hope," said Fanny.

However, they were lucky and escaped unnoticed over the Iron Bridge.

And at noon on the next day, when the de Mellin party were peaceably sipping *apéritifs* of iced vermouth in the hotel lounge, Frau von Langenberg came majestically to join them, escorted by her son. They brought the news—the lady announced it—that they were leaving Venice in the early afternoon. "Homeward bound," said Frau von Langenberg. For her part she could suffer no more of this preposterously over-rated town, and indeed she feared it had not agreed well with dear Otto.

The latter, whose face this morning was a perfectly rigid mask, murmured an inaudible protest. But Frau von

Langenberg swept on with her correct speeches of regret and farewell, and of delight at the happy encounter which had given such an unlooked-for interest to their journey in Italy.

She sat a moment between Countess de Mellin and André, but refused an *apéritif*. Otto accepted one, however, and drew up a chair near Lucille.

The German lady's decision must have been vigorously enforced upon her son during the morning, because there had certainly been no hope of this good news when they all parted after supper, and Otto seemed positively sulky now, Lucille thought. Indeed to Patrice he looked as if he desired with his soul to give his mother a good beating.

Frau von Langenberg, of stronger stuff than the Countess, and greatly to the latter's delight, had gone with the young people to the concert—because it was given by a German string quartet of which she had heard excellent reports. But she had declined to stay with them for supper at the Bauer-Grünwald, so André had escorted her home from the Goldoni and then had rejoined Otto's party.

Surprisingly, this was gay.

The concert had been stimulating and beautiful, and after it the night seemed still to be full of seventeenth-century music. Otto was a good host, at his best when in charge and in command; and under the influence of beautiful Moselle everyone became amused and amusing—Signor Maffetoni perhaps most amusing of them all. They lingered contentedly at their round table, laughing, admiring each other, and admiring their own jokes, urging Signor Maffetoni on in foolish reminiscence.

". . . And yes, Miss Fanny, an Irish lady she was—oh, delicious! . . . in the little city of Toulon we met—a curious chance! A little widow, very little. . . ."

André savoured his wine with pleasure and let his eyes have their pleasure of Fanny.

"In the little city of Toulon," said Patrice, lovingly. "But how very little widow was she? Could you say?"

Otto drank Moselle copiously and gravely. But his eyes shone, and sometimes he could not help singing over a phrase of Corelli that the violins of the concert had left in the night.

"I think I begin to understand Venice, Miss Lucille," he

146

said. 'How distinguished she looks,' he thought. 'Where in Europe could I find a wife at once so decorative and so correct for me?'

Walking home across the *Piazza* Lucille felt less tolerant of her host than she had been in the restaurant, for he took her arm in a painful grip and pinned her to him almost as if he desired to carry her, as he might a sword, on his flank. But she twisted away and ran forward, so that he had to follow her to where the other three, Patrice and Fanny and André, strolled in peace together. And then politely he let her be, and studied the line of her head in the clear moonlight, and hummed the Corelli phrase.

"Where's Maffetoni?" asked André.

"He felt unsettled," said Patrice. "He went towards the Rialto."

So the party had ended, in sleepy friendliness.

Now this morning Lucille, listening to Frau von Langenberg and looking at sulky Otto, guessed that the latter had dutifully gone to say good-night to his mother, but being full of wine must have expressed himself over-enthusiastically about her, must have revealed himself as rather too rapidly growing 'inclined' for her. She was sure that Frau von Langenberg did not like her personally, however much she liked her suitability, and that she did not wish Otto to commit himself save after long reflection. Hence the simple decision to withdraw from Venice without further parley. The quarry the German lady really pursued in de Mellin territory was André; and Lucille reflected that had Augusta been with her mother on this tour they would not now be tasting this sudden relief, this truly refreshing news.

Yet, in detachment and benevolently remembering how he had enjoyed his own party last night, she almost felt sorry for Otto as he sipped his *apéritif* and glared down at it in silence.

Frau von Langenberg rose, and with her the three men. She must be excused, as she required to lunch early. She would say good-bye, as she and Otto would be gone before the siesta hour was over. She could not say she envied them their remaining days in Venice, but she wished them all a safe return home, and she sent her most cordial greetings to

M. le Comte. And at last all the bows and flourishes were ended, and she withdrew towards the dining-room, followed by her handsome son.

André asked the waiter to renew the *apéritif*.

The Countess sighed.

"A commanding personality," she said.

"Bad persons don't like Venice," said Patrice. "It takes a good person to like a good thing."

It was July. The days were hot and Venice seemed to the Countess more crowded and noisier than it had been in June. She grew wistful for Brussels and desired to be at home in time to prepare for the holiday return from *Place des Ormes* of the three little daughters.

So on Tuesday, the day before he left them for Vienna, André made their travel reservations for the others. They would leave Venice on the following Monday morning, to join the Paris Express at Milan on that afternoon. They would spend Tuesday and Wednesday nights at the Meurice in Paris, and be at the *Villa des Glycines* in time for dinner on Thursday night.

The Countess's eyes brightened with happy tears as she listened to the schedule.

Patrice refused to take charge of any tickets, vouchers or time-tables, save his own.

"Give me mine, André," he said, "because I may tire of human society and decide to travel alone."

"Dear boy, I hope you won't," said the Countess plaintively, for male protection was essential to her peace of mind in the perils of travel, and Signor Maffetoni, who was better than no man at all, had expressed his intention to visit his aunts in Bologna, and therefore had that morning concluded his appointment of tutor-courier and, handsomely rewarded, gay and grateful, had departed southward.

But Patrice would promise nothing, so Lucille and Fanny took joint charge of the remaining days and of the journey home.

"And look at the folder I've bought for you to keep them in," said André, as he placed the various papers in correct order in the pockets of a beautiful green wallet of Venetian tooled leather. "And here's another—a red one—for the different kinds of money you'll have to carry, Lucille."

"The one for the tickets should be black," said Fanny.

"That's certainly what your two solemn faces are saying! Oh, don't be sad! What would we all do, in Brussels and in Dublin, if in fact you didn't come home, you silly girls?"

"But we want to go home," said Fanny.

"Indeed we do," said Lucille. "It isn't that."

They locked the wallets away in Lucille's dressing-case. When they were empty, when the tickets and the *lire* were gone, not only would Venice be an insubstantial dream, but grown-up life would stare them insistently between the eyes. They both felt chilled and solemn, but they managed to smile at André and they thanked him for having been so efficient and solicitous for them.

That evening at dinner he was charmingly gay and fussy and paternal with his mother and with them all. And Fanny, watching him, understood that he was happily excited to be setting off alone the next morning, for Vienna and his normal concerns. He had had, she thought, this pleasant month of foolery, and now was perfectly willing to let it go, and to give his full attention to what lay ahead. He would remember Venice quite accurately, as a surprising town and 'picturesque'; but she was prepared to wager that he would find Vienna incomparably more attractive. In leaving the flock which he had shepherded with serenity all these weeks, he had made every possible arrangement for their safety and comfort, and that being done he would, as he drove over the Mestre viaduct in the morning, banish them contentedly from the front of his mind. But the flock would miss him, she surmised; she herself would miss his brotherliness, his sweet temper, and the constant, gay appreciation of her that his bright eyes did not trouble to conceal. And in any case his going stirred melancholy in at least three of those he would leave behind because, as Patrice was saying, it was the beginning of an end.

"It's like the 'ten minutes' bell at school," said Lucille.

"Yes; we'll be counting everything from now on," said Fanny, "every day, every hour——"

"Last sight of Torcello," said Lucille.

"Last walk along the *Zattere*," said Fanny. "Last look at The Presentation of the Virgin——"

"Last ride in a gondola?" said André, mischievously.

"Goodness!" cried Fanny and Lucille.

"Last photograph of me among the pigeons," said Patrice.

"Children, children, what a dreadful litany!" protested the Countess. "Do try to eat some dinner, please! And since you're talking of last things, isn't it a pity, dear André, that your last dinner in Danieli's should be this poor attempt?"

"The wine is good, Mother. Let's drink a toast? I give you Venice," said André, and lifted his glass.

"Venice!" the others echoed gently.

"Venice, and us in Venice!" said Patrice.

The Countess said she would take coffee in her sitting-room.

"I like Florian's coffee," said André. And as they left the dining-room he said to Fanny: "Will you be kind and companion me in my last walk around the *Piazza*?"

"I'd like to," she said.

The night was cool; they sat in one of the little open, mirrored rooms, and looked out from its bright square across the shadowed, humming colonnades to a scene of perpetual movement and gaiety set about hundreds of café tables, and spread under silver light. Florian's string band scraped at a waltz near-by; music and singing floated across from Quadri's too, and randomly from many directions.

They drank coffee filtered into glasses.

"I haven't offered you *grappa*, Fanny," André said, "as I don't suppose it would be good for you." But he tasted his own small glass of it appreciatively.

"What's it like?" asked Fanny.

"It's a little like vodka—perhaps you're a vodka addict? But it's cleaner, sharper to the taste, and, unlike vodka, it is truly exhilarating. Would you try it?"

Fanny was feeling low-spirited but decided nevertheless not to experiment with her moods tonight.

"What are your messages for Dublin, for Mespil Road?"

"I was thinking of Mother this very minute," said Fanny. "Please tell her, tell Father, that I'm ashamed of my selfishness in staying away so long—but that it was irresistible——"

"Was it?"

"I'll not forget it, ever! It, it leaves me helplessly inexpressive—perhaps it won't always——" she paused, grown shy under his attentive eyes.

"Go on, Fanny."

"Nothing—I'm only babbling. But truly, no matter how long I live there will never be anything, there couldn't be, to equal this first being in Venice. I think it's knowing that, that makes me—well, so reluctant to go away." She laughed at herself.

He laughed too, gently.

"You are eighteen," he said. "You are a baby. Yet how can you be so babyish as to suppose that a mere pleasure of travel, however surprising, however delightful, should possibly be the unmatchable experience of a life which will surely be long, Fanny? And—I should think—vivid."

"It will have been that, honestly. I can't explain it to you."

"Don't. I wouldn't understand. Because I know that an experience which can only have been, shall we say, aesthetic, and possibly even, young as you are, a little intellectualized—such an experience, believe me, Fanny, is not the fullest event that life provides for such as you."

"You don't see what I mean. I know that many exacting things must happen to anyone who lives a reasonable number of years. I don't mean that my life is over now!" They both laughed. "Indeed, the trouble is it hasn't begun—and I suppose it must begin soon——"

"That's what I think," said André.

"But still—this being in Venice, in peace and with Lucille, at the very start of things, and even while I'm still such a green fool, if you like—truly, whatever you say, it's something that will never be matched, for me. If I lived for ever I could not say enough 'Thank you's' for it, to your parents and Lucille!"

"Oh, as to that, sweet Fanny, I think you make it clear, your lovely gratitude. Nevertheless, believe a well-wisher. You're talking nonsense. And if you like we'll make a pact here and now. Let's undertake to sit here together, at this very table and at this hour of ten o'clock on any convenient day of the first week of July in 1917—when you will be twenty-eight and I thirty-four. Let's sit here together—you'll be old enough to drink *grappa*. And you can tell me truthfully then, in the light of your added ten years, which of us had the right of our argument tonight. Shall we do that?"

"1917! How far away it is! How old we'll be, André!"

"Yes, indeed. Do you make the pact?"

"I do. It would be fun—and an excuse for coming back to Venice."

"It might be that we'd be coming here together, Fan, to keep our pact. By then, who knows?"

"No, we won't keep it that way——"

"But how do you know what I mean?"

"I'm eighteen," she said. "Not eight. And I'm getting used to your idiom."

"But you don't like it?"

"I don't either like or dislike it, André. Simply, it could never be mine."

He drew a deep, comical sigh.

"That's sad news, Fanny. I suppose I must take it that you are, at present, a very religious young lady?"

"No."

"You're not?"

"I'm not. I'd rather not talk about—difficult things to you, André. Do you mind?"

"Certainly I do. Am I so stupid? And how are we going to know each other if you won't talk to me?"

She smiled.

"We know each other by now, André. As well as we ever shall."

"What nonsense! See how little I know you, when you've just shocked me to the soul by announcing coolly that you are not religious! You—a respectable young lady from *Place des Ormes*!"

Fanny laughed with him.

"I don't care much for that word 'religious', anyway," she said. "I admire holiness, and I envy those who are holy. But I am not—not the least bit."

"Good news! Well spoken! I think I'm getting over my shock! Let's have more coffee——" he spoke to the waiter.

"But tell me then, unholy one, why you lecture your fellow-men about their hedonistic habits of life?"

"I don't lecture my fellow-men. All I say to hedonists is that I am not their kindred spirit!"

"What are you then? What do you believe in?"

"Ah!" There was a silence. The waiter brought coffee and refilled André's glass with *grappa*.

"What do you believe in, Fanny?"

"Give me time. I'll tell you at this table in 1917."

"And you've nothing to say now?"

"Nothing offhand. 'The holiness of the heart's affections'," she said in English. "Will that do? And if I understand what he meant, 'the truth of imagination'."

"What *he* meant? You're quoting someone?"

"Yes."

" 'The holiness of the heart's affections'," he repeated, as if trying over the English words. "We all believe in that, Fanny."

"Heavens, André, we don't! Look at the world!"

"I believe in it," he said obstinately.

Fanny smiled.

"Some day, if you're lucky, you may," she said, "after your fashion."

He sipped his *grappa*, then set down the glass and turned to her a face that was cold, in which his eyes burnt narrowly.

"That was an arrogant and cruel thing to say."

She stretched out her hand and laid it on his.

"It was, André. I'm sorry."

He melted at once; his face was all sweetness as he secured her given hand in both of his.

"Go on being sorry, Fanny! I adore it!"

"Why will you wear your philosophy on your sleeve, 'for daws to peck at'?" The last words were again in English.

"Another quotation? Same gentleman?"

"No. I know a lot of quotations. Let go of my hand now, will you?"

"I suppose I must, for the moment. What a dreadful bore it is that you're not coming with me to Vienna!"

"Poor André!" she mocked.

A shadow fell across them. Patrice sat down.

"I'd like some *grappa*, please," he said. "I'm sorry, André, but Mother has gone to bed early, and she wants to see you before she goes to sleep—last blessings and entreaties, you know! She's really terrified of being forsaken in Italy with only Lucille and Miss Fanny and me for caretakers!"

"Yes; it's good of her to let us have this extra week," said Fanny, "when she hasn't even got Signor Maffetoni, who at least could speak the language!"

"But I think we all do wonders with our pidgin Italian, Miss Fanny. Which reminds me, André—I've just got creditably through a very difficult long-distance telephone call for you, from a lively gentleman in Milan——"

"Ah, I'd forgotten he might ring—name of Albi?"

"That's it. I think I got his message all right. Tell me, André, are you getting married in Dublin, or setting up a very expensive mistress, or what?"

André laughed.

"Actually, no. It's about the silk, isn't it?"

"It is. Signor Albi was happy to tell me that, contrary to his expectations, he had been able to get the seventy metres you required of what sounded to me a very expensive fabric, and I was to tell you, with all his compliments, that these seventy metres were dispatched to Dublin today, to the address you had given."

"Good. Well then, I've done what I promised. It was a commission I undertook, Fanny, for your brother-in-law and your sister, Mr. and Mrs. O'Connor——"

"Heavens! Seventy metres of Italian silk?"

"Yes, and what silk! Wait until you see!"

"What's it for?"

"For the drawing-room curtains at Stillorgan Road."

"But—seventy metres?"

"Well, you saw the house? There are those three long, great windows, which will take, we calculated, about sixteen metres apiece—each curtain four metres long, and double the width of the stuff—and then there's the great semi-circular window at the end——"

"You sound like a draper's assistant," said Patrice.

"Yes, doesn't he?" said Fanny. "Is it very beautiful silk?"

"You wait! I half-wanted your advice in Milan, Fanny—

154

but then I know that your sister, that they both want the drawing-room to be a secret, until it's ready."

"Except from you," said Patrice.

"I had been telling them about the fabrics to be had in Genoa and Milan," said André. "And they suggested I should send them silk for their drawing-room curtains."

"Suppose they don't like it?" said Patrice.

"But it's perfect," said André.

Fanny looked at him as if weighing the value of something other than seventy metres of Italian silk. Yet she spoke lightly and to the point.

"If I were in the position to be ordering myself drawing-room curtains," she said, "I couldn't let anyone else choose them."

"I have good taste, Fanny, and I know what your sister wants——"

"How could you?"

"It's an odd procedure," said Patrice. "And I daresay it will end in tears. But come on home now. Mother must take her sleeping-pill and settle off."

They went back to the hotel, André's last walk over *Piazza* and *Piazzetta*. Fanny said good-night to the boys outside Lucille's door. She would not see André again until she was at home in Dublin.

At last it was the last Venetian midnight. At eight in the morning their luggage would leave Danieli's in a *vaporetto* and at nine the de Mellin party would board a last gondola and travel once more over the Grand Canal, 'in the wrong direction', as Lucille said. The last things had been done, good-byes said, presents bought. Lucille had paid the last week's bill, and done all the requisite tipping, as instructed by André. The Countess, who had never paid an hotel bill in her life, or indeed a cab fare, was awestruck, even somewhat shocked, to discover that her nineteen-year-old daughter managed these functions of male prerogative without confusion, and without becoming as it were unsexed by them. But for Fanny the surprise was not in that Lucille could add up *lire* correctly and calculate *pourboires* as easily as André, but in the coolness with which a fortune of money, as it seemed to her, was paid down for one week's board and lodging. She had known indeed that with the de Mellins one habitually lived *en prince*, but until this last evening she had not seen any of their bills. When she did read over this one she told Lucille that it was the only argument, and an unanswerable one, for leaving Venice.

And now the Countess was asleep, and it might even be hoped that poor Séraphine had forgotten tissue paper, dressing-bags and labels, and had briefly closed her eyes.

Fanny, her packing done, her mother's letter of this morning in her dressing-gown pocket, paced between her own room and Lucille's, and came to stillness at last on the threshold of a balcony. Life sang and clattered on the *Riva* and over the radiant, black water; cool stars rode above the islands, and *Santa Maria della Salute* seemed to float like a white ship. Gondolas crowded darkly against the steps of the Dogana, whence came sounds of singing. Fanny, thinking that, as Patrice had said, one might in fact be remembering Venice when one believed one looked on it, turned her eyes back to the lighted room, and met Lucille's which rested on her. She stretched out a hand, and Lucille came and took it and leant against the window-pane.

"By the time we get to Milan—I suppose about three o'clock tomorrow?—it'll be truly in the past tense," she said.

" 'This insubstantial pageant faded. . . .' "

"English! How I have forgotten it!"

"How I have!" said Fanny. "But it will come back now. Everything will."

"You were looking—not so much sad, just now, Fan—as sharply troubled?"

"I've had a letter from Mother——"

"I know. Any special news?"

"No. Everyone seems as usual. I don't think she herself is ill, or anything. I'd say she's tired—it's a shorter letter than she usually writes. Naturally it is full of messages for your parents and for you, and they are infinitely grateful and happy that I have had this unmatchably lovely time——"

"Oh, go on, Fan——"

"Truly, there's nothing to go on to. You see, Lucille, Mother **is**, as I've often told you, a person of almost

156

maddening restraint. She can be even frightening—simply in her inhuman bewilderment—if other people get expansive, or—well, out of hand."

"But, your father——?"

"Oh yes—he's the exact reverse! And they love each other in a fashion which is, I think, entirely remote from the humdrum——"

"Yes, but——" Lucille laughed softly, "what has this got to do with your letter?"

"Nothing in the least. Thinking about Mother I got a bit irrelevant. But what I'm trying to say about her is that she's so restrained that for those who notice it she is, without her knowing it, the most tantalizing kind of film, or photographic plate, or something. Oh, a very bad one—because you can't make out what anything is that she's—well, I suppose, reflecting. She's an atmosphere, if you like, or an atmospheric register of some kind—I don't mean that she sees ghosts or makes prophecies, Lucille—she's almost primly intelligent!"

"I know. I remember your telling me once that you were never quite sure how much she isolated her real self from the world, or how much power of self-isolation she expected from others."

"Yes—but I think I was wrong. Mother is frightening really because she *isn't* isolated. I think she'd do anything for Father—and that her tenderness towards him is a little —mad. I mean, by now, after twenty-four years of always loving him a bit more, the plight of his dependent, fussy heart really alarms her. In a way it's—funny, you know, Lucille—to see where good, conjugal love has brought two well-mannered elderly people!"

"Sometimes you sound too old for your age, Fan!"

"Soon I will be. I'm not for nothing Mother's daughter! It would be easier just to be Father's!"

"His 'gentle maiden'?"

"It'd be nice to start off with being no one's anything!"

"Lord, I agree!"

"To have had all those lovely years at school, yes! I wouldn't give *them* up! And then this—this magic interlude with you—cloudless!"

"Cloudless, Fan?"

"Oh—well, let's say cloudless, curiosity-box! But then, then—giving thanks to God, to become someway anonymous, Lucille—and to disappear! Just to go off on the quiet!"

"How do you mean—on the quiet?"

"I mean the impossible. I mean to have no relations whom one loves and to whom one owes the normal considerations of love, and to have instead of them a little secret nest-egg— just enough to go off quietly and get some decent education and sort things out. That's all! You see how unselfish I am!"

"I see how you are. Your question is different from mine. Because you have no money, and much heart, and a kind of dangerous thing—a cynicism I have not. Now I have no money unless my father gives it to me—but he has more heart than I—so I *might* beat him. Anyway, if I love some of my relatives I love them not as you do, Fanny. I love them without *nuances;* I do not require always to feel with them; I will do them no wrong, I hope, and I like them because I know them so well. But I am confident, I am even maybe obtuse, where you are too subtle, Fanny. I will go off on the quiet, as you say, and I will, *somehow*, get educated, and get so that I live with my fellow-men, *as* a fellow-man!"

"I am sure you will," said Fanny gravely.

"You were shocked by the bill I paid tonight," Lucille went on. "But that was 'romantic' of you. I knew it would be very large——"

"I'd never seen a rich person's hotel bill!" Fanny protested.

"No; but you see how Mother and André assume things must be. You analyse your own parents, so surely, if it was only from Patrice's sweet mockeries, you'd know that he and I are aware of the absurd millionaire-assumption with which our family insults our fellow-creatures?"

"But we've all enjoyed this reckless luxury, Lucille! I'm afraid it's never occurred to me that I'm insulting my fellow-creatures!"

"Of course we've enjoyed it! That's the danger! Oh, Fan, believe me, I like, I like very much those parts of being rich that happen to appeal to *me!*"

158

Fanny laughed delightedly.

"Then explain yourself!" she said. "Why are your millionaire-assumptions less nefarious than your mother's or André's?"

"They're not! My only plea is that I'm aware of them, and feel guilty. They don't. But I'm better than they, Fan, bad as I am—because I do assure you that I will not live my one precious, small life in the way Mother has lived hers. I can't alter the family way of life, or its assumptions—all I can do is choose a way which will dissociate me from all that, and set me free. Of course, if I had happened to be André, then I'd have had an enormous social responsibility to face, which he does not see at all. Don't misunderstand me, Fan! I love being rich; I love not having to bother about things. So does Patrice. All I'm saying is that he and I are less beastly people—perhaps all I mean is, less absurd—than André. And we know that we must try to take the consequences of that. I don't think we're at all sure of anything, Fan—all we know is that we desperately require education!"

"Ah! So do I! So do I!"

"The thing is, how to get it?"

The two stared at each other; a bell rang from across the lagoon.

"Good-night, Lucille."

"Good-night, Fanny."

In the golden August morning they travelled up the Grand Canal, the whole weary and cantankerous party, and caught the early train for Milan.

CHAPTER SEVEN

MÈRE GÉNÉRALE

"I am perturbed, Lucille. I am even perturbed by my own perturbation. But this, I see, is a consequence of favouritism! And everyone knows how, in government of our Order, I have thundered against favouritism!"

Lucille, who knew herself to be a favourite of the old nun in whose study she now sat, yet did not know if she dare laugh at this piece of ironic self-accusation. Pupils and nuns of the house of *Place des Ormes* sufficiently intelligent to be allowed in due degree the 'favour' of *Mère Générale* knew very well, and often amusedly discussed together, that she allowed none of this, her own weakness, among those she ruled. Tacitly she made it understood that her favourites were beings whom inevitably she, in her indisputable wisdom, knew must be favoured. But for anyone other than her, *Mère Générale*, to admit favouritism in community room or in the study hall was flatly impermissible. Yet even when now surprisingly invited, as it were, to share this autocrat's joke, Lucille was not sure if she was meant to see it clearly. Moreover she was troubled, and in no mood to play comedy. So she did not smile, and weighed *Mère Générale's* word: perturbed. She conceded that that was what she had been herself for many weeks—perturbed, and sad, through the Venetian days.

"I have thought since Fanny's visit to me yesterday, of asking your father to come and talk to me——"

"Father?" Lucille's voice was vivid with question.

"Your father is also father of André," said *Mère Générale*.

"But—truly I don't understand, *Mère Générale*. If you say such—such significant-sounding things as that, then in fairness—oh, please forgive me, *Mère Générale*!—you must tell me something of what Fanny has said to you."

"That is just, Lucille. All the more so as, in effect, Fanny has said nothing to me."

Lucille could only laugh at this.

"Please, *Mère Générale*—you are very wise, very venerable, and I know how much you care for Fanny. Also, we all know you do not make riddles for riddles' sake. Why then—if Fanny says nothing to you or to me—are you and I perturbed?"

"Child—as to your perturbation—we must examine that. But mine is entirely a—guess, a foreboding of the spirit; and, I confess, a cloud born of tenderness. Fanny is in no commonplace trouble—indeed, I think that one of the difficulties that will be of the structure of her life is that she will never be capable of everyday disaster. A characteristic on which one might surmise immeasurably——" mused *Mère Générale*.

Lucille could not resist a mischievous rejoinder.

"Then why on earth send for Father?"

Mère Générale chuckled.

"Be careful, Lucille; you will be a witty woman, please God—but I do wish you were French!"

Mère Générale's snobbery, as a Frenchwoman, about all things French, but especially about what it meant to be French in contrast to being Flemish, was an accepted foible; Lucille treated this instance of it as the aside it was, and waited for the stream of confidence her flippancy had broken.

But the conversation swerved.

"What are you going to do with your life, Lucille?" *Mère Générale* asked, on a new, crisp tone.

Lucille looked out over the wire half-screen towards the elm trees of the square.

"I had hoped to talk that over with Fanny—in Italy," she said.

"I know. You told me you desired to. That's why I ask you now, dear child."

"We didn't talk at all. We were lazy, I think."

Mère Générale adjusted her steel-rimmed spectacles.

"Neither of you is mentally lazy," she said. "But Italy can be enervating."

"I don't intend to be married suitably in the fashion of my class, *Mère Générale*. I know that will mean a clash with Father—but that is something he and I will have to face. I do not desire to be married—until or unless I desire it myself, that is!"

"I am not surprised. Well then?"

"I have no desire to be a nun. I have strong religious belief —I am unlike Fanny in that. I know, from her, that I don't betray her in saying so. She has told me that she told you a long time ago why she couldn't go to Communion——"

"Yes. Fanny told me, when I was preparing her for Confirmation, when she was twelve, that she felt no response at all to certain Mysteries of our faith, but that of course she acknowledged that that meant nothing, except to her. Fanny has always been extremely polite. . . ."

"She told me about that, and that you and *Père* Anselme both asked her to accept the sacrament if she could do so, in the hope that the Holy Spirit might enlighten her."

"Yes. So we did. And she, who never had anything but welcome in her soul for the Holy Spirit, agreed with excellent humility. But constantly since then she has told me that it is no good. That she does not believe what the Church requires its children to believe."

"She believes in God, *Mère Générale*. I think she believes, roughly speaking, that we are made in His Image."

Mère Générale bowed her head.

"She does, dear Lucille. But she has asked me again and again what that means—"

"What have you said, *Mère Générale*?"

"I have said, child, that for me it is a blessed truth—unprovable on our general evidence, but every now and then suggested, in the sense that every now and then a human being has demonstrated it to be true that we are made as capable of being His Image. That it is our fault if we are not in some sense a reflection of God. But then, you see, I believe positively in the Good God, Lucille, and in His Divine Desire to raise us up to His own likeness."

"I don't quarrel with the Good God, *Mère Général*—and I've never had Fanny's difficulties about the Mysteries of Religion, or the Sacraments. I think that may be because—well, I'm not a dreamer, like Fanny. I mean, I don't examine every idea in the light of my *own* comprehension. If I find certain hypotheses working for the general good, I'm willing to let them be hypothetical—if I think them for the general good——"

"That is intelligent of you—and I trust you will be able to serve humanity thereby, Lucille——"

"Ah! That, that is obligatory! Oh, *not* to serve humanity —that's a ridiculous phrase, about *me*, *Mère Générale*! But simply to give back, to work, to do without, to stop being rich and favoured! I don't think I have any talent, but I *have* ordinary brains—and so I won't go on living the way Father requires me to live. I won't."

"No, you won't. Nevertheless, the answer to your intention is not round the next corner, my child. Since you will not take the decision of becoming a nun——"

"*Mère Générale*—I have no desire at all to live the life of a religious."

"What a pity! The two most promising ones of a whole decade escape me on cool denials! Dear God! I cannot be as clever a woman as I've sometimes thought myself! But if you are thinking of being 'independent', child, of being any kind of 'new woman', you will have a very painful battle with your adoring father—and I don't see how you can win."

"I'm only going to ask for some education, *Mère Générale*!"

"How polite you are to *Place des Ormes*, child!"

"And by the time I am somewhat educated, I'll be a grown-up woman, and Father will have been growing a little used to my foibles, perhaps. I don't know in the least what I shall want to do then—but I'll have started, and I'll have some equipment. I want to go to some foreign university, German perhaps, or English—and read a great deal in modern history and literature. I'd like to learn some languages really well—and to travel in many countries—by myself, of course, or with Fanny—and as ordinary people travel, *Mère Générale*. After some years of that I might be fit to earn an honourable living, you see!"

Mère Générale laughed.

"Your dear father won't hear of it, Lucille—and unless he does you are helpless."

"Yes. If I were to run away hysterically, and break their hearts—which I *couldn't* do to them—I could only become a governess or a shop-girl, in which I see little point. And I don't want at all to be melodramatic, but I'm determined to live my *own* way, that's all. It's not important, but it is my intention."

"Child, it's important, it's characteristic, it is legitimate. But—ah well, I can only pray for you."

Lucille smiled into the broad, ugly old face.

"If necessary you will do more. You'll talk to Father."

"You hussy! Do you think that you could get this old fox to quarrel with this convent's banker and chief business adviser, to say nothing of a parent who pays us very handsomely for the present education of three little daughters, who has always been so generous in gifts and endowments to the Order—and who will one day be sending granddaughters to school?"

"No, I couldn't get you to quarrel with Father. I didn't say that, *Mère Générale*. But that reminds me—why on earth did you say just now, in regard to *Fanny*, that you'd like to see him?"

"Because I would advise him—strongly—to have M. de Lainsade appoint André to represent his business interests say in America or Argentina—or Germany. Anywhere, that is, save in Ireland—where I cannot believe his labours are vital."

"Ah!"

"Lucille, I don't think it at all a happy thing that André, who is after all over there a very charming and delightful exotic, and not humdrum, should be living in Dublin, where Fanny lives."

"She is very good, *Mère Générale*; very wise and *isolated*, if you like, in judgment——"

"I know no better girl of her age, and none better balanced. And, like you, she craves education and to choose her own way. She will not marry, she announces now, and like you, I think she also means it now. Like you also she has a very loving father—but as he is not rich her difficulties in that will not be yours. On the face of it I think in regard to education and freedom Fanny's chances are better than yours. But, this Venetian episode, all of it, including André, has moved her in some subtle way, Lucille. You have felt that too."

"She always is, as if deliberately, a little misted off, *Mère Générale*—just a little as if about to vanish—but that was always——"

"True. That is her charm—so different from the 'Look At Me' beauty of her sister Lilian. It has puzzled me about those two sisters, who have such a marked physical resemblance, yet express themselves in everything, in movement and voice and thought and general air, in such amazing contrast. I never cared for Lilian—to my disappointment, because her mother and her aunt, dear Julia and Eleanor Delahunt, were girls of especially fine quality. However, she seems to have got what she demands of life. In return for that, I trust that she will be a good wife and mother. I pray for her, of course, as we pray here for all our children."

"I understand she is very happy—but I never knew her much at school, *Mère Générale*, so Fanny and I never talk about her. I think."

"Fanny is almost amusingly like her mother—dear, dreaming Julia. And I'd rather she took the simple path of domestic happiness, as Julia surprised us by doing, than weave her secret spirit into some cocoon of pain that no one but she will ever know about. That would not be good; it would be wasteful."

"Indeed, it would not be good." Lucille's voice was troubled. "But . . . André? He's hardly the man who could —cause her such pain. I mean, he's hardly fine enough to capture Fanny's sensibilities——"

"Let us hope not. But, he and Venice, and all the rare delights of these two months, my child—and his great charm and openness of manner! She'll be lonely when she goes back —and she'll be glad he's there. And he is superficially very like you, whom she adores. He has, alas, your touchingly beautiful eyes. In short, I do not like it. Since there is no question of marriage—and André *will* only seek a wife to promote his millionaire prospects—but since he cannot resist trying to charm where he is charmed, since he is a selfish young man, and since Fanny *does*, believe me, find him attractive; since she is fastidious, secretive and of a faithful heart, I deplore his being in Dublin any longer. Truly I fear he will hurt her—and I hold that to be a very grave offence."

"So should I, *Mère Générale*. Ah, so I do. I've been afraid already."

"Well, there it is. I believe that I *shall* speak to your dear father."

"Fanny says she must go home tomorrow. She has had a letter today from her father which seems to suggest that her mother is ill—she is very much distressed."

"Is that all he said to her? I had a letter this morning from Eleanor, asking for our especial prayers. 'Julia's time is now very short,' she said. 'May God take Father and me very quickly after her. Pray for us all.' We are praying for them all, I need hardly say—and I have written today to Eleanor."

"Fanny knows nothing of this—I mean, as you seem to know, *Mère Générale*! Oh God, her beloved mother! She's not going home to see her die?"

"She's going home to watch her die, Lucille. We all have to learn to watch death, and Fanny will watch it intelligently."

"But why, what?"

"Is it possible that Fanny's foolish father has not prepared her for the truth?"

"She told me that she must go tomorrow because her mother was not well and was anxious to have her back."

"When I saw Fanny yesterday I was greatly concerned for her return to Ireland, where André is. But I knew nothing of this other thing, any more than Fanny did. But today I have had this letter—of agonizing sorrow—from Eleanor. That is one very grave reason why I said to you just now 'She will be lonely when she gets back'. Ah, my gentle child, straight from the radiance and follies of Venice she is going back to an immeasurable, shocking grief!"

"Oh God! Oh, are you sure?"

"Eleanor says that Julia's recent increasing weariness has now become helplessness, and that the doctors say she has an acute anaemia, pernicious, for which they have no answer. That she is dying, rapidly now. Dear Julia! She will die well. She is just fifty, I believe——"

"Fanny knows nothing of this! Oh, *Mère Générale*, it will tear her in pieces!"

"Yes. And after the long summer in Venice. Her mother's last summer on earth. Poor Fanny! Poor dreaming Julia. They have both been my dear, dear children!"

The old woman rose laboriously and leant on Lucille's arm.

"Take me across the cloisters, child. Let us go to the chapel and pray."

Lucille's tears were pouring down her face. With the revered and great old nun she crossed the empty cloisters where on an autumn Sunday a few years ago she had first

heard Fanny's light, shy voice, and noted her detached good
sense and the careful beauty of her foreign French. She led
the old nun into the school chapel, gave her holy water, and
knelt beside her. The awkward straw kneeling-chairs were
all familiar. She dropped into one of them, and bowed her
head and sobbed. For Fanny she must sob and pray; later she
must find courage. But it was impossible to see in this moment
of shock what could be done or said or felt that could enter
the approaching pain, or at any point seize on it.

Mère Générale looked up.

"'Remember, oh most pious Virgin Mary'," said she aloud
in her exquisite French, "'that never was it known that anyone who fled to thy protection was unanswered. . . .'"

Lucille joined in Saint Bernard's great prayer, and fell into
quiet at its end . . . "'Oh Mother of the World Incar-
nate. . . .'"

"Help me, child; I'm very fat."

Lucille took *Mère Générale* up, and back across the school
cloister.

"I must go to Ireland with Fanny, *Mère Générale*."

"Good child. That is right. Whenever you love a person,
stand near in trouble—unless you are forbidden."

"Fanny won't forbid me to go to Ireland with her, *Mère
Générale*."

"Indeed she won't You are true friends. Only I wish
André wasn't so like you. Still, in view of the grievous news
she is going back to——"

"Oh, do I prepare her about her mother, or may they be
wrong?"

"I don't know. My dear Lucille, do what occurs to you.
You are a wise, good girl, in spite of being a beauty! Help
Fanny, and keep your brother away from her, in so difficult
a period. Leave your arguments about your futures until the
great grief she does not apprehend has been accepted, as it
must be. Time enough then, my child, for bracing at life."

"*Mère Générale!* You look weary! You sound weary!"

"Why should I not? I am seventy-five and very fat and in
bad health. And I hear this morning from my very dear
Eleanor Delahunt that her beloved Julia, lovely Julia as I
remember her, is dying rapidly, poor child. I taught her how

to read the French alexandrine—Julia took well to French, and was a reasonable actress too—as schoolgirls go."

Mère Générale paused, and sat on a cloister parapet.

"I'm glad I saw Fanny yesterday, Lucille—not today. Because yesterday I didn't know that her lovely mother was dying. I think I'm too old now to tackle such a complicated sorrow head-on. What do you think?"

"You're old, indeed, *Mère Générale*," Lucille answered.

"I remember teaching Julia how to speak Corneille—actually I taught her well, and she played *Polyeucte*. I remember how simply, purely she said her lines—'*Je vous aime, beaucoup moins que mon Dieu, mais bien plus que moi-même. . . .*' Ah, she was good! Dear Julia, she was unexpected, in those days. Well, she chose a good, exacting life, and now she is composed, I pray. Take me indoors, child. I feel better when I sit in my office chair. The cloister is sad. You were all so young and silly in this cloister——"

Lucille was startled to see tears in the eyes of the great old nun. Impetuously she put an arm about the heavy frame, so awkwardly robed in black serge.

"Come," she said, "come in. *Mère Générale,* you have loved all the generations of fools you ruled so well?"

The heavy old nun leant back against the young girl's arm.

"Lucille, there is no other way. Power is love, or else it is corruption. Remember that. You will rule, in some sense, some day. Oh, dear child, I'm tired!"

Lucille drew the old woman on her arm across the quiet hall to her little office, a lay sister running to help her. Together the two got *Mère Générale* to her chair, and *Soeur* Théophile ran then at once to fetch a warm *tisane*.

Mère Générale laughed as she understood the devoted flurry.

"Lucille, if you should win this impossible battle with your father—*don't* go to Germany. Oh, I know that this is an embittered old Frenchwoman talking, and that for you neutral Belgians our old argument is nonsense. You are a very new nation, and you are neatly placed outside allegiances. That's A.B.C. But the soul has allegiances, child—nothing to do with wars or frontiers. Your soul does not await you in any German place of learning. Lucille, you must lean towards

France. Believe me, France contains Europe. And that is much to contain—because it is Greece too, you see, that France contains, with all of our sweet Christian thought. Germany—towards which your wilful, charming father drives —Germany is still the unthinking Goth, a bully and a warrior. Do not seek 'education' in Germany, Lucille!"

"*Mère Générale,* may I seem very rude?"

"I cannot imagine your seeming so, Lucille."

"Well, then—I must say that I deplore your French bigotry, and that I cannot have the native land of Beethoven and of Goethe dismissed in your French style. As to your unceasing argument, you French and the Germans—it seems idiotic to all outside it; it's about a breath, it's nonsense. No one alive who is not French or German has any patience with it."

Mère Générale folded her hands, her rosary beads mixed in them.

"Child, you baby," she said. "To be alive on this continent now and be neither pro-French nor pro-German is to be a troglodyte! Ours is an *issue,* and on it hangs the new century! I tell your dear father that in our every business talk. You know, Lucille. I am the daughter of a very successful industrialist of Lille. He was concerned with iron mines, steel and rolling-stock—just as your family are. To the dear man's sorrow I was his only child, and my mother died when I was very young. So he made me, perforce, his confidante and friend—which is why your father and other business gentleman have met their match in me. But I had with my father when I decided to be a nun—that was in 1852, and I was mature enough, I was twenty, after all—one of those quarrels which ring in the heart right into its old age. Simply, we fought, Lucille—my dear, lonely father and I. And I won, God forgive me. But ever after he insisted on consulting me in business matters, and always I gave him a business man's advice—as I give always to your father, child. But frequently my father discarded my advice. And sometimes he was shown to be right in doing so. But always I advised against transactions with Germany, and always my father refused that counsel. He liked Germany, and thought my French snobbery, as he called it, hysterical. Well, after 1870, as he had made a great fortune out of rolling-stock trade with Germany—most of which he had willed, of course, to our Order—he was bankrupt, and moreover he was proclaimed a traitor. So the dear good man sent me a telegram—I was Reverend Mother in Rouen then. I remember its wording, because I pray every day and night for him in that moment when he wrote it."

Mère Générale paused. Her eyes were closed, and the withered, big face, very dark and heavy, seemed to Lucille to assume a composure which might be final, might be the expression of death. But, as she thought of this, the heavy old eyelids went up and the bright eyes swept her face affectionately.

"Tell me about the telegram, *Mère Générale*," Lucille said timidly.

"I will. Because it may help you—and because none of us know what is our precise importance to our parents. Listen now, Lucille. I have incorporated this extraordinary telegram in all my prayers for my father since 1870. 'Pray for me, my beloved son'. That is all it said. But when I read it I knew he was gone. And he was gone. By the timing on the telegram, he had handed it to his butler and then put his pistol in his mouth . . . God rest him."

"Oh, *Mère Générale*—it isn't true!"

"It's not only true, child, but it's in the newspaper files of every respectable public library. But I pray for him every day, and so do all the members of our Order—and it won't be very long now, until I meet him."

"'My beloved son'," said Lucille.

"Yes. All of this is only an anxious parable, Lucille. I developed it to show that I was right once in my fear of Germany. Nowadays, in protecting the Order's investments, I am compelled often to refuse flatly propositions towards Germany. Your father grows angry with me sometimes—and I think I worry him. Because of course all your own families' moneys are invested in the German Empire. For you de Mellins that may be all right—you are Belgians. But your French uncle, Paul de Lainsade, may well be heading for confusion, and carrying André with him. We want no more farewell telegrams, no more pistols in mouths——"

"For so wise a woman you talk strangely, *Mère Générale*. We all know that the Kaiser likes to dress up and rattle his armour. But he is a rather theatrical figurehead, and the Germans are serious and realistic."

"Undoubtedly. Serious and realistic. You have said you desire to read history, Lucille. Well, begin at once, dear child! And read it with detachment!"

Lucille laughed and touched very lightly the fat old hands through which the rosary beads were twisted as they lay in the nun's vast lap.

"Most dear and holy Frenchwoman," she said with tender grace, "if I do read history, I fear that I shall madden you with my detachment."

"It is unlikely that any earthly way of thought could *madden* me now, Lucille. I am near the end of thought, and awaiting God, who will be merciful to my errors—if you, sweet child, are not!" She patted Lucille's face, the rosary beads still swinging about her fingers. "But to be maddened is not the same thing as to grieve. And I sit and grieve—for Europe, and for all of you, my dear ones who are young. Ah well, this is a golden day, a jewel thrown down to us by our good God. So the bees think, child, in my little herb garden. Take me out to them, and to my rosemary tree. Poor patient *Mère Assistante* and all her vast account books!" She creaked up once again and Lucille helped her. "You said that terrible motor-car is waiting for you, did you not?"

Lucille nodded. They moved down the beeswaxed corridor to a glass door through which the old nun's little private garden gleamed.

"Go with Fanny tomorrow to Dublin. And come to me at once when you return. I said good-bye to her yesterday, but I shall see her again."

Mère Assistante came hurrying forward from a trestle-table, covered with papers, over which an old chipped statue of Michael the Archangel flung its shadow.

"I grow lazy, *Mère Assistante*; I must ask you of your charity to pray for me that I moderate at least that terrible vice." She sank into her basket chair by the table, and a sandy cat leapt into her lap. "This cat has a very bad character, poor fellow," she said. "Good-bye, for a little while,

Lucille; and for a little while also to Fanny. I shall see you both again, and often. It is Julia whom I shall not see—not yet, at least, not here."

Lucille kissed *Mère Générale's* hands, and then bowed in the correct fashion of *Place des Ormes*.

"Good-bye for a little while, *Mère Générale*. I hope I have not stayed too long?"

"I'm afraid *Mère Assistante* thinks you have!"

Lucille bowed apologetically to *Mère Assistante*, who smiled stiffly.

"And now, to these builders' estimates, and this awful overdraft! Which reminds me, dear Lucille, do tell your father that I desire to talk with him!"

"I'll tell him, *Mère Générale*."

"Quiet, sir! What is all this purring about? You drown the bees!" The two nuns put on their spectacles, and Lucille left the herb garden.

CHAPTER EIGHT

HOMEWARD TOMORROW

THE Countess desired very much that, whatever the strains and anxieties of Fanny's last sad day in her house, dinner should be wonderful, to cheer and distract the child, and truly nourishing, so as to strengthen her for the long journey and the anxious return to where her dear mother lay ill.

At noon she had heard from Fanny that her father wished her to return as soon as possible, because Mrs. Morrow was not well. Fanny, much distressed, had decided to catch the next midday's boat from Ostend, had sent anxious telegrams to Dublin, and had hurried into Brussels to arrange about money and reservations. In all of this she had had the smooth-making co-operation of all the de Mellins, and all their kind-ness; even Patrice, who detested places of business traffic, had stirred himself to accompany her in one of the family cars, to Cook's, to the family bank, and hither and thither in

Brussels while she called to say absent-minded, brief good-byes at the homes of school friends who had been hospitable to her.

All that was necessary was done as easily as possible, the de Mellins being the people they were; and the Countess felt when Fanny came back from town in the early afternoon that at least everything had been made orderly and simple for the child's journey. Yet, while they took tea in the Countess's small *salon*, as Fanny sat drinking politely from a beautiful Dresden cup, as she told her hostess how easy it had been to arrange for the passage straight through and a sleeper to Holyhead (she would not pause in London), as she made little jokes, and appealed to Patrice for support of them, the Countess's heart was wrung—she could not say why. All that Mr. Joseph Morrow had said in his letter of that morning was that Mrs. Morrow was not well, and that it would be good if Fanny could come home within the next few days. People were frequently unwell, and a lady of Mrs. Morrow's usually delicate health might well have some passing illness now. The Countess knew—she herself was fifty-six and had left *Place des Ormes* before Julia Delahunt came to school there—that Fanny's mother must be fifty. A bad period, wherein one might well, the general trouble of it apart, become ill. There was on the evidence nothing more to worry about than that one wished no one to be ill, least of all Fanny's mother; and that everyone had desired Fanny's Venetian holiday to end in a sunlit return home, not under shadow.

So the Countess argued with her gentle self. Yet some silly fear came to her when she talked with Fanny as they drank tea. It was nothing to express; indeed, even were it expressible, what more unkind or tactless than to try to word it? And there sat Fanny, as folded and reserved as a lily of the valley—yet the Countess felt her heart wrung. She felt afraid of shadows which she did not see, afraid of warnings which she did not hear.

And Patrice, who lay wearily in a *bergère* and drank four cups of tea, was of no help to her. His face was white and he seemed as if he could hardly lift his eyelids. And, asked the simplest question about the day's outing, he closed his eyes tight and muttered some noises which the Countess felt to be very disloyal indeed to his upbringing.

However, she advised Fanny to go to her room and rest after tea. She told her to trouble not at all with packing, that Séraphine would supervise Julie about everything.

"Rest, child," the Countess said, stricken against her optimistic will by some new darkness, new today, in Fanny's eyes.

"Thank you, Countess," Fanny had said, and had gone upstairs.

Later, in the hour of changing for dinner the Count came into his wife's room. He was newly showered and shaved, and wrapped in a white dressing-gown. He had two ivory hairbrushes in his hands, and he brushed his hair vigorously as he strode about. The Countess was leaning back on a small sofa, her torso and her hair covered in towels; old Séraphine was slapping timidly about her grease-covered chin.

"Oh, what is this nonsense, at your age? Stop it, Séraphine —go away. And wipe that mess off, please, my dear. I want to talk to you."

"It isn't nonsense. I'm tired, Marcel—and it rests me!"

"So am I tired!"

"Yes, no doubt. And you have the great relief of shaving!"

He laughed delightedly, as frequently through their life together she could make him laugh.

"Clean her up, Séraphine, and away with you. I've told them to send us up a bottle of Clicquot—I'm tired, and I want to talk to you."

"There's no better idea than a glass of Clicquot, dear Marcel. I'm tired too. But you have bought some bad Clicquot years now and then—you know that. I hope you directed them to the right bin?"

"Impertinent! Ah, you look better now—anyway, recognizable. Come in!"

A footman brought in champagne in an ice-pail and a salver with glasses.

"Off with you now, Séraphine; I can hook up Madame. Don't worry. We're dining at home, after all."

The servants vanished and the Count opened and poured the champagne.

"You look positively pretty," he said to his wife as he brought their filled glasses to her dressing-table.

"Thank you, my dear," said the Countess.

They sipped the wine.

"Lucille called for me at the bank this evening, and we came home together."

There was nothing unusual in this procedure, so the Countess wondered why it was mentioned.

"I heard you arriving," she said.

"Lucille desires to go to Ireland tomorrow, with Fanny. So I had to make the necessary arrangements for her rather hurriedly."

"To Ireland? Tomorrow?"

"Yes. Blondin will bring me her tickets and money tonight. He is having to telephone Euston, etc."

"But why?"

"*Mère Générale* has had grave news, which Fanny has not had. Her mother is extremely ill, and *Mère Générale* thinks that Lucille should be with Fanny in the coming weeks. She can stay with André; she will be no trouble therefore to Fanny's people, but she will be at hand. I have telegraphed André. I understand that he has rented an attractive furnished house, the dog!"

"But—how *sudden* you always are, Marcel! Is this really necessary? I—I have been counting on Lucille to be with her sisters when we go to Le Coq next week——"

"Well, she won't be with them, my dear. She requires to be with Fanny just now—and I see her point."

"You're very indulgent of Lucille."

"I don't call this indulgence. It's only sympathy. But were it indulgence, it might be that I know why I'm indulging in it!"

The Count laughed at his word-play, and drank off his glass of champagne.

"This *is* a good year," he said as he refilled his glass. "If it is true that Mrs. Morrow is extremely ill, then none of us would grudge that dear child Fanny any help we could extend, and I agree with *Mère Générale* that the proximity of

175

Lucille, her dearest friend, might well be a great assistance to her in what lies ahead. But apart from that perfectly true wish, my dear—Lucille desires to go to Dublin with Fanny. So I would not deny her that whim, just now."

"What do you mean? What is that sly intonation about?" the Countess asked.

The Count smiled.

"'Sly intonation'," he repeated. "For a really silly beauty you are sometimes rather quick, dear wife!"

"I should hope so. Still—no, no more Clicquot now, Marcel. Help me into my dress."

Together and quite efficiently they tackled her heavy, whale-boned, stiff-sleeved dinner-gown of pale grey brocade. They got it over her head and down about her, got her arms into the sleeves, without any disturbance of her coiffure; and then the Count set masterfully about the hooking-up.

"Stand stiffer, my dear. Pull yourself in."

"Oh, Marcel, you're pinching me!"

"Sorry, darling. This is a devilishly stiff bit of whale-boning. How on earth do you eat inside this kind of armour?"

"Truly I don't know. Oh, Marcel, are you sure that the news is so bad about dear Fanny's mother?"

"Well, Lucille seemed shaken by *Mère Générale,* who had heard this morning from Mrs. Morrow's sister——"

"I suppose then it is only kind to Fanny to let her go—but——"

"I hate it when Lucille is away. I've just had two lonely months without her and you, my pet—and now you are off to Le Coq, as you must go, with the little ones. I'd much rather Lucille stayed at home—at any rate did not tomorrow go so far from me as to Ireland. But this is a gesture of sympathy. And—do you ever observe our eldest daughter, my dear?"

"Of course I do, you foolish man! Am I not her mother?"

"I believe you are, but——"

The Countess, completely hooked up, sat down to retouch her 'Alexandra' coiffure, and to choose some jewels.

"You can refill my glass, Marcel—and then you had better hurry yourself into some clothes. I cannot have dinner spoilt tonight—we begin with *aubergines beurrées,* and you know how frightful can be overcooked *aubergines*——"

The Count marched to and fro between his own room and his wife's as he got himself briskly into the various items of his 'smoking'.

"Lucille is very like me," he said. "Have you noticed?"

"She has your very beautiful eyes, indeed—so has André."

"Oh, the devil take our eyes! She is like me—reserved and wilful."

The Countess smiled at him in amazement.

"I have never found Lucille wilful—and as for *your* being *reserved,* oh, my friend!"

The Count laughed.

"Heaven bless you," he said. "Still, I warn you, as I love Lucille I intend to win the last battle—and for her sake."

"The last battle? But, dearest, there never are any battles in our sweet family! Now, are there? When do we have the first?"

The Count took his wife's hand and kissed it.

"Come on, let's go downstairs. You look splendid. You look like someone who has a happy life."

"And so I have—thanks to the good God and to you and my good children. Let us try to make this last evening bright for Fanny——"

"We can hardly do that. She is frightened, naturally——"

"I fear she is, poor child. And we shall miss her—and Lucille. But thank God for André. He will be with them, and is a very rock of kindness—dear, pretty Fanny——"

The two descended to the salon.

*　　*　　*　　*　　*

Everyone put brightness forward at dinner. Fanny and Lucille wore the dresses they had worn at Savini's in Milan, and Patrice stared at them out of eyes that burnt darkly in his white face. The three little holidaying sisters, home from *Place des Ormes,* were allowed to sit up tonight and to eat through every course, to Fanny's astonishment. Small replicas of André and Lucille, lovely little girls of amber-gold, gentle and funny as kittens, they ate as solemnly as

177

three burghers of Brussels. Fanny wondered once again by what miraculous dispensation this beautiful group of de Mellins, young and middle-aged, managed to be so beautiful. She herself, touched by the Countess's absurd idea of a real banquet to help her in farewell and in her sudden grave anxiety, could only be as courageous as possible, and eat from each rich dish as it was hoped she would.

The effort was truly severe.

She was frightened, though baselessly. Her father's letter of the morning had frightened her because it said that Mother was ill and that he was glad that she was returning within a few days. His telegraphed reply to her telegram, which she had received before dinner, had been sent from Crahore, the postal village for Glasalla. It said: "Welcome darling Joey will meet you Kingstown Mother better and sends her love Father."

She could not explain to herself why this telegram frightened her; but it made her sick with fear.

Monsieur le Curé had been a young chaplain at *Place des Ormes* thirty-five years before, and remembered the shy and beautiful Delahunt children from Ireland. He had instructed them both for First Communion and for Confirmation. Enjoying now a beautifully grilled sole and a glass of Moselle, he discoursed gently to Fanny, who sat on his right hand.

"Your mother—she was Julia?—was a curiously intelligent little child. Perhaps Eleanor had more attack, more dash. And she did *not* marry? Curious. But I remember them both quite clearly—I shall pray for your mother's quick restoration to health, child. Tell her that *Père* Desmans remembers what a good, quick child she was, and is praying for her."

Tante Justine, the Count's eldest sister, was also present. She was very full of counsel, in all directions. First she admonished Fanny that nobody should be permitted to be ill in an Irish country house, and that her first duty on her return to Ireland would be to have Mrs. Morrow transported to a first-class clinic. If Ireland *had* a first-class clinic? If not, then at once to England, or France. It was madness to attempt to combat illness in an isolated country house, let alone an Irish country house. They must see to that im-

mediately. Nothing simpler; and *essential,* she warned
Lucille.

Lucille bowed her head, and smiled with all the reassurance she could muster at Fanny's desperately polite and
attentive face.

Patrice ate nothing, pushed every plate away untouched.
The Countess observed him, and began to fuss.

"Mother, I entreat you——" he said, in a tone so husky
and unusual that she had to pause, bewildered.

"Cécile!" the Count said softly, sharply, and made a small,
commanding flick of his left hand. The poor lady knew that
small signal, had always obeyed it, and now, in anxiety,
allowed Patrice to starve himself.

The sweet little girls ate on, as merry as wedding guests.
Roast ducklings—"They are ducklings themselves," said
Fanny, gaining an appreciative laugh from their father.

Tante Justine had much heavy advice to give her brother
about the plans and intentions of Germany; in her thun-
derous forebodings she was supported by M. le Curé; the
Count grew bored, and poured champagne and tried to keep
his obstinate old sister off matters she did not understand—
military alliances, for instance, neutrality pledges, and
Belgian finance.

Patrice drank champagne, and once leant over the table to
Fanny when the elders were thundering at each other, and
lifted his glass.

"To that awful luncheon in Savini's—do you remember,
Fanny? I have the rosebud."

She smiled at him, but could not answer. Her throat was
tight, and she felt sick at this well-meant banquet. Her heart
was racing to Glasalla, and Savini's was an irrelevance,
indeed a wounding frivolity now. Mother, Mother,
Glasalla.

The Countess was distressed—but if Fanny, Lucille and
Patrice were obviously in very poor appetite, at least everyone else was showing appreciation of a reasonably good
dinner. The young were difficult and rarely knew what was
good for them.

After the salad came the very flower of the garden's
nectarines and plums and peaches.

Fanny looked about the beautiful wide table, at the gleaming glass and heavy silver, at the Sèvres plates and dishes; she smelt and appraised the radiant fruits; she tasted her golden wine and looked with attention at the many splendid faces, ageing and young and very young, about her in the gentle lamplight. 'It is a lovely scene,' she thought; 'all this civilization, generosity and peace; all this blind, easy grace, this taking for granted of perfection in small things; all these radiant eyes, all this well-mannered affection, all this assurance, this polish, physical and even mental. But I belong to another place. I have dallied, I have dawdled. None of this is either mine or what I want. Mother, I am coming home.'

She found Lucille's eyes, and her own rested on them. Neither girl smiled. Lucille knows, Fanny told herself. Lucille knows what I'm afraid of, and she is coming home with me tomorrow. She will see what I mean.

"Your nectarines are better this year, Marcel," *Tante* Justine said. "I think that new man you have does seem to know about wall-fruit. . . ."

A footman came in to say that Monsieur Blondin awaited M. le Comte in the library. Monsieur Blondin was the Count's secretary.

"That will be your reservations, etc., Lucille," her father said. "Have coffee served in the library for Monsieur Blondin and for me. And, if you will excuse me——" The Count rose—"An excellent dinner, dear Cécile——" He bowed to his wife, to his sister, and left the dining-room.

At eleven o'clock the evening's long strain was over. *Tante* Justine and M. le Curé had departed in the former's carriage-and-pair; the Countess had gone to bed, after many kind blessings to Fanny, whom she would see for farewell in the morning; the Count had withdrawn to his library, and the three little girls were fast asleep. Fanny and Lucille, alone on the terrace, surveyed the noble summer night and listened to its sighing. The stars were high; the Flemish plain lay veiled, though pricked with living light. Smells of verbena and roses lingered on the cool air; from eastward the murmur of Brussels drifted towards them.

"I've always loved this view from your house, Lucille—in light and dark. I wonder when I'll see it again?"

Hand-in-hand the girls descended through the garden and turned under an archway into the kitchen-garden. The dew was heavy; the moon was up, and light and shadow cut each other sharply.

"Are you cold, Fan?"

"A little. Thank you for coming with me tomorrow. Why are you doing it?"

"I don't know."

"Mother can't be more than—ordinarily ill? I mean, she's fragile, but she's never *ill*. All of a sudden—it couldn't be much? Could it?"

Lucille decided to bide her time, and to help Fanny to have a night's sleep before the long journey.

"I don't see how it could be," she said, "from what you've told me of your mother."

"Besides, Father says in the wire that she's better. Oh, it'll be lovely to be at home—and show you everything!"

They paused at the top of the kitchen-garden to test the figs on a corner tree.

"No good," said Lucille. "They never ripen until mid-August. I adore figs."

"So do I. There's a great fig tree at Glasalla, Lucille. It's an extraordinary tree for County Clare. You'll see."

They passed beyond the kitchen-garden and climbed the slope which the de Mellins called The Hill, to the little temple-grotto on its crest. Fanny mounted its two shallow steps and leant against a slender pillar of the portico; below her across the steps Lucille sat on the flat balustrade, and in her gold dress, her long legs crossed, her gold hair catching moonlight, she looked, Fanny thought, like some androgynous myth.

"I shall be glad indeed to know Mespil Road and Glasalla —at last," she said. She turned her face upward, smiling to Fanny. "And I've had to invite *myself* to those places, after all," she said.

"That's true, most welcome one," said Fanny.

They heard a sob, a choked, swallowed sound, within the grotto. They turned to its darkness and saw a boy's head gleaming dimly, heavy gold hair falling forward over the edge of the stone table; they saw a white hand clutching the table's edge.

"Patrice!" Fanny said softly. "Patrice, why are you crying?"

Patrice raised his head. Then slowly he rose and came and stood on the grotto's threshold. He looked at Fanny, then at Lucille, then back to Fanny.

"Because you are going away, Fanny; because I love you. That is why I weep. My situation is absurd, I know; but I know that neither you nor Lucille will mock at it."

"Indeed it is not absurd," said Fanny. "How could it be absurd to love and cry? Patrice, I think it is more like absurdity to love and laugh."

"You are grown-up sometimes of late in what you say," said Patrice. "But that only makes things more absurd. You are eighteen; I am eighteen and just out of the Lycée. Love can only be for me the kind of thing André instructs me about—which I can, of course, explore. I am sorry you found me crying, but I am not sorry to have been able to say to you, before Lucille, that I love you. I know you will remember that I said it."

Lucille had not moved from where she sat. "All that you have said, Patrice," she said, "seems to suggest that you also are grown-up, like Fanny. But—I imagine this is the first time you have loved, I mean, really loved——?"

"Indeed it is."

"Then you will bear it, dear brother. And you will get over it. That seems to be the law of first love."

He smiled.

"When I have got over it I will bear it, Lucille. That seems to be the law. But tonight, believe me, I am not bearing it. If you like, it is bearing me! Fanny, Fanny—forgive this demonstration!"

He turned to her and took her hands; she could see that his face was still all wet with tears. So she raised her hands from his and put them round his face, his neck. She too was crying now.

"Oh, dearest boy, dear friend!" she said.

Lucille stood up.

"I'll go indoors," she said softly.

Patrice turned to her, as he drew Fanny's hands away from his face.

"Yes, you and Fanny both go indoors now, please. We'll meet tomorrow for good-bye. Good-night, dear ones—I'll stay here awhile."

He bowed over Fanny's wet hands, but did not kiss them.

"To bed, ladies," he said gaily, and disappeared into the dark temple-grotto.

CHAPTER NINE

MESPIL ROAD

Joey Morrow and André de Mellin awaited Fanny and Lucille on Kingstown Pier.

The morning, of early August, was tranquil and brilliant. Fanny had come into this harbour at least twice a year, and in various weathers, during five years of school-life abroad, and had departed from it a similar number of times in varying evening weathers. So she knew the aspects of Dublin Bay. But she did not tire of them. And on this lovely morning, anxious as she was to get ashore, and irrelevant as the familiar prospect was to her preoccupation, she could not help feeling at once proud and touched before Lucille's delight as the Irish coast curled out to draw her in.

They stood on deck, in a throng of returning holiday-makers and schoolchildren, while morning rose and arrowed the Wicklow hills, struck the shelving terraces, white and green, of Killiney and Kingstown, and sought to pierce the lazy cloud of Dublin, further in. The silken water rippled past the ship; seagulls cried, and from the shore came the ringing of bells, for Mass.

"Fan—oh, Fan, you never told me——!"

"I did. You didn't listen."

"I always listen to you. I tell you, you never said a word——"

They drew alongside and the two young men welcomed them eagerly. With dispatch they and their luggage were clear of the landing-stage confusion and climbing into André's car. 'How familiar it is,' Fanny thought with a pang of mingled anxiety and remembrance as she mounted it. Verona, Vicenza, Milan—how sophisticated we felt ourselves to be, climbing up to this perch and down from it!

They were to go to Mespil Road for breakfast, and there they would talk.

Fanny searched Joey's face.

"How is Mother?" was all she could say.

He was turned sideways to speak to her from where he sat in the front seat with André.

"She is a good deal better, thank God. She gave us a fright last week—but now the news is good, Fan," he said kindly. And she could read nothing more than what he said from his handsome young countenance. But he went on giving her the outline of family news, as the car hooted and snorted along Seapoint Avenue and up into Blackrock.

"It's a pity there's no one but me at home for your return, Fan, and to meet Mademoiselle Lucille—but you'll be seeing them all in a day or two anyway. You see, the youngsters, Stephen and Cockle and Muscle, all went off to Doon Point a couple of days ago—with Aunt Edith in charge, and her old Betsy. Decent of Aunt Edith, who hates Doon Point, and thinks that lodge there a hell of primitiveness. But, you see, Father had almost cancelled the booking—only when Mother heard that just because she was ill the children were not to have their sacred month of August at Doon Point she read the Riot Act, from her bed in Glasalla—so good old Aunt Edith volunteered. Kitty couldn't—Bill being troublesome and wanting to go on some kind of spree at Biarritz in a week or two. Kitty, by the way, very decently came round to the house at dawn this morning on my appeal—as I wanted to be sure that your rooms and breakfast and everything were as Mother would wish them to be. I do hope, Miss Lucille, you'll make allowances for the fuss we've been in in the last fortnight or so——"

"Ah, but what nonsense," said Lucille.

"But where are Lizzie and Nora?" asked Fanny.

"Oh, they're at home—and wild to see you again, Fan. We didn't let them go to Doon Point, in case Mother wanted suddenly to come home. That's why Aunt Edith took old Betsy instead. And of course someone has to look after me!" he said. "You see, Mademoiselle, I'm an industrious apprentice, and I have to stick to my last."

"You are becoming a chartered accountant—have I got it right?" asked Lucille in cautious English.

"Perfectly right," said Joey.

"You will learn English very rapidly in Ireland, Lucille," said André. "Beautiful English. They compel you to talk here—and oh, how well they talk!"

"Mademoiselle Lucille talks beautifully already," said Joey. "In any case, if I tried my French it could only embarrass her very much!"

"Father is well?" asked Fanny.

"Yes—now. Last week—ah well, last week! I dashed down there for two days, with the specialists—André very kindly drove us down, Lilian and me——"

"Specialists?"

"Yes—the doctor down there, O'Curry, wired our own man, Mother's old Redmond, you know, to bring some blood and heart experts. So we were all terrified."

"But why wasn't I told?"

"Because you were travelling across France—and by the time you were in Brussels the panic was over, thank God! And then, when he was calm, Father did write and ask you to come home, after all."

"Is Lilian at Glasalla now?"

"No. She couldn't stay—she's here, in Stillorgan Road. Heavens, she's letting herself go with grandeur in that house! Michael must be out of his mind!"

"Why couldn't she stay—a little while? Aunt Eleanor must have been so anxious and weary——"

"Well, there's this Exhibition thing going on in Herbert Park, you know—Dublin is packed for it—and next week is

Horse Show Week—and the O'Connors are somehow involved, in connection with cattle displays and sales, in both.
And so Michael's wife has to be here and have her house
in order, and entertain foreign merchants, etc. All very
natural. It's Lilian's duty. And she seems to be doing it well.
However, she'll tell you about these things herself. She said
she'd try to come over to breakfast, as she was afraid you'd
feel lonely coming back to the house with Mother away."

Fanny was touched.

"Mother was always there when we came home from
school," she said.

Joey stopped talking.

André had turned south at the Kiosk. The white, ugly
tower of St. Mary's, Haddington Road, shone against the
immaculate morning sky. He turned to the left before
Baggot Street Bridge. There were three swans in sail up the
canal. The little trees rustled dryly, dustily. The car turned in
at the green gate and drove to the rear of the house, to halt
before the greenhouse and the breakfast-room's glass door.

Fanny was home from Venice. And as she sat still in the
car and looked about her, at the dark brick house, at the long
shabby garden of which she knew every weed and bush, at
Rose, the aged collie, lumbering forward from the paddock
gate, at the dewy grass, at all of childhood lying still in the
tempered Irish summer morning light, she wondered, as often
in Venice she had wondered, whether she was indeed in this
place her eyes considered, or was once again remembering it.

Where was Snap? He wasn't barking. Ah, he's gone to
Doon Point with the others! Old Paddy Crowe came running, lame and eager, to help with luggage. "Miss Fanny!
Miss Fanny child, ye're home, praise be to God!" Out
through the breakfast-room rushed Lizzie and Nora, familiar
and natural to Fanny as her own hands, in splendid white
big aprons. 'How bright their eyes are,' Fanny thought—
'and Paddy's too. They are all crying; so am I. Oh, Mother
—how is it with you?'

Joey had assisted Lucille from the motor-car.

André leaned up and took Fanny's hand.

"Come, Fanny," he said. "Come, don't be afraid. You're
at home now, truly at home."

She tightened her hand on his and smiled into his sweet, familiar eyes. His simple and penetrative words had helped her.

"Yes, I'm home," she said, and let him almost lift her down to her paternal earth. Then she was in Lizzie's and Nora's arms, and Paddy Crowe was holding her hand, and Kitty Morrow and Joey were welcoming Lucille into the house— and at last, in confusion of tears, exclamations and kisses, the moment had been lived through and gone, of entering the house where Mother was not and where fear had taken her gentle place. Bright, faithful eyes—all, she saw, had been frightened; all were still concealedly afraid. So now was she indeed.

Lilian came in through the glass door to the breakfast-room where the travellers sat with Kitty, Joey and André. Fanny saw her before the others did.

"Lilian!" she cried, and André, who sat beside her, leapt to his feet as she did. The sisters hurried to each other. 'How slim, how elegant she is,' Fanny thought as if surprised. 'Goodness, how grown-up she looks!'

"Fan! Welcome home!"

They kissed, and searched each other's faces, conscious each, instantly, that meaning, content had increased in the other's features; that each according to her nature had grown fast, and subtly, since the April day of Lilian's wedding. Within this brief exchange of observation spontaneously they kissed again, as if afraid of whatever had been mutually asked; and Lilian said gently: "Mother will be all right. I promise you."

Fanny flung her arms about her sister's neck.

"Oh, swear it!" she said, and hot tears tore down her face.

"We all swear it," said Kitty Morrow. "Don't we, Joey?"

"Indeed we do," said Joey, coming to his sisters and taking Fanny's hands from Lilian's elegantly white-ruffed neck. "And now, Lilian, you remember Mademoiselle Lucille——"

Lucille had stood up and was waiting politely to greet Lilian. 'How *absolutely* beautiful she is,' she thought coldly, 'how much she is mistress of her beauty. She wears it like a weapon, like a coat of arms. Already she has mastered it completely; she knows it to be her estate; she will invest it for sound dividends all her life.'

It was perhaps curious that a young woman of formidable and powerful beauty, rich and brought up in that world where beauty can indulge itself in exaggeratedly careful cultivation, should have felt the shock of cold power from a beautiful Irish girl whom she had despised at school, whom now she despised, and whose sophistication could only be of the skin-deep kind, put on in three or four months' marriage to a rich, infatuated but necessarily naïve young Irish auctioneer. Yet Lucille did experience a bitter and alarmed *empressement* as now she observed again Fanny's unimportant elder sister. 'Is she a sort of Madame Récamier?' she wondered. 'Has she such dangerous vanity—or is she strong, does she feel?'

It is true that Lilian came out of the morning light into the shaded breakfast-room as if she were herself the morning light. She was exquisitely dressed; her close-fitting gown of white muslin was embroidered all over with tiny rosebuds; her little tilted hat was made of rosebuds; she wore immaculate white gloves and an immaculate white-gold skin and over her ears and about her snowy neck shone babyishly the soft gold of her hair. Her blue eyes were not dark, but translucent, aquamarine.

The two travellers were jaded; they had been travelling for twenty hours, and had merely washed their hands and faces before hurrying in great need to eat and drink. Yet they were young, and their authentic beauty could not for so small an ordeal withdraw or fade. But here to greet them at their journey's end came the world's eternal concept of lovely woman; here embodied, standing in the simple, quiet breakfast-room where she had been a baby and a child; and she was only Lilian, Fanny's sister, who had been a frivolous bore at school.

Lucille worried over these impressions as she watched Lilian greet Fanny, and as she waited to be greeted in her turn.

"Ah, Lucille! But of course I remember her, Joey! The thing is, dear Lucille, could you possibly remember me?"

They clasped hands briefly.

"Yes, I remember you," said Lucille. "You were the school beauty and you played tennis better than anyone."

"Good heavens! Did I? You were ages younger than me, of course—but you were intellectual, and even in my time you were way up in *Père* Anselme's Latin School where such as I could never even try to be received! So I'd remember you —even if you weren't Fanny's friend!"

During these exchanges Lucille continued to wonder. What is it all about, this exquisite morning toilet, this pseudo-graciousness which—give her her due—she never troubled for at school? Their mother is dangerously ill, and Fanny has come home in weary anxiety; Fanny is tired and wants to get quickly to the truth here. The elder sister would indeed come round to breakfast with her. But would she make an 'entrance'? And if she did, why do it?

Fanny, able to see her sister once she had turned to Lucille, was puzzled too. She never had so much to say, she thought; she was always lovely, but she never wore her clothes as if she —well, as if she was in a Fragonard picture. Is she always now as 'finished' as she is this morning? She used to be most conceitedly slapdash. I suppose it's being rich, and having to be the wife of a successful Dublin man. I suppose it's her duty. But, thought Fanny, you'd almost imagine she had been put through some rapid course of schooling in the business!

And then the younger sister reproached herself. She cannot help it if you do not accept her view of life. She was warm and kind this minute. She swore Mother would be all right. Oh, more tea! This dear, dear tea we have at home!

Fanny turned to sit down. André was not in his place at her side, but Lizzie pushed in her heavy chair for her, and ran for the big silver teapot.

"A fine, fresh cup, children," she said, "and then off up with you! We have the water scalding for the bath—and into your own bed I'll thrust you then, and clap the sleep down on you, please God!"

"Yes, I'll have coffee, please," Lilian was saying.

Fanny was surprised. There was coffee for Lucille and André, but the Morrows—and the O'Connors—all drank tea at breakfast.

"Coffee, Lilian?" said Joey, in astonishment.

André was holding out a chair, into which Lilian settled herself, pulling off her pretty hat and handing it to him, as she shook her silky curls.

"Would you be so kind as to put it—oh, anywhere?" she asked André.

He bowed smilingly over the little hat.

"But not on my own head, I think, Mrs. O'Connor?"

Joey laughed and Lilian smiled.

"Good coffee. Thank you, Lizzie."

"Of all the foreign nonsense, Miss Lilian," said Lizzie. "A child like you, out of this house, taking up with coffee for your breakfast! What's on you at all?"

"Silly Lizzie! Do you know, Lucille," said Lilian, "there's only one person who is allowed to be capricious in our family —and that's Mother."

That is true, Fanny thought. Oh God, dear God, don't ask the impossible of us—yet!

André came back to his place beside her and Lizzie brought him fresh coffee.

"You are very weary," he said.

"I must go to Glasalla," Fanny answered.

"Of course. But not until you have had a long sleep."

"I'm afraid I must sleep. But perhaps there's a train to Limerick this evening, or to Ennis, and then in the morning I could get the little train to Moyasta, and get a trap or something from there. I'd wire Aunt Eleanor, and she'd send the trap for me."

"Leave that, Fanny; we'll see to all that. We'll get you there tomorrow."

"You promise?"

"I promise."

"Lucille says you're reliable in such things."

"Have you not found me so?"

"Indeed I have. Oh—oh, I must go to bed!"

She rose, white as a snowdrop her face, her eyes blue-black as sudden violets.

"Mother——" she whispered, and fell, fainting.

But André had stood up with her and caught her in his arms. He lifted her across them and she lay as if dead. Everyone was standing now, shocked and exclamatory. Lucille moved hesitantly, but Kitty Morrow lifted Fanny's head, which hung over André's arm.

"No wonder," she said. "Poor Fan! It's a perfectly ordinary faint. Can you carry her upstairs, Monsieur André?"

Kitty led the way out of the breakfast-room, and André followed with Fanny in his arms. Lizzie ran after, lamenting tenderly.

"The little love! Sure, she never faints, whatever! Oh, 'tis the way she's anxious, God help us! But wait now till we have her in the bed, the little dote! Sure, if the Mistress was to see Miss Fanny, of all, going off in a faint, 'tis the way she'd eat the lot of us!"

Five notes chimed prettily from Mother's little glass-encased clock on the mantelpiece. The drawing-room was beautifully in order, in its ordered shabbiness, as if Nora and Lizzie expected the Mistress home at any moment. Roses, singly or in twos, in slim glass vases, as she liked best to have roses, on her bureau, and here and there; every surface polished; the threadbare rose-patterned carpet newly back from one of its customary clean-sweepings up and down the dewy grass of the paddock, Fanny guessed.

She paused at the foot of the old green velvet sofa. The little tapestry pillow was in its place, and the shallow foot-stool too. At the end, where she stood, Mother's old soft foot-shawl lay folded and ready. She bent and stroked it, and her eyes, as she did so, considered Father's familiar photo-graph, silver-framed, on the table by the sofa. Everything ready, everything as and where Mother desired it to be.

Fanny could not remember that she had ever been at home when her mother was away. Julia needed always to visit Glasalla at least twice a year, but she went there infallibly during school terms, and was never absent from the drawing-room, this centre of her life, it seemed to Fanny, when her children were home from their schools. So she had never seen the room expectant, prepared, as now. Always she remem-bered the sofa-shawl unfurled, books with markers jutting from them, opened letters, letters half-written, scattered on the bureau, the fire burning, the window open, and Bella-donna, the beloved tabby cat, washing her face on the window-sill. Always there were voices in this room, and even if they were irritable or uncertain often, at least—whatever pitch they might take in the breakfast-room—they were perforce quiet here. And as she remembered this, Belladonna came in through the half-open door, stared about expectantly and, seeing Fanny, ran forward with a cry of surprise and leapt on to the sofa.

Belladonna, matriarch who had borne her part in the long lineage of Delahunt cats, was the mother of Grandfather's adored Teresa, and grandmother of incestuous young Iago. She would die soon, the beautiful, gentle tiger, and she was lonely now for the missing centre of this room. She came along the sofa to rub herself against Fanny's welcoming hands.

"She'll be back soon, Belladonna," said Fanny.

Outside the long window the August afternoon was hot and still. Dublin was packed with foreign holiday-makers, they said, with provincials visiting the Exhibition, and with the usual pre-Horse-Show throngs. But here—here, thought Fanny suddenly, one might almost be in Bruges. From far-off indeed the trams could be heard rumbling, but they rumbled also in Bruges, and with the same soporific, lazy purr that here all her life she had hardly heard. Beyond the short front garden lay the leafy road; beyond that the motionless canal. The design repeated itself on the other bank in depth and quietude; and over all lay the burning, speckless summer sky. Peace up to a point, Fanny thought, as she moved towards the window; as nearly peace as anyone could find who was exiled for life from Glasalla.

The house was very quiet, but its dear familiarness and her long, deep sleep worked together now in Fanny and were restoring her courage and her hope. She had woken at about three o'clock, astonished to find herself in her own bed and sheltered from the sunlight by the shaky old green Venetian blind of all her childhood. Bathed and dressed, she went down to the kitchen to Nora and Lizzie. There, with Belladonna on her lap and Nora's awful tom-cat, Sibby, roaring round her, she had sat on the table, and eaten cold chicken and hot soda-bread. Then she ate many of the first Victoria plums from the garden, and homely hope and courage silted back, and the familiar ring and smell of the day and the place reassured her. Yet she would not ask these two dear friends what had in fact happened to Mother. She could still see fear in their eyes, and she judged that they knew nothing save that the Mistress had nearly died. To question them would only be to make them cry, and they had cried enough for now, her heart told her.

"Mrs. Bill Morrow had to go home for a while, Miss—you see, it's the holidays, and she couldn't leave the little gerrls all day—but she'll be back to you this evening, she said———"

"She's very good———"

"Ah, she is that, the creature!" Nora paused, her discretion fraught with ominousness.

"And where is Mademoiselle Lucille?"

"Oh, the lovely young lady!" cried Lizzie. "Did ever you see a greater beauty, outside of yourself and Miss Lilian, God bless ye all! I declare to my God, I said to Nora over and over, and I in and out from the breakfast table this morning, didn't I, Nora? I said, if there's three greater beauties seated down together this minute in any of the four corners of the world I'm prepared to go before the Judgment Seat this instant!"

"Faith, she said it," said Nora, who was laconic, and a foil to Lizzie, who was not.

Fanny laughed.

"No need for the Judgment Seat, Lizzie. Where is Mademoiselle Lucille?"

"Fast asleep, God bless her, in Miss Cockle's little bed. She had a fine, boiling bath—thanks be to the Sacred Heart that those old dampers didn't disgrace us before her, for the first go-off, anyway—a lovely, foreign young lady—and she a Countess, isn't she, Miss?"

"Oh, not really."

"But that gentleman, her brother, isn't he a Count, Miss? And before I forget it—how do I address him right, Miss Fanny, if I have to? You see, I can't speak French, as well you know. Do I say 'Mister Count'?"

"No, no. Don't do that. Just say Mister André, as you say Mister Joey, or Mister Stephen."

"Like that? Are you *sure*, Miss?"

"Yes, honestly. Is Miss Lucille still asleep?"

"Oh, I think so, Miss. I peeped in a while ago and she was dead out. And do you know, the way her head was thrown back, the beauty of her, she reminded me of the Archangel Gabriel, God bless her."

"She *is* rather like the Archangels, I imagine. She's very beautiful, isn't she?"

Nora said in a practical tone: "We prepared Miss Cockle's room, Miss—although it's a bit simple, I know, for the young Countess; but we couldn't make out from the fussing of Mr. Joey and Mr. André whether she would be staying here or with her brother. So we thought we'd have a bed ready for her anyway, to start off."

"And faith, the child was glad to drop into it, God help her!" said Lizzie. "Isn't she lovely, the simplicity of her— as natural as the day she was born!"

"Hardly that, Lizzie!" said Fanny.

Healing, or gathering protection somehow, from all about her, Fanny wandered afterwards about the house and the garden, the stableyard and the paddock. So at last she came to the drawing-room, when she was sure she had weeded out fear and planted courage.

Now she sat on the window-seat, and was vaguely reminded of Lilian's wedding day, and so of Cousin Bill. Kitty had said at breakfast that Bill would come to see her—"he says he is curious to see if anything happened to you in Venice, Fan. He's somewhat impertinently interested in you always—deep calling to deep——" Kitty said all of this with perfect good nature. The bitterness which, being human, she felt and quietly contained, in regard to her husband, she did not extend to such as Fanny, who could not, she clearly saw, be held blameworthy if Bill chose to weave his ironic myths about them, wherewith to insult her. It sometimes occurred to her that his alcohol-lighted reflections and speculations on those human beings who attracted his interest—as his cousin Fanny always did—were more of an insult to them than to her. But truly she knew that his regard for Fanny was inno- cent, even brotherly, and that he watched her development in ironic pity—for reasons which, when he was in the vein, he would expand and decorate all night, let his partner sleep or not, as she chose. Kitty had reached, through suffering and insult, the more or less regulated plane where she could pity, and so in a measure love, her brilliant husband. Fanny, from afar, understood something of this, and while liking very much her disgraceful cousin Bill, admired his wife.

She sat on the window-seat and looked about the empty room. Slowly, oddly, her memory filled it with the crowds of Lilian's wedding day: all the discreet Morrows, poor Lady Rawlinson, Mother on the sofa sipping China tea, the O'Connors, loud Mr. Sam O'Connor, Cousin Bill. Muscle drinking champagne behind the door. *'Ah, si je pouvais deux fois naître. . . .'* She hummed over the tune. She had been sitting here, with Cousin Bill, when André was shown in to the room by Lizzie. How far away it seemed now, that first surprised impression of Lucille's brother!

> *' . . . Mon beau printemps et mon été*
> *ont fait le saut par la fenêtre. . . .'*

"Singing *that*?" said Cousin Bill. "And sitting where I last remember you—even if it isn't, for all I know, where I last saw you!"

"Oh, Cousin Bill!" Fanny stretched out her hands. "I *was* in fact thinking of you, and of Lilian's wedding day!"

He kissed her.

"Welcome back, young beauty," he said. "But never recall wedding days. They are unlucky days. Ah, welcome, little Fan! We've missed you, in our cups. Are you glad or sorry to be home?"

"Oh, glad! How can you ask? But—what is this about Mother, Cousin Bill?"

He sat down on a low chair opposite to her; the sunlight fell clear on his face and she saw, with surprise, that he was sober.

"I am not sure what it is, Fan. I was on circuit in June, and when I came home I was tired and took my own kind of repose. However, I gather that your mother became abnormally tired, even to positive weakness, about a month ago, and expressed a great longing for Glasalla. She was taken there—and everyone said: 'Rest. Rest and home air.' But suddenly she grew alarmingly weak, about ten days ago—so Kitty tells me. And the specialists dashed down; and now she is on a very strict regimen, and is out of danger. Apparently her blood construction—or composition?—is faulty, and will have to be nourished back to the requisite strength. These fellows have it under control, Kitty tells me—and now for a while she must lie very still and be a patient invalid on a heavy diet of meat and milk and porter and burgundy."

"Oh! she won't be able to swallow those things! Oh dear!"

"Fanny—she will. She intends to, and she will."

"Oh, I wish I could get down to her tonight! Bill, I can't help it—I'm afraid! Is there any way I could get to Ennis tonight?"

"But, child—you're being driven to Glasalla tomorrow, Kitty tells me."

"Am I?"

"Indeed you are. Oh yes—you fainted during breakfast, so you mightn't know. But Kitty says that that most obliging Belgian gentleman, Comte de Mellin, is going to drive you to Glasalla in the morning."

"Is he? I've seen no one since I fainted."

"They'll all be back. Evidently they fixed that that was best. He seems to be an obliging chap. Do you remember our talking here in this window *à trois*, Fan? And afterwards you got cross with me because I said what a pity it was for Lilian that he turned up on the afternoon of her wedding day?"

"Did you? I don't remember, Cousin Bill."

"Just as well. No good listening to prophets. How was Venice, Fan?"

"Have you never been there?"

"No. I'll go sometime. But no one is going to tell me it is more beautiful than Florence, which I do know."

"No one sane would pit Venice against anything, or argue about the place at all. For better or worse it is not comparable to other cities. You can say that without having seen many other cities, because clearly, whether you like it or not, it is a place which is *literally* unique. Bill, don't ask me to talk about it! Go and see it for yourself. I'm not going to gush."

"I know you're not. It's a pity, I think. Girls should gush, Fan."

"You're fond of telling me what girls should do. You told me once that I'd have to try to learn to amuse the Mistress of Novices!"

"Did I? And will that be necessary?"

"No, Cousin Bill."

"Well, I'm glad to hear it. But you're growing up. I begin to see that, now. I'm getting used to you again, Fan. You'll amuse—someone. Perhaps you'll even be witty."

"Ah, don't be tedious," she said impatiently, and her frightened eyes swept over the empty room again as if asking forgiveness of some ghost for momentary inattention.

"Don't, Fan," Bill said gently. "She'll get well, and she'll be back here very soon."

"Oh, but will she? Will she?"

She covered her face with her hands

Bill was not in fact sure of the answer, and found that to Fanny he could say no more in hope than what he had said, which was only Kitty's hearsay. He rose and paced about.

"May I smoke one cigarette in this room, Fan?"

She lifted her head and nodded.

"Forgive me," she said shakily, and she dried her eyes.

Kitty came in, helping Lizzie with the tea-trays.

"Hello, Bill!" She raised her brows at him and shook her head reproachfully when she saw that Fanny had been crying. He turned to the fireplace and snapped his fingers in impatience.

"Here's the tea for ye now, at long last," said Lizzie, unfolding the leaves of the tea-table. " 'Tis the way the scones went back on Nora, poor misfortunate woman, and she had to go at them again in a bustle! But the angel cake didn't fail her, faith! Let ye enjoy yourselves now, in the name of God!"

"Thank you, Lizzie," said Fanny.

Kitty raised the silver teapot, and Fanny crossed the room to the sofa.

"I don't want tea," said Bill. "May I have a drink, Fanny?"

"I imagine there are decanters in the dining-room, Cousin Bill," she replied.

He went through the folding doors. Kitty handed Fanny a cup of tea.

"Did you have a good sleep?" she asked.

"Very good. I suppose it's best to stay here tonight? But how long does the journey take in André de Mellin's car?"

"Oh, I believe he can average something amazing, like thirty miles an hour—with luck. Joey said he got them to Glasalla in very little over six hours last week——"

"Ah! So if we left at nine——"

Lucille came into the room.

"Welcome!" Fanny cried. "Come and sit here. Did you rest well, in Cockle's rickety little bed?"

"Wonderfully, Fan. And you? Are you better?"

"Of course. I'm very much ashamed of having frightened you all with that idiotic faint. Do you remember, Lucille, how we despised the fainters at school?"

Lucille laughed.

"Yes, I thought of that even when I was quite frightened, seeing you lying so dead in André's arms——"

"Did I faint all over poor André?"

"Oh, he was delighted with the drama," said Lucille.

"He carried you upstairs as if you were a small bunch of flowers," said Kitty. "Lucille, would you like very weak tea with lemon, or will you try our dark brew with cream?"

"The dark brew with cream, please, Kitty; and may I begin to eat some—what do you call them?"

"Scones," said Fanny. "And they're not spelt as we pronounce them."

Lucille, biting a scone, looked puzzled.

"I'm only teaching you English," said Fanny.

Bill Morrow was back in the drawing-room, glass in hand. He came towards the sofa, smiling.

"Oh, this is Cousin Bill, Lucille. May I present him? Mr. Morrow, Mademoiselle de Mellin."

"I am happy indeed, Mademoiselle." Bill bowed over Lucille's hand. "We have all been looking forward for a long time to meeting you here."

"That is true, indeed," said Kitty.

"I've looked forward, too," said Lucille, "but I could never get Fanny to invite me!"

"Do you think you're going to like Fanny's—well, all of us, Fanny's background, what you will?"

Lucille looked gravely at him, then at Kitty, and about the room.

"I like Fanny's background," she said. "Fanny can talk much, but she used few words at school to tell me of—all this, and of all of you. Simply I knew that here was her home, and that she loved it. But she must have said more things than I was conscious of hearing—because, in a sense, I recognize everything today."

"I agree," said Bill, "that Fanny gives an impression, for the most part, of being laconic about important things. But that may be illusory, because I, for one, most certainly recognize you, Mademoiselle Lucille."

"Ah, but you know my brother!"

"Yes," said Kitty. "And you do resemble each other extraordinarily."

"Do they?" said Bill. "I shouldn't say that."

"But, Bill," said Kitty, "you must be blind! Why, they're the image of each other—they might be twins!"

"Oh, twins, not at all! What do you think, Fan?"

"I don't think André and Lucille are like twins. But sometimes either can remind you amazingly of the other."

Bill looked at her.

"That surprises me," he said. "I must look out for it. It's parallel with everyone's saying that you and Lilian are like twins—which is nonsense. I'd know you from Lilian in pitch darkness."

They all laughed.

"But that test would be irrelevant, Cousin Bill," said Fanny. "We're talking about appearances."

"So we are. I forgot." He turned again to Lucille. "Fanny has been growing up during her wonderful holiday with you, Mademoiselle Lucille. Do you notice it?"

"I've always found her rather grown-up—that's why she was such a relief at school," said Lucille.

"Oh, at school! Naturally, to meet an intelligent fellow-creature at school! Even I am not so old as to have forgotten the rare relief that was!"

The drawing-room door opened and Michael O'Connor, Lilian's husband, came in.

"Welcome back, Fanny," he said, crossing to her eagerly.

"To save Lizzie's legs I cut the front door and came in through the breakfast-room. I've left the motor-car in the road. How are you, dear Fanny? Had a wonderful time?"

"Yes, indeed I did. I'm very well, Michael. How are you?"

"Oh, splendid—but very busy these weeks——"

"I forgot—Lucille, may I introduce Lilian's husband? Mr. O'Connor—Mademoiselle de Mellin."

The two smiled and shook hands,

"Happy to meet you, Mademoiselle," Michael said shyly.

"Will you have tea, Michael?"

"No, thank you, Kitty."

"I believe you'd like a glass of whisky," said Bill.

"To tell you the truth, I would. I'm fagged."

Bill went again to the dining-room, and returned with a salver bearing a decanter and glasses.

"May I bring it in here, Fanny?"

Fanny nodded.

"Well, if you'll forgive me, Fanny, in your drawing-room and at this hour——" Michael poured himself a stiff glass, and drank almost half of it in one gulp. Bill refilled his own glass.

Fanny thought that Michael was looking very well, handsome, dark and bright-eyed as she remembered him; and in his manner he kept that brotherly boyishness which she had liked in him in the brief time of his engagement to Lilian. But in worldly details he had improved; his clothes were excellent and well-chosen and he wore them stylishly; he was much better barbered than had been his wont, and he had grown thin, had lost the somewhat too athletic or bucolic outline of a few months ago. He was no longer the lusty cattle-man from the plains of Meath but a young man of the city. Marriage had groomed him, Fanny observed, as complementarily as it had groomed Lilian. But there was a hint of near-feverishness in his manner, in his movements, which was entirely new.

"I came round first of all just to see you, Fanny; and then to ask you, on behalf of my father and my uncle, as well as myself, to take all our very best wishes to your dear mother and father, and to say that we are delighted that the doctors have got her to obey them, and that the news is so good. Will you tell her we all send our love?"

"Indeed I will, Michael."

"And Lilian said that she'd have loved you to come to dinner tonight, you and Mademoiselle Lucille, but that she knows you'd loathe to, especially as you have this other long journey tomorrow. Anyway, unfortunately we have two Dutch cattle-men and their vast wives dining—and they'd just simply exhaust you! God knows they exhaust me, and I'm used to their kind!"

He looks exhausted at this minute, Fanny was thinking, as he laughed very pleasantly about his Dutch guests.

"Thank Lilian, won't you, Michael. But she's quite right. I simply couldn't go out to dinner tonight."

"Naturally. But Lil wants to know exactly how you are, after this fainting business. You scared her, Fan!"

"She scared us all," said Kitty.

"Oh, I'm grand now. Tell her not to be silly—it was complete nonsense."

"That's great. I must say you look perfectly well—doesn't she, Bill?"

"I think so," said Bill. "She's getting into perspective too —sooner than I thought she would."

"What the dickens do you mean?" asked Michael. "May I?" He turned back to the decanter, and poured himself more whisky. "It's beautiful whisky. Trust Morrow & Sons!"

He smiled at Fanny as he lifted his glass.

'He does look thin, tired,' she thought. 'And he's an athlete; he has always been fussy about keeping fit. I thought he drank very little. Perhaps he is especially tired today. He seems as if he were in the thick of some race or contest which he must win at any price. I do not remember that he was formerly so tense and quick.'

"How is the house, Michael?"

"Oh!" exclaimed Kitty. "You never saw such extravagance, Fan!"

"But it's going to be very beautiful," said Michael. "And, after all, Lilian simply calls out for a beautiful setting. We *are* being extravagant—but then, once these things are done, it's over, and you have your house forever—haven't you?"

"I'm dying to see it," said Fanny.

"Indeed, we're dying to show it to you, Fan. When you're back from Glasalla we'll have a house-warming—all the relations——"

"We'll have to get into training for that—in our different ways," said Bill.

Michael looked at his watch.

"I hope poor Lil's head is better," he said. "She wanted to come round with me now but she simply had to lie down —in view of these Dutchies tonight especially!"

"Naturally. It was good of you to come."

"But I wanted to, Fan. No time now, however, to hear all the Venice adventures! You must save them up for us! Oh —we're sending round a small hamper to Monsieur de Mellin's place in the morning, to be put in his car—just a few delicacies for your mother, things Aunt Eleanor might find difficult to get in County Clare——"

"Thank you very much, Michael—Mother will be very grateful to the two of you."

"Nonsense! I wish I could have driven you down, Fan —but it really would be difficult to get away this week, and since de Mellin is so kind, and he's a far better motorist than I, I'm sure you'll have an easy journey, you and Mademoiselle—oh, I must fly——"

He kissed Fanny's brow lightly, bowed to Lucille and to Kitty, and was gone.

Kitty smiled.

"Poor Michael! What a pace he's going at lately! He's really killing himself over the business of being happily married!"

"But marriage is death," said Bill. "Doesn't he know that? It's the death of us all."

"He's looking well," said Fanny sternly. "He's got thin too, which suits him."

"And he's dressing to kill," said Bill amusedly. "But he'll only kill himself that way, poor innocent!"

Lucille, who had surmised somewhat bitterly about Lilian during breakfast, had now at the tea-table been interested and, inexplicably, touched by Lilian's husband, at first en- counter. As Bill made his insolent and not very fresh

202

aphorisms she said nothing, but handed her cup to Kitty for more of the 'dark brew with cream'. 'Michael O'Connor,' she thought, 'suggests to a stranger that from having been completely self-confident he has suddenly been frightened.' Bridegrooms may often go through that experience, she supposed, before they are moulded as husbands. Lilian could not ever be an ordinary wife, and probably she had married a young man very passionately in love with her who nevertheless needed for his ultimate peace that his bride should become an ordinary dear wife. There was plenty of time for that to happen, but were the elements of ordinary dearness in Lilian? Was this young man already afraid of the glory he had won at the altar? Or was the anxiety that burnt through all his gaiety no more than a compound of those commonplaces which novelists charter for the newly married? Was he working too hard because in pride about his beautiful wife he was spending too much money? And was he loving too much, both sensually and with his heart, because he could do no other? Lucille wondered, and wondered what Fanny's impressions had been today, first of Lilian and now of Lilian's husband.

But Fanny's attention was only politely turned today, when it had to be, to all these kind relatives coming and going. Left to itself it pressed ahead, it was fixed on Glasalla.

She rose now and crossed to the window. The scene outside was very quiet and, save for lamps pricking awake one by one as the lamp-lighter passed, seemed almost emptied of life; but the canal waters shone and so still did the western sky as evening handed the hour on slowly to the near command of night.

"What a long day it's been," said Fanny.

"Yet you slept through most of it," said Kitty.

"Even so."

Lizzie came in and, helped by Kitty, removed the teathings; not exclamatorily now, but praying softly as she clattered in and out, as if the time of day subdued or frightened her. Kitty left the drawing-room with the old woman, and closed the door. Bill lighted candles on the desk.

"Shall I put a match to the fire, Fan?"

She did not hear him; he knelt and lit the fire. Then he

poured himself another drink, and savouring it looked at Lucille and then at Fanny's back, framed in the window.

"I'll go now, I think," he said. "I'm not fit company——"
He went and put his arm round Fanny's shoulders. "Good-night, sweet coz; dear, beautiful Fan, good-night."

He came back and bowed to Lucille.

"Good-night, Mademoiselle." They smiled at each other, and he was gone.

"Come to the fire, Fan," said Lucille. "Look how it's flaming! A fire like this is a real novelty to me."

She had spoken in French, and Fanny replied in French, which was their language together.

"Yes, of course it must be—with all your central heating and your *lovely* porcelain stoves."

"But *this* is much more lovely."

"It *is* lovely."

Fanny sat near the fender on a little stool.

"Queer to be sitting with you here in Mespil Road. Ah, Lucille!" she stretched out a hand for the other's. "It was good of you to come with me! Why did you?"

"Because I've always wanted to, and because I did not like our summer to be broken off so suddenly, with everything I've wanted to talk to you about still in the air, Fan. Also, I knew you were coming back to anxiety——"

"Thank you, dearest. It'll be a long drive tomorrow—but you'll like Glasalla, I know."

"Listen, Fan—I hope you'll agree with me about this. I'm not going with you tomorrow to Glasalla. Oh, I'll go to you the very first day after tomorrow that you telegraph for me! Truly I will. I'll be dying to. But at present I think that to arrive *with* you, a total stranger, when you've been away so long and when they've all been in such distress—truly I think you must arrive alone tomorrow, pet."

"But there'll be André——!"

"Oh, they know André and he's been there before—and anyway he'll be leaving the next morning. He's only the necessary chauffeur! But I—well, I'd prefer to come to you when you've been a few days alone with your parents and Aunt Eleanor—I think it is what they would wish now, Fan —and that it would be easier."

"I see what you mean, in a way. But it's an enormous barrack of a house, you'd be in no one's way——"

"I'd be a stranger and they'd be anxious for my comfort and entertainment—and after all, they're under a great strain. With two nurses in the house——"

"Two nurses?" Fanny sat upright.

"Yes—didn't you know? Naturally they'd have a nurse for night and for day. Two 'Blue Nuns' I think Kitty called them."

"Oh! Oh, Lucille! If Mother is tolerating nurses, even Blue Nuns, round her—she is ill indeed! Oh, oh God!"

Fanny was stricken. She stared into the fire.

"But it's only because she simply must not exert herself just yet, Fan! It's the most obvious precaution, pet."

"I suppose so."

"So you see, don't you, that I don't want to descend on a visit to your people until you have been there and can see what you think about my joining you later? I swear I'll come the minute you summon me."

"Perhaps you are right. I ought to be alone with them first."

"Of course, I should chaperon the long drive tomorrow, I know, but——"

"Good heavens! Chaperon André and me—after Italy?"

"I know it's nonsense—but people talk."

"Lord, let them talk! André is a good friend in this hour of need—and *he* certainly won't trouble about 'talk'!" She laughed. "Dear Lucille! What a queer idea for *you* to have!"

"I know it sounds silly——"

Lucille was troubled about her decision to let André take Fanny home while she withheld, stayed in Dublin. She heard always *Mère Générale's* warnings: 'She will be lonely . . . keep your brother away from her. . . . I fear he will hurt her, and I hold that to be a very grave offence. . . .'

Lucille would have preferred that Fanny travelled under other escort than André's to County Clare. But she apprehended, rightly, that until Fanny reach Glasalla she would be quite simply blind to any mood, emotion or approach upon her sensibilities which was irrelevant from her mother and that sea-washed, westward-facing house where she lay in shadowy danger. Lucille knew that Fanny could at present travel endless deserts under escort of unimaginably unscrupulous voluptuaries, and so long as they pressed for Glasalla she would notice no other action or idea they might advance. And André was, after all, what was called a gentleman, and he was truly willing to be helpful in this trouble; and having delivered Fanny safely, he would have to return the next day to his business in Dublin. Moreover, Lucille had watched him during the morning, and at breakfast particularly, and had been impressed by his reserve, his self-suppression, a kind of detachment, or guardedness, which she had not noticed in him formerly. She was inclined to think that the Venetian flirtation, if it was even that, was over, and that now André was preoccupied, a business man —though as always most willing to be kind to any friend in trouble and, naturally, to be as kind as possible to their dear Fanny. And as for Fanny—it was only too touchingly clear that nothing lived for her or reached her now save that fragile life that waited for her coming in Glasalla. Whatever light impress André's charm might have made upon her in Italy might remain, might re-assert itself; but at present Fanny had forgotten it, Lucille was assured. She had room now only for the fear she had come home to, and for all the homely loves, anxieties and memories that rose and swarmed about that fear. André would be kind and reliable and get her safely to where she must be; Fanny would be grateful for that, but otherwise would be, at present at least, unaware of him.

Lucille wondered indeed if *Mère Générale* had not been talking somewhat old-fashionedly, making a mountain of a molehill, in her accepted, protective tenderness for her favourite, Fanny.

As for her own decision not to go to Glasalla yet—she felt that to be right. She understood family life, and she knew that Fanny must not come to her parents in this hour encumbered by any stranger. So, in the sad circumstances, she felt compelled to disregard *Mère Générale's* injunction in this one instance, and to let André alone take Fanny to Glasalla.

"You have to be alone with them all at first, dear Fan— after so long, and since they have been so much disturbed.

I'll come, as I've said, when you send for me. But, I've a favour to ask—may I ask it?"

Fanny smiled.

"Of course you may not," she said.

"May I stay here, with Lizzie and Nora, and not go to André's house? Would that be giving a lot of trouble?"

Fanny leant her head back against Lucille's knees and laughed.

"Fearful trouble! You wait till you hear how Lizzie and Nora will kick up! Considering they have already decided you are the twin of the Archangel Gabriel!"

"Have they? Could I sleep in your room, Fan, while you're away?"

"How like you it is, how sweet, to want to stay in our shabby house, when André——"

"I'd like to be here in your house!"

"But André has a perfect jewel of a furnished house—a little Regency one in a terrace off Leeson Park. He was telling me at breakfast. He says he's taken it for six months, and that it's exquisite in every detail. And he has his manservant from Charleroi there, and in fact he says, as if surprised, that he is able to live a civilized life in this outpost! Are you sure you wouldn't prefer that? Here, you know, the range is old and hot water is uncertain for the bath, and you see how shabby things are, and the mattresses aren't very good——"

"Please, Fan—may I stay here? And may I use your room?"

Fanny's head was still against Lucille's knees. She did not turn it; her eyes were on the leaping fire. She stretched her hand up only, to touch Lucille's face.

"Stay here, sweet friend, until I send for you. But you must come to Glasalla."

"I'll come."

Silence fell. Fanny leant forward and placed two small logs of applewood on the fire.

"The moment of death is something I think about often, Lucille."

"I know. You used to talk about it at school."

"It is the only moment that we all know we will face. I think that many more people than cowards die many times before their death—don't you?"

"In a sense. But perhaps we all become cowards when we really face the idea of death."

"I hadn't turned it that way. That is probably true."

Fanny knelt and began again to adjust the fire and add wood to it.

"It must be a cold moment, if you see it coming—no matter what your faith, or hope or charity. Lucille, is Mother dying?"

"I think she is gravely ill. But this unhoped-for rally—I understand that it was unhoped-for—must surely be a very good thing?"

"I wonder. She'll be fifty-one on 18th September. Father and she had their silver jubilee last year. Lilian wasn't born until they were nearly three years married, I think."

"You've told me you never remember her being ill, Fan. Surely that will help her now?"

"True, she's never ill. She's always delicate, but more in the way of being fastidious than in the ordinary meaning. I mean, she hates noise and loud voices, and she likes to be alone a great deal, and to lie here and read. But she can walk for miles and miles, and she never minds about weather, one way or the other. She adores to be warm in the house—and she loves to see this fire roaring up, and to lie still there where you're sitting and watch it, and watch out for the different stars that come up there over Wilton Place. She knows the stars—she's nearly always right about them. She says they were the chief excitement of her childhood in Glasalla."

"She can see them better in Glasalla than here——"

"I wonder if she's able to sit up and watch for them? Ah, yes, Belladonna," Fanny stroked the purring old cat. "That's the sort of fire you're used to here, isn't it?"

Joey, back from his office, came into the room.

"Good-evening, Mademoiselle! Good-evening, Fanny! Did you both rest well? Are you better, Fan?"

The girls responded and he came to the fire.

"Funny how cold the evenings are—although it's August. I wired Father, Fan, to expect you by car tomorrow afternoon. André wants to leave here at ten—will that be too early for you?"

"Too *early*?"

"I called at his business place on the way home, and he sent his greetings, Fan, and his love to you, Mademoiselle. He would have liked to call here, but is being delayed at the office, and has a dinner engagement tonight, to his regret. Lovely, I must say, to come home and find the drawing-room alive, and two such agreeable companions sitting here! It's been lonely these last evenings."

"That reminds me," said Lucille. "Will you find it very unconventional, Monsieur Joey, if I am here for a few days, when Fanny is gone?"

Joey looked surprised, and Fanny explained Lucille's plan.

"So you'd prefer *not* to go to your brother's delightful house, Miss Lucille? Well, of course, we are only honoured—and I think, don't you, that Lizzie and Nora will take care of the conventions?"

Joey was very cordial, but both Fanny and Lucille noted with amusement that he was in fact somewhat startled at a breach of correct custom which might easily lead to what he called 'talk'. However, he was too young and, give him his due, too modest to protest. And he admired Lucille exceedingly—so he swallowed his surprise, and took his chance like a man with Dublin's scandal-mongers.

"I'll have to show you Dublin, Mademoiselle Lucille," he went on. "But, heavens, it's crowded! And everyone making for Herbert Park at the same time! Still, the lights do look exciting! Will you let me take you to the Exhibition one evening?"

"I'll be delighted if you will," said Lucille. "But I chiefly want to see Dublin."

"Oh, you'll see Dublin, of course." Joey's eyes fell on the tray of decanters. "Cousin Bill been here?"

"Yes, and Michael," said Fanny.

"Ah! Poor Michael! Lilian's making him spend far too much money, I'll swear. Oh, by the way, Fan, just as I was turning in at the gate there was a carriage drawing up—and whose was it but old Lady Rawlinson's! The poor old girl wanted the latest news of Mother, and was going to call—but I told her that there was no one at home but you, just back from abroad, and that you were in bed and asleep——"

"Oh! She's terribly fond of Mother, Joey."

"I know. But I didn't know you were up—and anyway, you didn't want to be bothered with the poor old bore——"

"I'd have liked to see her. Mother would have been glad to have news of her."

"Well—give her news. The old girl sends her love to Glasalla, and is writing to Mother—and I told her that the reports are good now, and that Mother is responding to her treatment. She sent her love to you also, Fan."

"How did she seem?"

"Shaky. After all, she's a good age. She cried when she spoke about Mother—she said: 'I had hoped to see Julia again.'"

"'To see Julia again . . .'" Fanny repeated.

"Yes; I think she feels very near her end, poor old lady. When she was crying she struck me as very feeble. Still, I'm glad I fobbed her off—you and Mademoiselle are too tired today for that kind of thing. I think I must go and wash before supper——"

He bowed to Lucille and left the room.

The sky over Wilton Place was deep black now, and pricked with the stars that Julia could have named. Fanny crossed to the window and drew the curtains.

CHAPTER TEN

THE LIGHTHOUSE

AUNT ELEANOR was standing in the grass-grown drive, about a hundred yards south of the ha-ha bridge, and out of range of the house.

André pulled up the car. It was a wild, blowy evening, and the wind rattled through the drying leaves of sycamore and ash. Eleanor's silky grey hair was tossed about; she looked gaunt and cold. She came to Fanny's side of the car.

"Welcome," she said. "I've been on the watch-out for you since four. The thing is, will you get out here, Fanny, and walk up to the house. I'll send a man down for the luggage

—and in a while you can bring the car up to the yard, Monsieur de Mellin."

"Of course, Aunt Eleanor," said Fanny, scrambling down to her. "But why?"

"It's because your mother has been counting the minutes until you'd arrive—and now she's dozing a bit, and if she woke up and heard the car arriving I'm afraid the excitement would be too much for her."

"Oh! Oh, is she very ill?"

Eleanor looked at Fanny appraisingly, but did not answer the question.

"We'll just walk up to the house in silence, and then I'll go to her door and tell Joseph to tell her if she wakes that you are here safe and sound. Until she has seen you she must not hear the car."

"I understand, Miss Delahunt," said André. "The car won't be in anyone's way, I think——"

"Not in the least. Anyway, the avenue is wide, God knows. Come, child—you must both be cold and tired. It was good of you to drive her here, Monsieur de Mellin."

"I was only too glad to be of the least small service, Miss Delahunt."

In silence the three crossed the ha-ha bridge, where the low white gate was hooked back. The vast Georgian house loomed up, grey and lonely in its embankments of ilex trees and escallonia bushes. Beyond it the west sky was preparing for a stormy sunset, and Fanny could hear the thrash of the sea, and could smell the bright seaweed below the kitchen-garden wall. It was not yet time for the lighthouse to strike up, but the evening was dark. The hall door was open, and a lamp had been lighted already in the hall. Above, the windows of Mother's room were wide open, Fanny noticed, and the curtains drawn back. There was a dim light beyond them, across which someone, Father perhaps, moved.

They went up the shallow steps; Teresa and Iago were asleep on the flags of the terrace. Fanny bent and stroked them, and then followed Aunt Eleanor into the house. They paused at the drawing-room door.

"Perhaps you would like to wash, Monsieur de Mellin?" said Aunt Eleanor. "You know the bathroom?" She waved a hand towards the stairs. "And you will find decanters and sandwiches, and a good fire, I hope, in the little study. My father is there, I imagine, and will be glad to see you."

André bowed and opened the drawing-room door for Eleanor and Fanny.

The two crossed to the fire and Eleanor pulled the bell-rope.

"You must be longing for tea, you poor child," she said. "Honoria will have it up in a minute. Oh, come in then!" She went to a window where Teresa and Iago were screaming, lifted it and let them in. "You're a bold pair, making all that row," she said as they raced to the fire.

"Belladonna has got very old," said Fanny.

"She's twelve now," said Eleanor. "I was tempted to ask you to bring her down—Julia misses her."

"Oh, why didn't I think of it?"

"Did you see *Mère Générale* before you left Brussels, Fanny?"

"Yes, of course, Aunt Eleanor."

"Had she had a letter from me?"

"No; not when I saw her."

"Ah!"

Honoria came staggering in with a vast silver tea-tray, heavily laden. Fanny jumped up to help her and pull out the table. When Honoria had landed her load she expected the customary assault of greeting. But the fine, strong woman only turned to look at her.

"Miss Fanny!" she whispered, once only; then with her apron to her eyes she actually tiptoed out of the room.

Fanny stared after her, and then stared at Aunt Eleanor. But Aunt Eleanor was pouring tea and did not look at her.

"While you're drinking this cup I'll go upstairs and tell your father you are here. And eat some of these good scones, pet; this is this year's raspberry jam, and truly it's excellent, if I do say it myself."

Fanny did not recognize this somewhat formal Aunt Eleanor who left the drawing-room now with a caution of movement as unexpected in her as it had been in Honoria. She drank some tea, and listened, with quickening heart, to the great humming stillness of Glasalla.

The cats purred about her ankles, recognizing her. She gave them a saucer of cream. She was very tired. André had been throughout the day absolutely efficient and considerate, but the drive was long, with anxiety racing ahead of every mile. So she was afraid as yet to ask direct questions, and alike Aunt Eleanor's strange composure and the unrecognizability of Honoria frightened her. However, before she saw Mother she had better drink tea, and eat something. She was addressing herself to this task when her father came into the room.

He almost ran to her, and he seized her in his arms.

"Welcome, darling Fan! Welcome home!"

She looked closely into his face.

"Thank you! Oh, Father, it's nice to be home!"

"Good child! God bless you!"

She saw that he was tired, that his eyes had a drained and faded look; clearly he had suffered much since she had last seen him; but with sudden sharp relief from panic she realized that he was happy now, that he was released from fear.

"I'm to have tea with you, Fan. And then Sister Guadalupe says—did you ever know such a name for a nun, and she's just a nice little Irishwoman!—Sister Guadalupe says that in about fifteen minutes you are to go up and see your dear mother! Oh, she'll be so delighted to see you!"

Fanny poured him a cup of tea.

"How is she, Father? How shall I find her?"

"Wonderful. Oh—I forgot—of course when you went away she was perfectly well, and since then she has been very seriously ill—so you'll see a great change. But I see a different kind of great change, from last week to this. So I find her wonderful—she's fighting back magnificently, Fanny!"

"But what happened?"

"It's difficult to say," Joseph said wearily. "She simply got so tired towards the end of June that we didn't know what to do about her—and yet she wasn't ill; I mean, she had no symptoms. But she kept hankering for Glasalla, and Redmond advised a total rest here. So I brought her down. But after a few days here she collapsed completely, and although she was in bed all the time she kept fainting. Oh my God!" Joseph put down his cup and rose and paced about. "It was terrifying. Well, we got that young fellow O'Curry out from Doon Point—and I must say he seems to know his job. He said it was advanced anaemia. She had been very much frightened, for some weeks it appears, by a knocking sound behind her ears. Apparently she thought something terrible was happening to her, and was afraid to speak of it—afraid of frightening me, she said. Ah, dear Julia!"

He paused and stared out of a window.

"What did Dr. O'Curry say, Father?"

"He told her that the knocking in her ears was a classic symptom of acute anaemia, and that with her blood reduced as it was he did not understand why she was alive. This diagnosis relieved your dear mother extraordinarily, as you can imagine—and then O'Curry got Redmond to come down with a couple of specialists on heart and blood. But somehow in spite of them, last week—last week was bad, Fan. The treatment seemed beyond her strength—and, we had to let her receive the Last Sacraments."

"Oh, Father! And I didn't know!"

"The night she was anointed you were in the train somewhere between Milan and Paris, darling. And after that she rallied—and there was no need to frighten you, but only to ask you to come home, as she was missing you."

"And now?"

"Now—she is very weak, and will have to resign herself to a long period of invalidism, and to eating and drinking a great deal more than she likes to. But—she will be well again. She has told me that she knows she will. And I know she will. We must take great care of her, great care, henceforward." He moved back to the window, mopping his tired eyes with a silk handkerchief. "Oh, Julia, Julia!" he whispered to the garden. "Oh, thank God! Oh God, I promise——"

Fanny refilled his cup and brought it to him.

She felt heartened. If Mother had said that she knew she would get well, and if he, Father, who was so exceptionally sensitive to every vibration in his wife, her mother, if he also knew this good certainty, then she believed them both, Mother would be well again. Patience was all.

"I think I'll go up to her now, Father."

"Do, pet. Go into the dressing-room, and Sister Guadalupe will hear you there, and if your mother is awake she will let you into the room. But—no tears, Fan—and be very, very quiet."

Fanny suppressed exasperation at these instructions, which, after all, were natural enough. Carefully she climbed the staircase and paused a minute by the great window on the landing. The lighthouse was getting ready; she could see the preparatory flickers in the lantern.

"Tell me what Venice is like, Fan."

Fanny laughed softly.

"I could never do that, Mother."

A carefully-shaded lamp burnt on the table, but there was still some daylight in the sky, towards which Julia's face was turned, as also towards Fanny, who sat at the window side of the bed.

After the first agonizing shock, expression of which the girl had only been barely able to suppress, Fanny was beginning now to see that her mother was indeed herself, and only changed inasmuch as she was recovering from an illness the crisis of which she who looked at her now had not witnessed.

Julia lay propped against vast white pillows, and so thin was she, so hollow and shallow her torso, that almost it was as if no frame at all lay within the smocked and tucked white night-gown and the silky pale blue shawl. Her hands, it seemed to Fanny, were now no more than long shadows of those always shadowy hands, and it startled her to discover how high and domed her mother's forehead was and how profoundly socketed her eyes. Yet, after a moment, hearing the voice, meeting the calm, dreamy glance, welcoming the slow-curling smile, she was assured. There, out of an ordeal indeed, was Mother; but Mother unmistakably, and beautiful, and looking outward, to the sky. She understood her father's gladness; clearly Mother would get well again.

"You must try to tell me about Venice," Julia said. "Truly, pet, you must."

"By degrees I'll try, Mother. But I couldn't begin just this minute."

"Were you happy there?"

"It's a place which—compels you to be happy."

Julia closed her eyes.

"Like Glasalla," she said.

Fanny laughed and stroked her mother's fingers.

"Some people might find Glasalla sad," she said.

"Not I," said Julia. "Are you glad to be here again, Fan?"

"Delighted, Mother."

"I hear Lucille came with you. Won't you bring her in a minute? I'd like to see this wonderful Lucille."

"I left her at Mespil Road for the present. She'll come down here in a few days."

"Do you think she'll be comfortable there, Fan? The shabby old house. Ah, Lizzie and Nora will do their best. But—send for her soon. She should be with you."

Julia's eyes were closed again. The lighthouse beam had begun its nightly swing, and its first hard stroke flashed over the bed.

"Shall I draw the curtains, Mother? The lighthouse has started."

"I love it. I grew up with those strokes of light."

"I know. But when you're so tired——"

"I sleep to its beat," Julia whispered. "I always did."

"I don't see how you ever learnt to read the stars against it."

"That was the excitement. Eleanor and I learnt to read the sky by flashes of lightning—you know, pet, like Edmund Kean playing *King Lear*. It was great fun. . . ." The voice trailed into a mere breath. Fanny took Julia's hand, which had been hot when she first touched it; now it was very cold and damp. Startled, she bent above her mother's face, and saw that it was covered in cold sweat. Julia's eyelids lay upon her eyes as if forever sealing them.

"Sister Guadalupe," Fanny whispered, afraid to speak loudly yet also afraid to let go of her mother's hand.

The little bespectacled nun was at the bedside instantly. She disengaged Fanny's hand from Julia's.

"Let you run downstairs, child. 'Tis only a bit of a faint. She's very weak, you know—and we've had hard work with her all day over the excitement of your coming. Run off now, please. She'll be all right, I tell you——"

Fanny obeyed because it seemed the right thing to do.

"There, there—God bless you, take your time . . ." she heard the Blue Nun saying, and heard the clink of spoon on glass.

Slowly she went downstairs, and out to the chill dusk of the terrace. Night was in full descent now, and all of Glasalla sighed in its acceptance. In spite of the threat of the evening it looked to be a noble night of August. The moon, its very silver edge appearing to the south-east, was at the full, and would engage the lighthouse presently in follies of illumination—as long ago they all had watched it do in the late summer. Fanny desired to go up to the top of the kitchen-garden, and sit on the wall there and watch and listen to the sea. But also she was at this moment disinclined to leave the house. She had never seen her mother faint before; she had never known her hands and forehead drenched in chill, or seen her eyelids closed as if never again would they open. She had been full of fear for many days, then for an hour or so irradiated by hope; now, she felt uncertain.

The lighthouse beam blazed on Aunt Eleanor as she stood in the stone archway of the stable-yard; she was piling up buckets for Corney Keane to take away—she had been feeding the hens. Fanny heard her then in the darkness, her goloshes squeaking as she came towards the house. The next flash revealed her, weary and beautiful, on the steps.

"So there you are, Fan? You've seen your mother?"

"Yes, Aunt Eleanor."

"Corney brought up your luggage, and I've told the young Frenchman that he can take the motor-car to the coach-house now. He's a polite young fellow. He has been keeping Grandfather quite happy and distracted in the study."

"He's always very kind. They all are, the de Mellins."

The two crossed the hall together.

"You look terribly tired, Aunt Eleanor."

"No, mind you, I'm not exceptionally tired. Those hens are devils, of course. But they're good layers. Come into my office, will you, Fan?"

Aunt Eleanor's office was a very small room at the back of the back hall, with a window overlooking, below, the inner kitchen yard, and beyond, at eye level, the Atlantic Ocean. A lamp was lighted now on the table-desk, and a fire burnt strongly in the small grate. The curtains and the window were open, and the noise of the sea and its exquisite smell filled the room. The lighthouse beam did not strike this side of the house directly, but its reflection swept past over the sky every minute.

Eleanor sank into a creaking basket chair by the fire, and bent and pulled off her goloshes and then her shoes. She curled her long, narrow feet for a few seconds before the fire, and then thrust them into a pair of shabby woolwork slippers.

Honoria came in, bearing a salver on which was a decanter, a beautiful Waterford sherry glass, and a small silver box.

"Thank you, Honoria."

Honoria paused by Fanny.

"I was too glad to see you a while ago, Miss Fanny—I couldn't speak, child. How did you find your mother, God bless her?"

Fanny took Honoria's hand.

"Better than I had hoped for, Honoria," she said. "Really, a good deal better."

"Ah well—please God! Please God!"

Honoria went out, still subdued out of Fanny's recognition.

"I have to have a glass of sherry at this hour, Fanny," said Aunt Eleanor. "Your grandfather disapproves of the practice, and says it will make me 'horsey'! But without it I could not nowadays face the evenings of accounts and worries, after having been a farmer all day. What he does not know, dear man, since he never enters this room, is that also at this hour I smoke two cigarettes. That would absolutely revolt him! A lady smoking! He has seen the spectacle occasionally at point-to-points, and it has always as good as broken his heart! But I think that it is on this glass of sherry and these two cigarettes that I run Glasalla!"

She leant forward, filled the glass with pale gold sherry, opened the little silver box and selected a cigarette. There were tapers on a jar on the mantelpiece and carefully she lighted one at the fire, and carefully from it lighted the cigarette.

Fanny watched with affectionate amusement. Austere Aunt Eleanor, taking her small and long-postponed indulgence with such deliberation, such delicacy, and an attractively mischievous hint of guilt.

"They seem little things, to do so much, Aunt Eleanor."

"Maybe. Ask your grandfather."

"I saw Mother, as you know, Aunt Eleanor. I—I was reassured. I had been frightened. But, considering everything, after a few minutes I could see that—that Father is right——"

Eleanor sipped from the sherry-glass and said nothing.

"However," Fanny went on, "she grew cold and tired all of a sudden, half-fainted, I think. Sister Guadalupe said it was the excitement of my arriving——"

"Very likely," said Eleanor composedly, and she knelt down to replenish the fire.

Fanny had very seldom been allowed even to look round the door of Aunt Eleanor's office, and certainly had never sat in it before. It was a crammed place. Glass-fronted bookcases packed with volumes, of history, of theology, of French and English literature; books on agriculture, on birds, on trees and flowers, dictionaries and reference books covering vast areas of possible human inquiry. A great steel safe, and near it shelves of box files, clearly docketed; the table-desk heaped with catalogues, diaries, letter-baskets, pens and pencils. Everything crowded, but the whole a triumph of the spirit of order. No dust anywhere, and whatever should have a polish on it shone to its zenith in the lamplight. Fanny was surprised; this room expressed a part of Aunt Eleanor which she did not know. Aunt Eleanor, with her soft grey hair always escaping from hairpins, in her easy, untidy tweeds, conducted Grandfather's household with a loose authoritativeness which produced comfort always for those who could take the essentials of good living as generally understood in West Clare. She was incapable of fuss, and preferred that people should suffer some passing inconvenience, if they must, rather than have housewifely 'scenes' about an overdone roast or a smoking chimney. But she had authority, and Glasalla responded always to her crack of the whip.

This little room, however, where—as Fanny now discovered with amusement—the mistress of the house drank the sherry her father frowned upon, and smoked the cigarette that it would have broken his heart to see her smoke—this room was a very private piece of self-expression, and bore no relation to the rest of the vast, haphazard house.

In spite of all it had to contain, orderliness gave the little room an extreme austerity. Over the mantelpiece hung a very fine print of da Vinci's Madonna of the Rocks; to the left there was a bad old photograph of the cloisters of *Place des Ormes*. There was on the same wall a pleasant drawing in red chalk of Grandfather when he was young, and in an oval silver frame on the mantelpiece a fading Brownie snapshot of Julia in the garden at Mespil Road, with Belladonna in her arms. In the middle of the mantelpiece, under the da Vinci print stood, about nine inches high, a singularly beautiful crucifix, the cross and its base in heavily wrought iron, the figure of Christ in brass. On the wall above the safe a small brass-faced carriage clock ticked gently.

Fanny studied all these things with pleasure.

"I know what this room is like, Aunt Eleanor," she said. "It's like *Mère Générale's* study."

"Oh no, it isn't," Eleanor said. "That old autocrat doesn't have to crowd all her books and papers into this small space." But she smiled nevertheless as she looked about her cell.

"For that matter, you needn't either," said Fanny. "The house is huge."

"For what this room means I need privacy, Fanny. You can't spread privacy over an Irish country house."

"Mother would like this room. Does she ever sit here?"

"Only she. Until you, tonight."

Silence fell. Aunt Eleanor drew delicately on her cigarette.

"Where are the cats?" Fanny asked.

"With Grandfather, in the study. I don't invite them here, in case he'd come looking for them and catch me smoking. But I brought you in here now to discuss something secret with you. May I begin?"

"But—of course, Aunt Eleanor."

"I don't know whether you know or not that I own Glasalla. Your grandfather very sensibly wanted to spare me death duties, and also as he loathed everything to do with running the place, farming and all that, thought it was only fair that whoever did the work here should be the owner. So about ten years ago he transferred all the title-deeds to me—and has been truly happy ever since. He adores the place, but couldn't bear the anxiety of running it. Did you know that?"

"No, Aunt Eleanor."

"Well, I am fifty-three now, and the weather and the work are ageing me fast. I've been discussing my will with young Hallinan in Ennis. I'm going to leave Glasalla to you, Fanny——"

"To *me*? But, Aunt Eleanor——"

"I have not spoken of this intention to anyone, except your grandfather, who delights in it. I have not told Julia, although I know it would please her—but she would instantly tell your father. Marriage is a fearful thing in some ways, Fanny. Julia would tell your father. And dear Joseph would instantly say that if any of Julia's children *were* to inherit Glasalla it must be one of Julia's sons. And Julia would agree with him the minute he said it! Isn't that so?"

Fanny, dazed though she was, had to laugh.

"I think so," she said.

"Well then—we say nothing to anyone except Hallinan the lawyer," Eleanor went on. "But like my dear father I believe passionately in cheating on death duties—and anyhow this is not a valuable property, although I have managed at last to clear it of mortgage, and hope to keep it so, with any luck. But, I propose now nominally and legally to make it your property, Fanny. With only one proviso—

a gentleman's agreement, if you like—that Grandfather and I live out our days here, that I run the place for you as long as encroaching rheumatism allows me, and that, subject to ploughing back any profits there might ever be, I take our living out of it exactly as I am doing now. I'll show you all the books, of course—and you can always examine them. But, if you accept that condition, I give you Glasalla. I shall give it to you this week."

Fanny sat astounded; her heart thumped painfully.

"But *why*, Aunt Eleanor?"

Aunt Eleanor sipped some sherry.

"Because you are very like Julia. In memory of her, I will give it to you."

"In memory of her?"

"Yes. What you'll do with the place when I'm gone, God knows. I'll make no conditions for after my death. Perhaps you'll have to sell it, or let it. Perhaps you'll be a poet or a novelist and so be glad of its silence. Perhaps you'll find someone to farm it for you; perhaps you'll marry someone who will farm it, finance it. There's very little money in it, save what hard work can compel it to yield. And I don't see you as a farmer, like me. But—you'll be free to do as you will with it—and at present anyway it is unencumbered, and a good bailiff or a good husband could keep it on an even keel for you. And I'll have left it to the right descendant—and when I'm in the vault in Crahore I won't know, after all, what that descendant does with the old stones. What do you think, Fanny?"

Fanny had believed herself, in the moments of listening to this absolutely unforeseen news, to be dumbfounded. Now she sat silent for some seconds, and gathered up what she had heard. And gently it sank into her and took its natural place. She looked about the little crowded, orderly room, and thought of *Mère Générale*; perhaps she prayed to the old nun. She heard the suck and rattle of the sea over the stones below the yard; she looked out to the stars in the darkness and saw them pale, as every minute of every night they paled, under the lash of the lighthouse.

She rose and came near the fire and stood in front of Aunt Eleanor.

"Thank you, Aunt Eleanor," she said. "I'll take care of Glasalla."

Then she fell on her knees and bent her head into Aunt Eleanor's lap. She shook from head to foot, as if in ague. This day had been too much, too full. Sobs tore through her. Aunt Eleanor stroked her head and smiled, unperturbed by the childish crying.

"There, there," she said. "There, there, you're just like Julia—'sh, don't cry!"

Honoria came in. The scene she met stirred her to some of her natural exuberance.

"In the name and honour of God, Miss Eleanor, what are ye at at all? Sure the master and the poor young foreign gentleman are wild to be at the bit of supper, God help them! Ah now, Miss Fanny child, don't let you tear yourself into tatters this way! Sure, who knows, and God is good—come on now, my pets, the pair o' ye——"

At supper Fanny met Grandfather at last, and played the sweet comedy of the cats with him, ritualistically, lovingly. But with pity now, after long absence, she saw him to be a very old man, and one newly shaken by some fear no one must name.

"That's right, Fanny! Ah sure, look at them, they remember you, the clever pair! Yes, out with them now for their parade on the terrace—go on with you now! Go on, you ruffians you!"

Joseph came down belatedly, to supper. He sat opposite to Fanny, and she could not help watching him for signs, although she had seen her mother and been reassured. He was bright, and bright-eyed.

"Is she eating her supper, Joseph?" asked Grandfather.

"Yes, sir. She's having some broth—and there's good port in it, which she doesn't know. And she sent good-night to you all—because Sister Eucharia says that except for saying her night prayers with me there must be no more social life until tomorrow."

"Oh!" said Fanny.

"Oh, damn it, can't I just say good-night to the pet?" whimpered Grandfather.

"We both will, Father," said Eleanor. "She'd be unhappy if we didn't."

Joseph frowned, and tried to swallow some food.

André smiled across the table at Fanny, and lifted his glass of claret towards her.

"You look happier now, Miss Fanny," he said. "You were tired and anxious when we arrived. But now—you have seen your dear mother?"

"Oh yes, thank you, André! It is a great relief, and I owe it to you!"

"Indeed you do not!"

"She does," said Eleanor. "You are a very chivalrous and truly friendly young man. No wonder Fanny loves your sister Lucille so much—since I gather you are very much alike!"

"Ah, but, Miss Delahunt, Lucille is a very good character, really good—and I am not!"

"I find much that is good," said Grandfather, "in a handsome, gay young man who yet is willing to drive far into the lonely country to be of use to friends who are anxious——"

"So do I," said Eleanor.

"Only last week Monsieur de Mellin took all this same trouble for Lilian and Tony," Grandfather told Fanny. "And you can't tell me, young man," he said sweetly to André, "that you haven't your own life to live meantime. I was young one time too, and I remember, do you know, about how it was to be young—*et ego in Arcadia*—is that it, my dear?" he asked Eleanor.

"Yes, Father, as far as it goes," she said affectionately.

"It *is* good of you, André," said Fanny. "Say what you like, it's anxious work driving over the awful lanes of County Clare."

"But I love it. It's my job to pioneer those cars. Every village I go through is valuable to our factories, Miss Fanny."

She smiled at him.

"Hardly yet, in Clare. In Dublin, yes. But you do waste your firm's time driving down to the last glimpse of Erin."

"Maybe. But I don't waste my own time," he said. "How exquisite these mushrooms are, Miss Eleanor!"

"Corney's twins brought them in this evening. They're

about a foot off the ground, Larry and Stephen, and they're seven years old. Two large canisters overflowing they had, just gathered. They put the canisters on the kitchen table, and they looked round very threateningly, and were surprised to see me. But they stood their ground. 'Sixpence is the price if you want them, Miss Eleanor,' said they. 'But we won't take a penny less.'"

"Did you haggle?" asked André delightedly.

"I didn't. And I think Mrs. Hession threw in a few cuts of hot soda-bread and jam. Anyway, I paid down the six coppers, and left the kitchen."

"Do try to eat something, Father," Fanny said gently. She saw that he did not know what to do, for politeness' sake, with the beautifully creamed mushrooms or the thin, well-grilled rashers before him. He was trying to eat some salad; Fanny was puzzled by the anxious brightness of his eyes and how it falsified, as she saw now, the crumpled, grey aspect of all his other features. 'He has been too much frightened,' she thought with pity. 'So he dare not yet believe that she is safe, that he will keep her. That accounts for the fight between his too happy eyes, and the rest of him.'

"Please, Father," she repeated softly.

"But I eat like a horse down here, Fan," he said. "I ate enormously at tea-time—you saw!"

"Try a glass of claret, Joseph," said Grandfather.

"Oh yes—do indeed, sir," said André. "Your own shipping and very, very beautiful, may I say? Look, *Château Larose* 1894!"

Joseph took a glass of claret, sipped it speculatively, and settled to enjoy it.

"Do you hear those two?" cried Grandfather, leaping to his shaky feet. "Where *is* that idiotic Honoria?"

"I'll let them in, Grandfather," said Fanny, running to the hall in answer to the shrieks of Teresa and Iago.

"And so you'd better," shouted Honoria sweeping past her. "Idiotic, how-dare-you, sir! And I with a cheese *soufflé*, no less, to place before ye! Come on here, Miss Eleanor, and let you whip it on the plates before it's destroyed! I think it's out of her mind Mrs. Hession is going, with her *soufflés*, I thank you!"

Eleanor served the platefuls deftly from the sideboard.

"I think it's very nice of her to try to show us up well to our foreign guest," she said. "And on her lucky night she *can* do a *soufflé*, Honoria. Here, eat it quickly, Monsieur de Mellin. It looks a lucky one, to me!"

"Delicious!" said André. "Oh, I must go and thank Mrs. Hession!"

"She'll adore you if you do!"

Fanny came back, the two cats cantering before her.

"Do you know," said Grandfather, "those two are champions. They always clean a *soufflé* dish, and the way they were screeching means they knew they were due in for the job! My loves, my little pair of grandees, come over here to me——"

André refilled Joseph's glass.

"She'll be all right now, she'll sleep," said Joseph. "Only I must go and help her to say her prayers. She gets troubled if she can't remember them all. She prays for a lot of people. You'd be amazed. . . ."

After supper Fanny stood on the terrace with André. Westward there were still a few streaks of gold above the water, signalling the hour-long vanished sun; but darkness commanded the east, and had gathered the ilexes and the spruce trees into its great depth. The stars fought their minute-by-minute argument with the whirling lighthouse; but the moon, commanding, full and brilliant, did at least direct the heavens now as forcefully as did the lantern of Loop Head. The nightly battle was engaged.

"I'm going up to have a look at the tide," said Fanny.

The two went down the shallow steps and along the gravel track to the iron gate in the wall which admitted them to the slanted kitchen-garden. They walked up the hilly central path. Fanny smelt far off to the right the crushed, early mulberries and the rotting gold plums below the south wall; right and left under the overladen apple trees she caught the glimpse and tang of over-grown phlox and dahlias and bush roses—all dying, falling; nicotiana and evening primrose—the moon and the lighthouse flashed thin shadows to her, and great globe artichokes stood, as if processional ornaments, against the rank, low run of lesser vegetables. Small creatures scurried over the path and through the stiffly rattling cabbages; little bright eyes flashed and vanished; glow-worms shone, and small bats whirred over Fanny's head, over André's.

"This is the place," said Fanny.

She turned to the right at the curve of the hilly path; she found the mossy steps she knew, and climbed to reach the top of the stone wall, in a western angle, beside the fig tree.

André climbed after her. They sat on the flat stones.

"Look," said Fanny. "Look down."

The tide was full in on the Golden Rocks below and, Fanny knew by its murmur, just about to turn. The stones were rattling on its backward suck. The water foamed and frilled, but gently; the night was gentle. Beyond, where the moving flood lay black, gleaming, radiant black as diamonds might be black, it was the Atlantic Ocean, and had to bear the minute-to-minute eye of the lighthouse lantern.

"Would it irritate you if I smoked?" asked André.

"But no—of course not."

Fanny might have preferred to be alone for this walk through the kitchen-garden and up to her look-out place, the childhood perch of summer afternoons. But she gave no sign other than kind to André.

She pointed northwards along the rocky coast.

"The children are over there," she said, "at Doon Point, with Aunt Edith."

"The children?"

"Oh, Stephen and Cockle and Muscle. You don't remember them? They're nice."

"Yes—yes I do."

"Have you ever seen Doon Point?"

"I don't think so, Fanny."

"I must take you there. Every summer holidays until this time the rule was that the minute we got back from Belgium, Lilian and me, we came straight down here with Mother. Then on the first of August the whole family, with Father and Lizzie and Nora, came to the lodge in Doon Point, and we went over to join them. And then through August we came and went as we felt inclined between here and there. It was lovely."

André marked, but did not comment on, Fanny's use of the past tense. Yet for all the sadness implicit in that, for one still so young and so touchingly close to her memories, there was, he thought, a new vibration in her voice, a ring of strength he had not heard before. He wondered about it lazily. It was indeed amusing that the long beam from the lighthouse gave no peace to the lovely night in this angle of the world otherwise cast for deep and blessed darkness after sunset. And perhaps the force, the resistance he thought he heard for the first time tonight in Fanny's voice, was no more than a characteristic answer to the maddening challenge of the every-minute beam of light.

"It must be difficult sometimes," he said, "to live with this lighthouse."

"It should be," said Fanny. "But I've never resented it. And I don't think I shall, either."

"That's easy to say," André laughed. "After all, you won't be living with it."

Fanny was leaning backwards, her hands braced against the cold stones and her face lifted to the sky. Now she lowered her eyes and swept the inland scene, the kitchen-garden below her, the massed group of the house and stables, the crowding, dark trees and the bare, stony hill beyond, with a searching, appraising look, a proud and happy look which her companion, whose pleasure it always was to watch her closely, observed with curiosity.

"You have a commanding air," he said amusedly. "I had not seen this aspect of your face before. Are you challenging the lighthouse, Fanny?"

"No, André. I'm fraternizing with it."

"Is that necessary?"

"Yes, indeed."

Fanny's spirit had been rent by a surprise which seemed almost unendurable when Aunt Eleanor told her that she was, and now, and at once, giving her Glasalla. The gift was unforeseen, immeasurable, and must revolutionize and dominate her thoughts henceforward. She had cried at Aunt Eleanor's knees, in sheer shock. And at supper, with her

228

father and with Grandfather, and conscious in every second of Mother in her shadow-place of life-and-death upstairs, she had, as she thought, folded away the extraordinary news, as something she had not rightly understood, something Aunt Eleanor had not meant, and which might be explained, examined and, perhaps, dismissed at another time.

Yet, unconsciously she was, all through supper, assimilating the stated fact. Unconsciously she took it home, and weighed its meaning: the responsibility, the power, the burden of piety such a clear inheritance would carry; and the sharp orientation it must give to her purpose in life. So, as she walked up the kitchen-garden path, she was moving from unconscious acceptance of Glasalla to clear consideration of it. And, surprised, delighted, she was aware that all her intelligence and all her impulses were rushing out together—in dangerous impetus, perhaps—to meet the multiple challenge of the place.

So now as she sat on the wall, her knees drawn up into the embrace of her arms as she turned her back against the outer branches of the fig tree so as to be able to look west and east, and face the lighthouse—now she felt inclined at once to laugh and to pray, she who did not pray.

She did not need to look at any one of Aunt Eleanor's account books to know that Glasalla was a poor and struggling estate; indeed she had been surprised and impressed to learn that it was clear of mortgage. She did not desire to become a farmer, as Aunt Eleanor had, who would have chosen, Fanny guessed, to have been a nun. But Glasalla was something else besides being an estate which had to be farmed, and to be its inheritor was an intoxicating honour. She would find a way to look after it. Aunt Eleanor would be in charge for many years yet, and by the time she, Fanny, was alone with it, she would have educated herself, made money in some way, and considered how to take charge of Glasalla. However, already as she sat on the wall above the sea and looked from the fierce lighthouse beam back to the dim lights of the house, she understood that henceforward all her studies, hopes and dreams would be anchored to her responsibility for Glasalla.

She shivered a little.

André was watching her.

"Are you cold, Fanny?"

"No; not really."

"What are you laughing at?"

"I'm not laughing."

"Your eyes are. They're shining—very firmly—almost like diamonds."

"That doesn't sound attractive."

"Well, they are a little alarming."

Fanny observed that André did in fact seem troubled as he said this. She was feeling remote from him in this moment, entirely full of herself and her new power and possession, but looking at his familiar, sweet face, so like Lucille's and so poignantly associated with the golden summer of Venice, she was touched with kindness towards him.

"I'll tell you a dead secret," she said. "You must *never* tell Grandfather, or anyone, but Aunt Eleanor told me tonight that every evening before supper she smokes *two* cigarettes on the quiet, in her office."

He laughed gently.

"I'm glad," he said. "She's lovely, your Aunt Eleanor."

"Well, I was thinking, do you think I could smoke one? Would you let me try one of yours?"

"Oh Fanny! It'll be such fun! Only I do hope mine won't make you sick!"

"I think yours are lovely. Much nicer than the smelly things poor Aunt Eleanor was puffing at tonight!"

"I'd love to offer her a really good cigar one night! Come now—look, don't take so much of it into your mouth! Now, pull—there, easy!"

Fanny coughed a little, and then settled seriously to the experience of smoking a cigarette. She was at pains to do this quietly and without too much comedy. André watched her with amusement.

"What has possessed you suddenly?" he asked. "You would never try the shocking practice in Italy."

She laughed.

"The descent of the mantle," she said. "I have to prepare myself."

"Riddles, Fanny?"

"Yes—riddles tonight. Oh, this is lovely, sitting here!" She felt among the branches of the tree behind her. "The figs aren't ripe yet. They are superb on this tree. You wait."

"I can wait—for figs. They come in their season."

"That's all that anything can do," said Fanny. "No need to sneer at figs!"

"I wasn't sneering. I suppose I was sighing!"

"You—sighing! Oh, dear André!"

The lighthouse beam flashed over her laughing face.

"Glasalla seems to have made a point of breeding beautiful women," he said. "I suppose as an answer, a counter-irritant, to this damned lighthouse! Imagine what it would be like, Fanny, to be very plain and live under this mad beam!"

"Lots of plain people live around—we don't notice it, you know. It's just the lighthouse—it can be helped!"

"You're very grown-up tonight! Very off-hand. Throw your cigarette away."

Fanny leant and watched the little red ember curl its way down to the dark rocks.

"I'm not fond of smoking," she said. "Oh, it's cold! It's lonely here."

André slid off the wall to the mossy steps below where Fanny sat.

"I must take you indoors."

"Yes. I hope Mother is asleep. Perhaps, if she is, Sister Eucharia will let me look at her."

They went down the steps and back between the hieratic artichokes and the heavy apple trees. The night was drenched in dew and silence. Fanny paused half-way down the path, listened and looked towards the house and all about her.

"Thank you for bringing me here today, André. In spite of all the anxiety, in spite of seeing that Mother has been indeed extremely ill, the—the relief of being here is—inexpressible; and, I am happy tonight."

"I have felt that, Fanny. It has puzzled me."

"I should be puzzled too—I'm not."

He took her hand and they walked a few more paces through the still garden. By the iron gate he turned and took her in his arms. He bent and searched her lifted, quiet face.

"Most beautiful," he said. "Oh, Fanny, most beautiful, have mercy!"

"Mercy on us both," she said surprisingly, and kissed him.

He took her to his embrace with astonished but very delicate pleasure; for as his tastes were usually drawn to difficult delights, so was he sensitive in acceptance of them. And Fanny was someone whom he had understood already in Venice to be at once unattainable and irresistible; unattainable, because she was a lady and a very young lady, just out of school, by no means to be dishonoured, but certainly not, for a thousand practical reasons, to be sought in marriage; but irresistible, because she could do no other than delight his spirit and his senses whenever he was in her orbit. However, used as he was to expressing his sensualities delicately, imperiously, but with due regard to the difficulties imposed upon them by varying social and religious codes, he had decided when he left Venice that he must consider his delicious attraction towards Fanny as abortive, and as too dangerous to be worth any momentary sweetness which a more pressing audacity than he had used in Italy might ever extract from it. He had indeed decided that his tenderness for Fanny had in it enough true affection, enough of Lucille's kind of love for her, to make him forswear any attempt at self-gratification which could only hurt her true spirit, while smirching his own credit.

Then, she had returned to Dublin with Lucille; weary, anxious, but carrying all about her for him the sweet remembered light of Venice. He had been angry with himself for being so much moved by seeing her again; but she had fainted in his arms, and he had carried her upstairs, a featherweight, to her bed; today he had driven her south-west across Ireland; and here she was, as ever unattainable and irresistible, and she was in his arms, and this was indeed her exquisite, cool mouth on his.

André had sufficient grace to feel uneasy in one part of his spirit now; but also he had much pagan grace in him, and understood how delightful is the expression, the mutual expression, of human attraction. So he controlled uneasiness, and wondered, and delicately, delicately took and gave delight in this first kiss to Fanny.

For Fanny there was none of such complicated uneasiness, but surprise chiefly that she should be doing that which she had frequently contemplated, in observation of fellow-creatures, as unimaginably difficult. Surprise she felt, but also an amused sense of peace; and indolently almost, her hand running through André's gold hair as if in the habit of years, she thought, felt herself smiling as she thought: 'What a simplification, after all! How easy it is to kiss so dear a face! What fusses we make!'

The stroke of the lighthouse fell harshly on them, and passed and fell again, and fell again. Fanny kept still, and gave as she took the isolated benediction of the long moment. 'I am glad of this extraordinary day,' she thought; 'glad to be here, glad to have seen Mother at last, glad about what Aunt Eleanor has told me. I'm glad I'm going to own Glasalla—oh, André——'

He was looking into her eyes, and she was startled by the dark anxiety in his.

"You're going back to Dublin in the morning, aren't you?" she said.

"I have to," he said.

"Well, don't be troubled," she said. "Thank you for everything, and forgive me for this—impulse."

"Fanny!"

"No. We'll go indoors now. No more. Don't trouble, I tell you, André. There need never be any more of what I know is forbidden to us both—for different reasons——"

"But Fanny——"

"Some day I might try to explain to you why I—why I had to kiss you tonight, André——"

"It was I who had to kiss you——"

"Oh, no! Believe me, if I didn't want it, you'd never kiss me——"

"Fanny, how dare you——" he laughed, and bent over her again.

"For good-night then," she said. "It's been an extraordinary day. Let it have an extraordinary good-night——"

She kissed him slowly, tenderly.

"You are not to trouble, I repeat," she said. "I know your worldly obligations, and for my part I refuse all sworn devotion, anyway. I was glad to kiss you tonight. That's all. Do you understand?"

"No, Fanny; I don't."

"Ah! You're sad. Please, please, André. I was only saying something private and transitory, and conceited!"

"Say it again!"

"I couldn't say exactly that again—no, no—come in! Aunt Eleanor will be panicking. Come, André—good-night."

He kissed her hands, and then he opened the iron gate. Slowly, hand-in-hand they returned to the house, subject to the beating, bright admonition of the lighthouse.

When Fanny was ready for bed, washed, brushed and in her school dressing-gown of blue flannel, she crept from the wing where she slept to the main bedroom corridor. A very small lamp burnt there. She saw that the dressing-room door beside her mother's room stood ajar, with a soft light gleaming through. She went to the open threshold.

Sister Eucharia saw her shadow, and came to meet her.

"Go down and fill this kettle for me, like a good child—with the *well* water, from the stone jar in the larder. And at the same time bring me up a big jug of soft water from the tap, will you?"

Fanny took a candlestick from the table where the little lamp was, lighted it and went downstairs. She was not so familiar with the basement of the house as to move easily through it at midnight by the light of one candle, but she was half aware, as she groped, of a new interest in her breast for the old, worn steps, the smell of damp, the dull glow in the great kitchen range. 'I'll come groping like this, along this very same passage, when I'm old like Aunt Eleanor. Strange. I'll live here. This will be my house. Not many people can see their old age in advance like this.'

She came back, cautiously, carefully, to the dressing-room threshold with her heavy kettle and jug. Sister Eucharia beckoned her in.

"Thank you, child," she whispered. "You are Fanny?"

Fanny nodded.

"She was excited all last night, expecting you today. But what are we to do? The least of us—and your mother is far from that—is so much more than the poor body we fight to protect."

The lean and dark-visaged nun was standing by the open window, the brass crucifix of her rosary beads in her restless hands.

"May I just look at her before I go, Sister Eucharia?"

"It is almost midnight, and I am tired of warning your poor father off this threshold," Sister Eucharia whispered, with a broad smile. "Still, you may just look at her. But not a *sound!* Her sleep is paper-thin—and she needs it! Ah, she needs it!"

The nun took Fanny by the hand and led her round a screen beyond the door into the bedroom. A night-light in a bowl was all that guided the two to Julia's bed. Fanny was saddened for her mother when she saw that immense, enveloping, heavy curtains had at last defeated the unmerciful, beloved lighthouse. 'I sleep to its beat,' Julia had boasted. But not now. Sister Eucharia was seeing to that.

Fanny considered again the extenuated, noble face, lying as if sculpted into the pillow. Very peaceful, full of hope and sweetness it was, as it lay in its tenuous rest. But hardly had her eyes traced the beloved features in the solemn dimness when Sister Eucharia's hand tightened on her elbow and she was led back again behind the screen, into the dressing-room.

"Sit there," the Blue Nun whispered commandingly, and pointed to a small chair by the window. "I have a cup of thin broth heating for you, and I'll put a drop of sedative into it. You have had a very hard day, and you look extremely tired. Sometimes when one is overtired it is necessary, oddly enough, to take a sedative. Sit still now."

The nun fussed deftly with a saucepan and a spirit-lamp. Fanny sat still in obedience and considered the strong, quiet figure. This middle-aged nun was visibly disciplined; she made active and definite movements in this ante-room to where her charge lay only thinly but yet most importantly asleep—but she made them without a sound above the whisper level; she spoke, as fully as she chose and audibly to Fanny, but strictly at whisper level. She was precise as a scientist in her arrangement of sick-room equipment—Fanny took in the orderliness with an appreciation which contained a grateful sense of comfort for her mother. She admired too the physical aspect of this plain, dark Sister Eucharia; most excellent, lean and accurate she looked, stripped of her romantic blue hood and cloak, and bound immaculately in a large white overall and stiff white head-dress. 'To be Sister Eucharia, to be disciplined, impersonal and sure of purpose like her, is to have a vocation,' she thought enviously.

The Blue Nun brought her a little bowl of steaming broth, with a dry biscuit. As she gave it to Fanny she broke into it a small white tablet, and stirred the mixture.

"There!" she said. "That'll quiet you."

Fanny smiled.

"Have I been kicking up a row, Sister Eucharia?"

The Blue Nun smiled slowly back to her.

"How would I know?" she said. "But you look as if you might have been."

Fanny took a spoonful of the broth.

"It's lovely—but it's very hot," she said. "Won't you have some, Sister?"

"No, thank you, child. I had my supper at eleven. I'm going to Holy Communion at eight o'clock Mass in Crahore."

"Ah!"

"You don't go to the Sacraments, your mother tells me."

Fanny lifted her head, surprised.

"Sick people talk of their anxieties in the night, my child. I am only your mother's nurse, and your problems are not my affair. I only mention what your mother has told me, because you strike me as surprisingly young to be so—decisive."

"I'm *not* decisive, Sister Eucharia. Only, I can't do any serious thing unless I'm certain I believe in it. What I am is indecisive, I think."

The Blue Nun sat down and looked attentively at Fanny.

"You seem intelligent, anyway. Too intelligent for me."

Fanny laughed.

"Please don't be ironic!" she said. "It wasn't I who talked about my—indecisions!"

"That is true, child. But I was not being ironic."

"To have a vocation—any kind of vocation, I mean—that must be marvellous! A marvellous help! Is it?"

"Is it?" Sister Eucharia echoed gravely. "I expect it might be useful, in a way."

Fanny stared at the nun's dark face.

"*Must* you make fun of me?" she asked.

"'Sh!" said the Blue Nun, and pointed towards where Julia lay.

Fanny fell silent, compunctiously remembering the place and the hour, and shocked to observe how this tangent or that could carry her attention off from sorrow.

Guiltily, politely, she finished her little bowl of broth in one rapid swallow, and then she stood up.

"Thank you, Sister Eucharia," she said. "That was lovely soup." She paused then and looked at the dark-browed nun whose eyes were fixed on her.

"Mother will recover, Sister Eucharia? Won't she?"

The Blue Nun smiled a little, and busied herself with washing up Fanny's soup-bowl.

"Please, Sister Eucharia—she *will* get better?"

Sister Eucharia turned from her washing-up, the little bowl dripping in her immaculate hands.

"How old are you, Fanny?"

"I was eighteen in April."

"Then you have left school? You are entering life?"

"Yes, Sister Eucharia."

Sister Eucharia dried and polished the little bowl, then slowly dried her beautiful, gleaming hands.

"Your father—he is foolish, poor man. But your aunt is a strong woman. However—since you are compelled to ask me, child, I will answer. Your mother will not recover."

"Will not?" Fanny's whispered words startled even this experienced nun—but more so did the exposed terror of the young, white face.

"I am not your mother's doctor," Sister Eucharia said. "But I have been nursing for thirty-five years. There is no answer now—there will be—but there is no answer now to

237

pernicious anaemia. So your mother must die, my child, and she is dying quickly."

"Dying? But I was talking with her a few hours ago——"

"Yes, thank God. And you may talk with her tomorrow. It is a blessed illness in that it inflicts no agony, but only weakness, and also it leaves intellectual lucidity up to the last short coma. Anaemics die simply of fatigue, Fanny. And if they know they are going they are usually very glad to go. There is no pain; there is only weariness, and frequently they are asleep, just normally asleep, when they die. Your mother is ready—and so——?"

"But—she can't die! Not now! Oh, you're wrong!"

The Blue Nun stroked the crucifix of her rosary.

"Your mother is ready." she said, "and this is her time. Believe me, child, she is dying. Be good now, and pray for her, and for your poor father. Kneel down and say a prayer with me."

"I'm sorry, Sister Eucharia, I—I don't pray."

"You don't pray at all?"

"I pray—if you like—to praise God. I often thank Him for—oh, for sudden things. But I can't pray any more to *ask* for anything."

"I see. That is a dangerous arrogance. It surprises me. But you must work it out. Meantime, could you not kneel down now and praise God with me for your lovely mother, for her good life and her calm, good patience now as she looks at death? You don't have to ask for anything, young lady. So far as I can judge, your dear mother is in no need of *your* intervention between her and Our Blessed Lord."

"Oh! Oh, please—need you sneer?"

"I wasn't sneering. But kneel down now, young intellectual, and just thank God for your mother—that amount of condescension will be something. God is good, you know."

Whipped, humiliated, Fanny knelt down.

"*Te Deum laudamus . . .*" Sister Eucharia began to whisper, and Fanny picked up the familiar antistrophes and gave them back fluently, through tears.

As they knelt and prayed, Joseph came in, grey and lonely, in a grey dressing-gown. He dropped on his knees, and murmured the Latin too.

When the psalm was ended, Fanny got up, smiled at Sister Eucharia, touched her father's bowed head in good-night and went to her room.

* * * * *

At Mespil Road Lucille was restless. On the day when Fanny had been driven away to County Clare by André she had set herself resolutely to walking about and getting the shape and quality of Dublin, and in so doing had been distracted and refreshed. And in the late evening, strolling in the environs of Mespil Road with Joey—Joey already too much her admirer—she had gone round, as André had desired her to, to inspect the little house off Leeson Park which her brother had rented. His valet from Charleroi, in command here, had welcomed Mademoiselle Lucille and Monsieur Joey with great pleasure, had served them with exquisite coffee and *fine*, and had shown them over the extremely pretty little Regency house with enthusiasm. Etienne was enchanted by Dublin, and amusingly surprised that his master had found therein so elegant a dwelling, and that in fact one could actually live, and eat, and drink, elegantly in Ireland. Certainly Number Two Rosetta Terrace was a pretty little house, but clearly it was expensive. Joey whistled softly as he considered its amenities, and Lucille, saying nothing, reflected on some of Patrice's aphorisms about his brother, and wondered why André required so much *chic* in a simple, friendly town. However, that was his own affair, a question of taste. Lucille might have said, if pressed, that to require so much elegance was bad taste. Certainly it occurred to her, as she studied her brother's expensive setting for a brief bachelor year in a simple, beautiful city, that he was, he must be, the least likeable member of their family. Her mother might be absurd in hotels and with head-waiters, but she was homely; her father was an imperious man who could do without any material comfort, or could perversely make hell for those who denied him a sudden whim; Patrice was spoilt, impatient and hypersensitive, but could be all of those things in a slum as he was in his father's ordered house, and cared not a damn for order. She herself would not like slum life—but she detested *chic*, save in its accidents. She detested the presentation, the pathetic fuss, of people who were 'elegant'. So she smelt in André's little Dublin house that part of André that she distrusted—the 'public' André, the success, the picturesque, self-flattering bachelor. 'It is a pity he is posturing like this in a nice place like Dublin,' she thought wearily. 'A room in a good hotel would have been more suitable. But I suppose that Patrice would tell me that our elder brother always has to have his decorative private life. And, in a way, so much the better, because undoubtedly if there is one thing likely to turn Fanny against him it is all this excessive interest in his own comfort, his own *décor*.'

Joey was impressed, however, and, while anxious to convey to Lucille that he was very serious, yet was troubled by the atmosphere of wordliness which the French manservant, even more than the gay little house, had conveyed. Indeed as they walked home down Mespil Road together Joey did not know what he ought to think or feel. All he did know was that Mademoiselle Lucille was beautiful, beautiful to madden a man. But he knew no way of saying that, or of managing the pain of not saying it.

So the two parted, in most friendly politeness, in the breakfast-room, and Lucille went to the kitchen to drink cocoa with Lizzie and Nora—and Belladonna.

Lizzie and Nora were not cheerful about the mistress. Old Dr. Redmond had been in that evening to see to Nora's varicose vein, and he told them he didn't think much of what the two specialists had had to say. But he had great faith in prayer—and he thought, and Nora and Lizzie agreed with him, that a good novena now to Blessed Margaret Mary A La Coq—'the Sacred Heart was revealed to her, you know, Miss Lucille'—and then, maybe, if the mistress got her strength up a little, if the master could maybe take her to Lourdes later on—anyway, that was Dr. Redmond's opinion, and there could be no better, said Lizzie to Nora.

During the sad, late twilight of the next day, an old priest stumped in out of the garden to the breakfast-room, where Lucille, tired from lonely sight-seeing, was sitting by the fire and drinking strong tea, to which she was becoming addicted.

She stood up; the old priest stared at her in vague resentment.

"I don't know you," he said. "I'm the Morrows' parish priest. Name of Whelan. Canon Whelan."

"Oh—I'm sorry, Canon—I'm only a visitor from Brussels, a friend of Fanny's. All the family, except Joey, are away in County Clare."

"So I hear." The Canon sat down, leant on his umbrella, and looked at Lucille. He laughed sharply. "And do you know," he said, "I've had a couple of old harrapins in already this very day to tell me that Joey Morrow has a French-woman installed here, in the tragic absence of his parents!"

The old man threw back his head and snorted fiercely.

Lucille was at a loss. Her English was good, but the Canon's rapidity and adenoidal Dublin way of speech confused her. Yet she had gathered his drift—without catching his mood; and she did not propose to offend the old man.

"I am a school friend of Fanny's, Canon," she said. "I wanted to go direct to Glasalla with Fanny, where her mother is ill. But I thought it better to let her go there alone, and wait for her instructions. That is how Joey has installed me here!"

She laughed, and the old priest laughed louder.

"Good girl! Sure I was only trying you on! Not that it isn't true about those old damsels! But, dear and blessed God, wouldn't it be an ease if we could push a few of those into that quiet old canal?"

"I think there are a lot of people who should be pushed into canals," said Lucille.

"Yes; you and I think so. But God doesn't. That's what makes it tiring to be a priest, I may as well tell you. That from the human standpoint you can't be bothered with God's mercy—but, if you are his priest, you have to try to be, God save us! It's a weary business."

Lucille hesitated.

"I should have thought," she said slowly, "that being a priest brought compensations with its anxieties——"

The old man groaned.

"Colleagues tell me that. Holy men. I can only say that I find humanity impossible—and if that is the sin against the Holy Ghost . . ." Canon Whelan paused and out of his pale

241

old eyes stared about the room. "How often I have argued with her, here and above in her drawing-room, about the sins against the Holy Ghost! Dear Julia! Ah, how is she? Is she gone?"

"Gone?"

"Is it over? I heard today from old Redmond that there's no hope at all, that it's a matter of hours."

"Oh, no Canon Whelan. So far as I know there is still hope of her recovery."

"That isn't true, my child. Julia's time has come, untimely. What foxes me is how to pray for her. She used to argue with me about prayer—prayer, I mean, for special things, or for named people. She said all such labelled prayers were nonsense——"

"Did she? That's strange."

"Why is it strange—I mean, why do you say it is strange?"

"She was very orthodox, I understand?"

"Oh, with her children ruthlessly so, thanks be to God. Never a word to left or right allowed—only the teaching of the Church. But Julia was, is, an absolute believer. Don't misunderstand me. It's only that she was always a bit austere and choosey about the principles involved in prayer. She absolutely hated that prayers should be said for any ordinary necessity. I always told her that was conceited of her."

"What did she say to that?"

"Oh!" the old man sighed. "She was clever. Once she said about that that I missed her point, but that even for argument's sake she couldn't be so conceited as to claim that her idea had to do with humility. She could confuse you, that Julia."

"I've never met her. She sounds very like Fanny."

"Fanny is like her. But Fanny will venture further in life, I think, and maybe fare worse. Julia's life hasn't been bad —and she has liked it." The old man stared about him again, as if trying to memorize the shadowy, familiar room. "I'm tired. Could I have a glass of whisky, child?"

Lucille, shocked at her stupidity, leapt to her feet, and ran to summon Lizzie.

"Ah, sure, is it the Canon? God help us, the poor old saint!"

242

In a moment the charged salver was at his side, and Lizzie was his minister.

The old priest found a cheerful mood for the old servant. He lifted his glass.

"How is the bride, Lizzie? How is the grand young Mrs. O'Connor?"

But, oddly, Lizzie did not make a routine answer.

"I don't know, Canon," she said. "God bless her, I don't know."

"Well, here's to her, and to her dear, dear mother!"

Lizzie dabbed her eyes with her apron and hurried back to the kitchen.

The Canon sipped his whisky.

"Do you know at all, are they going to let her die in Glasalla? If they do, that'll mean she'll be buried with the Delahunts, in Crahore."

"That would be natural, I suppose."

"Maybe. At my age it's a terrible journey, from here to Glasalla. But, as her parish priest——"

"Oh, surely, Canon, at your age. . . ?"

"Never mind my age, young lady—the Morrows have been important parishioners here for about eighty years—so one doesn't offend them. . . . Ah, Julia! Ah, God help her now and in her last agony. . . ."

The room was deeply dark.

Lizzie came in with a taper and lighted the shaded gas-brackets over the fireplace.

The old priest blinked.

"Damned excessive, this acetylene gas! However, good-night, Lizzie, and thank you."

"God bless you, Canon sir. Good-night."

The old priest levered himself into standing by means of his umbrella.

"I hate funerals," he said. "Well, it's time I was home. Time we were all at home——"

He wandered out through the glass door into the twilight of the garden.

At supper Joey begged Lucille eagerly to come with him to Herbert Park, to the Exhibition. There was to be some especial display of fireworks, and in general he was anxious to be gay tonight and to show her the wonders of the Somali village, the water chute and the coloured fountains. But she was tired; she did not choose to sadden the boy with report of the old Canon's visit, and it was clear that he was confident and happy about his mother's progress back to health. But his exuberance bored her, as did also the fatuous admiration of her that his too easy eyes expressed.

"No, Joey; thank you very much. But I'm tired. Another night, yes. You go, please, by all means. But I have letters to write, and also I think André may turn up——"

"Yes—I thought he might be here when I got back——"

"He was due back at his office this evening."

"Well, a chap in our office saw the car—you know it's famous?—in Nassau Street this afternoon."

"That's where his office is, isn't it?"

"Yes. So he's sure to be in to see you when he's through with business."

"I'm anxious for news from Fanny."

"Of course. I understand, Mademoiselle Lucille. Any other night will do for the Exhibition."

"Oh, but you go, Joey! You must!"

"But—would you mind?"

"I'd be most unhappy if you didn't."

"It's only—they say the new fireworks tonight are going to be extraordinary! Oh, Mademoiselle! I don't think it would be polite of me to go off and leave you!"

"I think it would be most impolite of you to turn me into some kind of dreadful nuisance by having to stay at home on my behalf!"

He laughed.

"Well, there is that!"

"So please, Joey, have sense. I *don't* want to go to the Exhibition, and you do. I want to see André. So why can't each of us have what we want?"

"You're sure you won't be lonely? Say André is late in turning up?"

"I couldn't be lonely with Lizzie and Nora to talk to."

"You're nice, Mademoiselle. My goodness, you're natural!"

"Did you expect me to be unnatural?"

"Oh stop it! You know what I mean!"

So, supper ended, Joey, as much in love with the fantasies and ebulliences at Herbert Park as he was with the beautiful exotic Lucille, raced off from the latter with some regrets, but in anticipation of a variety of pleasures, nevertheless. For he was only a boy, however regrettably he contained within him the makings of a chartered accountant. And Lucille saw him go with relief, and waited for André, and read *Villette* by lamplight, sitting on the velvet sofa in the drawing-room, while Belladonna purred about her feet.

* * * * *

Nine o'clock rang from some far-away tower. Saddened by the lovely sadness of *Villette,* Lucille removed Belladonna gently from where she slept on her ankles, and crossed the room to the wide-open window. Stars rode high and proudly over Herbert Place, and the canal lay drenched in light; the full moon, which she could not see, must be sailing up from the south-east.

'I'll walk up Leeson Park to Rosetta Terrace,' she said to herself. 'I must hear how things are with Fanny. Silly of him not to call in.'

She threw a coat over her shoulders in the lower hall, and called to Lizzie that she was going for a walk and would not be long.

There was a light gleaming through the elegant fanlight of André's hall door, and light filtered through the silk curtains of his drawing-room window. As Lucille rang the bell she turned a handle in the door, and found that it opened. So she was in the dim, pretty hall when André came to receive her. She flung down her coat.

"Welcome, dear Lucille!" Her brother kissed her. "Etienne is out, and I had to get my own supper. Otherwise I'd have been round to see you earlier. Come in——"

"I'm anxious for news——"

"Naturally. So was Mrs. O'Connor——"

Lilian was standing by the silk-hung window, tall and lovely.

Lucille felt disconcerted, even countrified, but instantly nevertheless she began to think fast, and angrily.

"Oh, Lucille—how fortunate you came round," said Lilian, with beautiful grace. "I was about to ask your brother to take me down to Mespil Road—we've all been so anxious for the Glasalla news!"

"Yes," said Lucille. "I was expecting you ages ago, André. I couldn't wait any longer. How is the situation? How is Fanny, André?"

"Fanny is still hopeful, like her father, I think," said André. "But Miss Delahunt, and Dr. O'Curry whom I saw for a minute this morning, are in no doubt that Mrs. Morrow is dying——"

"Oh! Oh God!" said Lucille.

Lilian twisted her lovely hands together.

"All through the summer it was frightening," she said. "Why can't they do *something* for her? It isn't as if she had a disease!"

"She has a disease, O'Curry says," said André. "They haven't a cure for this disease of her blood. They can't halt it."

'So,' thought Lucille; and looked about her. Beyond the archway in the inner room she could see candle-lit débris of supper on a lace-clothed table. Figs and silver knives and bread and roses. Here in the lamp-lit foreground all the apparatus of coffee-making; champagne, opened, in a silver cooler; the exquisite smell of Turkish tobacco; roses, more roses drooping, and a pretty fire in the pretty grate. 'No wonder you could not come round earlier, André,' she thought; but still she was unable and unwilling to assemble the evidence, might it be, of a dreadful thing.

"May I make you some coffee, Lucille?" asked André.

"No, thank you."

He indicated the champagne, in an impertinent kind of invitation.

"No, thank you; nothing," said Lucille. Almost she admired his unapologetic coolness in this odd situation, and certainly she admired the serenity of Lilian. So sure was this that it seemed as if indeed there was no explanation of the position save that Julia's eldest child had come round impetuously to André for the Glasalla news. Almost, against the evidence of supper and luxury and indolence and roses,

246

almost such evidence might be accidental, a routine of André's life in which briefly Lilian found herself pausing, on her way home, to hear about her mother. Certainly it was a relief, even if only to immediate tension, that neither Lilian nor André was offering excuse for their being together in his house at ten o'clock of night. For that restraint Lucille saluted both; and their outward ease made her withold her racing surmise, her fear, her indignation. Nevertheless she was startled; and, inexplicably, as she surveyed these two perhaps guiltless worldlings, so elegant, so graceful before her uncertain, assessing eyes, she was filled with anxiety for Fanny, with hungry tenderness for one, her friend, who was so alike to this present beauty, and so blessedly, gently, her opposite.

"Well, since now we have Lucille with us and don't have to go to Mespil Road, perhaps you'll be so good as to drive us home?" said Lilian to André. "Or shall I send for a cab?"

"By no means," said André. "The car is just up the road. I'll drive you both home at once."

So it was done.

When the Mercedes turned in at the gate of Lilian's mansion in Stillorgan Road, the young matron invited the two de Mellins to come in—"You haven't seen my poor, raw house, Lucille—do come in a minute and advise me——"

Lucille decided she would go in. She wanted to see Michael again. She was interested and alarmed.

But there was no Michael. It seemed that he had had to go to England on urgent business connected with the oncoming Horse Show. He had left on the evening boat, and would be away for three days—Lilian had seen him off at Kingstown, and now here—"This always happens when he's just gone," she said amusedly—here was a great box of white roses, and hidden in them a little velvet box with a diamond inside, a starry clasp. And some message, over which she smiled.

"Dear Michael," she said. And her guests murmured admiration of the roses and the jewel. Lucille did not look at André, but kept her eyes on Lilian, who was imperturable, pleased and beautiful. She handed the roses to her parlour-

247

maid, and ordered more lights to be brought to the drawing-room.

"Heavens, how grand you are!" said Lucille, not without mischief in her voice.

Lilian seemed to catch the mockery.

"Dublin doesn't have to be all shabbiness, Lucille," she said. "And after all, what's a bit of our grandeur to you de Mellins?"

"*Touchée*," said Lucille. "But we overdo it, you know. Still, this is a superb, great *salon*. You'll have to sharpen your wits, Lilian, and become a *salonnière*!" She felt with pleasure the exasperation of the self-centred beauty to whom she spoke, but she never could care whether or not she annoyed Lilian. She stroked a curtain. "Is this the famous silk from Milan?" she asked.

Lilian looked surprised, but André was ready.

"Yes, indeed it is!" he said. "It got here with miraculous safety. I think I forgot to tell you," he said to Lilian. "but there was quite a lot of telephone fuss about it, and your silk was news on the *Piazza* one night in Venice!"

"Ah! Anyway it's lovely—even if Michael was a bit staggered by the bill!" She turned from a salver the parlour-maid had brought in. "*Fine? Grappa?* What will you have, Lucille?"

"Nothing, thank you."

"*Grappa* for me," said André.

"How on earth do you know about *grappa* in Dublin?" asked Lucille.

"You have a poor opinion of us," said Lilian. "But anyway we learn as we go."

She brought a glass to André.

Lucille, watching the two as they smiled to each other, was suddenly inundated with wild and bitter sorrow. The vulgarity of the beautiful pair in their shocking concern with themselves smote her for a second violently. All around lay the lost, dark world, all its revealed and hidden pains, all its fears, its sins, its agonies and crimes; and close up, close in to Lilian's very breast lay the imminent, lonely death of her mother; close in to even Lilian's cold mind must lie the present knowledge of her father's woe, of Fanny's waiting and Aunt Eleanor's, and of the fear, the solemn wonder in which her mother must be now from hour to hour engaged. And André, who had wooed and weakened Fanny all through the Italian summer, André who had got between Fanny and herself, who had set Patrice's nerves on edge, who had taken Fanny home to Glasalla in this grave time, and who had seemed too dangerously to care for her—here now he bowed and smiled with exquisite unconcern before Fanny's beautiful sister, and in vulgarly elegant settings which expressed the vulgar egotism of the two who graced them.

"Oh God!" said Lucille out loud. "You don't have to drive me home, André. I'm sure I can find my way. But will you help me to make arrangements to get to Glasalla tomorrow?"

André's impeccably sweet manner put his sister in the wrong at once.

"Of course, Lucille," he said. "Don't be silly. I'll drive you home this instant. And of course I'll drive you to Glasalla in the morning!"

His gentle tone confounded her. She covered her face and cried.

"Lucille! Lucille!" said Lilian gently. "Oh, Lucille, you're tired!"

"I'm anxious for Fanny," she sobbed.

"Come on, dearest. I'll take you home," said André.

Lilian found her coat and put it round her.

"Tell Lizzie to give her a sedative, in hot milk," she said to André. "Don't cry, Lucille. Good-night."

Lilian kissed her and André tucked her into the car.

They drove to Mespil Road in silence.

André took her in through the glass door of the breakfast-room. Lizzie and Nora were there in the gaslight. They looked anxious.

"There's a telegram for you, Mademoiselle Lucille," said Lizzie.

Lucille opened the telegram.

'Mother is dying rapidly,' she read. 'Tell them all there is no hope now and come quickly if you can love Fanny.'

André took the telegram and read it carefully and clearly to Lizzie and Nora. Neither made a sound or said a word, but both went down on their knees and made the sign of the cross. Lucille looked at them; then she picked up Belladonna, and knelt down with Lizzie and Nora and made the sign of the cross.

André took and folded the telegram.

"I'll go and tell Lilian," he said. "Be ready to start early."

On the morning after her arrival at Glasalla Fanny slept almost into the full noon. Aunt Eleanor bent over her at ten o'clock and at eleven, and although a high, hot sun was streaming through the thin curtains of the little room, there was no stir in Fanny, and Eleanor could not decide to wake her. But at half-past eleven young Mr. Hallinan of Ennis was in her office, about various matters of business, he having been at the District Court in Doon Point, only to find the R.M. was ill and that his time was wasted. So he had whipped up his high-stepping cob and made a side-turn for Glasalla and Miss Delahunt.

So Eleanor sent Honoria up to Fanny's room, with instructions that the child was to be in the office within twenty minutes. And she employed some of those minutes in explaining to Mr. Hallinan that here and on that day she desired Fanny to sign some rough-drafted paper, however hypothetical, which secured her ownership, if possible in escape of death duties, of Glasalla.

"But what is the hurry, Miss Eleanor? I understand your niece is eighteen——"

"Yes—but at eighteen you can inherit, surely?"

"Indeed, yes. But with provisos. Why not wait for her majority?"

"I want it made certain. Even if she cannot be full owner now, I want her to have signed for this inheritance and to be sure of it. It isn't only, Mr. Hallinan, that my dear sister's suddenly desperate illness—and she is three years younger than I—has made me question my own tenure on life. It is that I believe my niece to have some powers, some intellectual talents, which will have to be educated. The father has neither the means nor the desire to give her such freedom of education. He has sons, he is not rich, and he is selfish and sentimental about his daughter. I want, therefore, to put a weapon in her hand, at the right time. Three or four years from now would be too late. Education, to be vital, should flow onward from school. It would be an arid, staccato business, to start one's self-education when one had fought out into the twenties—having fussed round over Father in the intervening years! Don't you agree?"

Young Mr. Hallinan laughed gently.

"I don't agree at all, Miss Delahunt," he said. "I see no harm in a nice young lady 'fussing round over Father'—and as to self-education——!"

"Well, so be it! Your opinion is only that of a sweet and silly young man, Mr. Hallinan! But I desire my niece to have in her hand as from today a weapon of independence which she will use or not, as she may choose, in the immediate years, not to say months. So, as I have told you before, I desire you to draft some document which, when Fanny signs it, will mean that before the law, and before any bank manager on earth, she is the owner of Glasalla."

"I can arrange that, of course, Miss Delahunt. You are the unencumbered owner of Glasalla, and it is perfectly simple for you to transfer your ownership to your niece. But, does that niece require a large, difficult property in Co. Clare —and how is possession of such property going to forward her education, as you call it? How is it going to be a weapon in her hand?"

"It is unencumbered. It is insured and valued for six thousand pounds. So—she can encumber it, surely, if she likes, for a thousand or two, with which to educate herself?"

"Unwise," said young Mr. Hallinan.

"I knew you'd say that," said Eleanor. "All the same, I'd have hoped for better sense from you. Your father would have spoken closer to the point, young man. Anyway, keep your opinion, and produce a right piece of paper. Time presses, in a sense you don't understand—and I desire Fanny to be the owner of Glasalla at once. So have a drink now——" she waved to the decanters Honoria had brought in—"and rough out a rudimentary bill of inheritance——"

He laughed.

"You're grandiose, Miss Eleanor!"

"What harm? Get to work, young fellow. I'll have my

inheritor awake and down here in ten minutes. And I hope you'll take luncheon here?" With these words she strode from the study. Young Mr. Hallinan looked after her with a broad smile. Like his father, he was very fond of Miss Delahunt. He poured himself a drink, lighted a cigarette, and set to work.

So, at noon on the day on which her mother was to die, Fanny became the owner of Glasalla.

Late in the afternoon, after anxious, quiet hours in which the news had been that Julia was asleep and that no one must disturb her, Fanny, carrying up Sister Guadalupe's tea-tray to the dressing-room, had found her father seated on the window-ledge of the great landing, and crying with a childish, weary control that smote her fearfully.

"It's all right, Fan," he said. "Go on up."

"Oh, what is it, Father?"

He covered his face and shuddered.

When Fanny set down the tray in the dressing-room, Sister Guadalupe came to her.

"Thank you, Fanny," she said.

"Father is crying," said Fanny.

"I know," said Sister Guadalupe.

"How is she, Sister Guadalupe?"

The little old nun stared at her, and then sighed slowly.

"She is dying," she said. "Haven't you understood that? Your aunt has, at least."

"I've understood too—in a way. But——"

"There is no 'but' now, my child. Perhaps she will breathe for another six hours, perhaps another ten——"

"Oh! Oh Mother!"

"Quiet, if you please, my child."

"I'm sorry, Sister Guadalupe."

"Your aunt has sent for Dr. O'Curry and for Father Brosnan. But neither is needed, may I say? Your mother is dying beautifully and naturally. None of us can help her now, and there's none of us she wants. That upsets your father, poor man. He can't understand that she's all right, that she's travelling naturally, and has forgotten him, and doesn't require him at all——"

"Ah, but, dear Father——"

252

"Yes, of course. Only she's past all that. Believe me, she's dying beautifully, as she should——"

Fanny heard a long sobbing breath from the next room; the sound frightened her, and she looked for help to Sister Guadalupe.

"Don't mind," said the old nun. "Breath is difficult in our latter end. But she isn't noticing that. She's gone forward, child. Our Blessed Lord is taking charge of her——"

"May I go to her?"

"Not now," said Sister Guadalupe. "I'll call you soon. But I'll be with her—don't be afraid. She's in no trouble. She's happy indeed, God bless her. Let you go down, like a good child, and have a telegram sent to the children in Dublin. Well, wait below till the doctor comes—but then he'll tell you to say she's on her way. She is, the good creature. She'll be looking into the face of God in a very few hours—and what greater joy could you wish her, child? 'Sh now, and away with you. I must go in to the pet, God help her——"

Dr. O'Curry came and, in Grandfather's study, told them all, Grandfather, Joseph, Eleanor and Fanny, that Julia must die within the succeeding ten or twelve hours. Father Brosnan, experienced, grey-haired priest, was standing in the room as the young doctor spoke his verdict, but Fanny thought that even he, wise-faced man, must have been amazed by the effect of the not unexpected news on Grandfather. Because the old, frail man stared for a second at Dr. O'Curry, his blue eyes empty as if he was about to become insane.

"She'll die tonight?" he cried. "Julia, my darling, will die tonight? Oh, how dare you, sir! How could that be? *I* wait for death! It's my turn and I insist on it! Yet you come cawing that my lovely child must go and I hang on! Oh, out, out of the house, you crazy little fellow! Out and be gone—I want to die, I tell you! Have you no brains! Can't you let me die, in my right time?"

Dr. O'Curry crossed the room in two strides. Gently, lightly he took the screaming old Grandfather in his arms. He took the old man firmly, masterfully and pressed him into quiet.

"Mr. Delahunt," he said, "good, dear, sweet Mr. Delahunt, don't you know that we'd all do anything to spare you this, and let you go first? Now listen—I promise you it won't be long. Sure, the way you're going on, sir, you might nearly be off with her tomorrow! God's truth, you might!"

"He's right, Father," said Eleanor. "Quiet now—it won't be long——"

Fanny could hardly suppress a smile as she watched the young little doctor stroking her grandfather's fluffy white hairs, as if they were a girl's silky locks.

"There now, Mr. Delahunt," Dr. O'Curry said. "Mrs. Morrow is absolutely peaceful—and when your turn comes —any day now, sir!—I hope you'll be half the man she is!"

Father Brosnan came and took the old man from the doctor's arms.

"Did you hear what he said, my friend?" he said jocosely. "You'd better be getting ready——"

Fanny watched this scene with amusement, but also with a feeling of tender gratitude towards Doctor O'Curry. She surmised that she would seldom in life see a young man do anything kinder and more surprising than take her screaming old grandfather in his arms and stroke his wandering white hairs.

When the young doctor was gone, Fanny gave her telegram for Lucille to Cornelius, to take to the village. Father Brosnan said that he would stay awhile.

"I know she's confessed and ready, Eleanor, but I think I'll anoint her again. I've never known, if there was a gleam of consciousness, that the words of the Viaticum didn't help. And anyway, I'd like to be with her, and be sure that the necessary prayers are in her ears."

Joseph, who had been sitting in pitiful stillness, sprang up with a groan.

"I must go to her," he cried, and ran from the room as if someone had whipped him.

"Stay with Father, will you, Father Brosnan?" Eleanor said. "Do have a drink——" she waved towards the salver. "There'll be supper soon——"

"It's only those cats," said Father Brosnan. "You know I can't stand them!"

"Oh, stand them tonight," said Eleanor imperiously. "Come, Fanny—I want to talk to you in my office."

In the office Eleanor lighted her illicit cigarette with eagerness; tremblingly almost she poured herself her glass of sherry. But, sherry untasted, cigarette undrawn, she sat and laid her head on her orderly desk.

"Julia!" she whispered. "Oh, Julia, please, oh please, please, Julia!"

Two hours later, supper over and the lighthouse in its nightly command of Glasalla, Sister Eucharia summoned the household to Julia's death-bed.

"Si ambulam in medio umbrae mortis, non timebo mala. . . ."

Fanny listened, and wondered why Father Brosnan was repeating this especial psalm. But perhaps he knew her mother, and chose his words to assert her quality now. . . . *"Alleluja, Alleluja—In te, Domine, speravi, non confundas in aeternam. . . ."*

Ah, what tranquillity! What noble peace! Fanny stood near her mother's bedside, and was certain that Julia heard and understood the words Father Brosnan said. He said them carefully, gently. Julia's white lips moved as if she strove to say them too.

Incredible—a foolish dream—to be standing at Mother's death-bed. But watching the beloved eyelids Fanny understood that darkness, in human terms an absolute and frightening, lonely darkness, weighed them down, and that they would not rise again.

"Julia!" Joseph cried.

The eyelids stirred, vainly. Julia gave a great, strange sigh.

"Lilian," she whispered. "Oh Lilian——"

"Speak to *me*, Julia!" Joseph cried.

"Lilian—child—I beg you——"

The eyelids folded, for ever. Without another attempt at breath Julia was gone.

Sister Eucharia bent over her. So did Father Brosnan, as the nun lifted her head, and took her outflung hands and folded them.

"Requiem aeternam dona...."

"Ah, so—my lovely Julia——" said Eleanor.

"No, no!" Grandfather screamed. But Eleanor put her arms about him, and almost carried him into the dressing-room and down the stairs. Joseph fell on his knees beside the bed.

Fanny stood and looked at her mother.

"Is she gone—really gone?" she asked.

"Yes. God bless her—it's over," said Sister Eucharia.

"She wanted to speak to Lilian," said Fanny.

But Father Brosnan went on, in a soft mutter, with Latin prayers.

"What can I do now, Sister Eucharia?" asked Fanny.

"Go down and tell them in the kitchen, child, and have Cornelius send a telegram to Dublin—and have tea made for everyone, including myself."

Fanny stared at the dear, folded face.

Sister Eucharia almost pushed her away.

"Do as I say, Miss," she said—"and tea for everyone at once."

CHAPTER ELEVEN

VIGIL

IN THE morning Fanny, at the dining-room window, saw one of the Doon Point barouches, the best one of all, Micky Marrinan's, come up the drive in the sunlight, red-nosed Micky on the box, whip in hand. Forgetting everything, she jumped for pleasure. From as far back as memory reached, the Doon Point barouches were symbols of excitement, picnic, pleasure, festival, fun. But in a second, as Micky drew up with style before the steps, she recollected herself. He brought the children, with Aunt Edith; here came pale, thin Stephen, fat Cockle and sweet Muscle, having driven in morning light along the cliff road from Doon Point, because Mother was dead. She saw Aunt Eleanor descend the steps; she turned away from the window. Often in Italy she had thought lovingly of these young ones, especially of amusing Muscle, her secret pet. Now she must wait; by no means was she ready for their dear faces now.

By noon all was in ceremonious order. Knots of black crape fluttered correctly from the front and back gates of Glasalla, and also from the knocker of the hall door, and the back doors. All of these were set wide open to the beautiful August day, and the dusty, long-forgotten Venetian blinds were carefully lowered behind the open windows of the house. A lovely green light, dust-laden, streamed thereafter in long shafts across the rooms. The noonday silence was so deep that the familiar Angelus bell from the Mercy Convent actually startled Aunt Eleanor as she sat in her office, writing telegrams.

"Ah, of course! Twelve. The breeze must be from the north-east. I hadn't noticed."

She went on with her telegrams.

'Mère Générale, Sainte Famille, Place des Ormes, Brussels,' she wrote, *'Chère Mère, Julia est partie en paix nous exigeons tous vos saintes prières Eleanor Delahunt.'*

In the early afternoon the tide of local kindliness was on the flow—flowers, notes, callers of high degree and low, were on their way to mourn Julia Delahunt. Fanny, stricken by the children's helpless woe, suggested to Stephen, who knew something of sea-birds and sea-anemones, that he scramble down to the Golden Rocks; she asked Honoria to take Cockle to the kitchen to help her, and then she put her arm round little, slender Muscle.

"Come, pet," she said. "We'll go and see Corney in the harness-room. He's busy today—there's a lot of things you could do for him."

She felt Muscle shaking; she had had the impression that he was shaking all through dinner. But, talkative as he always was, she had not heard his voice since he had reached Glasalla. Now, as they passed under the big yard-arch, he began to whisper. She bent down.

"Yes, Muscle?"

He buried his head against her.

"Father was—was upset," he sobbed. "But I—I couldn't go in to see her! The others did. But I'm afraid! Oh, Fan, I'm afraid!"

Fanny stroked his head.

"I know, I know," she said. "Darling Muscle, that's all right. You don't have to see her, love—she looks simply lovely—there, there—remember her the way you last saw her, pet——"

"She looked very sick that time."

"Well, she doesn't now. She's finished with being sick, Muscle—Oh, here's Corney!"

"Ah, is it Master Muscle before me? Well, look at the size of you, for God's sake! Is it as tall as the house you're going to be on us, young laddo?"

"He wants to give you a hand, Corney——"

Corney bent and lifted the slight boy to his shoulder. Muscle was still crying; the big man stroked his head and nodded with sorrow in his face to Fanny. Then he carried the child off towards the loose-boxes.

The afternoon wore on.

Handsome and helpful, Aunt Edith Morrow took charge in the drawing-room behind the silver tea service, and received for the family the sighs and hand-pressures of the 'carriage class'; Joseph, wandering like a ghost from garden to house, and from the hall to Julia's bedroom, did his best in fits and starts to recognize old acquaintances and reply to their kind murmurs; but Father Brosnan was in the house and looked after the courtesies—dining-room hospitalities of sherry or whisky-and-soda—which were correct for such callers as the Rector, Colonel Standish, old Jack Sheridan and so on. (Dr. O'Curry had called at one o'clock, given Grandfather a merciful, strong sedative, and forced him to swallow a bowl of soup. So the old man was deeply asleep on the sofa in his darkened study, his two cats sleeping with him.) Eleanor had sometimes momentarily to face some particularly good neighbour or old friend; this she did with a great air of courtesy and with icy calm.

The friends who were hard to face, the ones who had known Julia and Eleanor from birth and who were able to express their feelings, came up and down the stairs from the kitchen, led by Honoria or Mrs. Hession, or by Corney's Kate, to take a last look at Miss Julia, God bless her, and to say a prayer. From these and from the love in their eyes Eleanor had to flee again and again into her office. These were her people, her friends among whom she worked; these could speak to her and they knew that she had undergone this day a mortal loss. Before what they would say to her of Julia she would be helpless. Later they must say it, and later it might be balm, even a kind of music against loneliness. But today these who were her very own, of her own faith and blood, these from Crahore and Kilmahon, from the shops and the farms and the Convent and the fisheries around the lighthouse, these people who could measure her pain must hold her excused in their mercy from the eloquent understanding they brought to her sorrowing house. And indeed she knew they did, and that all they had come for today was to look a last time at Julia, say a prayer for her and have a mournful cup of tea with Honoria and Mrs. Hession. All through the evening and the night these scores of friends of Glasalla would come and go, whispering and grave, and tea would be drunk and porter, and snuff and clay-pipes would be enjoyed, and many a rosary said, and many a *De Profundis*. Julia would be waked, quietly and as was fitting, in her father's house. Eleanor was glad to know that. There would be sorrow all night, ceremonious and vigilant, in Glasalla.

Fanny stood at the dressing-room window, and absently considered the garden through the uneven slats of the old blind. 'I'll get her some flowers in the morning,' she thought. She had been keeping vigil awhile by her mother's bed, watching the quiet women tiptoe in and kneel and pray, and lay their bunches of flowers on the floor. Some bent over and kissed Julia's hair; all came and pressed Fanny's hand. All said: "She looks beautiful, God bless her."

But now the Protestant Rector had come up, and behind him the Reverend Mother from the Convent, and some ladies Fanny did not know had brought up wreaths. The two rooms and the corridor were already oppressively enriched with flowers; the sharp-scented flowers of early

August, from all the surrounding sea-girt gardens—carna
tions, asters, roses, early dahlias, early Michaelmas. Fanny
closed her eyes, and leant against the dusty blind. She had
not slept the night before, and felt now as if afloat, as if
without weight; indeed in the craving of her young body
to be asleep at once almost she believed she was asleep. She
was not sure.

"Fanny!"

"Yes, Father?"

Joseph was standing near her and in his hands he had
some roses and green branches.

"I was looking for flowers for her," he said. "I have to give
her my own flowers, you know. I couldn't order any of those
wreath-things."

"Of course not, dear Father."

"But—it's how to make them look right?—You see—" he
sat down and looked up at his daughter, his flowers and
leaves carefully held. His face was grey. "—You see, I was
looking for things she'd understand, from me. I got this
rosemary," he touched it, "and ivy—she loved these little
young, tight trails of ivy—I hope I got the nicest ones? What
do you think? And I know she was devoted to this especial
rose—you see its golden centre? Often and often she told me
its name! Oh God!"

"Aunt Eleanor will know its name, Father."

He looked almost delighted.

"To be sure she will! And then you see I couldn't resist
the lavender. She worshipped it. But—is that an awful
mix-up, Fanny?"

Fanny looked at him out of pure love.

"Father, it's—oh, Father, she'll be so deeply grateful to
you!"

Joseph's grey head bent over, and his daughter saw tears
splash on to his flowers.

"Help me to put them together for her—will you?"

Fanny looked at the flowers.

"They are together, Father. If you like, we'll just tie them,
with some thread—so that they won't get mixed with any
other flowers."

He looked up gratefully.

"Yes, thread. I couldn't bear a ribbon, but I didn't know what to do."

Fanny went to Sister Eucharia's sewing basket, and found some strong cotton thread. Loosely she tied together, as her father held them, the ivy trails, the rosemary, the golden-hearted roses and the spikes of lavender. She looked at her father for guidance once or twice—"Is this right, Father?" —and he nodded. He smiled almost triumphantly when she had finished and he saw that the symbols he had brought up to Julia from her childhood's garden were safely and grace-fully bound together for her. He held the swathe of flowers, and listened.

"Is she alone?"

"I'll go and see."

She was alone.

"I'll take them to her," he said. "She'll know who they're from. Thank you, Fanny."

She sat down and began absent-mindedly to tidy Sister Eucharia's sewing basket. After a few silent minutes she heard sympathetic murmurs in her mother's room, and knew that, having tried to respond to them, her father had fled downstairs. But when in a little while she returned to where Julia lay, all was quiet, with only Sister Guadalupe reading her office in a rocking-chair near the big window.

Joseph had laid his flowers against his wife's left arm, left shoulder. They looked dark and wonderful on the blazing whiteness of the death-bed. Fanny observed that a feather of the rosemary touched Julia's neck.

She had not lied to Muscle when she told him that Julia looked 'simply lovely' and 'was finished with being sick'.

Her mother lay, Fanny thought, not as if to instruct that here was the cold, emptied case from which a spirit had fled, but rather as if she were that escaped spirit, resting on its way—the discarded shell forgotten, not in this room at all. 'This lovely mother that I look at now,' thought Fanny, 'does not appear to be the part of her that we will carry in a coffin to the Delahunt vault; this that I look at is the other part, surely—the part that lives and is gone?'

The girl sat on a low *prie-dieu* chair. A wax candle burnt

at either side of Julia's bedhead, but neither the wavering flames nor the dimming by the drawn blinds of the evening light outside could detract from the other-worldly, floating whiteness, the lost, proud peace of this bed of death. Julia lay flat, attenuated, her limbs hardly outlined at all under the white coverlet; her shroud, her habit was of white wool; her head was low on the pillow, and her silky grey hair shadowed softly back from her deep forehead. All of *rigor mortis* had gone in these last hours from her face, and with it all sign of her illness. Simply she looked ethereal, rested, and of a dateless beauty, Fanny thought.

With its faded pale blue ribbon they had placed about her neck her heavy silver medal of *'Enfant de Marie'*. Fanny knew the inscription on the back; she had received a similar medal herself . . . '. . . *Couvent de la Sainte Famille, Place des Ormes* . . .' etc. 'Are we all buried with those medals—is it *de rigueur?*' Fanny wondered. And she smiled as it occurred to her that Julia's air of reposing majesty now made the school medal seem like some ancient Papal honour, of measureless importance. Below this decoration the light, long hands of her mother were folded for eternal rest, the left one over the right and bearing as it would for ever now her loosely-fitting wedding-ring.

"Dearest one," Fanny said confusedly—for she was almost delirious for need of sleep—"dearest Mother, why did you want only to speak to Lilian?"

Sister Guadalupe, her fingers between the pages of her Office Book and her silver-rimmed spectacles sliding on her nose, was beside Fanny, and took a shrewd look at her.

"Don't let that bother you, child—yes, Eucharia told me she was talking to Lilian before she went. But don't let that hurt your father, or you, or any of ye. It isn't that she loved Lilian more than you, or your father. But she was a bit anxious about her—Eucharia and I both noticed that. She used to mutter to her often towards the end. Anxieties get expressed more than loves, I've noticed, on death-beds," said Sister Guadalupe.

"But why was she anxious about Lilian?" Fanny asked.

"Well, a newly-married—your mother's first-born—she might not have been sure yet in her mind that Lilian was really happy, after all? The first months are difficult, you know. Maybe your mother thought Lilian was being too extravagant, too grand—we've all heard she's that, you know! And I don't think your mother liked the O'Connors much, as a family——"

"Oh, she was pleased to see Lilian happy—and she liked Michael. Truly she did."

"Well, maybe Lilian's starting a baby! That might have made your mother anxious, do you think?"

"Surely not? It could only have pleased her, Sister Guadalupe."

"Of course, when it was all safe and sound. But anyway, 'twas only some vague anxiety she had, and she was very sick and weak, the child, and got it exaggerated, you can be sure, because she was so sick. It's always that way. But all I mean is let you not be thinking she didn't love *you* with her last breath. It was just this anxiety she was expressing, that's all! And sure, whatever it was, isn't it gone? Will you look at her? Did you ever see such holy peace?" Sister Guadalupe went over to trim one of the candles. "I don't care very much for this old bunch of flowers," she said. "Who put them up here beside her face, I'd like to know?"

"Father brought them to her, Sister Guadalupe."

"Ah, did he now? God help us, poor Mr. Morrow!"

"Don't touch them, please!"

"Sure of course I won't, child." The nun shuffled off to the dressing-room, and Fanny went and sat in the basket chair by the window. She closed her eyes. 'But I won't sleep, Mother,' she said. 'I promise I won't. She felt afloat again, and weightless, and the room, the house, was floating too. 'It's like Venice, Mother; it's like being in a gondola. You should have waited for me to tell you about Venice.' She fell asleep.

If people came to kneel by Julia in farewell they did not trouble her; if murmurs crossed her hearing they did not bring her back to the room she sat in. The slatted sunlight fell on her white face and it must have struck more than one tip-toeing neighbour how like it was, young and weary, to the beautiful death-mask on the bed. '. . . And may perpetual light shine upon her. . . .' Perpetual light—in Venice. Fanny's eyelids fluttered. That is André's car. But how? He can't bring it beyond Mestre. . . .

She woke and stood up.

Yes, there was the dark-green Mercedes coming up the drive. No need to halt it now below the ha-ha. It came, driven as quietly as was possible, to the steps. Joey sat beside André, and Lucille and Lilian at the back.

Fanny turned and looked towards her mother, some sudden wild entreaty in her face. She wrung her hands, and seemed as if she might go down on her knees and pray. But instead she tiptoed from the room.

Now the house hummed, as hushedly as it could, but at a great cost of fatigue, overstrain and nervous irritability to many of its inmates.

Honoria and Mrs. Hession had assembled a retinue of helpers and commanded them well, so that beds and stretchers were prepared, and the extraordinary amount of food and drink that occasions of sorrow seem to call for was forthcoming with an admirable minimum of fuss. Village boys ran up and down the steps all the evening with incoming and outgoing telegrams. It was clear that by tomorrow night, when they would take Julia to Crahore Church, a great number of relatives and relatives-in-law would have reached the neighbourhood—and beds must be found for them between Kilmahon and Doon Point, for Glasalla was now full. But Eleanor directed the elaborate arrangements required for saying good-bye to Julia with cold and untiring authority—and indeed embraced with gratitude the absurd demand on her. There would be time enough—she would prefer to mourn alone. The central thing had happened; Julia was gone. So this immediate fuss was nothing, save perhaps a helpful exercise.

Nevertheless, supper was an ordeal.

There had been an attempt to get Cockle and Muscle to have early supper and go quickly to bed; but Muscle had clutched at Fanny and almost shrieked that he wouldn't go to bed until Stephen went, with whom he was sleeping; and Cockle cried too and would not go alone to Aunt Eleanor's room, where a stretcher had been prepared for her. So argument was abandoned, and their elders were not to be spared, even for an hour or two, the extra tension created by these two, by their childish and for the most part touchingly controlled shock before what had happened to them.

An hour or so before supper Fanny had sat with Lucille on the bed in the shabby little room next to her own which she had prepared for her friend. These rooms were along a north corridor overlooking the yard—Muscle and Stephen would be housed in another of them—and when Glasalla was built in the eighteenth century the narrow little wing with its narrow staircase to the kitchens was the servants' quarters. But for years now, it had been unoccupied, Honoria and Mrs. Hession having their choice of much larger and much warmer sleeping quarters in the basement. However, where Eleanor's writ ran, all floors, walls and cupboards, used or unused, were kept scrubbed and convent-clean, and in her eyes shabbiness and poor equipment were not synonymous with sordidness. So it was easy when necessary to prepare these small white cells for honourable use, and Fanny had done her best, with flowers and books and silver candle-sticks, to ease the poor, monastic appearance of Lucille's room.

"You see—it's even more unlike what you're used to than Mespil Road."

"I love Mespil Road. But this—the whitewash and this tiny little iron bed, and the strange, lovely smell—the sea?—and then that grey, tidy yard down there—oh, it's amazing, Fan! It's exquisite! It's like being a nun!"

They both laughed.

"Without the spiritual compensations," said Fanny.

"But one could attempt those," said Lucille.

Under the shadow of Fanny's grief the two were still shy of each other. In the painful moment of arrival, when in the hall Joseph, Lilian and Joey had most understandably broken down and wept, Fanny, who had thought that she had no more tears in her for today, had been afraid to do more than touch Lucille's hand, and then present her to Eleanor. Lucille for her part also was afraid and quiet.

André carried bags and boxes of flowers into the hall, tactfully effacing himself from the family's moment of anguish. But as he laid down one load, Fanny, as much seeking escape from surrounding stress as desirous to welcome him back, came to him and took his hand.

"Welcome," she said gently. "You are very good to us, André."

He was tired, and very dusty and dirty from his hard itinerary. He looked almost as if troubled, Fanny thought. And that seemed to her so uncharacteristic of him that she supposed him to be strongly affected by the sad circumstances to which he had brought his passengers. She was touched by the unexpected weary gravity of his face.

"Ah, thank you, Miss Fanny. But there is nothing I would not do—I dare not take your hand, no! I am filthy! May I go and wash? I know my way——"

"Of course, André! And there are refreshments in the dining-room——"

"Thank you. Thank you, Fanny." He bowed, and she turned back to the others, and chiefly to Lucille. "Come—oh, Lucille, you're welcome!"

So, as the heart-broken, tired travellers, Lilian and Joey, tried to gulp tea in the drawing-room with Aunt Edith, Lucille had politely drunk some also, and then Fanny had brought her here.

But after Lucille had washed the dust of the road away— in soft, gold water, hot out of a brass can—in Glasalla's wonderful Victorian bathroom which did indeed make her smile in delight, both she and Fanny had had time to get used to the relief of being together again, let it be sadly to meet the assembled sorrow of Fanny's people. For Fanny in all that lay immediately ahead it would be relief unparalleled to have Lucille, it would be strength; and Lucille, troubled in many ways for Fanny, responded unconsciously but gratefully to the unexpressed appeal, the necessity she felt in the other. Therefore sitting together in the little cell, the two grew gently back to their constant certainty, and Fanny lost the sense of being on the edge of delirium which had possessed her all day.

"Oh! You're making me feel strong!" she said.

"You'll need to feel strong, darling," said Lucille.

"Brush your hair."

In the bathroom Lucille had shed all the dust-soaked clothes of the motoring day, and now in a dress of dark silk looked very beautiful; but her hair hung about her shoulders still. She got up obediently, took her brushes and quickly, as it were carelessly, put all in shining order, twisted up her *chignon* and secured it.

"Will that do?"

Fanny nodded.

"Oh, Fan—this beautiful grey stone! What is that little feathery tree in the corner?"

"It's a mountain ash—the prettiest one I've ever seen. I don't know whether it's a sport or a true variety, but its berries are crimson instead of scarlet, and its leaves are grey-green instead of—well, instead of leaf-green!"

"It's strange to be here," said Lucille. "You look wonderful in black, Fan. You know, it ought to sadden me, but after all, we were always in black at school—so—well, it knocks the years away!"

"I suppose we ought to go downstairs?"

"Yes, Fan. Could I—could I see your mother first?"

"Yes. Her room should be quiet now. Come."

Julia's room was quiet. Sister Guadalupe sat sewing by the window, but as twilight was advancing beyond the Venetian blinds she had lighted more candles about the bed, and a small lamp by which she could see to darn. She looked up when the girls came in, but did not move.

Lucille knelt down near the foot of the great bed, and made the sign of the cross; Fanny stood and looked once again, in desperate, weary grief, at Julia's face.

After a minute or two the two girls left the room. Fanny moved towards the staircase, but Lucille clutched her arm.

"Not yet! A minute, please!" And she turned Fanny towards the flight of steps that led to their corridor. Fanny could feel that the other was shaking. When they entered Lucille's little cell the intense last light of the day fell on them obliquely. Lucille, golden-skinned, looked almost pallid; and the tears that dashed along her frightened-seeming face shone alarmingly, unnaturally bright.

"Oh, Lucille! Oh please, what is it?"

Lucille turned and took her hands.

"You'd never told me! I—I wasn't prepared! Fanny, Fanny, she's the *image* of you!"

"But I always told you I'm like her! So is Lilian!"

"No, no! *Not* Lilian! You! It was seeing *you* dead! That is how you will look when you die. Fan! Oh, it was frightening!"

Lucille sank on the little hard bed and covered her face and sobbed.

"Lucille," Fanny took hold of her. "Oh, Lucille darling, don't! After all, I'll have to look someway when I die—and, if you're right, could I do better?"

Lucille laughed and hugged her.

"Oh forgive me! Simply—I was shocked, and I jumped forward. Oh, Fan, for a second I thought I was kneeling there praying for you!"

Fanny held her closely in her arms.

"And if you did think that, what harm? The prayer will keep, perhaps—if it was good enough——"

Lucille chuckled.

"And anyway," Fanny went on, "there's always the Communion of Saints, you know!"

Lucille kissed her.

"For an unbeliever you're a witty theologian," she said. "I'm all right now. I've got it clear. It's simply that you are the image of her—so it was like kneeling at *your* death-bed."

"I'm—I'm grateful to you. But one has to live, well, as Mother lived, to look like that when it's over."

"Yes," said Lucille. She got up and began to tidy her hair again, and sponge her eyes. "Yes. To look as she does tonight you have to have lived, I think, by the highest claims of whatever your nature happens to be. In any case you have to have lived by some discipline which can be saluted. But there are many kinds of high claim, Fan."

"I agree. But I won't live as Mother lived, so I won't look like her on my death-bed."

"You will. Your mother's discipline was in self-surrender, I imagine. I mean, I think she gave all her powers to making

268

her marriage with your father as good as possible—and when I say 'good' I mean 'good'."

"I know you do. It's a tricky word, Lucille."

"It is indeed."

"But, I repeat, I'm not going to live as Mother lived."

"No, you won't, I think. Still, all I mean is that you'll be 'good'—take the word with all its implications, take your choice, dear theologian! Anyway, you'll be 'good', because that is how you're made, Fan. And so, you'll look when you die the image of your mother as she looks tonight."

"Generous one!" said Fanny, suddenly shy; also stricken compunctiously that in this house and day of grief she had been finding relief, finding strength, even forgetting immediate anguish, in chattering with Lucille. "We must go down and help the others," she said. "You are such a consolation to me that I grow selfish."

"Let's go down," Lucille agreed. "But you're not selfish. Am I tidy and all right?"

"You're tidy and all right. Come on."

They went down the narrow corridor and the steps which led to the main part of the house.

"I hope André won't be miserable having to share a room with Joey," Fanny said.

"Why should he be?"

"He's not used to such vulgarities! But simply we can't help it tonight! Anyway it's a big room, and it has two reasonably good beds."

"Goodness! What are you worrying about?"

"I thought he looked very tired—and he is so terribly kind with his car. To ask him to share a room with Joey isn't what Aunt Eleanor or I would like, but——"

"Nonsensical child!"

The two, pausing on the landing by the great window, looked at each other through veiled questions. Lucille was thinking: 'She is oddly concerned about the temporary fatigue of a young man whose health might be said to be so good as to be a disadvantage to him.' And Fanny was thinking: 'What would she say if she knew that two nights ago of my own will I kissed her brother André?'

A breath of anxiousness, of estrangement, passed about

269

them. They stood by the window, troubled and unsure.

"The lighthouse is tuning up," said Fanny. "You wait. It takes getting used to, our lighthouse!"

"I can hear the sea," said Lucille.

"The tide is in. It's sucking over the Golden Rocks."

"You used to talk about the Golden Rocks at school——"

"It's the seaweed that's golden—saffron really. I'll show you."

Supper was, as has been said, an ordeal for everyone. The dining-room was large, the table had all its leaves in and seemed to be laid to accommodate a score; a side-table more-over was laden with silver, glass, plates, napkins, loaves of home-made bread, dishes of butter and honey. The main sideboard was charged with cold meats, cold birds, bowls of salad, silver platters of hot scones and baked potatoes; there was tea, there was cider, there was wine. It was easy therefore to select and settle down to some nourishment; but no one, young or old, seemed able to do so, though many of the family, trying to set a good example, went through the motions of helping themselves to food and drink, and even sat down, unfolded napkins and picked up knives and forks.

Callers drifted in and out, to press Joseph's hand, to have a drink, an odd bewildered one to sit down and eat a bit of chicken. Village boys still ran in barefoot with telegrams; Lilian seemed to receive a telegram every thirty minutes from Michael in London. Joseph paced about, politely accepting cups and plates and instantly putting them down and losing them. Father Fogarty was shown in; he was the devoted curate at Haddington Road who adored the Morrows. It crossed Fanny's mind, if no one else's, to wonder how the good young priest had got to Glasalla.

"Lucille, this is Father Fogarty—one of Canon Whelan's assistants at home——"

"Oh yes—I met Canon Whelan——"

"He is very ill, Miss Fanny," said Father Fogarty, who looked very ill himself. "I dared not let him come——"

"Of course not," said Fanny. "It's extremely good of you, Father Fogarty—do sit here, won't you? Lucille, will you please look after Father Fogarty? Some chicken, Father? A glass of wine? A cup of tea?"

Father Brosnan, in and out with various callers and in excellent command of them, came and put a hand on the shoulder of the exhausted young curate from Dublin.

"Good boy," he said. "It is right for you to be here. She was one of your very best ones. You'll stay in my house. And you should be the Celebrant—we are having full High Requiem. Can you sing?"

"Father Fogarty sings beautifully," said Fanny.

"Then maybe he'd better take the tenor of the Office and the *Dies Irae*? Well, we'll see."

Lucille came with food and a glass of wine.

"Talk to him," Fanny said softly.

Lucille sat down to do so. Tears were coursing down Father Fogarty's face.

"Which would you do?" he stuttered to Lucille. "Would you be the Celebrant or sing tenor in the *Dies Irae*?"

André and Joey carved manfully.

"Won't you eat at all, Miss Fanny?" Fanny waved refusal. "Look, Mrs. O'Connor, look, one sliver of this Irish ham——"

Lilian, who was looking as white as her name suggested, and very tragic, very beautiful, looked up into André's masked face and said under her breath: "No. Sit down. Pour yourself a glass of wine, and sit down. Here——" she tapped the empty chair beside her. "Bring your wine and sit quiet, please."

He obeyed her, fetched wine bottle and glass, and sat where she told him to sit as if very glad to do so. He filled his glass with Burgundy, lifted it to Lilian and drank, and said not a word.

Lucille, across the wide table and talking to Father Fogarty, did not mishear a syllable or a movement of this delicate interchange between her brother and Lilian.

But Fanny was far off! Grandfather had come in with his cats in his arms, and he was abusing Honoria in the loud tones which he summoned only for her on earth.

"The idea, you unfortunate woman, that I couldn't pass a night of twilight inside there, with a bit of toast? Sure of course I could! What do I want or entreat, Honoria Maguire, but the vault below that's opening now for her? And what do I want at all, my God, with pieces of toast? But the idea of assuming that either Teresa or Iago could consume a bite of supper elsewhere than on this hearthstone of this room—where is their bowl, woman? Where is their milk and their dish?——"

"Oh, God save us, sir, have I nothing to do this day and night, will you tell me, but bring you that ould bowl——?"

Fanny intervened.

"Here is their bowl, Grandfather. Look, would you show Cockle how to mix their cream and milk in it? It's time she knew. And, if you'll tell us whether it's chicken or ham or lamb they're to have, I'll show Muscle how to chop it up for them——"

So the old distracted man was made briefly happy, and the unhappy children were briefly distracted.

Eleanor moved calmly in and out of the room, assisted excellently in attention to the general comfort by Aunt Edith. The dining-room curtains were drawn and the old Venetian blinds were down as they would be until the day after Julia's funeral, so the stroke of the lighthouse was only a hint now through these ancient defences, imperceptible save to those who were habituated to it. And Eleanor, who was, found it hard to forgo. She missed the wild, white beam under which she lived. Its lack was a part of the absurd unlikeliness of burying Julia. In a day or two the lighthouse beam would be back, and with it thought of Julia. So it had always been. Let Julia be in Mespil Road or in Crahore churchyard, she and the light from Loop Head moved together for her sister. The light's being curtained out paralleled with Julia's unnatural state upstairs. In a day or two normality would be restored.

Yet another barefoot boy came in with a telegram, and was given a wedge of buttered soda-cake with a slice of ham on it.

Eleanor read the message

'*Rien à pleurer notre belle Julia était prête comme elle doit être heureuse de regarder Notre Seigneur courage donc mes chères enfants toutes nos prières. Cathérine Mandel, Couvent de la Sainte Famille, Bruxelles.*'

Eleanor read the message through twice; then she took it to Fanny.

When the latter had read it, she looked up out of bright, wet eyes.

"May I show it to Lucille, Aunt Eleanor?"

"Yes—but mind it for me."

The terrible evening moved slowly, but at last the 'hall-door mourners' ceased to flow (the quiet village people would be in and out of the kitchen all night), Father Brosnan took Father Fogarty home; Stephen, exhausted, was persuaded to go up to bed with Muscle, and Cockle fell asleep in Mrs. Hession's arms in the kitchen and was laid by her in her neighbouring warm bed and did not stir again all night. Joseph went upstairs to where his wife lay waiting for tomorrow's coffin. Aunt Edith seated herself at the study desk, to sort out telegrams, cards and messages. Joey undertook to put Grandfather to bed, and gathered the old man on his arm gently, at the foot of the stairs.

Lucille and Fanny, the last to leave the dining-room, where they had been helping Honoria and some of her friends to clear things up, thought of walking awhile in the garden and listening to the sea below it. But as they crossed the hall they met Sister Eucharia and Aunt Eleanor.

"Fanny," said the latter, "there is tea in the drawing-room, and Sister Eucharia needs some. Will you take her in? Old Christy MacNamara is in the kitchen, and I have to go and see him. I'll be back in a minute."

Fanny presented Lucille to the Blue Nun, and opened the drawing-room door for her. Lamps and candelabra beautified the general, unpretentious shabbiness and worn-out elegance, and the familiar room struck Fanny's sensibilities freshly, no doubt because weariness was making her dizzy, and altering her perspective. In any case, whatever the explanation, she was struck as never had she been before by warmth, beauty and memories in this vast old room.

Aunt Edith was seated, almost heroically it might now be said, by the tea-table, where a flame burnt under a silver urn. Lilian was sitting on a low chair on the other side of the fireplace. Between the windows at a tray laden with decanters and bottles André was slowly filling a small glass.

Sister Eucharia had not met Aunt Edith before, so presentations were made. Tea was poured.

"Mr. Morrow's sister? Oh, poor Mr. Morrow. Yes, Miss Morrow, I do take sugar, thank you."

"You must be tired now, Sister Eucharia."

"No. Our work is a natural routine, Miss Morrow; and Mrs. Morrow's death was inevitable, and easy. She died very well. It is nice to see the soul go off so gladly. Though indeed it's seldom that the spirit doesn't depart in peace."

"Mother asked for me, didn't she, Sister Eucharia?"

Sister Eucharia stirred her tea. Her dark brows drew together as she considered the beautiful young woman who spoke to her.

"You are her daughter Lilian?" she asked.

"Yes."

There was a moment of silence during which Fanny placed a little table beside the nun for her cup, and then brought her a plate and offered her some little sugared cakes.

"But these look delicious, Fanny! Which shall I have?"

"The pink or the coffee, Sister Eucharia, I think. I'll put them here beside you—but be sure you tell Mrs. Hession you liked them."

"Thank you, child. Of course I will." Sister Eucharia chose a coffee-sugared cake and put it on her little plate. Then she looked again at Lilian, towards whom André had moved, carrying to her carefully a small glass of colourless liquid. The nun's eyes turned ironically on him.

"What is that you're offering, young man?" she asked.

"An Italian liqueur called 'grappa', Sister," he said politely.

"Grappa? Here?" Fanny said involuntarily.

"I took the liberty of bringing some, Miss Fanny," said André. "You remember it in Venice, and that we did not consider you old enough to drink it?"

Fanny did not answer.

"But Mrs. O'Connor is?" said Sister Eucharia. "What are the properties of this cordial which it is inadvisable to taste when you are eighteen but to be commended when you are twenty-one?"

André smiled delightedly, really enjoying the nun's cynical turn of mood, it would seem.

"It is an excellent and very smooth stimulant, Sister

274

Eucharia. When Miss Fanny was very well and enjoying every hour of the day in Venice, to offer her, so young and radiant, this kind of thing——" he lifted the little glass—"would have been idiotic. But, at the end of a day of sorrow and long travelling, and with a sad night and sadder day ahead, I offer it with confidence to Mrs. O'Connor, and would even—did you allow me, Sister—offer it to Miss Fanny, young though she is."

'Imperturbable,' thought Lucille. And as she watched she had the idea that this good nun had penetrated to a bad secret. It occurred to her that Sister Eucharia, who was taking her ease over her tea and cake and whose chatty enquiries about the small glass of liqueur had been no more than time-marking while she summed up a few points—that Sister Eucharia suddenly saw what she, Lucille, had seen in the drawing-room of Rosetta Terrace, and was carefully considering its implications while she ate a little sugared cake.

"Ah! Here is Miss Delahunt!" said Sister Eucharia as Eleanor entered. And Lucille had the impression that the nun had been almost praying for Eleanor's presence, that for some reason she wanted her here.

Almost immediately it became clear that that was so, and that the nun desired to inflict some kind of lesson on Lilian which would not only be witnessed by those whom it might concern, but which should also be supported by the memories of those who had seen Julia die.

"Miss Delahunt," said Sister Eucharia, "Mrs. O'Connor was saying to me that she gathered that her mother asked for her just before she died."

Eleanor paused in the centre of the room.

"Yes, Sister Eucharia?"

There was in the pronunciation of these syllables a flick of comment on Lilian that was revelatory to Lucille, and made innocent Fanny turn in simple wonder to consider her aunt's composed features.

"I was about to tell her," said Sister Eucharia, "that her mother did *not* ask for her—in the sense in which we normally understand those words. May I go on, Miss Delahunt? You and your niece Fanny were present when

Mrs. Morrow died. It is important to be accurate now in reporting this death to others who were not present, but whom of course it concerns very deeply."

"It is indeed important, Sister Eucharia. You and Father Brosnan were the two present, I suppose, whose account of Julia's death might be clear of confusion——"

Joseph came into the room. To Fanny he was for a moment almost unrecognizable, so all-over grey, so frantic with the spending of grief. He sat down near his sister Edith. He was almost saintly, had been all day, in his attempts to be calm and give no trouble.

"Is there any tea, Edith?" he asked gently.

"It's not very hot—wait, I'll light the lamp under the kettle, Joseph——"

"Do please. What are you all talking about?"

"Sister Eucharia was telling me that you were wrong, Father—that Mother didn't ask for me," said Lilian.

"But——?" Joseph lifted his head.

"I was going to explain," said Sister Eucharia. "Could I have another cup, Miss Morrow, when the kettle boils? I was going to explain, Mrs. O'Connor, that your mother did *not* ask for you, in the sense of wanting for her own sake to have you especially with her in the hour of death. To say that she did would be simply untrue; it would also be a most wounding offence to Mr. Morrow, and to her children other than you. What she did express in her last breath, Mrs. O'Connor, was something which Sister Guadalupe and I had become familiar with in the three weeks we have been nursing her here. Her last words were: 'Lilian child, I beg you——' but they were nothing new to me. Constantly in her recent deliriums I heard them. All that they mean is this, Mrs. O'Connor—that your mother went into her last illness with something on her mind about you—you especially out of all her family. She loved every one of you, and in lucid hours, Mr. Morrow, she would talk to Guadalupe or to me about you, about Fanny, about Joey, about all of you, with what I can only call perfect love—and very calm, proud love at that. She was sure and certain about the whole of you, down to young Muscle. She said to me one night: 'Muscle will be the great one—the famous Morrow'."

Joseph leant forward and groaned.

"But—yes, thank you, Miss Morrow, two lumps, and cream —but all I want to reassure you all about is that those last words of Mrs. Morrow's were no more than the expression of an anxiety she had had when her illness reached its acute phase—either you and she had had some misunderstanding then, Mrs. O'Connor, or she was anxious about your physical health, or your earthly happiness—or—goodness knows what! Anyhow, you can all be assured that whatever was troubling her is resolved now—for her."

Joseph lifted his head.

"It is true that she was troubled about Lilian quite lately. But I tried to show her how silly that was! You *aren't* ill, child, are you? You aren't unhappy?"

Lilian shook her head.

Her father got up and wandered out of the drawing-room.

"Come, Lucille," said Fanny. "Come up to the sea-wall."

They went Fanny's usual way, between the rigid artichokes and under the too-old apple branches, to the corner high-perched beside the fig tree.

"Does the lighthouse madden you, Lucille?"

"No. It's beautiful, everything here—very much itself."

"I'll show it to you in daylight, when—when there's time. Come up."

They climbed the wall and sat between the fig tree and the sea. Ruthlessly the lighthouse beam covered them every sixty seconds.

"As we came near this afternoon, Fan, I felt that I recognized things. You used to tell me about Glasalla—I suppose you told me well?"

Fanny looked about her, down to the spread-out Golden Rocks, south to the lighthouse, and inward across the dark garden to the darkened house where her mother lay folded in cold death and whence she would depart at sunset tomorrow. 'I shall make the same departure some day,' she thought, 'down the same steps and to the same place where she is going. And when I am living here I shall sleep in that room where she is lying now; I shall die in that bed.'

Her thoughts floated off to André, and she wondered if he was still in the drawing-room, sipping *grappa* with Lilian, being charming to Aunt Edith and Sister Eucharia. Her heart had been asked for more, and more diversified, feelings than it could wholly answer for within the last two days, and under the strain she had self-protectively, temporarily forgotten, or half-forgotten, this and that exaction from hour to hour—in superficial self-defence. Nothing was really forgotten; she knew that all would return, each important thing in its time and place, once they, the family, had returned from the vault at Crahore. But at this moment, sitting on the beloved wall above the sea, she realized with some detached amusement that in the stress and exaction of the past forty-eight hours she had, apparently, forgotten that she was the signed inheritor of Glasalla, yet had *not* forgotten that she had of her own free will kissed André.

How do we account for ourselves? she wondered now. And as, impatient, wounded by herself, she turned to seek Lucille, instantly she shrank again—not only because the awful stroke of the lighthouse crossed her in that instant, but also because it occurred to her, with shock, with disgust, that she had kissed André—after long inclination and long resistance— simply in pride and safety at last. Out of the exhilarated mood of independence which Aunt Eleanor's amazing news had brought to her, she had felt that she might kiss or not as she chose; that she was in fact as well in desire as in ideal now her own mistress; so she need be no man's, and so might kiss the man who moved her—without fear of consequence or condescension. 'Aunt Eleanor,' she thought, as she reflected on her own inexplicable, silly weakness for André, 'Aunt Eleanor has so strengthened me that I may be as weak as I choose. But, of course, only as weak as I choose. That is where the joke comes in, and the paradox. That is why I kissed him. Ah, André, would you be hurt if you could follow my thought? Ah, dear André——'

Lucille was troubled; admittedly the lighthouse beam exaggerated and bewildered, yet in this beautiful, innocent face which she loved she observed tonight variations of stress and a kind of mock maturity that made her anxious. Since she had come to Ireland she had understood almost with panic how profoundly right were *Mère Générale's* intuitions about André; indeed, every time she caught Lilian's eyes resting on him she felt, on the one hand, thankful to Heaven that at least the old nun need not take up the implications of such a pause, such a guilty question in the eyes of one of her children, and, on the other, impatient with Fanny who had not long ago perceived this dangerous, slow surmise, but instead looked with self-concerned and foolish interest upon a vain, indeed a wicked young man. Lucille was troubled; but respected Fanny too much to dare to speak or act rashly. And in these days of profound grief she could not introduce so undignified a matter as her brother's sensual vanity. Yet she was afraid for Fanny, and saw that *Mère Générale* was more right than she knew in wishing André out of Ireland. She leant down, her hands on the wall, and looked over the gold seaweed and the foaming tide below. 'It will all pass,' she told herself. 'He will go away, and he is shockingly fickle too; Lilian is very young and only at the brink of a very complicated married life which will soon engross her. And Fanny—ah, Fanny has brains and dreams, and she must come with me and learn to use them.'

"Glasalla is mine, Lucille. I forgot to tell you that."

"Yours? But—how on earth? How could it be?"

"Aunt Eleanor has given it to me. That is, she has given it to me from when I'm twenty-one, but meantime it is—provisionally, I suppose you'd say—mine. She wants to hand it over legally during her lifetime, and she has made me her heir."

"She has chosen well. You, and not one of your brothers."

"Yes. She is giving it to me because she has always loved Mother most on earth, and she says I'm like her."

"When did she tell you this?"

"When was it?" Fanny frowned. "The day before yesterday? We—we even signed papers and things with her lawyer. But, do you know, I had forgotten about it until this minute! Superficially forgotten, I mean."

"I can understand that. These must have seemed two very long days——"

"No—I'm wrong. It was yesterday only that we signed the papers. But the night before she told me about it. Ah,

279

Lucille!" She leant back into the fig branches. "Aren't they delusory, our ideas of time! Whole years of schooldays seem to me at this minute like a memory of one empty, sunny hour; and in twenty-four hours here, only a day ago, three vast things happened to me—grown-up, heavy things. And each of them a thing that can only happen once!"

"Three things, Fan?"

"I was given Glasalla—and, and I took a decision of my own," she laughed a little at Lucille's watchful eyes—"Oh, nothing portentous, simply odd and grown-up and altogether new!"

Lucille said nothing.

"And then, to conclude the twenty-four hours, I stood and saw Mother die. And already everything's tangled in confusion. Things float about; happenings seem to get detached, Lucille, and sail out of the calendar—do you know that feeling?"

Lucille moved nearer and put an arm about Fanny.

"Perhaps, a little. At any rate I can imagine it. But it is temporary. And tonight, at all costs, you must sleep."

"Yes. I must sleep. So must you, you dear one. Sister Eucharia has a wonderful potion. Come, Lucille. Come— I must say good-night to Mother. Good-night! Ah, ah God! I'd nearly forgotten—for a minute!"

Her head went down into Lucille's lap, and she broke at last into wild sobs—no more the weary, hushed, unceasing tears of all the night before and of today, but sobs that tore and shook her. Sobs through which she cried and prayed aloud.

It was well. It was a good thing.

Lucille held her and murmured to her, and let her own gentle tears fall down. The lighthouse beam passed and re-passed relentlessly over the two bent heads.

CHAPTER TWELVE

CRAHORE AND EVENING

THE small church at Crahore was crowded for Julia's Requiem Mass, and many of the country people had to stand outside the open doors and along the churchyard paths. Canon Houlihan of Doon Point presided in the sanctuary; Father Fogarty was celebrant of the Mass, assisted by the two Crahore curates; Father Brosnan was Master of Ceremonies, and the sanctuary and the upper nave around the coffin were crowded with surpliced priests, to sing the Office of The Dead.

Family and friends were massed there too, on the lovely August morning, to say good-bye to Julia, already lost and smothered under flowers, already secured in her handsome inflexible coffin.

Bill Morrow knelt beside his wife Kitty on the outside of one of the further-back family benches, and considered the mourners in front of him. He was reminded of Lilian's wedding. 'But I'm in time today,' he thought. Morrows, O'Connors—many more, of course—poor old Mr. Delahunt and Eleanor, and Mr. Delahunt's feeble old sister—Mrs. Halvey Foxe—from Ennis. Various other faces of Delahunt connections. Still nevertheless, in black and in sorrow, this was the April wedding party. There, grave and handsome, stood Michael O'Connor beside his beautiful, mourning bride, and one or two benches behind him other O'Connors, his father, his uncles, his two young brothers. There, near the coffin, stood Uncle Joseph Morrow, with poor old Grandfather Delahunt and Aunt Eleanor on his right hand; behind them stood Joey and Cockle, Stephen and Muscle, and beside Muscle, her hand through his arm, Fanny; Fanny in black and very straight, rather tall; Fanny with a clear, white profile—misty no longer. Ah Fanny, grown-up and visible today, in sorrow.

Cousin Bill stared at her in pity.

The beautiful Belgian school friend and her handsome brother the Count were in the bench opposite to Bill and Kitty. The girl—Lucille was her name?—was following the

Office in her Missal; the handsome Count stared towards the altar.

Bill heard all around the sobs and sighs of old country friends, of loving servants; he listened to the prayers at the altar: '. . . *ad te omnia caro veniat. Requiem . . .*' Yes, here they were, the April wedding party, brothers, fathers, aunts and cousins; all in their best again and on their best behaviour; but black gloves this time, and flowers on the coffin only, in no buttonhole, on no breast.

He smiled, and caught Kitty frowning at him, so he covered his face with his hands and tried to pray for Aunt Julia.

At last the long, beautiful Mass for the Dead was over; at last the coffin was blessed again, and the men who worked at Glasalla came deftly and gently, their reddened eyes dried, to gather up the heaps of flowers. At last Julia was raised, for her very last, very short journey out to the churchyard, Joey and Michael O'Connor at her head, Corney Keane and Martin Hession at her feet, young Stephen and young George O'Connor at either flank. Joseph could not carry her, could only stand behind her with her trembling father.

Julia was light indeed, but her slender, worn-out frame was majestically encased now in lead-lined, silk-lined oak with silver plates and ornaments; so she was carried difficultly by the six, though four of them were strong. But they brought her out into the sunlight and across the grass to the little stone vault of her people.

The surpliced priests chanted in Latin, and the people of Crahore repeated 'Hail Marys'. They slid her into her place.

"There'll be room for me beside her, won't there, Eleanor?" asked Joseph.

It was over; Julia was gone.

Eleanor looked about the scene for one second as if for ever abstracted herself now from human life—or that is what Lucille thought. But instantly then she put her arms about her father and took him to the waiting carriage.

Sunlight streamed on the little moss-stained vault. Fanny stood with Muscle and watched the Glasalla men piling up the flowers. She saw that her father's rosemary and ivy and

282

roses were carefully left where he had put them, over where her heart lay inside the coffin.

The day was lovely. The sea gleamed radiantly across the fields, and the white tower of the lighthouse shone against the gentle summer sky. Tonight when its inexorable beam passed and repassed over the house that Julia had left, it would also find this other little old house where they must leave her now.

Lucille came to Fanny's side.

"Come, Fan. We'll drive you back later to see that the flowers are all right."

Fanny took the outstretched hand and, keeping hold of Muscle, turned away and left the churchyard.

Throughout the terrible ensuing day, crowded, exacting, fantastic, Fanny, doing what she could in the general grotesque effort of sociability, paused sometimes to admire her father. Joseph's life, she knew, had lost all value for him with Julia's departure into the Delahunt vault, and he was weak and helpless; almost, suppressedly, he was insane with grief, Fanny suspected. Nor was he a man at all to be described as of strong fibre. Julia had been his strength; Julia he worshipped, and in Julia he had found the help he needed along his quiet, ordinary road. But her taking off from him was not a quiet, ordinary event; it had ravaged his sensitive heart. Julia was the flower and the fire and the pride of his life; that she had loved him, and never had ceased to love him, and never had failed him in all his irritable and pompous years of married life, had been—because he was a sensitive person—a source of unfailing, forever fresh astonishment to him. Fanny realized today that unconsciously she had for long understood this, and had even —without forgiving her mother—seen why as wife she had sided with Joseph and against her in the matter of the *baccalauréat*. Mother and Father had been, she saw now, in love. And so this was for Father the day on which he too should enter the little vault at Crahore. He wanted to be nowhere else. Yet—she admired him as he faced the assault of sympathy. He said nothing to all the loving outcry. Ashen-grey of face in his black clothes, he stood about, shaking hands, murmuring "Thank you", and "Yes, I know"; he offered drinks and plates of cold ham, and he was as quiet as a mouse. His old friends, the O'Connors, Sam and James, did not like this 'unnatural' quiet, as they called it, and plied him with whisky, which he refused to drink, and with elaborate speeches in praise of Julia, to which he bowed his head.

Fanny observed him in wonder, her ordinary, weak, pompous father.

By degrees the crowding round Glasalla thinned. Local gentry went home quickly after the funeral, and Grandfather's little old sister, Aunt Angela, Mrs. Halvey Foxe, was packed into her carriage with her old cousin-companion, and, weeping and shaking, was driven off towards Ennis. André kindly took the two Blue Nuns, Father Fogarty and Joey to Limerick in his car, the former to their convent there, the other two so that they might catch the evening train to Dublin. He himself would return at nightfall, to see of what service he might be to other travellers later in the week.

Michael O'Connor would leave for Dublin in his car early the next morning, taking Lilian and his father and Uncle James; the young O'Connor boys had got a lift to Moyasta Station from Dr. O'Curry, and were on their slow way home. Bill Morrow and Kitty, who were staying in the hotel in Crahore, would leave in the morning, and it was decided that the next day also Mickey Marrinan had better return and take Aunt Edith and the children back to Doon Point, to finish their sad August by the sea. So within twenty-four hours of Julia's Requiem Glasalla would be quiet again, Honoria and Mrs. Hession stripping beds and folding things away.

Towards evening of the funeral day, the house assuming a semblance of order and Fanny and Lucille feeling that they had given as much assistance as at present they could toward that end, the two decided to take the young desolate ones, Stephen, Cockle and Muscle, down to the Golden Rocks. It might not be correct to suggest a swim today, but they could paddle, and look for shells and sea-anemones. So they went down, the children pathetically grateful to them.

Grandfather, exhausted, dozed at last in the study, a rug on his knees and his cats on the rug; Joseph sat in weary patience in the drawing-room with Sam and James O'Connor and Father Brosnan; Michael and Lilian O'Connor paced along the leaf-strewn drive in desultory talk with Bill and Kitty Morrow; and Aunt Edith was devoutly hoped to be resting, heroic woman, on her bed.

Eleanor sat at her office desk and surveyed neat piles of letters and of telegrams. But without panic. There was no hurry; there would be time for everything now, and whatever had to do with Julia would receive full and meticulous attention.

Honoria came in with the small salver, which she placed on a table by Eleanor's left hand. It carried the usual Waterford decanter and sherry glass, and a little silver cigarette-box.

"Thank you, Honoria; it's good of you to remember, today."

"It's a pity I wouldn't remember the one and only bit of comfort you ever bestow on yourself, poor child! Yah, you're tired out, God help you!"

"Naturally. And so are you, Honoria. You've been angels, you and Mrs. Hession—all of you——"

"Ah, 'tis an angel that's gone from us this day——"

"Please, dear Honoria——"

"I know, I know. God help you, child."

Eleanor poured some sherry carefully into her glass.

"If you see Miss Lilian, Honoria, would you ask her to come to me for a few minutes?"

"She's abroad in the garden with young Mr. Michael, Miss. I'll send her in to you this instant."

Eleanor selected and lighted a cigarette. Delicately she sipped some sherry. After a moment or two Lilian came in. She seemed to bring some of the poignant light from the summer garden with her. She was taller than Fanny and her fairness had more accent. She did indeed look very lovely in her fine, close-fitting dress of black merino.

"Yes, Aunt Eleanor?"

"Sit down, won't you, Lilian?"

Lilian sat down, facing the window and the late afternoon

light. Like every other member of the family she looked strained and white, and her beautiful eyes were almost without beauty, so many hot tears had burnt them. The young, long bones of her head and neck flexed delicately under her delicate thin skin. She sat elegantly, and with an aristocratic tranquillity that was indeed admirable, but—Aunt Eleanor always felt—faintly mannered. 'Fanny is twice the lady this one is,' the older woman thought now, as often she had done. 'She's worldly always,' she reflected; 'that perfect little string of pearls, she wouldn't forget it even today—and how much did it cost that poor young husband, I wonder? And that amazing solitaire diamond guarding the wedding ring on her elegant left hand!'

'How uncharitable I am,' thought Eleanor.

"That's a beautiful diamond," she said.

"Yes—isn't it?" said Lilian. "Michael brought it to me from London yesterday."

"Oh! I supposed it was your engagement ring."

"Oh no, Aunt Eleanor. My engagement ring is three emeralds—don't you remember?"

"Not in the least," said Eleanor, with a benevolent smile. "Would you like a glass of sherry?"

Lilian shook her head.

"I don't suppose you smoke, Lilian?"

"No, Aunt Eleanor. And I'm amazed to see that you do!"

"Only in here, and only at this hour. But don't tell your grandfather!"

Lilian laughed.

"What is it you wanted me for, Aunt Eleanor?"

"Something a little difficult, Lilian. But as you're leaving in the morning and as it is on my mind, I think I'd better say it, and have done."

"Yes?"

"As you know, your name was the last your mother spoke. So far as we know she was in the very presence of death when she said—very distinctly, 'Lilian child, I beg you . . .'"

"Yes, Aunt Eleanor."

"But I—and I think I alone—know something of what lay behind that—that plea to you, Lilian. The Blue Nuns often heard her talk to you in half-delirium, they said. But she only

286

spoke to me, while she was still well and coherent, about what lay behind her uneasiness."

"And what did lie behind it? What on earth are you getting at, Aunt Eleanor?"

"Something simple," said Aunt Eleanor. "You were married in early April. Do you remember that while you were on your honeymoon your mother and Fanny came here for a short rest, and you and Michael called in on us for a night? And shortly after you went back to Dublin your mother and Fanny returned to Mespil Road, and Fanny left then almost immediately to go to Brussels to Lucille?"

"Yes—of course I remember. I was very busy with Stillorgan Road, and Mother was—rather severe with me. I think she thought I was being too extravagant."

"She did. She hated pretentiousness, as you know. She told me in a letter then that you were being far too grand, she thought—but that you would probably learn sense after a while."

Lilian's chin went up.

"If Michael wishes me to run his house well, why is that pretentious?"

"Don't get angry, Lilian. It was not your running of your house that made your mother grieve——"

"Grieve?"

"Yes, she was grieving over you when she came here this last time—for the last time, as it turns out. It was on the second evening that she was here—she was very ill, I feared she was very ill, but none of us knew it then for certain, and she least of all—well, she came in here; she always liked to watch me smoke my cigarettes and drink my sherry. And she sat in that chair you're in, as she always did. And she told me, all of a sudden, that she was frightened about something to do with you—and that she must talk to someone about it."

"Oh, but what mystery is this? If she was frightened about something to do with me, why didn't she talk to me?"

"You must judge for yourself why she didn't, Lilian. One night in May, about a week after Fanny had gone to Belgium, your mother went out of the gate and for one of her wandering walks. Your father was at some business dinner and she was feeling lonely, she told me, for you and for Fanny. It was a lovely night, she said; she didn't tell me where she went. But she told me that she was descending some little leafy, quiet side-road when she saw a cab stop at the foot of the hill, and a beautiful young woman get out, and pay the cabby. She was struck by the grace and beauty of the young woman, and —'Do you know, Eleanor,' she said to me, 'I was so silly that I even thought with amusement that she could only be up to something illicit, and romantic.' Well, as you turned in at the little gate directly across the road from which she stood, your mother recognized you, Lilian. She said she ran across the road almost to stop you—but you were expected where you went. The door was flung open, and the moonlight revealed your host also to your mother. She did not tell me who he was; simply she said she knew him. She did not know what to do then. She leant a while on the railings. There were no lights inside the house, but the long french window of the drawing-room was open, and she saw your host embrace you as you stood together near it."

Lilian stood up.

"It's hallucination, from beginning to end! Such a thing never happened to me! Mother can only have been far more ill than we understood!"

Eleanor lighted her second cigarette.

"That may be," she said. "Anyway, she felt ill then, as she leant on the railings, and decided she had best creep home."

"Oh, but what a crazy mistake for her to make! Oh, Mother, Mother!"

"Later, before her last illness quite engulfed her, she spoke to me of a letter your father had had from your father-in-law. This letter worried Joseph very much. Sam O'Connor said in it that he hoped Joseph and your mother would advise you and Michael to go a bit easier over the house, and that Michael didn't seem well or happy, and that he was sorry to say he was drinking a lot——"

"He's hard to please," said Lilian hardly. "And he *does* drink a lot lately."

"I understand he didn't, before his marriage?"

"Oh, how do we know? Anyhow—this dream, this nightmare Mother had is sheer hallucination! I swear to that, Aunt Eleanor!"

"You swear it?"

"Yes."

"Then—more's the pity! Ah, Julia, Julia!"

Eleanor got up, and moved to the window.

"That's all, Lilian. No one knows of this experience of your mother's but I—and I know no name in it, save yours——"

"It *wasn't* me she saw!"

"All right. It wasn't. But I thought it better to tell you what she told me. Now she's gone, and there's no more to be said. You'd better go. I expect Michael is looking for you."

Lilian bowed, and left the little room. Aunt Eleanor stared down at the yard.

Supper was early, and eaten languidly.

Fanny, to help Grandfather and the children, made Cockle and Muscle go through the solemn ritual of the cats' supper, and even went so far as to say that naturally no one would ever mix their bowl of cream and milk as perfectly as Mother did. She knew that her saying this made Aunt Eleanor wince, but it gave delight to Grandfather, and that was why she said it.

André came back from Limerick during supper; handsome, polite and a little weary, he sat down and gave his news of the journey; gratefully he smiled at Fanny as she brought him a glass of wine. Lilian had not come down to supper; she had a headache, Michael said, and was having some tea in her room. Michael himself and Bill Morrow, though both decorous and submissive to the house's mood of grief and emptiness, had neverthless been drinking too much. Kitty Morrow looked worried, and so did the two elder O'Connors, who were very kind with everyone and very well-behaved.

"We've an early start tomorrow, Michael," said his father. "It was wise of Lilian to take a good rest. We must all hit the hay in good time tonight."

"Indeed we must," said Kitty. "Bill and I have to catch that extraordinary little train at Moyasta at cockcrow."

"I like Crahore," said Bill. "I doubt if I'll trouble Moyasta tomorrow morning."

Everyone ignored this troublesome flourish. Towards the end of supper Joseph, who had been as good as gold all day, suddenly let his grey head fall on to his elbow on the table and broke into wild, hysterical sobbing. Everyone was frightened by the sudden noise—and Honoria gathered Cockle and Muscle into her great arms and swept them out of the room.

"Your poor, sweet father," Fanny heard her saying loudly and lovingly to the two—"sure he's so lonely that 'tis like yourselves he's feeling, just like a little child, the poor man!"

'Oh, wise and quick Honoria,' she thought. She ran to her father, who clearly was at last in severe hysterics; but Michael O'Connor had picked him up, and was holding him most gently in his arms.

"I'll take him to bed, Fan."

"I'll help you," said the other O'Connors.

"God! God!" said Grandfather. "God, are we all going to go mad without her?"

"No, Father," said Eleanor. "This is the sort of day when people seem mad. But it isn't easy to go mad all the same."

Bill Morrow laughed.

"That's true, Aunt Eleanor. Fanny," he said suddenly, and he walked down the room, glass in hand, in Fanny's direction. "Fanny, I used to think you were the very image of your mother. But do you know, since you've come back from Italy —I see it now—you're much more like Aunt Eleanor——"

"But she *is* the image of her mother," Lucille protested.

"To look the least bit like either of them is good enough," said Fanny shyly.

Supper came to an end, and Bill and Kitty said good-night, and good-bye.

"I'll go round to Mespil Road early on the day after tomorrow, Fan," said Kitty, "and I'll see Lizzie and Nora, poor things, and tell them everything——"

"Yes, and Joey; he'll be lonely. But we'll be back in a day or two——"

"I'll tell them. Everything will be ready. Don't worry."

Bill was out on the terrace by the steps.

"The lighthouse would set you mad," he said. "Fanny, come here! Do you remember that song you said you learnt at school?"

"I learnt a lot of songs at school, Cousin Bill—but they were all in French."

"I know. Do you remember—'*ah, si je pouvais Deux fois naître. . . .*'"

"Ah, please—Cousin Bill! Mother's only just gone—to hear anyone singing, under her very window——"

"Oh, I'm sorry, Fanny! I'm sorry, pet!"

Kitty took him back to the hotel in Crahore. He was very drunk.

By noon of the next day Glasalla was indeed quiet. All the O'Connors, and Lilian, were gone; Aunt Edith and the children were gone, and so were Bill and Kitty Morrow. It was exquisite weather—late, bright summer, not yet autumnal, even though some leaves crackled and fell already, and even if the brilliant blue Atlantic was whipped and streaked with white.

Joseph fidgeted all day. He wanted now to be back in the house where he had lived with Julia, where their lives had been one life. Once she was gone out of Glasalla he had no more use for it; it was not their house. He required now to go at once and find his wife, his happy years, his love, in Mespil Road.

Dr. O'Curry told Eleanor and Fanny that it would certainly be best now to take him home. So it was arranged that on the following day André would take him and Fanny and Lucille back to Dublin.

In the late, lovely afternoon Lucille walked over the farmlands with Eleanor, who was pleased to show her the cattle, the sheep, the mountain spring, the pastures. In the beginning of the tour of examination Fanny and André had been shadowing near; but Lucille had the impression that Fanny wanted her to talk alone with Aunt Eleanor, about this inheritance and about the future in general, so she was not surprised when she saw the two scrambling down to the Golden Rocks.

She helped Aunt Eleanor to feed the Rhode Island hens.

"At home we have some hens not at all so pretty, Miss Delahunt. I hate their looks but they are supposed to be a fine breed. Ancona, they are called."

"A wonderfully good hen, the Ancona, child! Why do you object to them?"

"Simply I think their plumage is very ugly. They look like —well, like some old piece of weaving that's gone wrong!"

Aunt Eleanor laughed delightedly. She clanked the buckets down in the yard arch.

"There you are, Corney!" she called out. "Come in to the office with me, Lucille. I'm tired—but I want to talk to you."

In the office the ritual, new to Lucille, was what Julia and now Fanny knew. Eleanor apologetically pulled off her shoes, stretched her thin feet and then thrust them into the old wool-work slippers. Honoria came in with the salver.

Lucille looked about her with pleasure, with measuring care.

"Now, don't say it's like *Mère Générale's* room," said Eleanor.

"But it is, Miss Delahunt. For character, I mean—not in any detail."

"Fanny said it was—and of course as I envy *Mère Générale* at once her character and her life, I can't help feeling there may be some feeble imitativeness here."

Lucille laughed.

"Don't think me impertinent, Miss Delahunt, if I say that whatever is here there is no 'feeble imitativeness'."

"Yet there might be, you know. Because I have all my life admired *Mère Générale* above all creatures I have known."

"I think that in a way perhaps I do also; perhaps even Fanny does, who differs from her on many issues. But——?"

"Yes, I heard your 'but' to my statement before you spoke it, Lucille. The person I have loved most on earth, I think, was my sister Julia. But I did not *admire* her in everything. I loved her—and not merely because she was my only sister and because sisters are assumed to love each other. Not at all. I could easily have hated her for being my sister, had I found her a distasteful person. But I found her lovely, and without a stain of—oh well, untarnished by 'the world's slow stain' is what I mean, I think. Nevertheless, I didn't unmitigatedly admire her. Can you understand that, Lucille?"

"Not yet, Miss Delahunt."

"Well, all of us in our generations have admired *Mère Générale* because she is an irresistibly forceful personality. She is courageous, cynical, holy and strong without pausing to debate these truths in herself—and if she is guileful, as indeed she is, she does not in the least mind your knowing that. Guile is a part of her necessary mastery of life, and she would blush to be found lacking in it!"

Lucille laughed.

"Has she *ever* blushed, Miss Delahunt?"

"Hardly! God help us, it wouldn't become her! Did you ever see an uglier woman?"

"You were speaking of Mrs. Morrow——"

"I know. I said I did not unmitigatedly admire Julia. You won't misunderstand me. I loved her above all creatures. But —I did not understand the life she chose. I never understood her decision to marry Joseph."

"It is clear she loved him, Miss Delahunt."

"Clear indeed. But is that the same thing as comprehensible? Anyhow, my judgment is questionable, because had she chosen either of the two good local suitors she had—poor Standish whom you saw crying at her grave today, or George Hickey who was killed in Africa—if she had married either of those, she could have lived in Glasalla, as she always longed to, her husband would have run the place for her gladly, Father would have been happy, and I could have gone to *Place des Ormes*."

"To join the Order?"

"Naturally. But Julia chose Joseph and Dublin, so I took on Father and Glasalla. I not only never understood her infatuation for Joseph, but I always resented that she never once questioned what her choice cost me. Never once, in all our life. She was Father's pet—and mine, of course. And always when she came here she was adored, by all of us. But never once did she ask me whether I had liked the effort of learning to farm Glasalla, or whether I was content in looking after Father. It was this dreamy selfishness in her, darling one, that makes me explain that whereas I loved her entirely, I did not unmitigatedly admire her. And—that brings me to my point—it was an exposition from her characteristic

293

dreamy selfishness only last May, when she and Fanny were here, that made me decide overnight to give Glasalla to Fanny."

Lucille thought it better to ask no question. Simply she looked her wonder at Aunt Eleanor.

"Julia was emphatic and wifely about Joseph's denial to Fanny of her *baccalauréat*. I was shocked, that's all. I thought —she has, by sheer gentleness, made my life that which I had no desire to have it be. And in the night I thought that although I had nothing immediately useful with which to back up Fanny, I had at least Glasalla, which I could give her."

Lucille did not speak at once.

"It is a complicated inheritance, Miss Delahunt," she said slowly.

"On the contrary," said Eleanor. "Let me explain. Glasalla was encumbered with debts thirty years ago. It is solvent now, simply because my father and I live without extravagance, and I have learnt to breed good cattle and good sheep. It's taken me a long time—my whole life—to get the place on its keel, but it's been there a while now, and should stay there. The point about leaving it to Fanny is this: in April 1910, not quite three years from now, she will be twenty-one, and will become absolute owner of this place. In April 1910 my father will have passed his ninetieth birthday; you will agree, having met him, that it is unlikely that he will be alive then? If he is, I think Fanny will hardly sell Glasalla over his head. I think she'll let him die here. But if he's gone when she becomes possessor, she truly can do exactly as she chooses with Glasalla. I did not give it to her as a sacred relic, or a holy duty to be carried on; I do not want her to plague herself with farming if she desires to read and study and travel. I'd be very glad, in fact, if she'd sell Glasalla when Grandfather is gone—I only gave it to her because it's a piece of property, a means of raising money and independence—the only thing I had which might help her to be free."

"But you, Miss Delahunt? In three years *you* will not be ninety," said Lucille gently.

"When my father dies," said Eleanor, "be it one, two, three, four or five years from now, I shall leave Glasalla. I shall say good-bye to them all in the vault at Crahore, and I shall go to Brussels. I shall pay for a room in *Place des Ormes*—I have a small income from Railway Shares and such things—and I shall become one of those eccentric old women, *religieuses manquées*, who grow old so happily in the holy, good place where they desired to be when they were young and strong. I look forward to that end. Do you think I shall be granted it, Lucille?"

Eleanor spoke simply, and without a hint of sentimental appeal. Yet Lucille did not know how to answer. Her imagination was engaged in surmise about the lost years, the love, the acceptance, the belated, modest hopes of Eleanor Delahunt's interesting and dignified life.

"But—you *did* love your sister—didn't you, Miss Delahunt?"

"Love Julia? But, heavens, how could I not? I've loved her all my life, in every way I could."

Lucille inclined her head. The impetuous answer contained a life of love.

"Your intention in giving Glasalla to Fanny *now*, Miss Delahunt, was that if she desired to raise money on it for her education she could do so?"

"Exactly. There hasn't been time, so far, to go into details with Fanny; but I had discussed it fully a month or so ago with my bank in Ennis. My desires are perfectly understood, and when Fanny returns to Dublin these documents young Hallinan drafted for us will have gone to the bank's head office in College Green. The manager there will take charge, and explain everything to her. They'll have their insurance doctor run her over, they'll take her specimen signature, then they'll give her a cheque book, teach her how to write a cheque, and paternally allow her I should say not more than three hundred a year on her estate, until she comes of age."

"Goodness!" said Lucille. "Does Fanny know all this?"

"No—in principle she must guess that it's so, but I don't think she knows that she actually has an income now, if she likes to use it."

Lucille stared past Aunt Eleanor, at the darkening north-west sky.

"Fanny is free," she said softly.

"Oh no," said Eleanor. "It's only that I've been trying to arrange for her to be free. After all, in a sense when we were young her mother and I were free—yet neither of us lived as we really wanted to. Well, perhaps Julia did? Dearest Julia, perhaps she did. Anyhow, I'm doing the only thing I can do for Fanny——"

"Miss Delahunt—you know my father is a rich banker, and also my mother's people are rich and in the natural course when I'm twenty-one—two years from now—I shall inherit a great deal of money?"

"Yes, Lucille; I've understood that your family is wealthy."

"Well, I am going to have a tussle with my father about my views on my future. I love my father very much, but I know that he is going to be wilful and absolutist with me when I say that I must go to a university, and will not stay at home and play the Brussels social game—and I won't!"

"Naturally," said Eleanor.

"You say 'naturally'," said Lucille, "but you have taken all this trouble to release Fanny to her own decisions! Isn't it grotesque that I have no weapon against my father, such as you have given Fanny against all comers?"

Eleanor laughed.

"Do you know," she said, "I'm going to light a *third* cigarette, for the first time in my life? And what's more, I'm going to have a second glass of sherry!"

"But why, Miss Delahunt?"

"Because I've had a good idea. I don't know what your views on your future are, Lucille, and I don't know whether Fanny or you are, in the end, unusually gifted. But for me that is not the point, about either of you. For me the point is that when the young have ranging spirits, their spirits should range. Few of such there are. Too many are satisfied with the muddy lane ahead, and with boiled mutton, for certain, on Saturday——"

Lucille laughed.

"I don't agree," she said.

"I don't mind," said Eleanor. "And I'm not supposing that either you or Fanny is a genius of any kind. Only I think it would be a good thing if two like you could try out

296

your brains. For your own sakes—and because of the pleasure it might give us to see you at it. Therefore—and this is an ironic idea, Lucille, which I hope will not offend you—it occurs to me that if you were to say to your rich banker father that my bank, Fanny's bank, would allow you on my guarantee to borrow, in reason, what you might require for the next couple of years——"

"But Father would go mad!"

"That's what I mean! And say he went mad, and stayed mad, you could still go off to Paris or wherever you chose with Fanny? It wouldn't cost so much more for two than one, if you lived together—and why shouldn't you live poorly, the two of you, so long as you were doing what you desired to do? I mean that if my bank is prepared, as they are, to let Fanny borrow up to three hundred a year on her estate for three years, they would certainly let you, on your name, borrow another hundred a year for say two years. And surely you and Fanny could live excellently together with four hundred pounds a year?"

Lucille laughed in wild pleasure.

"Miss Delahunt, of course! It would be princely! But Father wouldn't hear of it! He'd go mad at my living on borrowed money!"

"Exactly. Let him go mad! Meantime live on borrowed money!"

"Oh, it's an amusing idea!"

"Lucille, it's an effective idea. Almost as effective as my giving Glasalla to Fanny. You young ones don't see how much some of us desire to promote freedom of action among the intelligent. Oh, you can be disappointing!"

Lucille stood up, aghast, embarrassed.

"Miss Delahunt, I used the wrong word, of course, when I said 'amusing'. It was simply that I was frightened of confronting Father with such a gesture of independence as you are offering. Can't you understand that? As for what you're doing for Fanny—I could not even try to tell you what I think of it. But I imagine that Fanny's life will be worthy of your generous decision, and I'm sure you'll be here to see how great and lovely Fanny will be."

"Thank you, Lucille. I have an idea, as you seem to have,

that Fanny is gifted. I suppose her gift can only be literary?
I mean, were she mathematically or scientifically or musically
gifted—in any considerable way—we'd have noticed by now.
Or so I gather from what I've read of geniuses. And as for
painting or drawing—well, in our family, dear Lucille, I can
assure you that no one has ever been able to draw as much
as an apple or a pot of geraniums that a Christian could
recognize. So—in so far as I have this recurrent idea that
Fanny is a talented creature, I can only assume that she is
talented in the literary direction. And literary talent mani-
fests itself relatively late, I believe?"

"Yes, Miss Delahunt. I believe that is so. But except that
it is quite clear that Fanny is unusual I could not guess yet
how that unusualness is going to come out."

"Never mind. The thing is to be sure, if we can, that she
can ride easy to life. And you, Lucille? You are very beautiful
and brilliant. What are your talents? You can defy your
angry father now—you can go wandering with Fanny,
cheaply, modestly? What do you desire to do?"

"Oh, I wish I knew! I think Fanny is calm at the centre of
her imagination, Miss Delahunt. I think she would like, if
she can, to read literature and history—but she would read
them calmly. She is no kind of a partisan, I think. But I'm
not like that. The immediate social scene distresses me—
and I feel engaged with it, yet useless. However, neither of
us is much use—in any direction—until we collect a bit of
education."

"And Glasalla, of all unlikely assets, will provide you with
some of that, my child. You tell your proud father that he
doesn't have to bother—that an old, shabby farmland in
County Clare will see you through!"

Lucille laughed delightedly.

"I couldn't be better armed," she said. "I cannot say how
grateful I am to you, Miss Delahunt, and I'll certainly use
this terrific weapon you have given me. But, poor Father,
he'll nearly die of it!"

Honoria came into the room.

"I didn't like to sound the gong, Miss Eleanor. Somehow,
I can't get it into my head that she's gone from above, and
I'm afraid of disturbing her, the creature——"

"Oh, Honoria, I know!" Eleanor leant back in her chair. "Did we really bury her today? Is she gone?"

Lucille moved to her side. Eleanor's eyes were closed, and the shadows about them were darkly brown and blue.

"Miss Delahunt?"

Fanny came in and bent over Eleanor, taking her hand. Eleanor's eyelids fluttered wearily, and she smiled.

"Julia, pet," she said to Fanny.

"Oh no, Aunt Eleanor," Fanny cried.

Honoria put her strong hands under Eleanor's thin shoulders.

"Now come on, my love," said she, "and let you make the necessary struggle to get the poor master and poor Mr. Morrow through their bit of supper, God help them. After that, 'tis in my own arms I'll carry you up to bed, love—and you won't know at all the potion I'll pour down your throat, my gentle child. Come on now—and make a bit of a stand for the poor master's sake—I'll see you get your rest tonight —my lovey, come on——"

Eleanor stood up and smiled at Honoria.

"I've told you before, Honoria," she said. "You're worse than the lighthouse."

"I know," said Honoria, "and that's bad."

CHAPTER THIRTEEN

'WHITE COLD VIRGIN SNOW'

FANNY had much to do after her return to Mespil Road.

Lucille had found letters and telegrams awaiting her there which meant she must go home at once; one of the little sisters had contracted some kind of fever at Le Coq-sur-Mer, the Countess had a *migraine*, the Count was vaguely *souffrant*. So the strong Lucille, contemptuous of their whimsical ills, had, because she loved these people, to hurry back—understanding though she did that all the complaints and outbreaks were only a test of her loyalty, and a jealous intrusion on Fanny's need of her. However, momentarily Lucille had to go, and for a reason she could not speak of to Fanny she was indeed eager to get home. For she desired to advocate at once to her father André's withdrawal from Ireland; she would enlist *Mère Générale's* authoritative help in this, but she hoped to spare the old nun the real reason for her anxiety. If necessary, however, she would tell her father of what she read in Lilian's eyes and André's every time she intercepted their long glances. That would indeed shock Marcel de Mellin and sting him into action.

Lucille, though saddened and puzzled by Fanny's persistent tenderness for André, which she still could not discuss with her, and though unable to gauge how deep the bruise inflicted, saw it now as a transitory weakness in itself; because Fanny, she believed, was so made that she would continue to love only where the love she was given was true, and André was incapable of sustaining even a pretence of attraction towards any woman, however much her beauty, youth or unusualness might allure him, once it was clear to him that he had no chance whatever of obtaining from her the satisfactions he insisted upon. It seemed to Lucille that her brother's commonsense must be asserting itself already in this regard, and that once he had admitted to himself that he had no hope on earth of seducing Fanny he would quickly cease to trouble her with his charm; and Fanny, hurt no doubt, would have learnt something, and secretly would laugh at her own scars. No, it was no longer Fanny's tenderness for André that Lucille feared, but first of all the appalling menace of a pitiful and ignoble scandal about the so recently wed Michael and Lilian, and secondarily the repercussion of suffering and disillusion such a dreadful thing would hurl upon Fanny. So all she hoped for now was to get André ordered back to Charleroi before anyone guessed how bad and vain he was, and let Fanny weep if she must, and learn to ignore her own innocent heart for a while.

The two friends talked, of course, of Glasalla, of Lucille's conversation with Aunt Eleanor and of the change her unlooked-for inheritance could make in Fanny's future.

"Aunt Eleanor was very forthright and secretive about it all—wasn't she?"

"Yes, but once she had made up her mind, she seems to have wasted no time?"

"No, indeed! It was almost, you know, as if she was afraid I'd—I'd marry someone, or do something sentimental too soon!" Lucille cocked an eye at Fanny, but did not speak. "I think Aunt Eleanor never really liked Mother's marriage——"

"She told me she didn't."

"Ah! But why on earth? Father and Mother were devotedly happy—and after all they had some nice children, and a harmonious life together!" Fanny smiled gently. "I don't see why people shouldn't be happy if they can—do you, Lucille?"

"Are you thinking of trying—that sort of happiness?"

"I? Oh no, you silly! Who with? But I don't see what Aunt Eleanor meant by objecting——"

"Oh, easy enough. She adored your mother, and simply thought your father not half good enough for her——"

"I suppose so. Poor Father! I must tell him about Glasalla and all this business with the bank. I can't go off and become an heiress behind his back, whatever Aunt Eleanor thinks!"

"But I should think he'll be very pleased—after all, it's a great piece of luck for you, Fan."

"Yes. That's why I find it awkward to talk to him about it yet—this isn't a time for good news."

"No. I see that."

"And I can't talk about—about our 'education', Lucille, just yet—not until I've talked to Father. Anyway, at present it all seems remote, hardly an issue at all—since Mother went."

"Still—it will be an issue, and one over which you will have power now."

"That is true."

"I'm going to talk to my father about my plans, anyway. We'll have a most terrible quarrel—at first. But how staggered he'll be when he hears about you, and Glasalla!"

They both laughed.

"Their two letters, your mother's and his, are the very expression of their dear, dear kindness, Lucille. I'll reply very soon. Will you give them my love? And to Patrice. I'll write to Patrice, too, of course. His dear, long letter. I'm glad he's winning about Harvard. I thought he would. It's a good idea, isn't it?"

"I'm not sure. I thought he might have entered a German university."

"*You* don't want to study in Germany, do you, Lucille?"

"Well, not yet. I think I'd like to go to the Sorbonne first. Shall we begin there, Fan?"

"It's what I've always thought would be perfect—but then, when they didn't let me do the *bachot*, and when I saw there wasn't going to be any money, I put it out of my head."

"But now there is money—and you could go to Paris and cram for the *bachot* whilst provisionally taking university lectures!"

"Could I? I hardly think so."

"We could find out."

"I don't know. I must talk to Father. It may have to be Dublin for me for a while—after all this——"

"But, oh, Fan——"

"Well, I could matriculate, and enter Trinity or this Royal University, whatever it is——"

"Aunt Eleanor didn't give you Glasalla for *that*, darling Fan!"

"No. That's true. Ah!" She looked about her, her eyes dismissing all but the current day. "This evening when you're gone! How shall I face this house tonight? Lucille, Lucille!"

Side by side on Fanny's bed, in the middle of Lucille's packing, they sat and cried.

Fanny found it hard to stop, though she fought to, and did indeed take warmth and help from Lucille's murmuring love, and from some promise of power and growth a part of her answered within Lucille's embrace.

"I don't know what I'll do when you're gone! Lucille, I'm frightened!"

"If I could only take you with me! But I'll write and I'll

write! And I'll be back the first minute I can! You know that, Fan! I'll come tearing back, pet, as soon as ever I can! And then will be time enough to decide on what we're going to do! Leave it all! Rest, rest, go easy—I'll be back—and everything will be a little better then!"

Fanny laid her burning forehead against Lucille's neck, and rested, and stopped crying.

"How good you are! As good as bread, Lucille! Where did I find you?"

"Where I found you." said Lucille.

"Patrice is good—like you. Not *as* good, perhaps—but good. André isn't, I think—although his eyes are exactly yours, and yours are the *best* eyes I've seen so far in the world, Lucille. Isn't that queer—about eyes, I mean?"

Lucille looked anxiously about the room, over Fanny's head.

"You're right, I think, Fan," she said. "I mean about André's not being good. I don't think he is good. Neither does Patrice. Don't let him charm you."

Fanny had not been sleeping sufficiently since Julia's death; now in the warm afternoon, weary and grieving, she grew sleepy for a moment as her head lay on Lucille's neck.

"But he *is* charming," she said, as if talking in her sleep. "He's very like you, Lucille."

That night she stood beside André on Kingstown Pier, and through the most harsh and burning torrent of tears which she had shed, of all her tears, since her mother's death, she strained still to see Lucille, who waved and waved, tall and lovely, as the mail boat carried her over the still water and out of the light of the summer evening.

Fanny stood there, acceptant and helplessly forlorn, until the steamer was only a string of lights in the darkening east. And as she stood and fought for control of her tears she became at last, unexpectedly and in some measure of command, detachedly aware of the strange violence of her gentle mother's quiet death; she was visited, as it were, by apprehension of the several cavernous sorrows it had established; she saw her father's unassuageable pain, her grandfather's and Aunt Eleanor's; she saw the faithful woe of Honoria and Mrs. Hession, of Nora and of Lizzie; she saw the fretting mournfulness of poor old Canon Whelan, the vague, uneasy grief of Lady Rawlinson; she saw the blankness of her brother Joey; she looked into Muscle's childish terror, and through the folded mask of Lilian to where memory ground upon itself in silence. And behind them all she saw the little vault at Crahore, dark and locked, the flowers dying, and the lighthouse beam preparing to strike on it, and strike again. Mother asleep in that cold place, for ever and for ever. And all this mortal pain in too many hearts—and Lucille gone.

She could see the moving lights no longer.

André took her arm.

"Come, Fanny. I'll drive you home."

During the smooth journey into Dublin Fanny stopped crying, and gratefully received the sweet evening airs on her aching head. She did not speak and neither did André. The latter was, in Fanny's knowledge of him, a young man of unfailing grace and kindliness of manner, and she was touched by his patient silence as he drove her home and allowed her to recover self-control.

But what Fanny did not know was that whereas André was still prepared to be as respectful and helpful as he could be before grief, he was growing somewhat tired of it. He had done everything a friend could do to be of service to the Morrows in their bereavement, and he would continue to do whatever he might; but he could not live too many days in close alliance with breaking hearts; he could not bear more tears than seemed to him reasonable, and he grew uneasy in social situations upon which he must not, in propriety's name, exercise his especial personal gifts for lightness, for impudence, for comedy. Moreover, that a beautiful young woman whom he admired should have to blow her nose vigorously in his company affronted his taste. And Fanny, half-convulsed with crying, had to blow her nose two or three times on the drive back from Kingstown to Mespil Road. This set André's nerves on edge.

He had been ravished with triumph that Fanny had, of her own free will, kissed him in the garden at Glasalla on that night when he had driven her down to see her dying mother. He had not understood why she had done so, had simply felt

304

exultant, and was far too delicately clever to question the exquisite impulse, or to force it beyond its light span.

Then death had come, and all this grief; André certainly knew better than to intrude his own desires, however light, however carefully harnessed, upon the mourning in Glasalla. But on her last evening there Fanny had seemed happy to walk about the lands with him, to show him the place and explain it. So when they climbed down together to the Golden Rocks, and she talked of childhood mornings, crabbing and shrimping among the pools, swimming off Seals' Head, he had been glad to see her smiling, and had skilfully led the talk to Venice, to herself, and at last to the kisses she had given him only a few nights before in the garden up above them.

She had laughed quite simply.

"Yes, I wonder at that now, André. Oh, not in regret. Only, it seems so extraordinarily long ago. I remember that suddenly, after all the arguments in Venice, I *wanted* to kiss you." She paused. "It was the first, the only time I've wanted to do such an extraordinary thing!"

She laughed.

"You called it an 'extraordinary thing' once before, Fanny," he said gently. "But it isn't, you know."

"Maybe not. To me it seems extraordinary."

"Even now?"

"Yes—more than ever now." But her sweet shy laugh gave mystery rather than sting to her words.

"Will you ever—try the extraordinary thing again, do you think?"

"I don't know. I hope not."

He looked at once hurt and amused.

"It might become—an addiction," said Fanny.

Unable to suppress a very proud laugh, André moved towards her on the rock, and seized her hand.

"Lovely one!" he said. "Lovely Fanny!"

She took her hand away and stood up. She looked about her, over the blue water, and backward to the overhanging trees and walls of Glasalla.

"No, no," she said, and he could not but note the sudden grown-up sorrow of her voice and face. "We were talking about another time and mood, André; we were just trying to remember something far away. It was a pleasant, foolish thing, and I'll remember it. But now—oh, please——"

"I'm sorry, Fanny," he said, with his customary grace.

They climbed along the rocks, and homeward slowly, up by the rough ledges to the yard. His manners were charming and gentle; but he felt that he had been found guilty of a failure in technique, and whether he knew this of himself or not, André never forgave whomsoever caught him out, in his rôle of lover, in a lapse from style.

So tonight, though beautifully-behaved, he had felt weary on Kingstown Pier, bored with Lucille's possessive love of Fanny, and, in the cold centre of his heart, indifferent, it might almost be said, to Julia Morrow's death, and resentful of the toll it was taking on pleasant life. However, he said to himself as he drove down Pembroke Road, Lilian grieves, but she does not cry. She is more beautiful at present than this red-eyed young Fanny. Still, he remembered, still with a surprise which surprised his sophistication, the exquisite movement of Fanny's innocent mouth to his—the cold truth, the searching courage of the girl's kiss. There are moments like that, he thought gratefully, even in a life as calculated as mine.

At Mespil Road they went into the house through the breakfast-room door. There was nobody there.

"I expect Father is in the drawing-room," said Fanny. "He spends a lot of time there now—it was so much Mother's room. Come up and talk to him for a minute."

Fanny dreaded the house so darkly tonight, without Lucille to help her, that she felt a desperate need to be sociable, hospitable.

"But you're tired, Fanny; so is your father, I'm sure——"

"Oh, he likes to see people. And you ought to have a glass of wine, or something."

They went up to the drawing-room. Lizzie was there, having lighted the fire, engaged in lighting the gas brackets on either side of the mantelpiece.

"No, Miss Fanny. The master had a cup of tea after ye left for Kingstown, and then he decided to go down to Westland Row to the devotions. There's a big novena on there, it seems—and sure, what can it do the poor man but good? Master Joey went with him. Would you like a cup of tea, Miss?"

"No, thank you, Lizzie."

Fanny sank on a stool near the fire and Belladonna rose from the window-seat and came to her.

"Ah, you'll be missing Miss Lucille, God help us! Well, she has a fine night for her voyaging, praise be!"

Lizzie left the room.

"Do have something to drink, André. There are wine and things in the dining-room."

He demurred.

"I'm sorry Father isn't in, but do stay a few minutes, if you can. It's—so terribly lonely."

"Of course, Fanny. I'll fetch some wine."

He lighted a candle on Julia's desk and took it through the folding doors. Quickly he came back with a tray, glasses and a long-necked green bottle of Moselle.

"This looks beautiful," he said, "and won't hurt you. It's very delicate."

They sipped some wine.

The curtains were open; stars shone, leaves shivered. Fanny was glad of the crackling fire, and Belladonna purred at it.

"We drank a Moselle very like this at Savini's in Milan—do you remember, André?"

"I do indeed! How disgracefully you all behaved!"

"Poor Otto von Langenberg!"

"Why 'poor'?"

"Oh, only if he's set on marrying Lucille!"

"You think he won't get her?"

"André—I know he won't."

"Indeed?"

André felt sharply irritated once again; Fanny and Lucille had been tiring him all through the evening, and now this kind of impudence reminded him of their exasperating free-masonry, the too-much force they seemed to generate when together. 'How untidy her hair is,' he thought now. 'And all this crying may end in ruining her eyes.' He looked about the shabby, melancholy room, consecrated, he knew, to memories

307

that were crushing this girl's heart. He looked at the sad old tabby cat. He took an impatient step or two, and refilled his glass. Fanny shook her head when he offered to fill hers. He drank his wine. But he had had for today all he could take of sorrow and of women's tears. Suddenly his whole nature insisted upon selfishness, upon Rosetta Terrace and its impersonal elegance, upon the suavity of Etienne, upon his *own* way of taking life. 'There might be a message,' he thought. 'She might be there——'

"Fanny, you're dead tired. I'm going now. You must go to bed."

Her face was frightened as she looked up to him.

"You couldn't stay—until Father or Joey comes in? It's lonely, André. Could you sit and talk a little while—about Venice, or anything? The way Lucille could, or Patrice?"

She had stood up while she spoke, Belladonna in her arms, and moved restlessly about the room, in her fear of being left alone in it.

"Father won't be long now," she pleaded.

"I'm not Patrice," he said irritably. "*I* have kissed you. I can't sit and chat to you like a seminarist!"

She laughed; she felt warmed by his unexpected bad temper.

"André," she said, "I need your kind company for a little while. And I've told you that, though I fear the dangers of addiction, I was glad, that once, to kiss you. So, if I must buy your company until Father comes in, most gladly I'll kiss you now——"

He came to her, his eyes shining angrily, she thought. He was in fact indecisive between the immediate temptation of her sweet audacity and his stronger need to flee from her sorrow and her innocence, and get back to where he was master, and where no tears fell.

But as she put Belladonna down and turned to pay her forfeit, Joseph and Joey came into the drawing-room.

In bed, crying again, she re-read Patrice's letter. It was hard to read through tears, because it was very closely written, in small 'seminarist's' handwriting, on thin sheets of paper. But it was phrased in Patrice's fastidiously beautiful French, and although it was grave in content and Fanny remembered Patrice as in general very gay, it brought him to her almost as if she sat with him on the *Piazzetta*.

'Brussels, August 7, 1907.

'MY DEARLY LOVED FANNY,

'Yesterday at noon we received Lucille's telegram, and learnt that she and André were on their way to you. That, oddly enough, was of some slight comfort to us—how peculiar we all are! Yet definitely I was with Father and Mother in feeling comforted that two of us, Lucille and André, would be with you before the end of that awful yesterday.

'I believe that Mother and Father telegraphed our sympathy yesterday, and also wrote to you, dear Fanny. But you will understand that I could never telegraph to you about this grief, and you will understand that even now, having considered it and you with all my heart for twenty-four hours, I do not know what to say to you—save this, Fanny, that as I love you, and I have told you that I do, so my whole mind is with you now, in pain. That is no good, of course; indeed, it is an impertinence to imagine that one may set down such a fatuous statement to you at present. But I only mention it as a bald truth—and because, for my own sake, I must say it.

'But, as you know, I am selfish, and so I do not allow myself fully to consider what you are now going through. Firstly because I love you I am unable to endure the idea of your grief while feeling so far from it, both in space and in my non-existence for you in relation to it; and secondly, because it frightens me, close in my own heart. You must know how much I love my dear "Countess". Yesterday she cried and cried over your news, and recalled that she was at least four years older than your mother—at school, she said, she had been a year or so ahead of your aunt, Miss Delahunt. Well, I looked at her and I thought: this has happened to Fanny. Fanny is saying good-bye for ever now to her "Countess". When shall I be saying the same to mine? You know, Fanny, I cannot foresee how I shall focus the world, or behave myself, when my "Countess" is not in it. And I assume that you are now undergoing that black, unimaginable bewilderment. So I can hardly bear to think of you— that is my selfishness. But my love, my whole love, is with you.

'Will you be here at all in the immediate future? I am

winning my battle, and shall enrol in Harvard before October is ended, I think—however my sweet "Countess" weeps. There is a man there, a Spaniard called Santayana whom I read—do you read him?—he is an Aristotelian, and an aristocrat. Have you read *The Sense of Beauty*? I hope you haven't, because I want to give it to you. But I am set on Harvard because he is there—far though it takes me from Lucille and you! But perhaps there is some hideous little house of learning for young ladies hidden in Cambridge, Mass.? Do you think there might be?

'There is also knocking round Boston and Cambridge, Mass., an individual I'm not as sure of as I am of Santayana, but whom I'd like indeed to listen to—one William James. (Brother of Henry, whom I know you read.) You will gather from these two enthusiasms that I am driving towards philosophy—but I'm not sure. I shall attend any lectures I can get from either, but I shall read history too, plain history. It should steady the mind as Euclid does—or as a drop of cold water clarifies coffee. Anyhow, one can only begin—and hope to learn, "get educated", as you and Lucille are always saying. And I hope you both *do* get educated. We all need that very much.

'Come here before I go away—will you, Fanny? But if you don't, it doesn't matter. I carry you with me, in so far as my notions claim or invent you. Do you know what I mean? All I mean, dear one, is that you are to forget me. I suppose—history suggests—that I shall forget you. But at present your lovely head is die-stamped in eternal-seeming bronze upon my memory. And that is only a pompous way of saying what I have said before, that I love you. Remember, love, that I do indeed love you. And in your grief do not entirely dismiss the helpless grief I feel for you. *Stáli!* Do you remember? It meant that *you* turn right, not I. That is what only you and I grasped—and possibly Maffetoni? Ah, the golden summer! Why should it end in all this pain?

'Good-night. I shall write again in a day or two. I warn you I shall write very often—until I forget you in Cambridge, Mass., which is thronged, I suspect, with infinitely more beautiful and more intelligent girls than you. But meantime, while you remember, write to me, in the name of grace.

'I love you, I grieve with you, and I wish I had just once seen your mother.

'Your devoted
'PATRICE.'

310

She folded the letter carefully, replaced it in its envelope and put it under her pillow. Then she blew out her candle, and tried to go to sleep. But she cried for a long time in the dark, staring at the stars and wondering which they were. Would Mother have known them?

The next day Fanny had to go, by appointment, to a vast banking house in College Green. She had never entered a bank of any size in her life, and felt frightened on the threshold of this place; but she was handled most paternally, and a handsome, grey-haired man, who seemed fully informed by Aunt Eleanor and Mr. Hallinan, explained the rudiments of banking to her, took specimens of her signature, gave her a cheque-book and taught her how to write a cheque. He then informed her that for the present it had been agreed between her aunt, her lawyer and the bank that within each quarter-year she could, if she required to do so, draw up to £75. That was, she could control and use £300 a year, provided that she directed these monies mainly towards her own education and, in general, expended them usefully.

Fanny went home amazed and uneasy, with her cheque-book in her pocket.

"I must talk to Father," she said. She knew that she would regard herself as flagrantly dishonest did she as much as study her cheque-book, let alone draw out one pound, until her father knew what had been arranged for her. But he had gone that day, for the first time in many weeks, to his office, which, for his own sake, everyone had been very glad to have him do. So she would not see him until evening.

She walked home slowly through the sun-baked streets. Lizzie brought her a belated lunch of cold ham and lettuce and bread and butter, with a jug of lemonade, to the old rickety garden table under the red maple tree. She brought her also the midday post and a telegram.

The telegram was from Lucille, at Dover, just about to embark for Ostend. 'Thinking of you dearest Fan will write tonight God bless you love Lucille.'

'She'll be home about seven,' Fanny thought. 'I'll send her a wire to be there before her.'

Old Rose, the collie, came and lay at her feet. The post was thick, as always these days. Many of the letters were for Father, two for Joey, three for her.

She opened *Mère Générale's*. She had been expecting this letter.

'Couvent de La Sainte Famille,
Place des Ormes,
Bruxelles.
Le 8 aôut, 1907.

'MY DEAREST CHILD,

'You will apprehend many of my reflections today, because this is the morning, I understand, of your dear mother's Requiem Mass and funeral. The Mass is being celebrated as I write, I think, and although I sit under my rosemary tree at this moment, child, in self-indulgence, and with my self-indulgent cat incommoding my pen, I am, you will believe, as much united with you all in this Holy Sacrifice of petition as it is possible for a weak mortal to be. Three Masses of the Dead were offered this morning in the school chapel for our beloved child Julia, and naturally I attended all three, and I offered Holy Communion for her, for Eleanor and you. But now, believe me, I am present, in that far-away Irish chapel, at her Requiem.

'I have never been in Ireland, and therefore cannot see the externals of her obsequies. I imagine that the little church and the graveyard may be something like ours in Brittany. But that does not matter. The Eternal Church is, like its Founder, the same today, yesterday and for ever; and in our hours of human tribulation we all know, throughout the globe, that its prayers will be the same for all of us. Today, in your little parish, and everywhere where general prayers for the dead are being said, the Church, through the Communion of Saints, is asking our Merciful Father to grant eternal rest to Julia, and to let perpetual light shine upon her.

'It has always seemed to me an immense and extraordinary petition, that we, unmitigated sinners, who can hardly conduct ourselves for five consecutive minutes as if even dimly aware that we were conceived in His Image, should present so confidently to Almighty God. Eternal rest and perpetual light. It seems to me that the greatest, the holiest of human creatures has never done enough to justify such a demand. Yet, whatever my many sins those two against the Holy Ghost are beyond my powers of guilt, and so I can neither despair of God's infinite mercy, nor can I imagine that we presume, if we attempt to understand it at all, by our poor rushlights* of intuition. And in any case, such reflections are irrelevant in this hour—it is only that the great plea, which is ringing through all our hearts here today, naturally—has never failed to make me catch my breath before God's goodness. And as I fear and know that you, my dearest child, have chosen to travel outside such reflections, and prefer to think for yourself, as you believe, and waive the whole Catholic idea of God, I pass on my unfaltering amazement before Him in this letter, which will reach you in a solemn time. Also, you see, dearest Fanny, as I know you are now, at this moment, decorously following the Church's ritual in your Missal, and thinking of its reference to Julia in her coffin before the altar, I pray for you. I pray that you may pause, and pray.

'But as to Julia—on her journey. We need not doubt that she will reach eternal rest, and enjoy perpetual light. Remembering her indeed in all the phases of her gentle, dignified and unselfish life—above all remembering its qualities of poetic gentleness, and of quiet, almost inexpressive, mercy— we can be sure that Our Lord, who clearly set gentleness and mercy above all other gifts, has welcomed her already, very gladly, into peace and light. Thinking over her these days, talking of her with nuns who taught her here, with old lay sisters who remember her as, one of them said, "the most beautiful and unaffected young lady that had ever come to *Place des Ormes*"—thinking over all I have known of her, Fanny, in childhood, and in the faithful letters and visits of her adult life, and finding so much of what she was—with a difference—in you, I have been telling myself—and I hope this will make you smile—that seldom must a candidate at once so tentative and so well qualified have arrived at Peter's Gate. And I take pride in the credit her arrival there will mean for *Place des Ormes*.

'I have no desire to be frivolous, child—only to make you understand how confidently I salute your mother's departure from amongst us. Our Lord took her too soon, according to our sore hearts. But her life had been good and full, and she was not made to grow old and gnarled and knotty, like some of us who sit around under the trees wondering if, after all our vain efforts to please Him, His Majesty has forgotten us now. (The great Teresa of Avila used to call God "His Majesty", and often she abused Him sharply under that title. I, wicked old woman, sometimes imitate her in that; I cannot help it.)

'My dearest Fanny, this letter is too long, but I grow garrulous with the years, and there is much I would wish to say to you—for it is you, not my happy, departed Julia, who engages my anxious thought. You know that.

'I have written, of course, to Eleanor. The loss of Julia is her chalice of Gethsemane. But she has courage, and although not so gentle as Julia she is also good all through, in a different kind of way. A very good strain, you Delahunts. Do not lose its essentials, Fanny. But you cannot. They are in your bloodstream, and in your immortal soul.

'I believe that I shall see Lucille within some days. The de Mellin family is mildly upset; little Adèle contracted some kind of fever—probably from drinking impure water—and everyone had to return in haste from Le Coq, the Countess very much fussed, and now not well, I understand. The Count, who called on me about your sad news, is tired and anxious. He feels, being a just man, that he must allow Patrice to go to Harvard if his mind is set on it—but he is sad about its far-awayness, and sad for the Countess's distress at the decision. He misses Lucille too, and I think he foresees some arguments with her about her future. I said nothing to his hints, but I felt for him, because he is a man of sensibility, who also has a conscience and a strong devotion to his family. He is still obsessed with Germany and the merits of all things German, including German scholarship, so it disappoints him that Patrice will not cross the Rhine in search of learning. I warned him all over again, but he told me, as usual, that I'm a bigoted old French snob, and that I don't understand the twentieth century. If I don't perhaps I don't want to. But my heart is heavy for it, Fanny, and for all my dear young ones plunging about in it.

'Now I must end. I imagine that your mother's beautiful funeral is over; and I am sure the bright sun shone on Julia's last journey, as it is shining here where we all remember her today. Write to me when you can; and when you can, as soon as possible, come back to Lucille, and come and sit with me here and we will talk together of your mother, and pray together that in our separate times we may be found worthy to greet her in Paradise.

'And here is *Soeur* Anastasie, whom you remember, come to help this helpless old religious into the house, to eat a luncheon she does not require. *Soeur* Anastasie is waiting patiently for me to end this letter, and she asks me to send her love to Mademoiselle Fanny, and the assurance of her constant prayers for your dear mother, and for you. I can only add my own love, therefore, child, and the promise of my unflagging prayers. Come back to us when you can.

'Meantime, be good, be humble, and reflect on true things. You will ask me which things are true—and I can only refer you, to begin with, to your own quite active conscience. Always may Our Divine Lord bless you, as indeed He does.

'Pray for this aged sinner, dearest child, and remember in these sad days the singular beauty, physical and spiritual, of your dear mother. Remember about outward signs of inward grace—and then remember her, as she lived and moved.

'Yes, I must go with *Soeur* Anastasie, to an unnecessary salad. I must disturb my lazy cat and say good-bye, dearest child.

'God bless you always,
'CATHERINE MANDEL
'(S.S.F.)'

It was a long letter, and less formal in style than *Mère Générale's* letters customarily were; it was less like a letter than one side of a conversation, which was probably what the old nun desired to give her now. It was indeed the voice, the warm voice, of a great friend, taking great trouble to reach her and offer natural comfort.

Fanny sat a long time under the maple tree, and read and re-read this letter.

About four o'clock she roused herself and went up to the drawing-room.

Joseph had an ordinary roll-top desk in the breakfast-room where he kept his papers and dealt with correspondence, but he had decided that all the letters and messages about Julia must be kept in her walnut bureau in the drawing-room, and now in the sad evenings, after supper and when Lizzie had lighted a wood fire, he sat in his wife's writing-chair and carefully, with tear-wet eyes, replied in order to messages of condolence—pausing to consult Fanny about this one, Joey about that. Fanny, sorry for his weariness, had undertaken to reply on his behalf to some of the more formal communications, and this afternoon she would sort and answer a few. So she sat at her mother's desk and began her work.

But she was almost immediately interrupted.

Cousin Bill came into the room.

"Hello, Bill."

He looked not quite as usual, she thought. He was always deathly white of colour, and untidy-looking; his thinning hair usually fell in all directions across his high, fine forehead, and when he was sober his face, which Fanny admired, had a somewhat alarming, mask-like composure. But when he was drunk his grey eyes crossed and darted randomly, and he smiled then, overmuch, his wide and very intelligent-seeming smile. But today he wore neither of these two aspects that she knew.

"Hullo, Fanny. Do I interrupt you?"

He went to the window-seat and sat down. He seemed weary, but he was often weary, through his own fault.

"No, Bill, I'm glad to see you. It's lonely here now."

"I expect so. Poor Fanny!"

Fanny decided that he must be drunk, but only, she admitted to herself, on the circumstantial evidence of its being mid-afternoon, by which time, she understood from contemptuous Joey, he usually was drunk nowadays, and also by the fact of his wandering here alone—a somewhat touching and inexplicable tendency which he had developed in recent months. For the rest, surveying him with an eye almost as experienced now as Kitty's might be, she thought amusedly, she saw no smile or trace of smile, and his eyes were not dancing about, but seemed to glitter almost angrily, very steadily, under his tired eyelids. She had never seen anger on Bill's face. He was always too cynical and too much in the wrong himself to be able to express anger against others. She had seen him being inexcusably ill-behaved and what he believed to be humorous sometimes at his wife's expense. Yet she had never seen his white strange face express anger. But that passion seemed to her to smoulder concentratedly now within his weary mask. He might be drunk indeed, but she got the impression that he was profoundly disturbed.

"What's the matter, Bill? Are you unhappy?"

"I'm always unhappy, through my own fault. But it's someone else I'm bothering about, for once. A lot of people may be unhappy and humiliated any day now——"

316

"Please, Bill?"

"I've come round here after a hell of an argument with Kitty, to tell you something that she says it's insane of me to tell you! But I have a reason, a special reason that I couldn't give to Kitty, for having to face you with this news, dear Fanny. You see, you are my pet—I love you very much. And so I think that even if we can smother up this thing from the world, it is necessary, I say *necessary*, to wound you with it. Kitty doesn't know of that necessity. So she forbade me to come here——"

"Bill, what *are* you talking about?"

"I met Michael O'Connor this morning, in a bar near the Four Courts. I was in the Law Library, by an odd chance, and he sent in a message to me. He wanted my advice, poor fellow! Well, I've been wondering lately *when* he'd want someone's advice, the fool!"

"But what has happened to Michael? Is he bankrupt? Isn't Lilian with him?"

Bill laughed gently.

"Lilian is asleep this moment, I imagine, between crêpe de chine sheets in Stillorgan Road. I expect she took a very good sedative in the small hours of this morning, and may presently wake up to ring for some China tea. More's the pity. An overdose of her sedative might cause Michael some inconvenience now, but in the long run—oh, my God!"

Fanny stood and tried to assess what truth or madness was working behind these features which she did not recognize.

"You are being rhetorical, Cousin Bill," she said. "That isn't fair. Tell me what you came to tell me, and be quick about it."

"It's quickly told. It's that your Belgian friend, the Count André de Mellin, has wrecked Michael O'Connor's married life within its first three months."

Fanny drew back, and leant aginst the ledge of Julia's bureau.

"Did I hear what you said, Cousin Bill?" she asked in a whisper.

"You did. I can repeat it. It's no delight to me to bring you this truth—because I love you, Fanny. But, for your own sake you must take it in. You must. You know why."

"It isn't true. You're making some—some drunken mistake."

"Ask Michael O'Connor then. Perhaps he is also making a drunken mistake. God knows he's drunk today."

"Where is he?"

"I don't know. He had to meet his father, poor fellow, about some Horse Show business, at one o'clock. And I was so much rattled by his frenzy that I actually went home to Kitty. Kitty and I have both seen this extraordinary, dangerous thing in the air—since the honeymoon, since before you went to Belgium. We thought it terribly frivolous of Lilian, but we supposed that—oh, the first difficulties of marriage, and the continental antics and compliments of Master André—then he went off—after you, apparently?— and we thought that the absurd and, may I say, very tasteless flirtation, or whatever it was, was over. But not at all— not at all. It was no flirtation."

Dead silence invested the sad room. Fanny leant still against Julia's desk and tried to assemble judgment before a hideous improbability.

Into the silence came Kitty.

"So you *did* come here! To this innocent child! Oh, what have you told her?"

"Only what we know to be true—and what must break in hideous scandal any minute now, or else be smothered up for ever, somehow."

"And it will be, Bill! It must, I tell you! That Belgian cad isn't going to throw the world away for Lilian—so all we have to do is make him run for it, make him see his danger. And then we'll all settle down, to applaud the domestic felicity of Michael and Lilian. So *why* torment this child, Fanny?"

"I agree with every word you've said about the Belgian cad, Kitty. But, if you must have my reason for this act of brutality towards the child, Fanny, I am committing it in charity— because I have observed her fall in love with our Belgian cad."

"Oh! Oh no! Oh, Bill how dare you! Oh, not that, Fanny?"

It was indeed to be a day of drama. Julia's drawing-room had not in her lifetime certainly known such ugly troubles as

318

were to crowd into it on this August afternoon. For Michael O'Connor entered, even as Kitty spoke.

"Oh, Fanny—I'm sorry. I just wanted a word with you."

"Welcome, Michael. We can have a word, whenever you like."

Michael sat down. He looked very white and weary, and his dark blue eyes burnt almost startlingly under his dark brows. But he was sober and calm. Bill decided that he had gone to the Hammam Baths, and while he bathed had his clothes pressed and sent out for a fresh shirt. He looked grave and strong and physically immaculate. Evidently he had decided to make some especial appeal to Fanny, and had taken measures to appear before her in order and in good credit.

Kitty took Bill by the arm.

"Come," she said. "Let them talk alone. *Your* conscience can be at rest anyway, you mischief-maker."

"I'm not a mischief-maker. Simply, I do love this innocent Fanny. Well, let's go. *Au revoir*, Fan! I'll be seeing you, Michael."

Kitty kissed Fanny; Bill kissed hands to her, and they were gone.

"May I smoke, Fanny?"

"Yes, Michael. Of course."

"What were they telling you?"

"Nothing specific. They made a grave accusation—based on your word, I gather—against André de Mellin, and Lilian. But they gave no evidence."

"Ah!"

Michael lighted a cigarette.

"I have no right to come to you, Fanny. But—I wondered if you *have* any influence at all with Lilian? And also I thought that, as you are such a close friend of Lucille de Mellin—if there was anything she or her family could do, to get him away from here, I mean?"

"But what has happened, Michael?"

"Nothing. Oh, a series of nothings, until last night. Fanny, you're a young child and I'm not going to say things to you that I shouldn't. But Lilian and I weren't very happy in the beginning—well, we've not been happy at all, I think. We'd be straightening out by now, I suppose, if—oh well, you know

319

de Mellin oared in very gaily and friendlily, about our motoring troubles, during the honeymoon. And we both took a great liking to him—and he was a kind of relief, a novelty, when things were strained between us. We encouraged him around a lot, and he was a great help to Lilian about furnishings and things—of which I know nothing. She's extravagant, of course, and has a natural sense of grandeur, which his high standards developed, so that I had to begin to worry. The house was too big anyway—but that was my own mistake. However, Lilian was impatient to have it perfect—and I naturally wanted things to be the way she wanted them. I had to borrow from the bank, and of course from my uncle and people. My father, who's very liberal with me always, began to get upset—and I had to ask Lilian to go easy on some details. I hated doing it—and I *will* be a rich man soon, Fanny—if only—oh well! Anyhow, André de Mellin went off to Italy, just when his attentions were beginning to be too much for my taste. This is a long, ugly story!"

The young man looked about him out of miserable eyes. "You'd better finish it, Michael."

"I have to, I suppose—since I began it. Well, anyway—when he was gone things didn't improve between Lilian and me, as I'd been certain they would. Oh, I know I'm crude—and you see, Fanny, I was brought up to, to behave myself—so I haven't any knowledge of—oh well, of the way women go on and all that. I mean, except for filthy jokes at school and that, I was innocent, as innocent as Lilian, when we were married. But I've been trying to learn to grow up, and to please her."

He stopped. He gave a strange, loud sob, and buried his face in his hands. Fanny looked at the handsome bowed head in astonished pity, but could only wait for him silently.

"It hasn't been any good. I think she has come to—hate my loving her. Anyway, when he came back the change was visible in her—oh, it was shameless! I've pretended not to see things, not to notice. And then your dear mother died —and that indeed did shake poor Lilian to the depths——"

Fanny, listening in amazement to Michael's story, tried not to smile at this aside.

"Yes—well? Mother is only a few days in her coffin,

Michael. What can have happened since then to create—distress?"

"Last night, Fanny——"

"Last night?"

"Yes. You know, my father's been annoyed with me, and with the Ballsbridge Show next week I've been having to work extra hard—and I was in Mullingar yesterday about some special cattle sales. I didn't expect to get back until today, but at the last minute I found I could leave last evening. I wired Lilian I'd be home late and drove back."

Fanny opened the drawing-room door to Belladonna, who was crying outside it.

"Come in, Belladonna, please," she said impatiently.

"Lilian wasn't at home, and the telegram hadn't been opened. She had gone out at about eight, the servants said. The telegram had come just after she was gone, but they didn't know where the mistress was. I knew, however—I walked down to Rosetta Terrace, and paced up and down it for an hour or so, I suppose. His car was at the bottom of the road, and the lights were on in his drawing-room, behind his elegant silk curtains. I knew she was there; I knew she was. And I had only one wish, Fanny—to go straight in and choke that bloody Belgian quickly, quickly, before her eyes. But I couldn't do it to *her*. To him, yes, with delight, and delightedly I'd swing for him. But, on account of her, I couldn't even make a noise, even a small scene. Isn't that absurd?"

"It's the exact reverse of absurd!"

"So I walked home again. But I waited round the end of the road—I've suspected him of dropping her there by the church before now, on nights when she's supposed to have been here, or at Aunt Edith's or God knows where. I waited, and just at midnight I saw her slip out of his car—as quiet as a ghost. I followed her on the other side of the road, and caught up with her at our gate. I asked her where she'd been, and she said that she'd been here. We went into the drawing-room, and I turned up all the lamps. I wanted to watch her face—and I let her elaborate her story. You, it seemed, were going to be very lonely last evening without Lucille, and she had gone down to comfort you. André, who had driven

Lucille and you to the mail boat, was at Mespil Road and had kindly driven her home. I thought that clever—because it meant she suspected I had seen the car stop at Donnybrook Church. So I said: 'It's a wonder he couldn't bring you to the hall door, Lilian?' However, as I knew she was telling lies, I told one. I said: 'You were not at Mespil Road, Lilian, because I've been there, looking for you.' "

"Oh! Oh God! Oh, Michael—what happened then?"

"She went half-mad at first. And then, poor child, she broke down completely. She cried and cried, and couldn't speak coherently at all. Oh God!—in the end I carried her up and put her to bed, and made her swallow a stiff bromide. This morning I talked with her very quietly, and had her doctor to give her a real sedative. She'll be asleep all day, and maybe all tonight. That's all, Fanny. I'm sorry to have to be so heavy, and sorrier than I can say to tell you such a story. But you have power in his family—and for all I know you might be able to help poor Lilian too. After all, you are her sister. And it isn't as if there could ever be any question of the blackguard being in love with her!"

Michael stood up.

"I assure you, Fanny, that if I *had* to face a great love-tragedy at Lilian's hands—if it was a real thing, you know, the sort of all-out stuff they play in the theatre some-times——" Fanny smiled—"I'd try to face it. Well, I'd have to face it. But to see my love, my lovely love, destroy herself to feed that bounder's momentary conceit——"

Tears poured down Michael's manly, handsome face. Fanny took his beautiful linen handkerchief from his breast pocket and dried his eyes.

"She won't destroy herself, your lovely love," she said. "It's all a blunder of vanity. But the sins of vanity blow away, I think, Michael."

Michael tried to smile.

"You're a good girl, Fanny. I'm not going to deal with that fellow until I've heard the whole truth from Lilian. I promised her that this morning—so I must let him stew in his juice until after tomorrow at least. It's just as well. I might kill him yet, you know."

He looked down with some satisfaction at his fine, brown

hands. Then he bent and kissed the top of Fanny's head.

"I'll let you know when it might be good for you to see Lilian," he said. "Meantime, pray for us both—will you?"

"Where are you going now?"

"To meet Bill."

"Oh! Don't get drunk!"

"I'm sure to, Fanny."

He smiled and left her.

As she brushed her hair in her room Fanny heard the bell ringing from St. Mary's, Haddington Road. The Angelus, she thought, or Devotions or something.

She had put on her new, best mourning clothes, a pleasant, simple dress of black poplin, high-necked and with a narrow white frill at the edge of the stiff collar and cuffs; when she was satisfied with the gloss of her hair she put on her new mourning hat of black straw, a simple, shady mushroom with a black ribbon round its brim; she found the thin black suède gloves which she had worn at her mother's funeral. Then as she glanced out at the tranquil evening she saw Lady Rawlinson's carriage at the gate, and poor old Lady Rawlinson, assisted by her coachman, advancing to tackle the steep flight of steps to the hall door.

She sped like lightning to the kitchen.

"Lizzie," she said, "Lady Rawlinson is just about to ring the hall door-bell. Let her in, of course, and tell her that Father will be home from the office in a minute. He'd love to see her. But tell her I'm gone out—and as soon as you have her safely in I will be gone——"

"All right, of course, Miss Fanny, but what's the hurry on you——"

The bell began to ring, and Lizzie mounted dutifully to answer it.

"You're looking pretty, Miss Fanny," said Nora. "Where are you off to?"

"To Benediction," said Fanny, seeking the obvious reason why anyone in this house of mourning should hurry out of it at sunset, but realizing as she said it that Nora and Lizzie knew full well that she, Miss Fanny, was never known, God help her, to go to Benediction. Nora, however, looked edified. 'I expect she's thinking that grief will bring me back to holy practices,' Fanny thought.

"Remind Lizzie to offer sherry or tea to Lady Rawlinson, and of course to light the drawing-room fire——"

"She'll do all that, Miss Fanny."

"Oh, and tell Father not to wait supper if he's tired. Not that I'll be long! I think I could escape now?"

She sped through the breakfast-room, and saw the carriage exercising itself in the direction of Baggot Street Bridge.

That was not her direction.

She was going to Leeson Park, to Rosetta Terrace.

She did not know whom or what she might find there. Lilian might have risen from her bromides and her silk sheets and gone to weep in André's arms; or Michael might have changed his mind and decided, after all, to strangle the Belgian; or, improbably, Cousin Bill might be there with a horse-whip.

For her part, she was going to Rosetta Terrace, in her newest clothes, because she had a few words to say to its tenant which she thought might be effective in the present circumstances. She had been rehearsing these words while she changed her dress and brushed her hair.

When she rang the bell in the pretty porch of the pretty little house, Etienne opened the door to her at once, and greeted her charmingly. As he announced her on the drawing-room threshold André was advancing through the folding doors, cigarette in hand, suave and welcoming to whomsoever might be calling. 'Evidently,' thought Fanny, 'the breaker has not rolled this far yet.'

"But Fanny! Sweet Miss Fanny! Thank you, Etienne. Fanny, what a charming surprise!"

She smiled.

"Is it, André?"

"Need you ask? I was just wondering, smelling those melancholy, lovely dahlias in there——" he waved towards his elegant dining-room—"what a man like me, of such dull equanimity, *is* to do with your exquisitely melancholy Irish evenings! Because they can be intolerable, you know!

And then, dear Fanny, dear wraith from Venice, in you walk!"

For a moment as she listened to him she thought that he must be frightened, and therefore overplaying himself. But she decided, rightly, that that was not so. 'This is what charmed me; this is what even yesterday I turned to with gratitude,' she thought—and she was astounded. 'This is the man I fell in love with—almost fell in love with—in Venice.' She smiled, and the cruelty in her smile was directed as much against herself as against him.

"Will you dine with me, Fanny?"

"No; I have only—just called."

They spoke in French, as always they did. But Fanny, over-alert this evening, drew some ironic English amusement now from the verb *'passer'* as she used it. However, that joke was for herself.

"Ah, that's a pity! However, you *have* called, which is very gracious of you. And, looking so lovely! What an enchanting hat!"

"Do you like it?"

"It's ravishing."

"Nevertheless, would it be very unconventional of me to take it off for a minute or two?"

"*Very* unconventional, I'm sure; but please——"

He moved forward with a conqueror's ease to take the hat from her head, but Fanny stepped out of his reach, and removed the hat herself. In a mirror she noted quickly that her hair was shining and in order.

"I can't talk in hats," she said.

"And you've come here to talk?"

"Yes, André."

He cocked an amused eyebrow at her. Fanny was almost sorry for him, so gay he was, so flattered; not a cloud in his blue sky.

"But you'll also drink a little something, won't you? A glass of Chablis, or Moselle?"

"Have you *grappa*?"

"Of course I have *grappa*. But you and I have an appointment to drink *grappa* together in Florian's in July, 1917. Don't you remember?"

325

"Yes. But you and I will not keep that appointment, André." She moved to the window and looked out at the chaste sky. "I shall taste *grappa* now, if you will be so kind as to offer it to me?" She smiled at him, and he laughed for sheer pleasure in her whim, and because she looked very beautiful against the evening light.

He brought the *grappa*, two little glasses on a beautiful little tray of Venetian glass. He put the tray down, gave her her glass, lifted his own.

"To Venice," he said.

Fanny paused. It was a toast she could not refuse, even here, even tonight. Yet she did not allow her voice to answer it. She inclined her head, and took a formal, careful sip of the potent, pure white liqueur.

"Yes, I can feel that it is beautiful," she said. "I'm glad to have tasted it." Then she replaced her glass on the little tray, and moved across the room, away from the window. But the evening light was still strong, and André's eyes followed her with pleasure. 'How elegant she looks tonight,' he was thinking. 'How *soignée*, how like Lilian! Yet last evening all tears and dampness and hair astray—really, these Irish girls!'

"André, I said I came here to talk. Have you any idea of what I might have to talk about?"

"Not the faintest, Fanny! But you've always been a delicious, and unpredictable, conversationalist—so——?"

"Unpredictable? Ah, André! Listen. I have come here this evening to blackmail you."

"Blackmail?" He repeated her phrase on a laugh, then looked at her white face on which the light fell, and checked his laugh.

He felt suddenly startled.

"Blackmail? But what joke is this, Fanny? What ugly joke?"

"It's ugly, and it's not a joke. You must leave Ireland tomorrow, André—I suggest the morning boat. I suppose Etienne can tidy up here and follow you, and bring your precious car. And I suppose your uncle can send someone else to sell your engines to us. But you must go—tomorrow."

"Fanny, what *is* this madness? What are you talking about?"

"*You* know. In general, André, your hedonistic practices are no business of mine, except in so far as that I was silly enough to become somewhat softened towards them, for myself, of late. I liked you more than I thought wise in Venice, more than I said, I think."

"I knew that, Fanny."

"I supposed you did. Yes, I had, I think, fallen in love with you, André. Oh, I had no romantic dreams—but you are disarmingly like your dear sister and brother, and you take a lot of trouble to please. Now, were I to hear that while you were playing pseudo-lover to me you were simultaneously making love to every raffish old matron in Dublin, I would of course wash you out of my acquaintance, but for the rest your unpleasant vanities would be your own affair."

André was pacing the room; his face was white and his eyes blazed.

"What *is* all this virginal insanity?" he cried.

"'Virginal insanity' is not a bad description of what I am feeling today, André; and it will be turned against you, if you do not do exactly what I say."

"And what exactly do you say?"

"I said it a moment ago. You must leave Ireland tomorrow."

"You are mad."

"That's as may be. Nevertheless I think I am right in feeling that Lilian and Michael—they are both only twenty-two, and they were both brought up to be good, and they married in good faith—I'm right in feeling that they must not be destroyed for a nonsense. And, in relationship to the true rules and difficulties of life, that is what you are, André—a nonsense, a festive decoration. I have understood that—even when I kissed you. But I was free—and I could kiss you, and leave you. Moreover, I have far more brains than Lilian. But Lilian—Lilian, beautiful, troubled, vain, unable to adjust herself to the innocent adoration of Michael—you, you have the gracelessness, in her first month of marriage, to turn your cheap, cultivated charms into competition against her young husband's pledged, eternal love? Have you *no* standards? How do you come from your excellent, honourable parents? Have you no principles, André?"

He paced about.

"Impertinent, jealous girl!"

"Impertinent, maybe. Jealous I might have been a few hours ago. Because up to a few hours ago I believe that I was in a 'virginal' degree in love with you, André. But if I'm jealous now it's for our family honour, and for Michael O'Connor's hope and dignity—and for poor Lilian's peace. You are not going to trample all those good things into the dust, André. That is what I am here to tell you. Either you leave Ireland for ever tomorrow, or I disgrace you."

"And how can you disgrace me? What are you raving about?"

"I'm raving about what I heard this afternoon from the quiet, desperate speech of Michael O'Connor. Did he not love Lilian as a decent man can love, you would be dead, choked dead, many hours ago. That is true. Had Michael only himself to think about and his own honour, he would have killed you last night. Don't try to look surprised. He told me all the wretched story this afternoon. You sophisticated persons from Brussels cannot fool us completely. One of you may have half-fooled me—but that is my mistake, and I have learnt from it. But while you were fooling Lilian, André, you weren't fooling Michael. You were just simply, in his presence, cheaply and rudely destroying his life."

"I still don't know what you are raving about, Fanny!"

"Then, if you don't, explain today! Explain to me Lilian's misery and Michael's! Tell me why you are so guileless, so guileless, among all our breaking hearts?"

"Breaking hearts? What theatre!"

"Theatre! Go and find Michael! Look at him, talk to him, and see if your conscience, if you have one, can answer what you've done! In their first month! In their very innocence of love! Oh, André!"

"I protest that you are raving. What is your accusation?"

"A very simple one. From three variously tempered but all reliable sources I have been told this afternoon that what had been suspected from late April—that is, the last weeks of Lilian's honeymoon—was now certain; that you have been

Lilian's lover, without reference to past, present or future, and without reference to the hurt that such selfish vulgarity might do not only to Lilian, but also to two proud families, the O'Connors and the Morrows, who would not take the insult of your sensuality lying down."

"What nonsense you talk!"

"All right. Maybe. But here is where I come in with my blackmail. Remember, André, I came here to blackmail you, and I shall do so."

"Yes. How will you blackmail me, Fanny?"

"It is not complicated. I shall simply tell some true things about you to all our respectable relations, in both families, I don't think anyone will doubt what I say—about your court-ing of me while you were adulterously seducing Lilian, even on her honeymoon. I couldn't make up so hideous an offence against life, against friendship, against hospitality. Your father and mine would both be agonized by the shame of it, and so would Lucille. Ah, don't be silly! If necessary, I'd tell lies and say you had in fact made far more love to me than you did. Because I think you deserve real punishment, André, and I don't care what might be said about me."

"And why should you not care? You're a hard-up Dublin girl who must earn a living—or so I've understood. You can't make gestures, Fanny."

"It turns out I can. I can expose you, even if I have to do what is called disgrace myself. I'm quite well-off, André. I own Glasalla—did you know?—and I draw an income from it. I'm not poor at all—so I can create any sort of scandal I like—and then go off to Italy or Spain or wherever I choose. Oh no, don't imagine *I've* anything to lose in being a scapegoat. I won't mind at all being shown up as the fool who fell in love with you while you were making love to my newly-married sister. That's the point I'm making. Don't you under-stand? That's how I'll blackmail you. Your parents and your rich uncle will be delighted with it all. Do you see, André?"

"You are mad."

"Maybe. But if being mad saves Lilian and Michael at the brink of their life from your vulgar sin against them, I shall be mad. Understand, I'm not changing. I shall protect those two from your frivolity. So, either you leave Ireland tomorrow, for ever, or else at noon tomorrow I start against you, throughout your family, mine and Michael's, a campaign of studied vilification. I warn you that I shall do exactly that, and begin tomorrow. And I warn you that I can afford to."

There was silence.

"Will you drink your *grappa*, Fanny?"

"No thank you. I just wanted to taste it—as we shall not be meeting in Florian's in 1917."

"That's a pity."

"Yes, it's a pity. But it isn't my fault. Good-night now, André—and good-bye. Let me be sure that I never see you again."

"Fanny!"

"Oh, don't behave like that! Go and pack. Please begone. You have been bad here—a bad thing. I was a fool to mistake you for Lucille's brother."

They stood on the steps in the rising moonlight.

"You are cruel."

"Yes. Some events develop cruelty in me—I notice that. Still, whereas a little while ago I despised Lilian, God forgive me, now, André, I love her. Good-bye."

She ran down the pretty steps, and walked home quickly.

When she got home she went in as usual through the breakfast-room, and into the kitchen to Nora and Lizzie. They were saying the rosary, but stopped to gossip with her. Why was she so long, God save us, at the Benediction?

"I wasn't long," she said. "Has the master had his supper?"

"Yes, Miss, and the poor old Canon is above with him in the drawing-room."

"Ah, good. Give me something to eat now, will you, Nora —a bit of chicken or something?"

She sat on the kitchen table, and ate what Nora brought to her, soda-bread and chicken wings and apples, and glasses of milk. And as she talked to the two good women who had so long served and loved her parents, and looked about the dear kitchen in which she had never heard an unkind word or seen an action that was not generous, the sordid sorrow of the day slid back from her. She was in her mother's house, where crudities such as she had had to wrestle with today were not acknowledged; she was where she had been reared, where her mother's two good friends commanded everything, where generosity ruled, and where the small fusses of the self were not even focused. Oh, it was restful here, it was clean, it was home. Mother might be gone indeed, but what her aristocratic spirit meant by home was in this kitchen, Fanny thought. So she had always thought, while Julia lived. And so she felt tonight, as if washed in the good sea, after the place she had come from, as she sat on the table and chewed chicken wings.

"Oh, Nora, it's lovely having such lovely supper as this! Did the poor Canon eat anything?"

"Yah, no, Miss. Sure he ought to buy a few false teeth, God help him! But they say he's mean——"

"Did Lady Rawlinson stay long?"

"No. Herself and the master had a glass of sherry together. The poor old lady is feeble—indeed, she told me that she's dying—she cried about the mistress, of course——"

When Fanny went up to the drawing-room she found her father in better spirits than he had been for many weeks. His reception at the family wine-shipping office, the kindness of old friends there and the reassembling of himself as a man of affairs had clearly done him good. Also, he had had some letters which had, for this reason and that, touched or pleased him. And poor old Canon Whelan, seated near the fire, was very kindly trying to teach him how to play Double Demon Patience.

"I'm sorry I was out, Father. Did you have your supper properly? Did you eat it?"

"Yes, child—have you had supper?"

"I've been eating it in the kitchen this minute. How was it at the office, Father? Did it make you very tired?"

"No, darling—on the contrary. Oh, it was hard at first, everyone was so extraordinarily kind—and the things they said about your dear mother—but, after a while, I got glad to be back in the old chair, you know—and there was an awful lot to be attended to——"

Fanny was cheered by his tone—an old, recognizable pomposity was creeping back.

"Well, look here now, Joseph, are you following or not—this Patience bears no relation, you see, to the stupid one you play——"

"I can see that," said Joseph. "Look, Fanny—here is a letter from your Aunt Edith which needs consideration. No hurry about it, dear. Yes, Canon, yes—don't be so impatient——"

"Well, look here now, Joseph—it all depends on good shuffling really——"

Fanny read Aunt Edith's letter. It surprised her.

Aunt Edith was Joseph's only spinster sister, and very fond of him. But she had always been irritable and what was called 'independent', the true meaning of that adjective, in application, being that the one so designated was exaggeratedly dependent upon her world's acceptance of some facet of herself which she chose to present.

Aunt Edith was a very good woman, and very good to Joseph and his children. But her means, her investments, were short and shortening; her old good Betsy was growing very rheumatic indeed, and desired to go home to her brother in Castlebar, and mind him, and relax, and live on doles from their rich sister in Philadelphia. In short, Edith desired to give up her small house in Sandymount, and come and live with Joseph, and pay her share, up to a point, and for the rest, work her passage. That was what the long letter meant.

Fanny thought well of the idea—for her father's sake, and for her own. Aunt Edith was a bore, but Father liked his sisters—and her being with him would release one—say to the Sorbonne? Fanny folded the letter, feeling amazed at the good fortune that can arise around and because of sorrow.

"We'll talk about this tomorrow, Father," she said.

"Yes, child; that's what I thought. There's no hurry. But if the arrangement were any convenience to Edith—and we're all very fond of her, after all—I don't see exactly what room she could have——"

"We could work that out, Father."

Canon Whelan gave a great sigh.

"I'm tired. Could I have a drop of whisky, child?"

"Oh, Canon, I beg your pardon!"

Fanny ran for the decanter and glasses——

"Really, Father," she said jocosely—"you might see that the Canon had what he wanted!"

Joseph stammered his apologies, and returned to his lesson at the card-table. But it was clear to Fanny that he was not going to be a Demon-Patience player in the evening of his day, whatever the benevolent intentions of the old Canon.

'Oh dear,' she thought in deep oppression, 'when do I begin to explain to him about Glasalla and my cheque-book? When do I tell him that I would like to go to the Sorbonne?'

As she watched him tonight sipping his tea, being wilful with the kind old Canon about the Demon Patience, and boasting a shade too much about his reception at the office—which had obviously restored, but also somewhat pathetically inflated him, she began to feel again the impatience she had customarily felt against him until her mother had died. His bewildered misery then, and sustained until tonight, had made her respect him. But, as he crept back to normality, as today had floated him back, with the accompaniments of all his sorrow, to his place as an indispensable business man and a citizen whose voice and counsel would be missed, Fanny saw all the miserable consolations of empty vanity inflating the poor man again, as before his sorrow he had been so easily inflated. And she saw why Aunt Eleanor, impatient and high-bred, had never been able finally to accept Julia's love of Joseph. Eleanor had never understood, I suppose, how Mother could bear his silly little vanities and so on. But Mother had fallen in love—he must have been enchantingly good-looking when he was young—like Muscle, very light and sweet. And once you have fallen in love, if you are Mother, Fanny reflected, you do not retreat from the position you have undertaken to defend. You die still trying to work your gun. That is, if you are Julia. And Father was so lucky, little slim, handsome man, as to win her. That was enough. Julia won was Julia his for ever. But Fanny, considering him now, tearful, gay and self-pitying, because he had had a day of personal gratification in the office—Fanny, thinking bitterly of the day as it had been for her, and as it had been for her mother in her cold coffin in Crahore, had an impulse of unjust anger against her father, and thought with longing of Aunt Eleanor, lonely, grieving in Glasalla.

"I don't know why I'm bothering with you, Joseph—you'll never learn this game, and my housekeeper can play me to a standstill, God between me and her at any time!"

Lizzie came in with a letter on a salver. She brought it to Fanny.

"The butler of the Count de Mellin brought this, Miss Fanny. But he did not wait for your answer. He said he understood that none was required."

"Thank you, Lizzie."

Fanny took the letter from the salver, but did not open it at once.

"What is it, pet?" asked Joseph, who was still amiably considering the Canon's patience cards.

"A note from André de Mellin," she said. She opened it.

> '2 Rosetta Terrace,
> Dublin.
>
> 'DEAR MISS FANNY,
>
> 'A telegram from my uncle at Charleroi makes it necessary for me to return there at once for a conference which may, I gather, necessitate my being sent to America at once. This may mean that I shall not see my dear friends in Dublin for some time, so I ask you to extend to them all, all your dear family, my affectionate greetings. I shall, of course, write to your father and to Miss Delahunt when I am in France, but meantime will you give them all my assurances of friendship and gratitude? Etienne will necessarily be in Dublin for some days—I leave on tomorrow morning's boat—but he and the car which as you know he drives beautifully are of course at the disposal of all of you until he leaves. I have loved Ireland, and I go away with regret. Will you salute all your charming family for me, and excuse the enforced haste of this message of farewell?
>
> 'Always I am, Miss Fanny,
> 'your devoted friend and servant,
> 'ANDRÉ-MARIE DE MELLIN.'

Fanny smiled as she folded the sheet of note-paper.

"Not bad news, I hope, pet?" said Joseph.

"No, Father. André has been suddenly recalled to Charleroi, and may be being sent to America, he says—so this is only a sort of flourish—he'll be writing to you, he says——"

"Oh—so? Well, Canon, where are we now with these ridiculous cards?"

"I don't know. To tell you the truth I'm getting damn tired. It's time to be gone. Will you see me a piece of the road, Joseph? I'm getting very blind."

"I'll see you to your door, Canon—don't talk foolish."

"Ah, thanks be to God. You're a good fellow, Joseph."

The Canon swallowed his whisky, and rose to his feet with a great sigh.

"You'd miss her," he said, and he looked round the room appraisingly. "Ah well, it's time to be gone! It's time we were all at home."

Joseph got the old man into his overcoat and found his hat. As the two went down the steps together carefully Fanny heard Canon Whelan say: "Sing, Joseph. Don't mind. She'd be glad to know you sang for me——"

So Joseph sang softly, tunefully—but only for the old Canon, as they went down the road towards Baggot Street Bridge:

> *"There's one that is pure as an angel,*
> *As fair as the flower of May. . . ."*

Fanny stood on the high-stepped threshold, and observed the lovely night with gratitude to God.